THE ROMAN CANDLE

A BONE GUARD ADVENTURE

E. Chris Ambrose

ROCINANTE PRESS

Contents

Chapter 1	1
Chapter 2	6
Chapter 3	12
Chapter 4	15
Chapter 5	19
Chapter 6	24
Chapter 7	27
Chapter 8	30
Chapter 9	33
Chapter 10	38
Chapter 11	42
Chapter 12	44
Chapter 13	47
Chapter 14	50
Chapter 15	53
Chapter 16	57
Chapter 17	62
Chapter 18	65
Chapter 19	69
Chapter 20	74
Chapter 21	78
Chapter 22	84
Chapter 23	87
Chapter 24	94
Chapter 25	97
Chapter 26	100
Chapter 27	105
Chapter 28	111
Chapter 29	114
Chapter 30	117
Chapter 31	122
Chapter 32	126
Chapter 33	131

Chapter 34	136
Chapter 35	139
Chapter 36	142
Chapter 37	148
Chapter 38	152
Chapter 39	157
Chapter 40	161
Chapter 41	166
Chapter 42	169
Chapter 43	173
Chapter 44	176
Chapter 45	181
Chapter 46	185
Chapter 47	187
Chapter 48	191
Chapter 49	195
Chapter 50	198
Chapter 51	203
Chapter 52	211
Chapter 53	215
Chapter 54	218
Chapter 55	224
Chapter 56	230
Chapter 57	236
Chapter 58	240
Chapter 59	244
Chapter 60	248
Chapter 61	252
Chapter 62	256
Chapter 63	260
Chapter 64	263
Chapter 65	266
Chapter 66	271
Chapter 67	273
Chapter 68	275
Chapter 69	278
Chapter 70	281
Chapter 71	285

Chapter 72   291
Chapter 73   295
Chapter 74   298
Chapter 75   302
Chapter 76   306
Chapter 77   310
Chapter 78   313
Chapter 79   315
Chapter 80   318
Chapter 81   322
Chapter 82   325
Chapter 83   330
Chapter 84   334
Chapter 85   337
Chapter 86   341
Chapter 87   344
Chapter 88   347
Chapter 89   350
Chapter 90   355
Chapter 91   360
Chapter 92   363
Chapter 93   368
Chapter 94   370
Chapter 95   373
Chapter 96   376
Chapter 97   378
Chapter 98   382
Chapter 99   385
Chapter 100   387
Chapter 101   389
Chapter 102   392
Chapter 103   395

More by this Author   403
About the Author   405

Chapter One

Jugow, Poland

Sirens, lights, police wagons. Polish, Italian, German, Israeli. Didn't matter the language or nationality, emergency possessed a rhythm all its own. The Italians might seem casual, but they responded quickly enough back on Lake Como, and even allowed a fellow professional like Moishe to ride along and give them a vital assist. Like most law enforcement, they imagined themselves with clean hands. Defend, protect, serve, those things. Moishe, too, defended and served, but he was more broadly open to any tool that would do the job. Still, they didn't call him the Fist for no reason.

Now, he waited with a cluster of townsfolk, watching the collection of emergency vehicles accumulate and depart in waves from St. Catherine's Church across the way. A young man counted the body bags—nine, ten? Didn't matter if you didn't know who was inside. Looked like these Americans got paid by the pound. Little wonder they called themselves "Bone Guard." Snow filtered down upon the heads of the gawkers and the police cordon in equal measure, then the breathless girl arrived.

"Did you see? That old garage by Rubavitch's place—it's not a garage, it's a tunnel!" She jabbed her finger back in the direction she'd come from, her breath clouding the air. Moishe alerted immediately.

"A tunnel?" He moved through the crowd, or rather, they parted before him, startled by his appearance. He'd been still and silent for so long, they'd forgotten he was there, or that he was human. Either way.

The girl nodded eagerly. "Straight into the hill from the mill road. There's that curve in the road—"she broke off, her gaze rising up, up, looking for his face. Her lips parted, and she swallowed, searching the catalog of her memory and finding no reference for him.

Moishe smiled pleasantly. He was capable of such, in spite of what they said. "Can you tell me where?" His Polish was rusty, but serviceable.

"I've got to see this," the young man said, the one who'd been counting body bags. "Come on." He waved Moishe along with him, breaking into a trot.

They came to a pool of light beneath one of the church's street-lights, and a pair of officers watched them pass. The young man waved. Skirting the light, Moishe melted ahead of his guide into the darkness, letting the man catch up again.

"So you're a stranger. From where? Are you with the Germans or the Italians? I think that's what they were." The young man panted a little from matching Moishe's pace. He grinned sidelong at Moishe as he led him around a corner and up hill.

From the school parking lot, headlights started up, and a big Land Rover with Italian plates grumbled out from behind the building. Moishe melded himself with the nearest stone structure. The Nazi sympathizer drove, and Moishe had a moment to absorb the fact of his survival—then he noticed the woman next to the dead man...Moishe would never forget that face.

Two people he never expected to see again, much less to see them together. The universe had no more power to astonish.

Moishe wasted no time on surprise at the man's survival. However he had accomplished his escape from the handcuffs, from the sinking ship, from the depths of the lake itself—these things mattered not. The fact of his survival merely elevated Moishe's own response level should they meet again. No. If he had the capacity for surprise, it would be for another question. Why would Sadie go with that man, knowing what he was?

In the back seat, a young man clutched a bandage to his throat, blood staining his hand and clothes.

Moishe closed his eyes briefly, the only part of him that shone, and heard the engine as the car drove away. Did they already have it? How could they?

"Seima? You coming?" The young man stood halfway up a short street.

With a nod, Moishe followed along. Tracks, already being concealed by sifting snow, led down the slope into the school parking lot the other vehicle just vacated, but the snow that trailed from the Rover's roof proved it had already been parked when the snowfall began. Some other vehicle had come and gone again in the meantime.

A smaller cluster of citizens hovered near a garage built into the slope of the hill diagonally behind the church. One of them held a phone with its light on, another had a giant metal flashlight shining into the gap where one door bent outward. The smell of burnt flesh coiled out with a stream of smoke. A woman covered her face with her scarf. "What is that smell?"

Death. What else? But whose? Not the sympathizer, clearly.

Moishe needed information. He walked closer, reaching out to lift the flashlight from the man's hand, over his brief protest. Moishe projected strength and official menace, and the man just spread his hands, earning Moishe's nod. Take it for gratitude.

From the gap in the doors led a mark like a single ski track accompanied by two sets of footprints, , as if the two people dragged a narrow object with them.

Soft voices echoed within. Moishe stepped to the side, years of habit ensuring he didn't obscure the departing tracks as he looked inside the tunnel.

Some four meters from the entrance lay a blackened form with a skeletal hand reaching out and glints of gold among the burnt scraps of fabric that still clung to the body. A priest, immolated. Given the position of the body, Moishe put odds it was the Italian, the Centurion of Operation Gladio, which explained the Nazi sympathizer's survival if not the presence of his companion.

Quick shadows moved within, and Moishe stepped back, keeping the light in front of him to dazzle and distract.

"Moishe?"

A woman stood there, stiffly, her hand hovering over her gun. Dafne Chadad, a katsa, Mossad field agent.

"What happened?" he asked in Hebrew.

Dafne shook her head. "What are you doing here?"

"Looking."

"For what?"

"Lost things." He ghosted a smile. "Have you found some?"

"A few. Who are you working for?"

"Not you. Nothing interesting?" He flicked the beam of his light toward the passage.

Dafne folded her arms. "You'd love to see inside, wouldn't you. Tell me what you're looking for."

"The end of days." His smile grew. She wouldn't tell him anything. But the other woman might. Moishe returned the flashlight to its owner and turned away.

"Moishe! That man on the boat at Lake Como—what were you doing?"

"Working."

"Ha. Not up to your usual standards. He survived."

Moishe paused and turned, setting his foot down in the snow. The young man who had guided him there also froze, then withdrew to the company of his fellow citizens. "Oh, Dafne. You always had to criticize."

"People know you're here, Moishe. You're hardly invisible."

He nodded. "Some day, maybe soon, I'll be gone, and so will you, and so will everything." Gone into a glorious nothing, annihilated at last.

The thought warmed him as he trudged back through the snow to his own car. Italian Land Rover. Shouldn't be that hard to find. Nice that his targets came with a coffin large enough for all of them.

Chapter Two

"You drive like my grandmother," Gooney called from the back seat.

"If I let you drive, we'd end up under a snow drift, eating each other to survive." Grant scanned for the hospital entrance, nearly missing it as the snow fell. He checked the rearview. Between Nick and Gooney, Dom sat partially hunched over, his hand to his throat, his ruined laptop still held close. The kid was beat. The nearest hospital turned out to be over an hour away, given good conditions, not a blizzard on unfamiliar roads.

Grant pulled up in front, D.A. and Nick already bounding out of the vehicle as it came to a stop. Nick took charge of Dom, helping him toward the glass doors as they slid open, light pouring out.

"I'm okay," Gooney protested as D.A. said something to him, then, "Fine, fine." He flung up his hands, then gasped. "Just...stiff. Too much sitting." He shot Grant a look then he limped toward the doors, they slid open, then shut behind him as a nurse came up.

"I don't think he's seriously injured," D.A. said, "but with him, it's hard to tell."

"If he's got a sliver, he'll be howling all the way to the first aid kit, but give him a broken leg and he says he's fine."

"That second part sounds like somebody else I know." She looked over at him. "You all right, after all of that?"

"Could use a replacement bandage—"he displayed his gouged wrist, evidence of his ordeal chained to the police boat at Lake Como—"but I don't need the international hospital system to do that."

She sighed. "If you say so."

A security guard lingered by the door, not quite close enough to trigger the automatic door, but clearly staring at them.

"Need to move the car." Grant tipped his head, and she resumed her place in the passenger seat as he moved the Rover to a lot across the street and killed the engine, listening to it tick down. He'd have to turn it on for heat, depending how long they waited here, but for now, he wanted the quiet.

No point delaying any longer. The two of them were alone with the weight of her choices. Grant said, "The Mossad. When did you bring them in?"

D.A. stared straight ahead as snow accumulated on the windshield. "I'm sayan, a citizen agent for the Institute. Since I resigned after Avram's death. I've never been activated. Once in a while, I give them some intel—never anything confidential," she rushed to add, "not Bone Guard intel, but other things I come across."

She'd been Mossad when she came to the Special Forces Intelligence Unit back in Afghanistan, but he'd taken her retirement for given, after her husband's death during a Mossad operation. "Until you gave them our client, or tried to."

"The Nazi," she pointed out.

Grant gave a nod. "You didn't think you could trust me with this. The truth about you?"

"That's not how the Institute works, Chief." Her head turned, her eyes glittering. "Besides, I didn't want to put you in the middle, to make you choose between your client and me or the Mossad. I know you, Chief. I know what you're like. You're already evaluating how much of the blame should be yours for everything that went wrong with this op, and that's on top of the ethical weight you were already carrying just working for that woman. Maybe you think you can change her, make her see some kind of truth, but—sorry." She drew a shuddering breath, then added, "The Mossad's got their own rules. They make their own path. I wanted to tell you, especially after Lake Como. Nobody on our team was meant to get hurt."

Or nearly drowned while chained to a sinking ship by someone the Mossad clearly knew. "We'll come back to that." He turned a little in his seat, facing her. "They're after the Warden, and her organization."

"Yeah. I reported on meeting her, after Arizona, and they wanted more, but none of the leads panned out. She's had literally decades to work on her defenses. Then she sent you that box. Half the reason the Institute exists is to track down Nazis, and there aren't many left, not the old-school kind. The Warden bridges the generations, giving a new breed some connection to the glory of the Reich." Her lips curled as she said the words, and her glance narrowed.

"I'm not here to defend her, you know that. And you know why I signed on." Snow felt slant-wise through the streetlight, gray-gold as ash. "I am assuming, when I agreed to help her, that you asked on your own behalf, not that of the Mossad."

She hesitated, her breath caught, and he gave a nod that released it. She didn't know, couldn't be sure about the purity of her own motives.

"You were looking out for the Warden, for a way to bring her down. Whatever it took."

She flinched and took a moment before responding. A moment that told him everything. "If you had faith in anything, Casey, you'd understand. My people, and the only nation where we can maybe feel safe among friends, that's worth some risk. It wasn't meant to be at the risk of your life."

What about his trust? "I used to have faith in my judgment, Silverberg. I'm human intelligence, I'm not supposed to be caught out by stuff like this."

"Yeah, well, sometimes even you get out-foxed." Her posture spoke of fear, a weight she held in her shoulders. "I've been in this game longer than you. I've had skin in this game longer than you, and Mossad business is as sharp as it gets. You're good, Chief. You're very good; Mossad is next level, and those are the people I learned from. So you didn't catch on until the op was almost over. That doesn't mean your judgment is crap."

He stared at her a long moment, committing her fire to memory in case he never saw it again. Then he said, very softly, "I'm hum-int. I used to have faith in my people."

If he hadn't known her for sixteen years, if he hadn't fought beside her, would he have seen how his words struck home?

Her eyes flinched. Her brow hardened, and a breath became a gasp so slight even he almost missed it. She was signals intelligence, her listening honed to note the smallest details. A word choice, a verb tense. She caught his signal loud and clear.

"The guy at Lake Como. Who was he?"

D.A. sank into her seat, gripping her elbows. "Moishe the Fist. Also retired Mossad."

"Nice name." Grant would take a long time to recover from the power of those fists slamming into his chest and stomach.

"He boxed for a while, until nobody would step into the ring with him." She pinched the bridge of her nose.

"You know a lot about this guy. Who was he to you?"

"Nobody, I don't know. A colleague." She straightened and stared him full in the face. "He was like Avram's brother, this weird kid, fostered to the kibbutz where Avram grew up. Like his sidekick. They went everywhere together. He was there when Avram died. He was there, and I wasn't." She wet her lips. "Moishe and I—we weren't close, but we resigned the same day."

More than she'd ever said before about her husband's death. He didn't want to push. At the same time, he needed some context for the man who'd left him to die. "Was he responsible for Avram's death?"

Curls shook. "The director says no. I don't know what he'd say. We didn't talk after that. I have no idea what he's doing here, or why he'd go after you like that."

"Because your friends think I'm a Nazi sympathizer. A collaborator."

She slapped the dashboard. "They've gotta know that's bullshit."

He smiled faintly. "Thanks." There'd been some moments these last few days that he'd begun to feel like one, a thought that left a bad taste in his mouth.

"Moishe said he could get in with the Carabinieri and find out what they knew, that's what he told Dafne—Agent Chadad—"

"The woman who tried to kill me in a museum."

Her fingers curled and she shot him a look. "I didn't know that."

"We haven't talked much lately," he said mildly.

D.A. flinched. "Anyway, the Mossad didn't get what they came for, but they helped the Germans bust some of her minions, and the Italians break up the Gladio, so score two for international cooperation. They'll keep looking, but they'll have to do it without me." She drew a deep breath. "When that boat went down, Chief, when I saw what Moishe had done—if I could've jumped in and gone after you, I would have. I need you to know that."

Those had been some of the longest moments of his life, plunged under water, dark and alone. "You went after the objective. Ours as well as yours. That's what I'd expect from you."

"What, because I'm not allowed to be your friend? Or because you think I'm a traitor, more loyal to Israel than to you?"

Grant turned and caught her shoulder, just for a moment, arresting her fury. "D.A. You'd have to be a superhero or an idiot to follow me to the bottom of a lake." The torn skin of his wrist seeped blood and he withdrew his hand. "You're not a traitor, neither do you have a death wish. Rule number one is we don't throw lives after a lost cause."

"Even if it's you."

"Especially me."

"Yeah, well, Mossad's done here, at least for now. Done with us. So Moishe should go back to wherever the hell he came from. If I knew where to get hold of him, I'd bitch him out myself."

Taking in her words, everything she'd said, Grant shook his head. "They didn't call him; he called them. We don't know what he wants, so there's no reason to think he's done."

D.A. blanched, and Grant cut her a glance. "What?"

"He's obsessive. Single-minded. The man doesn't multi-task, he goes after his objective, and he gets it. If he's after you for some reason..."

"There's no reason to think it's personal." At least, it hadn't been the first time they met. "His objective must be peripheral, something we don't know about. Maybe just tracking the Nazi stash?"

"If he cared about money or fame or anything normal, sure. With Avram dead, I have no idea what he'd invest in next. I haven't seen him since the funeral." She considered this for a moment. "He could've been hired to find the stash, or some part of it, like us looking for the library."

"In which case, he'll have to negotiate with the Monuments Men, and a handful of governments." Maybe the red tape alone would bind the Fist, at least for a while. In the rearview, he could just make out the blanket they'd thrown over the crate in the back of the car, the crate the Warden had delivered prior to her disappearance. The only thing she'd been interested in from the cache, and she left it behind. "Speaking of which...he's not the only one who didn't get what he wanted."

"She got it, didn't want it."

"Then I guess it's time we figured out why an art collector rejects an Old Master."

Chapter Three

Not so many hospitals in a short range, and only one open at that hour. Moishe drove a little faster than reasonable. Not so fast that he risked his own annihilation before he was done. Hospital was only a guess, of course, but one backed by a lifetime of intelligence work, and by his personal knowledge of the woman, at least. Her companions remained mysterious, like cards he had yet to turn up in an array. Sadie Silverberg. How long since he'd last seen her? Would she be a distraction?

Moishe rolled that over in his mind, tumbling it like a stone he would make smooth as he scanned the highway signs for his exit. Ah, there it was. For Avram's sake, he would prefer not to harm her. Did that make him soft? Even the Stoics admitted to preference.

The kind of woman Avram would marry, the kind who would join the Mossad, who would remain in intelligence work even after resigning from the Institute...this kind of woman could not be expected to allow his work to continue without protest. Especially if she had any attachment to the sympathizer. If it came to the point, he would do what must be done. He had obligations, after all, both morally and financially.

His wipers swept away the falling snow as a red sign lit the city street ahead, in the shape of a short-armed cross, the universal symbol for help. It wouldn't be enough.

Across the street from the entrance, a nearly-empty parking lot. Moishe slowed as if to turn. One set of tracks led inside. He did not believe in the sort of God who provided snow to aid the righteous. Nor did he think the term "righteous" would properly describe him, but the snow helped, and he accepted it.

Keep driving, pass the parking lot, turn beyond the hulking concrete apartment building and find a spot. Tire tracks, but no footsteps. Whoever parked the car remained with it, or left by another route. Hope for the latter, count on the former.

Moishe checked the twin pistols beneath his coat, and worked his fingers through a series of exercises, in case.

He emerged from the car hatless and snow sifted down between his coat collar and the back of his neck. Not fast enough or wet enough to be a threat.

He strolled toward the corner of the building, noting how a few lights illuminated the parking lot in blotches, and the falling snow diffused the light, creating a misty glow likely to befuddle the unwary. He moved between the lights, switching direction, gliding along the sides of parked cars, letting his shape merge with their shadows and part again when he felt it safe to do so.

At each crossing, he swept his gaze toward the entrance. No sign of tracks. Another row, another, and he earned his reward: the groan of a car door opening into the cold night. A second door followed. One more row between them. Moishe came to the rear bumper of a van and peered around it. Two people, one shorter than the other, opening the trunk of a large vehicle beneath a light, a moderately defensive parking location. As the door moved, he caught a glimpse of the Italian plate and the spiderweb of cracks on the rear window.

And here he stood at a different sort of crossing. Two people. They might have what he needed, but again, they might not. A matter of moments to deliver his gift, and find out for himself. But unexpected deaths brought attention, and he had no reason to think the man's friends would be any less persistent than himself. He could afford a little longer, to be sure.

Chapter Four

While Grant got Dominic breathing again in the secret passages beneath the church where they had located the Nazi stash, the Warden had been removing her reward, the only thing she'd claimed from the inventory her husband had left. Grant dispatched their enemy, defending her, then she and her lieutenant, Adolph, hurried away with the single crate she wanted. Finding it in the back of the Land Rover had been a surprise—one they greeted with caution, then ignored in favor of bringing their wounded to the hospital.

Now, the time had come to find out what the Warden sought, why she'd been willing to pay their hefty fees, including various bonuses, and undergo the dangers she had. And, perhaps more intriguingly, why she'd abandoned it in the end.

The pair of them tucked behind the trunk door, D.A. held a flashlight she'd found in the glove compartment, aiming it at their surprising gift—or maybe burden. By rights, it should go with the stash, to be returned to its proper owner, except that Grant already knew this item had no known provenance. They could always turn around and bring it back to the church. Let the Monuments Men take care of it, and make all of this somebody else's headache. And never know what they'd missed. Grant's pulse beat harder in his injured wrist.

"Go on," D.A. said. "We both know you want to." Then she added, "Who am I kidding? I want to know, too."

They'd gone through Hell for this thing, even the Warden herself—imprisoned and treated like a Jewish prisoner at a concentration camp. Time to find out what they'd been bleeding for.

Drawing the blanket out of the way, Grant took a moment to scan the crate itself. About three and a half by four and a half feet, maybe five inches deep, it rested awkwardly in the space of the trunk, propped slightly up with a long edge toward the outside. If they needed the third-row seating, they'd have had some trouble, but everyone had been so tired on the way here they hadn't bothered.

The wood looked smooth, gray mixed with warmer streaks, and old, not the pale, young wood of the swiftly assembled crates in which the Nazis toted their booty. Somebody must've opened it, in order to add it to the inventory, then closed it right back up again, leaving it in the same state it had apparently rested for a long time.

"Just the one intake-stamp." She tipped her chin toward the blue marks partially visible at the top corner.

"Maybe more on the sides or back." The Warden had left him a note along with the crate. "*I find this not to my taste. I trust you will see it home. Presuming, Mr. Casey, that I may trust you with anything,*" signed with a scrolling letter "J" for Julia, the name he'd never called her, and never would.

He picked up the far end and lifted it onto the seat back, then lifted from his end, pushing the lid over to rest in the back seat. Folded cloth padded the inside. Hope it was archival. Grant pulled this away with a theatrical gesture, and both of them stared.

A large painting in a faded gilt frame took up every available inch of space. D.A. played the light over the surface from top to bottom, the beam almost lost in deep red-brown paint, tracing along the fine cracks in the surface, to the balding man in the foreground. Depicted kneeling in a three-quarter view, he wore deep green and warm beige robes, the

Renaissance conception of Biblical clothing, his hands outspread in astonishment, a burning twig in one hand, upraised toward an unlit candle. The light stroked along dove-gray wings, a strong, young angel, gesturing back toward the man. And between them, the beam arrested arrested on vivid branches of gold.

Seven branches, three to either side of center, with a series of decorative elements at the junctions and spaced along the arms. Creamy-white candles, partially melted, occupied the sockets at the top, beneath where the angel hovered.

Grant drew a breath. "Well. I can see why she rejected it. Can't imagine a Nazi displaying a menorah in her home."

"That's not just a menorah," said D.A. faintly. "It's the Menorah. The original. From the Second Temple in Jerusalem."

"Which the Romans trashed when they conquered the city and carried all the fittings back home to the emperor, according to Josephus, anyway. So, Biblical scene, Old Testament, presumably, given the setting."

"I guess." She flashed a grin. "Wish I could've seen her face when she ripped open her prize and saw this. She must've been furious."

Or grief-stricken. She had envisioned this as a final gift from her husband, recently dead, but long separated from her.

From spending time with his religious grandmother and historian mother, Grant could recognize a number of saints and other religious figures from the things around them, the regalia of their martyrdom or the moment that most symbolized their value to the church, but this one didn't fit any of those images. "I know a few things about Biblical iconography, but for this, I got nothing. Any idea what moment this illustrates? Or who?"

She shook her head, curls bobbing. "Doesn't ring a bell. Most artwork from the period is Christian, though. New Testament. Catholic."

"So maybe it's a fake, made to look like the real thing." Grant leaned in, looking at the dark spaces. A faint sense of architecture arose in the empty space at the back, hard to make out in the poor light. The style and the appearance of age looked convincing enough, to his inexpert eye. No signature. No idea how to be sure what they were looking at. "The real question, is it a genuine Caravaggio?"

"Looks like it could be. Maybe we get a hotel with wifi and I can do some research. In the meantime..." She balanced the flashlight in one hand and snapped a few photos of the painting on her phone. She tapped out a message and clicked. "Sending to the guys. Dominic's from Naples originally, and Caravaggio's practically their hometown hero. I think one of Dom's friends is an art historian. Maybe they've got some insight."

Grant leaned in to pull the lid back onto its crate.

The window over his head shattered, wreathing D.A.'s head in a halo of glass.

Chapter Five

Naples, Italy

Tonight was the perfect night to occupy a garret in a decrepit apartment building not far from the Palazzo Zevallos Stigliano, the art museum where Jacinta Scipiano held an internship as restoration assistant. On the easel in front of her stood a minor family portrait from the nineteenth century, somebody's beloved, or nearly forgotten ancestors: one of the private hires that paid her rent. Clipped to the easel, a pair of scissor lamps illuminated the painting as she lightly brushed the surface with a cleaning solution and tried not to think about Dominic. Five hours since she'd last heard from him, and then it was a terse, excited message. :*Nearly there! More soon.*:

He didn't even say where. She left two voice messages, sent three texts, and alternated between fuming about how much fun he was having with his new American friends, and imagining the lot of them shot through the head and left in a ditch like a bad Mafioso film. Or like the history of Sicily not so long ago.

The younger son in the painting reminded her of Dom, with his intense, deep-brown eyes and full lips. At any moment, this fop would put down his feathered hat and deliver a history lecture before apologizing profusely while she laughed. The garret smelled of linseed oil and antique dust. Italian rock music pumped into her earbuds. With a monocle pinched in her eye, she swiped the brush across the painted face. Why didn't he—

Her phone lit with a sudden burst of vibration that threatened to shuffle the phone from its place on her workbench. Jacinta dropped the brush and snatched up the phone, flicking off her music. Dom!

She stuck the paintbrush behind her ear and popped the monocle into a pocket. "Buon giorno, cretino! Do you have any idea how worried I've been?"

On the other end, a long pause, then a vaguely familiar voice said, "Ciao, Jacinta. C'e Tony, uno degli Americani—"

Tony. One of Dom's over-sized, dangerous American friends. Ex-Army, or so they claimed. She switched to English. "Tony? Where is Dom? How do you have this phone?"

"Because he gave it to me. Let's slow down a minute okay? Dom's right here, but he can't talk right now."

From the background, another voice, deeper, said, "Hand me the phone, Gooney. You're making this sound like a hostage situation."

Jacinta dropped both earbuds on her bench and clutched the phone closer to her head. "What's going on?"

The second voice took over, with a soothing tone that made her want to believe—and made her increasingly suspicious at the same time. "Jacinta. Hi, there, this is Nick. Dom assured us you wouldn't be sleeping, so I hope it's all right that we called. He didn't want you to worry any longer than necessary."

That did sound like Dom. "What happened? Why doesn't he call himself?"

"We ended up in a dangerous situation, as you, and all of us, feared that we might. Dom's throat has been injured, and he's just gotten some stitches. He'll be fine, with some recovery time, but he won't be able to talk for a few days."

Tony's voice muttered, "Yeah, you do this better than I do. I don't know why you ever let me talk to people."

"Show me. I need a photo," Jacinta demanded.

"He's not looking his best," Nick said, in that same tone, "but give me a minute, okay?" Away from the phone, he said, "She's asking for a picture. Do you want your glasses?"

Then Tony, "Here, hold this—she'll want to see."

A moment later, her phone buzzed for a message. Propped up on pillows, Dom lay in a hospital bed, wearing a stained shirt missing a few buttons, his throat bandaged under the chin. Dark waves of hair coiled around his face, the sweat making them gleam not unlike the painted hair in the portrait before her. His eyes managed to look weary and aglow in the same moment. He held a tablet in his hand, pointing with the other, but she studied his exhausted, excited face. Quanto è bello.

"Did you see the article?" Nick inquired.

Jacinta's glance dropped to the tablet. The Guardian, International News. *Nazi Treasure Recovered!* "*Author and historian Dominic DiMarzio led the effort to locate a stash of stolen treasures lost since the Nazi occupation of Italy...*"

"È vero? You found it?"

"We sure did—hang on."

"She's the art historian, right?" Tony muttered. "We gotta show her."

"Dom says no." The conversation continued a little softer, then Nick came back on. "Unless you have any questions that'll be hard for Dom to answer, I'll hang up in a sec and he can text you. Does that sound good?"

"Sì, certo." Harder to get much information, but a little more intimate than to have these American intercessors.

"One question for you though. Can you recommend an art historian? Somebody who's a real expert on the Italian masters?"

Jacinta glared at her darkened window. "Si, sono io. I am an expert." Even if she'd be stuck in this dead-end internship until the curator dropped dead at his desk

Nick let out a long breath. "That's what I thought, but...this is a little awkward. Dom prefers that you not get involved, and I think his objections are valid. He doesn't want you to get hurt."

Un obiezione valida: to not wind up in a foreign hospital, recovering from surgery. "Hang up. I will text him." She rang off, the phone heavy in her hand. She'd been waiting to hear from him, she knew he was safe—and yet...Jacinta moved from her stool to the overstuffed chair in the corner and flopped into it. :*Ciao, Bello! Glad you're alive.*

:*Anch'io. Someday, I'll get to tell you all about it, with my own voice.*
:*Can't wait.*

Then she tapped, :*Why do they need an art expert?*
:*It's not safe.*

Jacinta scowled at the phone. Should she be pleased he cared enough to protect her, or annoyed at his paternalism? :*How far apart are we now? I don't even know what country you're in, so what's the harm if they have some questions?*

:*Poland. Another country for my list! City name with lots of z's*

Poland? Che—? And now he was being flippant. This was Dom— he'd memorized the city name the moment he saw it.:*You're a thousand miles away, how dangerous can it be?*

Then the dots of a reply pending. Then nothing. Then dots again. And again, nothing, as if he typed out and deleted his words over and over.

She pulled up her long legs, clutching the phone as if she could make him respond faster by focusing her tension through the connection. :*I can feel you trying to lie to me. Since we were seven years old, you can't lie to me.* Since they became blood siblings with a dagger from her father's collection of arms and armor. Her ex-father, head of her ex-family. No wonder she was so close with Dom and his own family.

The phone lay silent in her hand, and finally, :*They need to identify a painting. Maybe a Caravaggio.*

Her lips parted in a silent laugh. :*From the Kaiser Friedrich? The paintings are found?* But those three paintings were well-documented, easily found in any catalog of the artist's work.

Another long hesitation followed, then, :*No, e si.*

No and yes? Those paintings were found, this wasn't one of them.

Jacinta's throat went dry, and for a moment, she almost shared the acute stinging he must feel from his wound, but in her case, it was the sting of desire. *:They think they found a Caravaggio. An unknown one.*

:It's unfamiliar.

And he had a photographic memory, easily capable of recalling the entire known oeuvre for an artist like Caravaggio, his life cut tragically short—then she connected the last detail. *:You've seen it.*

:Just a photo.

Her heart raced. Her best friend, her amati, though he'd yet to know it, caught a glimpse of her future. Jacinta had lost so much these last few years, even before her own family disowned her. These Americans had tracked a Nazi treasure across the EU. They'd fought, and killed and nearly died for it, then given him the credit. Thanks to them, he was made in his chosen career, while she—

:Show me.

:Have to go—sorry!

:What's happening?

No answer.

:Dom, you can't just leave me like that!

Trapped once again on the blade's edge between fear and longing, Jacinta sat alone in the dark. The man she loved stood between her and her destiny. Or maybe he died there.

Chapter Six

The spare tire neatly defended Avram's widow, but the man leaned in at precisely the wrong moment. Moishe had no time for curses. He already stood ahead, his shape merging with the shadow of the van. Now he charged past the open trunk, pivoted and fired again. The shot chunked into wood, a panel half the size of a door, rushing at him.

The wood panel slammed into Moishe. He slid back through the snow and crashed into the hood of the car behind. A shrill alarm howled from the abused vehicle.

Moishe's hand, flung wide by the assault, banged against the hood, but he didn't drop the gun.

His assailant shoved the panel upward, jamming into Moishe's chin.

Moishe rocked hard to the side. If the snow-slicked ground worked against him, let it hurt them both.

The man's feet skidded and Moishe turned, swinging his gun up, but the man used his own sliding momentum to whip the wooden panel back again, smacking Moishe's hand. Too late: he'd drawn the second gun.

The man finished with a back lunge, disengaging, then whirling the panel sideways, the corner jabbing into Moishe's gut.

He absorbed the impact and kicked back, sweeping the man's legs out from under him. The man landed atop his erstwhile shield and weapon.

"Moishe! Stop!" Sadie braced behind the Land Rover's open trunk, her gun extended.

The man kicked high with both legs as Moishe turned. The double-blow pressed Moishe into the car and launched the American across the parking lot on a makeshift sled. Moishe blinked. Had he meant to do that?

Moishe fired, both shots spitting into the ground as the American slid between two cars. From the apartment building a window slid open, someone shouted outside. A few more lights flicked on. Moishe dodged around the car with its worthless alarm howling into the void. He raced down the side, around the back of the noisy car.

An engine started, with the mighty roar of eight cylinders. Moishe slipped one gun away, running hard, his off-hand reaching ahead into the gloom.

In the trunk of the Rover, a flash of the painting: golden arms in a darkened scene. The trunk door slammed and Sadie sprinted, picking up speed alongside the car, then popping a door and leaping inside. The vehicle's spare tire formed a solid marker like the moon rising against the emptiness where the rear window should be.

The vehicle swung a turn, angling across the lot, but it had to turn wide, dodging the other cars. Moishe ran an intercept, like the hero of somebody's football team. He ran up the back of a coupe and launched from the hood, arms wide to embrace that spare tire.

He landed against it with a thump, gripping the tire case as if it were an opponent he must stop at all costs. His feet dragged a moment along the pavement, then he pulled his legs up and planted his feet on the bumper.

In the back seat, Sadie spun about, her eyes flaring wide. "Chief! We got trouble!"

She twisted in her seat, bringing up the gun.
Moishe's pistol was still in his hand.

Chapter Seven

The Land Rover lurched as their pursuer somehow leapt onto the back, and Grant caught a glimpse of his face in the rear view mirror: flat and expressionless, displaying neither fear nor fury. D.A.'s shout said they had trouble. No kidding.

He cranked the wheel, and the big vehicle ground across the lot in an angry arc, dangerously close to one of the metal streetlights.

D.A. fired out the back. "He's still armed!"

Ducking low in case of gunshots, Grant flung the vehicle into reverse, the change of course hurling him forward, then he turned in his seat, peering back. Moishe's gun arm wrapped the spare tire, his free hand groping. For what? Trying to open the trunk.

The Rover mashed him against the light pole. The overhead light flickered out as the metal groaned. Grant yanked the vehicle back into drive and the tires squealed.

"It's open!" D.A. was scrambling toward the back.

A half-dozen warning lights flashed across the dashboard, including the trunk open indicator. With another spin of the wheel, Grant backed into the light pole again, slamming the trunk. Moishe's arm briefly flailed, then fell back as Grant accelerated away.

"Do we still have the painting?"

D.A. gulped. "No. Shit, Chief!"

The sound of sirens rose somewhere beyond, and the onlookers from the apartment complex shouted and cheered. Who were they for, and who against? Grant jolted to the side as he finished his turn, the headlights raking across a bizarre sight.

Next to the tilting light pole, a huge man grappled with the wooden crate, heaving it up from the ground, holding it to his chest as he fought inertia and the snowy ground. In the windows above, a group of people pumped their fists, then started screaming, pointing toward the vehicle. Grant was about to look like the world's biggest bully, shaking down the guy for his hard-won treasure.

Moishe got moving, turning sideways to put another car between him and the Rover. D.A. leaned out the back window, pistol in hand. "Put it down, Moishe!"

Too late, the guy slipped between two parked vehicles as the first whirling light of police response rushed into the parking lot at the back. Great. About to be on the wanted list in another country. "Call Nick!" Grant shouted.

"Calling Nick," the car responded in a smooth robotic voice, and Grant almost laughed.

Nick picked up. "What's on, Chief?"

"Hot pursuit. Perpetrator on foot with the painting, heading north out of the parking lot. Armed and very dangerous."

"Casualties?"

"Negative, but we've got company." Grant turned the wheel and squeaked the Rover between the apartment wall and a storage shed. He spared a glance for the rear view, and saw D.A. pull in from the window, tumbling onto the backseat as they bumped over the sidewalk and onto the street. "We're too conspicuous. Ditching the tail, can you—"

"Already moving, Chief. Gooney's out the door, I'm after him."

"Go to," said Grant. "Over and out." He raced down the near-empty street and ran the light, turning sharply into heavier traffic. They'd only just found the painting, and now it was gone. How had this Moishe even known to look? "D.A., you all right back there?"

"Yeah." She sighed. "A-and-O times four, Chief. I thought he meant to shoot us, but he only wanted the trunk latch."

"Copy that."

Flashing lights appeared from the alley several blocks behind them now. The police. Go to ground, or race for it? Neither seemed a good choice in a foreign city, against cops who knew the streets. Really tempting to ditch the car. Dom's grandfather's car. Or what was left of it.

"Pull over," said D.A. "We don't want to get too far from the target."

"You want me to let them catch us."

She bobbed her head. "Follow my lead." Her face, half-lit, wore shadow and hurt.

"You don't have to prove anything to me, not right now."

"Please."

Trust. Maybe this was step one of getting it back. Grant pulled over to the side of the road and left the engine running. Trust, but verify.

Chapter Eight

All things considered, Moishe's retrieval had been a success. Smashing success, if one wished to be funny. Now, he flattened himself into a doorway, hefting the painting in front of him, counting on the flat square crate to become just another piece of the visual detritus behind the apartment building. The police car blasted by him, pursuing the vehicle.

Moishe lugged the crate, cradling the painting against his chest. An old cloth lay back over the surface, so it had some defense, but to have a stray button dent the canvas, or a stray bullet puncture it might destroy its true value. He'd caught only a glimpse, but it confirmed, for him, both the subject and the artist. This was the fist step, only, but a large one, on the path to the great dissolution. The great disillusion...

Coming to the corner, he paused and scanned both ways. The street to his left led back between the parking lot and the hospital. To the right, his modest vehicle waited, among a few others. From the windows above, a few voices tossed speculations back and forth. Gunfight, car chase, in their boring old city.

A steady, but not strong, stream of traffic moved along the larger street. No pedestrians. Moishe turned the corner.

"Hold it right there." English words, American accent, punctuated by the sound of a hammer's click. "Put down the crate and back away."

Moishe hesitated long enough, a calibrated interval to show he considered the other man's words. Then he executed a spin, sharply around to smash this new assailant with the edge of the crate.

"Shit!" The American staggered under the force of the blow, catching himself before he hit the street.

"Freeze, or I take you down!" A new voice, further away.

No. Shifting the crate a little lower, chest to thigh, Moishe barreled forward, putting his full power behind the crate. He rushed at the man he'd just attacked, battering into him. Moishe ducked, bracing the crate, as he shoved the stranger off the curb.

The man's feet stumbled. He tripped left, pushed off, trying to get around Moishe's attack. A gunshot whizzed by to crack into the building's facade beyond.

Moishe pivoted and shoved forward with his left arm, knocking the man back again like a table tennis ball faced by an implacable paddle.

"Jesus!" the guy yelped.

The glint of water from a grate. Moishe surged forward, shoving with a flood of strength.

The American hit the ice. His feet slipped and he hit the ground, rolling, already starting up again.

Horns blared. Someone rushed from Moishe's unprotected back and side. He shifted the crate to defense and ran, kicking the downed man, forcing him into the street.

Tires screeched, and someone swerved.

"Gooney!" the other voice. A bullet sparked from the pavement near Moishe's legs. The other shooter was clever and cautious, aiming low rather than risk the artwork, or his compatriot who was already rising.

Moishe planted one foot, pivoted hard and kicked the American's gut. The man fell again, into traffic.

Finishing his turn, Moishe ran diagonally back to the sidewalk, up to his car, brace the painting, click the key fob and yank open the door.

The second American strode into traffic, arms spread, coat flapping and hands spread, forcing people to swerve around him and his fallen friend. Predictable loyalty. Perhaps commendable, if counterproductive to mission success. Streams of curses greeted them.

Moishe slid the crate into his back seat. Barely room.Something struck nearby. A bullet? No, a bit of road debris. He glanced back.

The second man stuck his arm down, not looking, the other man grabbed his hand and pulled himself up. The pair of them stood back to back in the street now, a gun in the white man's hand. Moishe slammed the door, jumped in the front seat, tapping the power button. The car purred to life, and he was pulling away from the curb even before his door closed. The traffic pattern had gone completely off, cars swinging across the lane to avoid the two men. That did not mean he must follow suit.

Moishe swung his car into an arc, into oncoming traffic—the traffic already disrupted and sent on a new course. He sank his accelerator to the floor, and the white American's eyes flared. White rims of panic and a desperate yell. "Go, Nick, go!"

The two men leapt in opposite directions.

Moishe clipped one of them as he rushed into the gap where they had been. Just as well. He should prefer not to damage the car he currently depended on.

He smoothly cut in front of an oncoming bus, wishing it godspeed to finish the job as he joined the other lane and drove, inexorably, toward his reward.

Chapter Nine

Jacinta let it rest a long moment, counting heartbeats, and waiting for Dom to pick up again. *:va bene. I'm calling. You just listen.*

As she was about to call, his reply appeared: *There were shots. Outside. Nick and Tony have gone.*

She bit her lip. *:But you're all right?*

:Si. Ma, same as before. Already hurt.

:I'm definitely calling.

A few dots, nothing, then *:Video call? I'd like to see your face.*

Sure, but he might not like what she had to say. *:Two minutes!* And a few emojis. Jacinta crossed to her school desk and propped the phone in its cradle, then she poked the app and tapped his profile shot, one from a couple of years back, after a haircut. Should replace that with a new one.

The sigil circled for a moment, then he picked up, answering with a half-syllable, and a soft moan. They winced almost in unison, and he gave a half-hearted wave, the hospital lighting giving his face a greenish cast. Maybe she should stick to kindness for now, treating him extra gently, at least until his friends came back from wherever they--

Shots. As in gunshots.

Jacinta swallowed and offered a wide smile. "Dominic, shh, shh. Va bene. You don't have to talk, I know it hurts."

He started to nod, then exhaled softly, and held up a finger. Fumbling to put on his glasses, he picked up the tablet from the bed next to him and moved his hand over the surface, then displayed the screen with his careful writing. "Ciao! It's good to see you."

"I hope you don't have to stay there long? It's better to heal at home, I think."

He gave a thumbs up, glancing briefly away from the screen, then back with a faint smile.

"You're worried about your friends. Of course you are. They must've been through worse than this, no? I'm sure they'll be fine."

Another thumbs up, then, "You won't believe the things they've done, just the last few days." A tap to erase, and he wrote, "They're giving me the book rights, to write the whole thing!"

Jacinta leaned in closer. "Fantastico! Have you checked your book sales since the article? You must have."

His lashes fluttered as he glanced down, his cheeks slightly flushed, then he wrote again. "Up times 100...o."

"You're kidding."

A tip of his shoulders stood in for the usual Roman shrug. "Sales weren't so good lately, so it's not so much as it sounds. But also one of the conspiracy groups has amplified the story. Already it's with the AP, worldwide."

"And that's before any interviews or the big outlets. You're set, Dominic! You can quit your uncle's and finally just write."

Thumbs up, then he set down the tablet to give both thumbs up. Then—did his hand tremble a little?—he pointed toward her, and wrote, "I can finally come home to Naples."

"Bravo!" She clapped. He was in good spirits, knowing his future improved, in spite of his injury. What better time to remind him of her own future.

Jacinta took a deep breath and pinned him with her gaze. "Then I think you understand, Dominic. This painting, this maybe Caravaggio. If I can help to identify it, and publish my results...this could be my career, Dom. This would make me."

His brows pinched together over those warm brown eyes. Adorable. Then he gestured toward his throat and his surroundings, lifting an empty palm.

"You don't think it was worth it, Dom? For a thousand times the sales in a few hours?" Her throat ached. She reached out as if she could touch him. "You know how hard this has been for me. How hard everything has been. I could work for a decade, and get nothing, get shut out of publication, much less of a decent job. You think I want to be touching up portraits, living in an attic?" She indicated her own surroundings, the cheapest place one could rent without leaving the city limits—nine blocks from the family house where she'd never be welcome again. Her eyes stung. Stupido.

A long time ago, her father taught her and her brother to shoot, hunting rabbits and shooting targets. Last time she had considered shooting anything, it was to reject the idea of suicide. Dom was the only person who knew. The only person who'd been there, even then.

He sagged against his propped pillows, and his glance fell aside, to the streaks of blood down his shirt, like a martyr painted on a church wall, drawing attention to the wounds of his own death. How much was it worth to her, to claim this chance at a career-making discovery?

"It's just a painting, Dominic. Just a look. Your friends need help, and I can help them, you know that I can. Please. If not for me—"

He slashed his hand through the air, erasing her? Her words? His finger traced over the tablet, his gaze not returning to the camera, then he held it up. "Of course for you. Of course you deserve it." The tablet fell to his lap as he buried his hands in his hair.

"You don't have to protect me, Dom," she added.

He pulled his knees up, drawing the tablet close again, then finally tapped a few other things. Her phone buzzed, and the blip of an incoming message appeared.

"Grazie mille, Dominic!" She blew him a kiss. "Spetta..."

Picking up the phone, she tapped open the new message, obscuring Dom's face in the hospital bed. Expanding the image to fill the screen, she drank it in. If it were not an autograph work of Caravaggio, it was one of the finest imitators she'd ever seen. Jeremiah knelt in the Temple, before the golden Menorah, startled by the angel who brought him the news that his wife, thought barren, would bear a child after all, a baby who would grow up to become St. John the Baptist.

A most unusual subject, she tried to recall if she'd ever seen another depiction. Caravaggio could be original, an iconoclast who chose prostitutes and street people as models for saints, but to devise a completely new image to represent the life of the Baptist? She sent the picture to her cloud.

"Dom. We might have to go." Nick's voice in the hospital room.

Jacinta stared at the image. Something else about it...her eye traced the richly detailed branches of the Menorah.

"Don't worry, I'll be okay. Head wounds always bleed a lot." The other American, Tony.

Jacinta's head jerked up and she flipped back to the app. Tony leaned heavily on the side of the bed, clearly winded, fresh blood streaking his forehead as he tried to catch his breath.

"What's happened?" she asked.

Tony jerked upright, out of the image, and Dom waved a hand, then patted the air in a gesture of calming, pointing toward her, toward his phone which must be propped nearby. The Black man, Nick, leaned in, smiling at her with a little wave of his own. Dirt and water streaked his coat and his palm showed the parallel scratches of recent injury, bits of skin poking up, bits of dirt trapped. Whatever had befallen them, they hadn't even stopped to clean their wounds.

"Hey, Jacinta. Good to see you. Thanks for keeping our man company while we stepped out." Nick swallowed, glanced away, then gave a nod, as if he'd received a message outside of her hearing. "Our other team was attacked, rather unexpectedly. We thought we'd be safe here for a while, and get a chance to recover. It's not looking that way."

"Is the painting all right?"

Nick regarded Dom, who gave that lifted palm gesture again. "It's been stolen."

Her heart fell. "You have to get it back—right away!"

Tony leaned in on the other side, looking grim and battered, but unbowed. "Don't worry, lady, we're on it."

Chapter Ten

D.A. stepped out of the car as the police car pulled in behind them. "Thank God!" Her voice shook, all sign of the strong, fierce operator vanishing in a moment. "Thank God you're here, officers! Did you get him? The man who stole my painting?"

"Hands up! Where we can see them!" the officer barked, but his gun stayed low.

"The man shot at us, he attacked us in the hospital parking lot—people were watching out the windows, they could tell you, I'm sure. A big man, huge!" She indicated his size with sweeping gestures, standing on her toes and shaking with the fervor of her tale. "You see how he's damaged our car? He almost killed me, and my husband had to drive like a crazy man just to get out of there. This maniac, he jumped on our car!"

Ninety-nine percent true, like the best lies always were. Grant picked up his part. "We're safe now, sweetie, the police are here. It's gonna be okay."

Another officer approached on Grant's side, saying something in Polish.

"Do you want me to get out?" Grant offered. "I'd rather sit. I'm not used to that much excitement." He lifted his hands from the wheel, keeping them in view, letting them shake a little as if with an adrenaline rush.

The officer looked to his companion, speaking again. Did the men even understand what she was saying?

Then, from behind came a blaring of horns and angry voices. The officer on Grant's side spun about, shouting.

"That's him! He still has the painting," D.A. shouted. "Get him, officers! There he is!"

The mirrors showed chaos building a few blocks behind, cars swerving wildly into the wrong lane. What the Hell was going on back there? Grant had a horrible feeling he already knew, and he wouldn't like the consequences.

The officer on Grant's side started running, shouting, and now his gun was in his hand.

"It's all right, we see him," said D.A.'s man, as he was retreating rapidly. "Don't worry. We take care of this."

"Thank you, officers! I'll pray for you!" D.A. hollered after them, waving enthusiastically.

The officer leapt into his tiny car and spun the wheel, peeling away from the curb and heading back in the direction of the latest fracas. D.A. jumped into the front seat.

"Run or hide?" he asked.

"Hide." She kicked her gun further under the seat. At least the cops hadn't seen it. "Nick and Gooney are back there."

"Figured." Grant let the mess unfolding in his rear view cover his own escape. How much was this painting worth? Moishe might be willing to pay the price, but were they? The Land Rover became one of the tangle of vehicles grumbling through the snow, leaving the scene of some wild tourist action. "You get a look at Moishe? Where he went, what he drove?"

"Something low, dark and fast. Good turning radius. I'm a little surprised he fit inside."

"Yeah." He took a few turns, working back toward the hospital.

There'd been a repair shop a few blocks before the hospital, which might offer them protective cover. "Turns out Moishe wasn't done with us."

"If he got what he wanted..."

The man had run up one side of a car and leaped off of it to grab their own moving vehicle. Grant's first introduction to the Fist had been up close and personal, a beating that still ached in his flesh. If he'd gotten what he wanted, let him have it. The Bone Guard had enough to deal with. They'd completed their assignment, been paid rather handsomely—and a good thing, since they'd be liable for the damage to the Rover, and probably some hospital charges. Dom seemed unlikely to sue, thank goodness.

Grant envisioned loading the Land Rover onto an auto transport back to Naples, and the rest of them flying home. First class for the trans-Atlantic leg. Lord knew they'd earned it.

The car trilled suddenly and an image of a handsome young woman, her direct gaze framed by auburn hair appeared on the screen, "Jacinta" blazoned over the profile picture.

"Who's that?"

D.A. frowned. "Dom's friend, I think. The art historian." Her finger hovered over the control screen as the onboard system rang.

This Jacinta must know that Dom wasn't in the car. Did he want to know what she had to say? Yeah, okay, he kind of did. The painting drove further away by the moment, in the hands of a single-minded ex-Mossad agent, probably never to be seen again. "Go ahead."

D.A. tapped a key. "Hello, Jacinta? This is D.A. I'm another friend of Dom's."

"Sì, sì, fantastico!" said a deep, breathless voice. "I have been talking with Dom, and the others arrived, Nick and Tony, sì?"

"Right. Thanks for letting us know."

Grant flashed a thumbs-up. Good to know they'd gotten back to the hospital, apparently under their own power.

"Dom has shown me the painting the one he says you find with the Nazi things."

D.A.'s brow furrowed, and she muttered, "More civilians."

"Doesn't matter," Grant whispered back. "We're out. Let him keep it."

Louder, he said, "Jacinta, ciao. This is the Chief—"the only way that Dom knew him, so far as Grant was aware—"What do you think? Did it look like a Caravaggio?"

"I think yes, but I would need much more time, many more tests. He tells me it is stolen from you, your Nick? Is that right?"

Grant kept his voice neutral. "Nick and Tony would know more than I do at the moment."

"We have to get it back," she said, her voice urgent.

"First of all, there's no we. I don't want more people to get hurt over a painting. I know it's valuable, but—"

"No, no, no! You don't understand about Caravaggio. He paints only from life, he's famous for this. The others despise him for it, his competitors, and sometimes his clients."

Relevance? he wanted to say, but didn't. "O-kay."

Grant pulled into an unlit parking area filled with cars under tarps and propped on bricks.

"He has models for everything," Jacinta went on, "and he takes props, even the wings, they are meant for the stage. No imagination say the haters, si?"

"Looked pretty imaginative to me, I gotta say." D.A. found a water bottle somewhere, and offered it to Grant.

"Aspetta, aspetta—listen! Think of this! Where does he get this menorah? This is not from the city synagogue, and they don't give it to him if it were, do you see? Since Roman times, there have been stories, what happens to the items they stole from Jerusalem. Taken to Carthage, some say, but others say no. They say these things never leave Rome, and his patrons, they are some very powerful men. Caravaggio never paints from the mind, not ever." She paused, and concluded, "What if it's not just a menorah, this item he's painted from —what if it is the Menorah?"

Chapter Eleven

As Moishe accelerated away from the bus and the bodies that rolled across the tarmac, police lights flashed and a siren stabbed at him from the snow behind. This would not do. He had the painting in his possession, to be paused by the authorities, even for a moment, was unconscionable.

They drove a tiny, compact city vehicle meant for ticketing cars badly parked. It slewed a little in the snow but still gained as other vehicles let it pass. It drew closer, pacing him like a stinging fly vexing a racehorse.

With a terse command, Moishe brought up his onboard maps, watching the streets unfurl around him. The mountains weren't far. Streets getting narrower, turns sharper. Moishe sped up. A voice bleated at him from a loudspeaker. He need not hear every word to know grasp the essence of the message. His malfeasance in the city had been noted. His immediate compliance was required. He might have a few moments before they called for reinforcements.

Ahead, the dead space of a park on the map, a gap of darkness between the residential streets. They wished him to stop? Very well. He flicked on a turn signal, keeping his speed high as he pulled into the wider section of the road. Grand old trees sheltered the parking area and snow sifted down. Moishe turned carefully, ending with the car's nose toward the road. With the press of a button, he lowered his window.

Snowflakes filtered inside, speckling his sleeve, vanishing in his breath, resting gently on the muzzle of his gun.

The little police car skidded slightly making the turn, slowing already and pulling up as if to be sure he wouldn't simply drive away. Come, little people. He had no intention of leaving.

White bits swirled in the blue glow of their lights. Two officers, one of them reaching for a radio, the other starting to open his door.

Moishe met the eye of the man in the car, and pulled the trigger. The window cracked, a tiny hole appearing at the center of a spider's web. A corresponding hole in the forehead of the officer, his eyes still staring as blood trickled between them.

The first shot stopped both officers, the second man frozen for just a moment. Just long enough. Firing through the gap of the partially opened door, Moishe's second shot took the officer in the chest, and he squeezed off a third shot as the body jerked, just to be sure.

A fourth shot killed the flashing light, but stopping the siren required getting out of the car. Moishe used the dead driver's hand to trigger the siren off, and the park fell into blessed silence.

"You're welcome," he told the corpses as he walked away.

Chapter Twelve

Jacinta held the phone to her cheek, listening to the quality of the silence on the other end.

All great works made use of negative space, the areas outside of the subjects that showed the relationships among them. If only Dom had told her more about these people before now. She didn't even know with whom she was negotiating or what might win them to her side. Her chance at greatness slipped away by the moment, and she waited in her garret on the affirmation of strangers. Dom would be the first to tell her it wasn't healthy, this dependence on the word of others.

"Let me get this right," said the Chief. "You're telling me there's a chance that, not only did the original Menorah from the Second Temple survive the destruction of Rome, but that one of Caravaggio's patrons knew where it was. That person showed it to him, they commissioned this painting to include it."

He sounded skeptical, but rational, open, perhaps, to her argument. Too bad she hadn't honed it like a thesis before she made her defense. "Sì, esatamente. We have receipts and letters, we can show that even the armor in his portrait of Wignacourt, per esempio, that it's real, that he's borrowed helmets and other things. The wings for the angels—"she was repeating herself now.

She drew a deep breath. "I have only just put the photo on my large screen, and of course the light is not so good on the image, but the Menorah is so bright, and so distinctive. He's known to make such great detail mostly in his private commissions." As she spoke, she scrolled around the image, zooming in on the arms of the Menorah, then tracking down to the base. "This matches the descriptions, the blossoms from which the branches emerge, the number of layers at the bottom, every detail precise. He is not a scholar of the Bible, and has no interest in this, but only in painting and in earning money. So I believe has someone has shown it to him, loaned it to him for this work. Va bene?"

"With you so far," he said.

"And there is this subject at all. I think there are no other depictions of it, Zacariah. He's not so popular, not a saint or a martyr. Why should Caravaggio choose this? He doesn't. There is no church to hire for this work. It is about St. John, certo, which he frequently paints, but never this moment. This is the only scene in the New Testament which takes place in the Temple. If this patron wishes to have the Menorah shown, this is the only scene for it."

Another long pause, then the woman, D.A., said, "But why? Even if his patron has the Menorah, why paint it? It's been secret for, what, like a thousand years by then?"

Now it was Jacinta's turn to be quiet for a long moment. "Maybe he wants a commemoration for some reason. Or maybe it has been lost for a thousand years, and only just been found? There is much excavation in Rome at this time, things being discovered as they dig up to expand their palaces," she finished triumphantly.

As she spoke, she envisioned the whole thing. A treasure, hidden from the destruction of Rome, and then lost for centuries, maybe forever—until, as so often happens, a shovel breaks through the wall and something remarkable is revealed. Something lost for a thousand years returns to the light...like this lost Caravaggio itself, discovered in a Nazi stash only to be stolen again.

Jacinta wanted that painting. She wanted it so keenly she considered jumping a plane to Poland to search for it herself. The chance of a lifetime had nearly fallen into her lap only to spring away again. She would certainly not let it go so easily.

"Thanks for your thoughts, Jacinta," Chief said after a long moment. "We'll have to talk this over. Okay to call you at this number?"

"Si, certo—any time!"

"Great, thanks. Ciao." He sounded serious and distant.

"Ciao," she said faintly as he rang off.

Her phone felt dead in her hand, the connection lost. They would do nothing, would they.

They feared too much, but now that she, too, had seen her chance, she understood better how Dom was convinced to leave his boring and comfortable job, to be hurt in the search for something greater. Was she willing to lose some blood for the chance to confirm an unknown Caravaggio? Assolutamente.

Jacinta settled at her computer and got to work.

Chapter Thirteen

D.A.'s face barely interrupted the chiaroscuro of the car's interior. She raked a hand through her hair and a few chips of glass twinkled to the floor.

"The Menorah," Grant echoed. "From the Temple."

Giving a fierce shake of her shoulders that shook loose a few more shards, D.A. braced her hands on the dashboard, head bowed. "Could be all bullshit. She sounds pretty eager to get her hands on that painting, and we don't know enough about the artist to fact-check her. Even if it's not bullshit, if he really did see it--there's no telling what happened to it after the painting. Might've been melted down to make communion vessels."

"Copy that." He took another swallow from the water bottle.

Hydration. Rest. Safety. Really could use some basic comforts right now. He'd been knocked back a few rungs on the ladder of survival, and would really like to get climbing again.

"What if it's neither? Not bullshit. Not melted." He sat up a little straighter.

The snow had stopped, leaving the night clearer by the moment. Their hiding place had a diagonal view back toward the hospital parking lot. A lone figure moved among the cars, tall, lean, with a familiar stride. Nick paused, looking down, then bent a little awkwardly to pick something up. The wooden lid of the crate. Huh. Expected the cops to return and check the scene, or send reinforcements, or he'd've gone back for it himself. It might still provide some clue to the mystery he was determined not to claim.

Grant tapped out a quick message. Across the distance between them, Nick paused, bracing the slab to check his pocket.

D.A. remained silent.

Nick started walking toward the car lot, toting the big slab. Good. Grant turned his attention—most of it anyway--back to his companion. "D.A.?"

"It would explain all the interest," she murmured. "Moishe. Maybe the Warden even knew. Not the subject of the painting, but that it was a hint, the start of something bigger."

"Two maps, two different hunts, linked by the painting. What about your Mossad contacts?"

She flinched. "I don't see how they'd know anything about it, but then I don't know how Moishe knew. And yeah, maybe they have information we need, or maybe they have the right to know." She pulled back and faced him. "None of which means I'm just gonna give them a call."

He raised his palm. "I know."

With a gesture toward the window, he said, "Nick's coming."

She glanced in that direction. "I'm losing my touch."

"You've had a rough week."

"Not as rough as yours."

He shrugged and gestured Nick around the side.

"You're really okay with that? What happened to you? We thought you were dead that time. For real."

"Hasn't happened yet." Then he considered his ink, the tattoos that circled his neck and embellished his arm almost to the wrist, every one of them another ticket to the Lazarus Club: the place where a man might rise from the dead. "Or maybe it has, dozen times or so. What's one more?"

"Hey." Nick opened the door behind Grant and clambered in, still hauling the slab. The diagonal braces on the top made for convenient grips, as Grant discovered when he made it his shield.

Grant half-turned to admit both of them to his field of view. "Make yourself comfortable. What brings you to my office?"

"Couple of things. The first one, you know. Dom showed his friend the painting, and told her about the shots. She was on with him when we got back." He turned a palm up. "His room's no longer a secure environment."

A nod. "He's been through a lot. Regardless, he's not used to the level of confidentiality we expect on a mission."

Nick cut a glance toward D.A. as if this had been a dig about her own recent lapse. Definitely not Grant's style, as they should both know.

"What did you need to tell us?"

"We need a takeover on Gooney's phone, ASAP. He chucked it into the perp's car when the door was open to load the painting."

D.A. gripped the back of her seat, suddenly kneeling to face him. "We can track it?"

"You got it." Nick grinned. "Gooney may be an ass-hat, but he's also a genius."

Chapter Fourteen

The world of art restoration was a small, elite guild, and most of its higher-level members had specialties. The rest, like Jacinta, scrounged for scraps on the margins, like those creatures in the corners of Medieval manuscripts. Whoever had taken the painting couldn't risk just revealing it to a prominent expert in the field, though they'd want to do that later if they wished the piece properly acknowledged and added to the canon. No, if these people required the services of an art historian or restorer, they would be looking outside the establishment.

A person couldn't live in Naples for very long—certainly not if they knew the art world—without learning about its darker side. Many of the art collectors in southern Italy belonged to very old, well-established families, the sort of families you either worked with or avoided. Or you were born into them, and had to confront the truths about that. With the severing of her own family connections, Jacinta's path to avoidance became easier.

She had a couple of grad school friends who had chosen the other route, some of them freelancing as curators for very private exhibitions, or helping deep-pocketed buyers to make investments in art that might never see the light again. Most of the people she knew did not deliberately aid in money laundering through art, but she suspected a few had simply been looking the other way during elaborate games with invoices for works that never arrived, or were sent to a different buyer entirely. Nobody she knew had ever been hurt by this trade, and some of them had readily paid off their student debt and bought homes of their own or established their own galleries while Jacinta slaved away for the museum by day, and for outside clients by night, hoping one day to be recognized.

In truth, Dominic's righteous nature had encouraged her to pursue more upright means of support, in spite of her circumstances. If she were willing to capitalize on the family that rejected her, she could have done more. Yet his own step into a different world resulted in the kind of success he'd been working so hard for, while she lived in a garret eating canned meals. E basta. She'd had enough.

Besides, she reasoned as she opened an incognito browser, if she did get offers, she could simply turn down all but the one she wanted. Her fingers hesitated over the keyboard. These were not the sort of people who allowed one to publish their analysis, or to use before and after images for a restoration portfolio...would she settle for seeing it? For the chance to work with a masterpiece, even if nobody ever knew? If the money were good enough, would that outweigh the chance for fame and publication?

She had a fleeting glimpse of an undiscovered treasure—how would she live with herself if she never tried? She had not become who she was by dodging the risks the way that Dom had for so long. Was he sorry for his choice, now that his books climbed the best-seller lists? Now that he counted among his friends the sort of people he'd only written about?

Va bene. Also, she was jealous. At least she was adult enough to admit it.

Dom had shown her some things, showing off it seemed at the time, about how to browse the dark web, how to find information none were meant to have, and how to drop the sort of hints that upright citizens never noticed. First then, to place herself among her colleagues, and find a way to stand out from them. To make herself so appealing to this art thief that she'd be the clear choice to restore their stolen masterpiece —and to see what else she might discover.

She created her page in both Italian and English—the common language of the dark web, at least in the art world. Impeccable and carefully vague credentials topped her C.V., with a chapter from her thesis about how the darkness in Caravaggio's work reflected the tragic nature of his own life. Not the most distinctive material, but a subject that showed her interest without telegraphing her original research. She included cropped, close-up photos of finished restoration, fragments only that would not be readily identifiable, but served to show what she could do. It was one thing to place herself in the path of destiny, quite another for these people to know her address.

The finishing touch: a few broad hints about her need for money, and her absolute discretion. Taking a deep breath, she clicked "post."

Chapter Fifteen

Moishe drove some distance into the wilderness and back out again, and found a small hotel with their sign still lit, and a dangling notice about free wifi. When the receptionist chirped at him in Polish, he shrugged and shook his head, managing a pleasant smile. Ground floor, he indicated with gestures, using flowing, illegible lines to invent a name and address to write on the registration card she pushed toward him.

Hard to tell if she spoke more rapidly because she was nervous, or because the smile reassured her. In any case, she handed over the key, a genuine metal artifact of a by-gone day, with a big fob to prevent theft.

Her hands articulated the directions to his room, and a gesture toward a bell offered...what? Ah. Luggage assistance. Moishe shook his head. What he must carry should be left to no other hands.

He toted in his leather valise, depositing that on the bed. It would be short—they often were—but the width would do. He'd prefer a room with an outside door, but such was not on offer for most of this region. No matter, the place had large enough windows, and no sign of cameras. Moishe pushed open his window and leaned out. Bushes.

Snow. But the building had wide eaves, protecting a swath of ground alongside. He climbed out and returned to his car for the painting.

In the absence of the crate's wooden lid, an old cloth protected the surface. He must do better when he had the chance. He considered reusing the desk surface from his hotel room, but that would be noticed, leading shortly to noticing that all the information he'd filled out on the guest register was patently false.

The crate didn't fit through his window, and Moishe patiently removed the painting, putting it through onto the floor, on edge, then turning the crate behind a bush. Just a piece of hotel detritus.

He shut the window and secured it, then closed the blinds and got his first look at the piece. The artist had rendered everything with his typical darkness and striking expression, Zacariah's astonished face regarding the appearance of the angel, with the menorah between them. He placed the painting flat on the floor and removed a camera from his valise. Standing on the bed to capture the entire frame, Moishe documented every inch of the painting with various magnifications. He could not be sure what would be important. A few markings on the back as well, and he captured those. Paintings of the era sometimes bore the initials of the owner.

This completed, he sat down, and prepared his upload. The camera had a few features customized for his use, and the site to which he added the images was nearly impregnable, or as much as money could make it so. The transfer, over the hotel's rather feeble wifi, took longer than he'd like. Moishe spent the time cleaning his guns and re-loading.

It had been a surprise to see the drowned man again, face to face. No surprise the ferocity with which the man resisted him this time. It began to seem inevitable that they meet at least once more, and that one of them should die. This man appeared difficult to kill, but then, all men had weaknesses. Well. Almost all men.

The upload had finished. Moishe replaced his camera and took out the antique cellphone at the bottom of his bag. Repugnant, but necessary. He switched it on and placed it on the bed, moving the painting out of the way against a wall.

When the phone rang, Moishe picked up promptly.

"Good work, excellent!" Another chirpy voice. It was not in Moishe's nature to make people happy, had not been for a very long time, and here he had apparently done it again.

His associate hesitated, providing a space which he apparently, still, thought Moishe might fill. Finally, the man chuckled. "Any difficulties? Anything to worry about?"

Two dead police, four live Americans—more dangerous, but not significantly so. "Nothing not easily handled."

"I'm already looking into an appropriate scholar to take the lead on research."

Scholars who would work quickly, discretely. Scholars who could be trusted. Or wouldn't be missed. "Let me know where to deliver the piece."

The man cleared his throat. "About that...now that you have the image in hand, do you have any guesses where to go? Any leads? The photos are great, so clear, but they don't spark anything for me."

Moishe stared at the painting where it rested against the wall, even more in shadow now. According to some sources, the Menorah had been destroyed nearly two thousand years ago. He looked at proof it had survived. If he must hazard a guess, odious as that was..."It never left Italy. Possibly never left Rome. Someone concealed it during the sack of the city, probably Jews."

"I agree!" This affirmation was followed by a tink of glass, as if the man had toasted Moishe with champagne. "So, head south, and I'll be in touch!"

Already the voice grew a little distant as the man moved to dismiss him.

"And sourcing the items we need for the stretch goal?" The term was a sort of joke between them, along with an elite circle of supporters.

"We've received the first shipment of materiel to create fires in the sky, plus a few more controlled, to cause the right level of panic and destruction. I'd say we're well on our way. The return of what's been stolen should appear as the symbol we need it to, the light to call us to our proper homes."

Publicly, they spoke only of the first goal: that of re-building the Temple. Beneath this, as was so often the case, lay another, deeper truth. The true end would be a few months away, but his associate sometimes spoke as if the Temple were enough, and not merely a harbinger of what must come. Moishe had been patient this long, he could wait a few more months.

After all, until the Temple rose again, the world could not come to an end.

Chapter Sixteen

In the passenger seat, D.A. worked her magic, muttering about how much easier this would be with a real laptop.

After a moment, she crowed, "Seventeen miles away, northeast!"

Grant frowned. "Seems like he should be further away by now."

"Maybe the snow slowed him down?" Nick proposed.

"Negative. You've barely met this guy. It would take an avalanche to slow him down, and not for long." Grant scanned the parking lot again. Still no police follow-up. Something was wrong. Other men might pass it off as the lax discipline of a former Eastern-bloc force, but Grant knew better. "Moving?"

D.A. shook her head.

Grant pressed his thumb between his eyebrows.

"We going after it?" Nick shifted to the middle of the seat where he could see them more clearly. Whatever he read on Grant's face made him focus harder. "This guy we're tracking. He scares you."

Maybe. What the hell. Grant started the engine. "Observation, no approach. Tell Gooney and Dom to catch a flight in the morning."

D.A.'s thumbs hovered over the phone. "Where to?"

"Back to Italy, wherever they can get to easily." From here? Probably no place. "Tell them to get some rest and we'll deliver the car, or meet up with them on the way."

With a short laugh, D.A. said, "Gooney wants to know first class or business."

"Like he's got choices. He'll be lucky if the plane's not powered by a rubber band."

"He did get hit by a car back there," Nick pointed out, then he added, "But not very hard."

"I'm not unsympathetic, just cognizant of our location. He may have to take what he can get. Meantime, swap navigation to Nick's device," Grant directed, and D.A. frowned as Nick pulled out his own phone. "I'm betting your Mossad contacts are still in the mountains. I want to know his movements, everywhere he's been the last few months, and maybe further. If he targeted that painting, he found out about it somehow, and it wasn't from us or the Warden—she didn't know what it was beyond the name of the artist. I want to know what we're considering."

"Are we?" D.A. asked.

Grant tipped his head one way, then the other.

D.A. swallowed, then said, "But you want me in." She put on a chipper tone. "Makes sense if you need to interface with the Institute."

The Institute: an insider's name for the Mossad. "For now, yes," he said. "And yes."

Hadn't quite worked out how to feel about D.A.'s betrayal and the fallout. Her own contrition would keep her close and quiet. Yes, he needed her. He had few enough friends that he was willing to give her a little more time. Time to make it up to him? Time to prove herself unreliable? Who knew.

"Sounds like this is more than a painting." Nick gestured to trade places with D.A., and shifted the crate lid into the back seat. A piece of wood dislodged, and he winced as it fell to the floor. "Sorry about that."

"I probably loosened it up when I used it as a sled."

"Gooney's right, you do get all the fun." Nick came around to the front and immediately gave himself more leg room while D.A. moved to the back seat. Consulting his phone, Nick said, "Ahead then left."

"Definitely more than a painting, but how much more?" Grant started driving, following Nick's directions out to the main road, then rapidly out of town. "Dom's credible authority, Jacinta, says our man only paints from life, that if he painted the Menorah, that's because he saw it."

Nick gave a whistle. "That's big all right. Lot of people would like to get their hands on that."

"If nothing else, it's a lot of gold," D.A. said from the back.

"Give it to the Mossad. I'd like to go home," Grant said.

He guided the car down darkened streets, getting more narrow and windy. The breeze and rumble of the road came through the missing rear window. Probably killing their gas mileage, too, but given a vehicle of this size, their gas mileage was already on life support.

Nick's observation rolled through the back of his mind. Afraid. Of Moishe the Fist.

Made sense—the guy beat the snot out of him a few days ago, with an absolute lack of affect that made the beating seem so much harder.

Grant was used to that kind of abuse; he'd taken plenty of it, before, during and after the Army. But it was rarely so callous. On some level, the brutality had always personal, because of what he stood for, if not who he was. Because he was army. Because he was the enemy. Because he and his assailant were after the same objective. Sometimes because he pulled off something his adversary couldn't, making himself a target of rage or envy.

Moishe exhibited none of that. He came out of nowhere, twice now, with utter disregard for the lives of others, including the civilian drivers snarled up by his attempt to literally throw Gooney under the bus. The typical evil-doer didn't mess with civilians unless that was their sole intent. Better to remain incognito until your objective was in sight. Much easier to carry off your plans if you didn't have police, federal agents and angry relatives after you.

Come to think of it, that pretty much described Grant's week.

Afraid? No. Tired, oh, hell yes.

"Dafne? It's Sadie. Moishe came after us. Call me back." D.A. rang off.

"Sadie," said Nick. "Haven't heard that one in a while."

"I tried Reis Friedman, too. That's the other katsa. Don't know if they're not answering for me, or just—did you see that?" Her head turned slowly, tracking something out the window as they left it behind.

Grant nodded. Didn't slow down. A municipal police car in the gloom in a parking lot just off the road, one door open, one leg sticking out, lightly covered with snow. Living people didn't let snow accumulate like that. Didn't lie partially out of a car at that kind of angle.

One of those officers tried to reassure D.A. They hadn't even drawn their weapons when they had stopped the Rover. Grant pressed the gas. "Call it in. Those guys didn't deserve what they got."

D.A. addressed the phone in hesitant Polish in the back, speaking urgently as she delivered the names of the cross streets then hung up fast. They'd be well away before someone arrived.

Who else would get between Moishe and whatever he wanted? Maybe the bloodshed was over now that he'd gotten away with the painting. And if it wasn't?

Grant woke the car's onboard computer with a tap. "Nick, switch this thing to English and find us alternate transport. We need a flatbed rental to get the Rover back to Naples, and something for us, purchase maybe. No—make it two. SUV or van if you can, something big enough—"

"For the painting," Nick finished. "I guess we're doing this."

Grant fervently hoped they weren't, but he said, "If we have to. Otherwise, we're just surveillance until Mossad takes over. D.A., how much battery does Gooney's phone have?"

"Fifteen hours, twenty minutes," D.A. said. "I'm switching to low power mode. Should get us another twelve."

"Set up an alert if it starts moving. We'll pass the location and plan for watches. Nick—find us a hotel. I don't want to track this guy on three hours of sleep and a quart of adrenaline."

"Don't worry," said Nick. "We can stop off for chocolate."

Chapter Seventeen

The vibration stirred Jacinta awake, and she peeled her eyes open, squinting at her screen. A fresh notification, from a site she didn't recognize.

She snapped alert and sat up in her chair, shaking back her hair. Certo, she knew it. She'd installed it last night. Maybe this morning. What time was it, anyhow?

@Go4Baroque Available for work? @SecondComing

This person called themself "Second Coming"? È vero? Sounded like someone looking for a completely different kind of professional. Someone who thought a little too much of themself. Still...had she signaled gender on her new page? Unlikely—she was too sensitive to gendered language for that. Va bene.

@SecondComing What kind? Looking for the right job.

@Go4Baroque analyze, evaluate, possible restoration on an early-modern painting.

That all sounded reasonable. *@SecondComing Where is the piece? In situ or portable?*

Portable. Prefer you come to us. Can provide lab space.

Lab space? That didn't sound like a mafioso offer, but something else entirely. What, though? Jacinta ran her tongue over her teeth.

@Go4Baroque Your listing implied you would travel

No problem. Send photo for a quote.

No photos yet. Estimated size, 100 cm by 120 cm. Original frame or similar period.

That seemed reasonable from the photos she'd already seen. Her palms felt warm, the painting within her reach, but she mustn't seem too eager. *Condition?*

Excellent. Temperature-controlled storage, no light exposure.

Ma, si, if the painting had been crated in a cave for the last seventy years, and maybe not on display before that. She knew what the big names charged, but should it be less because of the clandestine nature of the contact? Or should it be more? Taking a deep breath, she quoted them double what she'd normally charge for an initial evaluation, to determine the extent of the work to be done. Plus a per diem to select lodging at her own discretion, then she would give her assessment and a second quote for the restoration.

Very good. Be in Rome, tomorrow at noon, or no deal.

The other party had agreed too quickly—she probably hadn't asked for enough. Well. She could make up for that in the next estimate, and it would still be more than she made at the museum. *Phone number for contact?*

The client delivered one, an Italian number, but of course, it only took a SIM card for that. Was she really doing this? She could stipulate a public meeting place, and see what she thought of them or their representative before committing. She envisioned a scene from a novel, or a romance film where the stranger must carry a rose or a certain book to be identified, and quashed her laughter. *What assurance do I have that the project is genuine?*

If you are what you say, you'll want to see this. The client sent an image, an extreme close-up of a painted eye, warm brown and wide with astonishment. It carried a gleam of hope and the painted flesh suggested a strong light source in a darkened space. Jacinta's core tightened. The same painting, *assolutamente*. The lost Caravaggio. Her fingers trembled, but she tapped out, *I'll be there.*

Her ingenuity landed the painting right in her lap. She wouldn't let it go again.

Chapter Eighteen

Grant woke to the buzzing phone, followed, on answering, by D.A.'s voice. "He's moving. He's got the crate."

"I copy." For a half-moment longer, Grant lay staring at the ceiling. The thin gaps around the blinds told him it was still dark, still too early to get alternative transport, regardless of the leads that Nick had found, and the Rover became increasingly conspicuous as a tail car. Steal something? Maybe. "Any word from Dafne?"

"Nothing. Coming for you. ETA, eight minutes."

Grant rang off. At least he'd managed to double his sleep quotient. He rolled out of bed, and Nick alerted in his own bed. "You going on watch?"

"Target's moving."

"Crap."

Grant gave a nod, pulling on his shirt, retrieving his jacket. "Wish I knew the destination, then maybe we could have a new kit waiting for us on arrival."

"You want some clothes, I've got some stuff in the back of the Rover." Nick sat up on his own bed, massaging the stump of his leg for a moment, then taking up the prosthetic from where it lay on the bedside table and working the upper sleeve over his limb.

"Yeah, I'll just roll up the cuffs and look like somebody's kid brother."

Rewarded by Nick's smile, slantwise, and a shake of his head. "Do what we have to sometimes." He assessed Grant's wardrobe. "Your jacket must've gotten most of the blood."

They finished their minimal preparations and stepped out the door as D.A. pulled up outside and cut the engine before she emerged from the Rover. The tourist hotel occupied a dark valley probably beautiful at another time of day, with a view out to the north across the highway. Stars above mirrored the scattered lights of the settlements stretching out across the foothills of the Owl Mountains.

"I'll take the wheel," Nick said, and Grant opened the back door. The dome light illuminated a slender beige shape on the floor and he recalled Nick's comment last night about a piece of wood coming loose. Only it wasn't. Looked like an over-sized envelope made of some off-white, waxy material, complete with a red wax seal. He bent to take it up. At the back of the vehicle, headlights approached, turning in. Grant stayed low, sliding the envelope into an inside pocket.

D.A. spun about to face the newcomer. Nick dropped to a crouch behind the Rover's big hood, his gun sliding readily to hand as the car pulled around the corner.

Grant let the bulk of the vehicle conceal most of him, staying low, watching the tires of the approaching vehicle as they rolled across the gravel and came to a halt blocking the Rover's escape. A second vehicle followed, but remained at a distance, pulling over without approaching.

A pair of practical brown shoes stepped out.

"Dafne." D.A. relaxed a little. "What are you going to do about Moishe?"

"I told you before, he's not ours anymore. He hasn't been for a long time."

"But you haven't lost touch."

"We don't like to lose track of our former associates, as you know,

Sadie. For him, it wasn't so close. I've spoken with him a few times, visited when I'm in town. Like that. Distant."

Grant listened as he observed her sleek sedan, not ten feet away, door open, engine running.

He rose, moving around his end of the Rover. "Really. Which town is that?"

The Mossad agent replied, "Why do I think revealing this information would lead to more violence?"

"Oh, so you are concerned about violence. Then why are you hassling us? Your man shot two police officers back there. If not you, who is he working for?" He drummed his fingers lightly on the roof.

Near the hood, Nick straightened as well. He caught Grant's eye, listening to the rhythm, then he gave a wink. Message received. Nick put his gun away, squaring his shoulders and stalked around the front to lean his hips against the Rover as he regarded the Mossad woman. Must be her partner in the other car.

"Who he works for and what he does are not my concern." Dafne Chadad shot Grant a look. "I'd hoped our entanglement was at an end, Mr. Casey. And before you accuse your associate of disloyalty, no, she did not tell me where to find you." She added a thin smile. "It's a good thing I found you, though. Some items were removed from the abandoned vehicles that appear to belong to you. I have taken the liberty of bringing them along." She gestured toward her car.

Trying to distract him from the question of Moishe. "I'd appreciate if you didn't make assumptions about my intentions and attitudes," Grant said. "He killed two officers, and you don't care."

"Did you see him pull the trigger?" she asked. "If so, why didn't you stop him?"

"My guess is, there's a tracker on the Rover. Maybe since the cemetery?" Nick suggested, drawing Dafne's glance.

She didn't reply to Nick's supposition. Seemed likely he was right. They'd managed to ditch a Gladio tag but missed the Mossad one. Land Rover was a very popular model these days.

"Is that the standard of evidence you want to establish, eyewitness accounts? Pretty sure you watched him set me up to die." Grant walked a few steps closer to the sedan, and Chadad drew back a little. He continued, "You claimed you'd clear us with the German and Italian authorities, and we didn't kill anybody they're likely to care about. Will you do the same for him? Tell the Poles it's fine he killed those officers, and have them believe you? What's he after?"

She gave a derisive sound. "The end of days? Who knows. Did you, Sadie, when you two were so close?"

Another distraction. D.A. slammed the door and strode around the Rover to stand by Grant. "It wasn't him I was close to. If anything, I'm lucky he didn't get jealous about me and Avram and decide I was a problem. You said he had an 'in' with the Carabinieri. What was it?"

Chadad shrugged. "Last I knew, he'd gone for some kind of cult. Maybe he's a Mason, and so's the Carabinieri commander. I suggest you forget him, and leave him alone."

"He's the one who followed us," Nick said, strolling across her field of view.

She pivoted to address him. "I don't know what he wants, or why he'd do that. If he's taken off, then let him go."

Nick nodded, and Grant and D.A. shifted a little. Grant tipped his head toward the car.

D.A. lunged into the driver's seat, then tucked through the gap between the seats into the back. Grant surged after her, practically diving into the passenger's seat while Nick raced down the side, forcing Chadad to jump out of his way, further from her vehicle.

The driver of the other vehicle blared his horn, gears grinding as he tried to react. By then, Nick was in the driver's seat, foot on the gas pedal even as he slammed the door. They peeled out of the parking lot, pedal to the metal as the agent's shout fell away behind them.

Chapter Nineteen

En route to Rome, Italy

Moishe needed only the humming of his tires on the road to keep him focused. That and the knowledge that the moment long anticipated approached at increasing velocity. He already had a list of targets, high-profile people and locations guaranteed to provoke a response, and he had people with the munitions to make it happen. When the Temple rose again, with the Menorah in place, that would be the culmination of expectations. Not the first sign, but a nearly final one. By then, the cascade of events would have escalated beyond the control of any human agency. Not the UN, not Mossad, his dear, old friends.

Others would join forces with him, ignorant of his cause or identity, merely because the signs that he delivered would confirm their own beliefs. Because he sent up the signal that the end was near, he could, indeed, make it so. It was not easy, nor simple, but if Moishe possessed nothing else, patience was his strength, with a certain doggedness that enabled him to succeed so far.

He paused only for gas, for certain physical necessities that even he still required, and to replace the lid for the wooden crate to keep his prize secure. Darkness turned to dawn, turned to day. Empty mountain roads became broad highways, became crowded, rose to mountains and emptied out again. So many cycles of day, night, humanity, emptiness. Soon, all cycles would be ended.

Rome arose in the same grubby industrial fringes that encircled so many cities now, the weary repetition of human behavior. He steered his vehicle inward, through the labyrinth, toward the secret heart said to contain enlightenment or peace. Only one pathway led to peace, and that, also, Moishe pursued with all diligence.

In a strip of identically made roll-up doors, he found the one designated for his use and entered a code to open the way. On the other side of this low structure rose a mixed-use complex of strikingly unappealing concrete and metal blocks. Moishe didn't care, but that did not mean he never noticed the aesthetics of things.

The door rolled down again behind his car, leaving him in a gloomy space with a single light. From the rear seat, he removed the crate, carrying it through the back door into the musty corridors to a freight elevator. Before the doors even opened on the third floor, the voice reached him. Deeper than many women's voices, but bright with enthusiasm. Too bright, perhaps, but then, she had a right to be nervous, brought to a strange location by a stranger who happened to be rich, for a purpose she could not yet fathom.

"—the setup is fantastico. Perfetto for this kind of work. Grazie, signore, you seem to think of everything."

"Call me Riccardo, please. I'm glad the facility meets with your approval. You will, of course, let me know what else you need, or if anything comes up."

"Certo, certo." She paused. "So, when will the painting arrive?"

Young. Eager. Moishe hefted the crate and stood in front of the anonymous door as footsteps approached from within. The door opened to a bright space beyond, to the brightness of "Riccardo's" smile. "Here it is now." He ushered Moishe inside.

Riccardo, for such he chose to call himself, presented no imposing character. He dressed well, but not conspicuously so, in European suits and leather shoes, his pale brown hair swept nicely back from his brow, his wire-rimmed glasses provided an air of intellect, his gold crucifix lapel pin hinting at his faith. At times, Moishe suspected their partnership began because Riccardo liked the contrast between them, his lack of presence counter-balanced by the mere bulk of Moishe, not to mention the reality of his background and training. Riccardo, too, had a past.

Statuesque and vividly dressed, the woman, too, might have been chosen for contrast to their little group. Auburn hair past her shoulders, held back by a band, cosmetics applied in a contemporary style Moishe had seen among other young women. Certain aspects of her skeletal structure suggested she'd been born in a male body and had recently corrected this. What sort of God would do that to people, make them suffer even to know who they are?

She put out a her hand. "Signore. So pleased to meet you." She pulled back the hand immediately, with a throaty chuckle. "Sorry, I'll wait until your hands are not full." Her glance had already dropped from the usual startlement at Moishe's size, to the crate he carried, and her face lit, the mascara and eyeliner emphasizing the greedy expansion of her eyes as if to devour what he carried.

"Buon giorno," Moishe said.

He marched through the eat-in kitchen, with its separate storage for chemicals, to the large studio beyond where a low easel awaited, and lay the crate on the nearby table. Coated windows down both sides permitted plenty of light, but no actual view, and heavy blinds allowed the light be eliminated depending on the artist's needs. On one side of the room, a couple of chairs and a coffee table gave a very home-like impression, while two doors interrupted the far wall. A few tools lay to hand, and he used a thin prybar to reopen the crate, lifting the lid and setting it aside, then reaching to peel back the cloth.

"Wait!" She pounced forward, pulling on a pair of glasses from a chain at her neck, glasses with inset magnifying lenses. "Do you know if this cloth is original?"

"To the crate, yes."

She picked up a corner and squatted down, studying the fabric in front of her face. "This unusual twill structure can be associated with the early-modern canvases. It will be interesting to see if the painting itself has also this structure."

Riccardo grinned across the table at Moishe, a silent, gleeful rebuke for Moishe's having doubted his recruiting methods.

"Va bene," she said, rising, but not moving away. "Go ahead."

It had been a long time since any woman stood so close to him without his intent to kill her. Men tended to stay close, pretending his size failed to intimidate. Too often, he could see the pulse that beat at their throats even before he felt it beneath his grip. Moishe complied with the command. They leaned forward, almost in unison, he revealing the painting, she leaning over it as each successive inch became visible. "We need infrared, x-ray and ultraviolet," she murmured.

"In the next room," Riccardo replied. "It's all been provided. The table has locking wheels, so you can transport the piece with all care. I know we spoke of a per diem for lodgings, but I've taken the liberty of setting up an apartment off the landing, in case you'd—"

"Sì, sì, is better to be close to the work." Her nose was already inches from it and she held back her hair with one hand, barely breathing.

She hungered for this opportunity: the perfect mark. Moishe felt vague disappointment, then she straightened and said, "Given that this limits my options for location and accommodation, I will accept half the per diem rolled into the sum we discussed."

Riccardo's neck wrinkled like a lizard's as his head retracted slightly, and he shot Moishe a look, then he spread his hands. "That's only reasonable. You arrived with certain expectations, and this arrangement was not among them."

With a flashing smile, she said, "It will be at least a few days for the initial documentation and cleaning. I'll just bring up my—"

"No need." Riccardo waved his hands as she started toward the door. "Moishe can fetch your valise and tool box. I shall point him the right direction. I feel ever more confident in our partnership, Jacinta. It's a fine thing to have you on board."

She whipped off her sweater and draped it over a chair, already rolling up her sleeves as the two men headed for the stairs. Funny that Riccardo should balk at the extra money. So far as Moishe knew, the woman wasn't expected to outlive her work.

Chapter Twenty

The men departed, leaving Jacinta alone with a masterpiece.

She gazed into the rapturous face of Zacariah as he regarded the angel, with the golden Menorah placed between, a link between the heavens and the earth, between God and his chosen people. Wait 'til she told Dom how she'd managed to bring the painting into her grasp, in spite of their attempts to cut her out. Dom had only her best interests, certo, but his dangerous friends had an agenda that did not include her. Va bene. She'd made this happen, gotten herself the best position in art restoration in this century. Eh, there had been that Da Vinci a few years back—that would have been something to see!

Riccardo insisted on confidentiality, certo, he did, ma forse Dominic already knew about the painting, so this was no breech to an unknown party, one who might wish to take it for himself. Dom would be happy for her when he knew, in spite of his misgivings. Still, better to be cautious for now, until she had earned her employer's respect.

The laboratory door opened with a dull creak and Riccardo approached with his rapid stride, his features intent. "I should have asked earlier, but I'll need to confiscate your phone, of course."

Jacinta recoiled a little. "My phone?"

He nodded. "You understand the magnitude of the discovery, I know you do. There can be no leaks whatsoever." He held out his hand. "It'll be in a locker just outside. I can arranged for supervised calls, maybe once or twice a day? To let your family know you're doing well?" A broad smile accompanied all of this. "We're placing your computer in there as well. I have one already set up for your use. Research and all of that. No uploads, of course. It already contains a library of materials on the artist for the sake of comparison. And look, we've got a complete reference library of books as well. Anything you could want about the artist, his life, his times!"

He spread his arm to show off the shelf packed with materials, including every known life of Caravaggio she'd ever heard of, and a few she hadn't, foreign language texts, general references on the Baroque period in Italy, even a few books about the Black Death—the Bubonic Plague that had carried off much of his family when the artist was a boy.

She cradled the phone inside her pocket. A complete library. A state-of-the-art computer system and virtual references. So she wouldn't be completely cut off. Even so...she'd known they required secrecy, but this sounded extreme. Had any of her friends had to work under these circumstances, even for the mafia? The bulk of his associate, Moishe, his thug, if she must guess, appeared in the doorway, her bag in one hand, and her toolkit in the other, like toys in the hands of a grown-up.

Riccardo strolled closer as Moishe shut the door with his foot and carried her things through the kitchen, depositing the toolkit on a low work table. "Tell me, Jacinta," Riccardo asked, standing with her by the frame. "What have you already observed?"

She returned her attention to the heart of her job. "There have been some changes, alterations to the image, I am certain." She indicated the lower left of the frame. "Sandals. Caravaggio nearly always paints such people barefoot, but often this is seen as ah...sconveniente." She frowned, searching for the right word.

"Rude?" Riccardo offered.

"Unseemly." Moishe emerged from the indicated apartment door, his hands now free. "Should I put it on the easel?"

"X-ray first, and examine the back, see la evidentia." She glanced around. "C'e una tavola, a covered table? Padded?"

Moishe vanished for a moment through the other door and returned with a blanket, offering it to her. When she accepted, he easily lifted the crate and waited while she spread the blanket over the table, then he set the crate on the floor nearby and her chest tightened as he lifted out the frame itself. She forced herself to keep breathing, not to try to help. Certainly a person of his obvious strength did not require help from her, she would only be in the way.

Instead, she held the blanket in place as he lowered the frame, face down, revealing a varnished canvas on the back, covering the stretchers and any support. That must be removed, of course, to be sure it concealed nothing important or dangerous to the work's conservation. In one corner something peeled away, a bit of parchment, it looked like, with old writing and a family crest of some sort. She started to take out her phone, to document, but Riccardo gave a cluck of his tongue and offered a high-end digital camera with an interchangeable lens. Exactly the sort of camera she longed for, but could never afford.

"It's worth the higher quality," he told her, and Moishe already had her phone in his hand, carrying it with great ceremony out to the hall where she'd seen the locker earlier, the sort of thing meant for storing hazardous chemicals.

"Do you recognize the seal? That's not the Cardinal Del Monte, is it?" Riccardo moved in that direction, pointing at the old paper even as Jacinta shook her head. Camera in hand, she followed, though her gaze lingered where Moishe had disappeared.

"This is none of his patrons that I know. So you see why I need research." She gripped the fancy camera. The work before her was more important, surely, than the temporary loss of her phone?

"Of course. We don't want to get in the way of your work. If this lens isn't suitable, the rest of the kit is in the first cabinet here." Riccardo slid back, giving ground for her to examine the label. "Angelina will be here shortly. She'll prepare meals and take care of cleaning so you don't have to, but please tell her if you'd like anything in particular. She knows not to clean your workspace, of course, but you may let her know how else to be of use—she's at your disposal."

The expensive camera weighed down her hand. He really had thought of everything. Was it so hard to be without her phone for a while? She'd have the computer, after all. If this were a prison, she'd been looking for one like it her entire life. Slipping the camera strap over her head, Jacinta focused on the antique label and framed the moment she'd been waiting for.

Chapter Twenty-One

The Bone Guard lost time shaking their Mossad tail, then finding a spot to sweep the car for bugs or trackers. Grant could only hope they succeeded.

While he and D.A. took care of that, using gear rigged up from a German electronics store likely convinced they were dealers or terrorists, Nick made arrangements to have the Rover picked up and lovingly delivered to the dealer in Naples. By that time, Gooney and Dom had left the hospital for the airport.

Their sweep of the car did turn up the belongings Chadad referred to: his and D.A.'s duffel bags, her computer kit, and the leather satchel he'd fought over back in Apicce Vecchia. Ironic, to have it returned now when it was unlikely to prove relevant.

D.A. regarded her laptop side-long. "The clothes and papers I can see, but the only way she'd return my computer is if they planted spyware on it. They're Mossad—it's what they do."

They drove the car over the computer and left the remains in a few different trash bins.

Moishe's car continued unerringly through Germany into Austria and south with the Bone Guard nearly three hours behind. They paused again to purchase a replacement computer, which D.A. configured on the fly. "Okay, Chief, lay it on me."

Grant pulled out the parchment he'd found on the floor of the Rover, the one detached from the stolen crate. In spite of the round wax seal, the flap hung open, and he handed it over.

He catnapped in the back seat while D.A. entered the letter into a translator. Their own grasp of Italian gleaned some useful information: the yellowed page originated in Rome and arrived near Naples, the correspondence linking one Cardinal Franceso Maria Burbon del Monte and an artist he addressed merely as "M." Michaelangelo Merisi de Caravaggio, commonly known by the town of his birth, simply, Caravaggio.

"Damn," Nick said from the driver's seat.

Grant's eyes flared open at the muttered oath. "Tell me it's not a traffic stop."

"Nope. Lost the signal on the outskirts of Rome, looks like the battery died."

Severing their link to the artwork, and the man who'd stolen it. The man the Mossad told them to leave alone. Happy to oblige, if he'd do likewise. If he wasn't out there killing people.

"Forget the painting for now," D.A. said, "Listen to this." She cleared her voice again began, "*To M, deservedly regarded as the greatest artist in Rome, and now in Naples, I have no doubt, from his beneficence, the most distinguished Cardinal Francesco del Monte, beneath the god-like presences you so graciously inscribed.*"

"A little grandiose, y'think?" Nick observed. "Do I keep on to Rome?"

"Confirmed," Grant said. "So, D. A., that's just the greeting?"

"Yeah, it goes on like that for a little while, flattering the artist, then it gets interesting. '*Some time must pass before His Holiness will be pleased to entertain the idea of a pardon, your most excellent portrait has also been exiled for now. With my own aspirations toward the Seat of Saint Peter again thwarted by the Spanish, I know not who may be our allies, and who our enemies.*'"

"From my understanding of papal politics," Nick said, "Sounds like Del Monte planned to be the pope himself, but he got shot down by the Spanish cardinals. Some of my local church ladies were all up in the gossip during the last papal convocation."

"I wouldn't know," D.A. remarked. "Guess there's politics in everything. Anyway, he goes on to say, *'Thus I ask you to keep in secret the Great Work which we have begun. I shall endeavor here to complete such tasks as I may in your absence. The mirror of the moons, the place of your confinement—these will point the way, together with my other pursuits.'*"

Grant frowns. "Moons, plural?"

D.A. skimmed again. "I'm pretty sure. The script is a little flowery. Anyway... *'For your part, you must deposit the item in its secure location on my behalf, being sure to leave—'* it's little unclear here, instructions, maybe? The handwriting's a little hard to make out. Anyway—*'for its later recovery. It goes without saying, I am sure, that these things should not be found in your possession or it will go the worse for you, as it did upon the stair.'*"

She paused for a sip of water. "No idea what that means."

"He was hospitalized," Grant said. "Late in 1605. Claimed he had tripped on the stairs. Sounds like the Cardinal doesn't think that was an accident."

"You were meant to be sleeping, Chief. Sounds like you were studying up," Nick remarked, guiding the car through a tangle of contemporary houses interrupted by the occasional Roman temple or mausoleum.

"I was sleeping. Mostly."

Grant gazed out the window as they wound toward the heart of Rome, the Eternal City, legend in its own time. It stood like an aging sentinel over the entirety of Western Civilization and beyond. Blocks of modern apartments gave way suddenly to the extended, columned fronts of Baroque palaces now turned to more apartments or fancy shopping. Instead of traffic islands and roundabouts, inconvenient eruptions of history distorted the flow of traffic, with buses, cars and Vespa scooters honking furiously around half-ruined marble arches made gray by decades of exhaust fumes. Columns, temples and broken walls emerged, with ancient stone incorporated into medieval houses, and those into modern hotels.

Nick chuckled. "Just can't help yourself, can you."

He tore his eyes from the city streaming around him. "It's Rome. City of emperors, heart of the Catholic world, origin of the Republic for which we stand. You never dreamed of coming here?"

"Capri's more my style, tho I'm sure they've got some nightlife around here, too."

From her spot, D.A. regarded Grant with a faint smile. "You're like a kid with his nose pressed to the window of a candy shop, Chief. We're not used to that."

"What, you want me to drive by the Colosseum?" Nick offered.

Grant shrugged. "Actually yes. The Arch of Titus includes a record of the items stolen from the Temple, including the Menorah. Seems like a good place to start."

"You believe Jacinta's story," D.A. asked.

He tipped his hand one way, then the other. "Your translation refers to keeping an item in a secure location, and the importance of secrecy. Could be the Menorah itself. In the meantime—"he flashed a grin—"I get another piece of candy."

Nick gave a thumbs-up. "Carry on, Professor Silverberg. What else you got?"

"Right. *'Eager as I am to view the completed work, with the unsettled state of Rome and of your reputation here, I deem it best you leave that with your other patron. I trust she shall keep it for us. We must strive to safeguard the pursuit we have in mind, to ensure that this treasure shall neither be lost, nor revealed prematurely. Were it to come to light, it should be taken for a sign, and not of the positive sort. Already, the rumor of its discovery has slipped my workmen, and there are some who would have it for their own, others who would hoist it aloft and claim powers reserved to the Church and to Her shepherds. Much as we all desire the*

Lord's return, I have tried to prevail upon all who know not to take this as symbolic of the end.'

"'You are less cognizant of history than I, but it seems that each successive age brings as well a new claim to the Apocalypse. Until the Lord himself shall deem it so, let us not supply fuel to a fire would destroy a third part of all mankind without sure knowledge of the Savior's advent.'"

In the driver's seat, Nick put up one finger for an interrupt. "There're still groups like that, people trying to jumpstart the Second Coming by killing off a third of all people, or claiming certain cities, anything they see in the Book of Revelations. Like, oh yeah, if we just make the rivers run with blood, then Christ'll have to show up. Some folks split off from my family's church to follow that crap."

"Just another reason to be agnostic," Grant said. "But it'll help to have an operative who's not."

D.A. scrolled a little down, and continued, "*'I shall, of course, be praying on it. And also for you, that you shall recover in good health and remain safe. I make bold to pray for your immortal soul, that the stains of your deeds shall be washed clean, and you will be welcomed once more to Rome and to civil company, as well as to the bosom of the Lord. Continue your devotional works as well as your dedication to our project lest your own flame fail too soon.'*

"'Go with the Grace of God, His Excellency, Cardinal del Monte,' and so forth. Phew!." D.A. took another sip. "May not be every detail, but I think it's pretty close."

"You sure you don't want to bring Dom in for translation, or his lady-friend?" Nick inquired.

Grant flashed in his memory to the image of Dom collapsed against the wall in the crypt, blood streaming from his throat, barely breathing. "I do not want civilians in on this, especially given we don't know for sure what it is. Maybe if we're stuck and we have an urgent need for intel to continue. We need D.A. set up in a hotel with the world's best wi-fi—"he aimed a finger at her.

"Got it, Chief. I'll find a spot and let you know where to rendezvous."

"That puts me on procurement," Nick said. "Gooney's landed in Rome and replaced his phone. He wants to get Dom settled in his apartment, maybe spend the night to make sure he's got everything he needs. Join up with us in the morning."

"And I'll see what I can at the arch. Meantime, I think we follow the cardinal's advice and keep this on the down-low, especially if he's not wrong about the people who want the Menorah as a rallying point for the End Times. D.A., is there any chance your old buddy is one of them?"

"Trying to re-build the Temple to spark the apocalypse?" She blew out a breath. "He went a little off the tracks when Avram died, and he wasn't real steady to begin with, if you see what I mean. His parents died in an early settlement attack in Israel, and Avram pretty much adopted him as his brother. They were inseparable right up until they met me, and half the time after that."

"So what happened to the Chief at Lake Como," Nick began. "Was that how this guy operates?"

Her chin dipped, her hands gripping the sides of the laptop. "Pretty much. He made money as a boxer for a while, until nobody was willing to fight him. He aims for incapacity, not just a knock-out. It takes a lot to stir him up, but once he's moving, he's damn hard to stop."

"The katsa said she thought he might've joined a cult. Would Avram's loss be enough?" Grant asked softly. "To turn him into a one-man *Apocalypse Now*."

"Could be."

"We're here," said Nick. "I'll look for a place to pull over. Then supplies. First aid, replace the gear we lost, fresh clothes. Maybe guns."

D.A. met Grant's eye. "Definitely guns."

Chapter Twenty-Two

The art restorer began slowly snapping photos, then the speed of her work increased, with bouts of leaning in, closely examining the edges and back of the frame, meticulously recording every inch. Additional cameras would record every moment of her work as well, as a security measure. Moishe felt the woman intelligent enough to understand all of that, yet motivated enough, and moved by the work at hand, that he was equally sure she didn't care. He suspected if he brought out his gun, right there, she would fear for the painting before she feared for herself. Be assured, good lady, that your blood will not stain the work. The two men backed away and returned to the landing.

Outside, "Angelina" adjusted her uniform to be sure the apron concealed her own weapons. A rounded woman, with streaks of gray in her braid, she came from MI6, the British spy agency. Certain things she witnessed had led her to a new service, and when her glance met Moishe's she looked haunted. He gave her a nod, which she returned.

"Jacinta is settling in. No trouble about the phone—bit of a surprise, there. Give it to her if you must, passive resistance," Riccardo said.

"Understood." She lifted a shoulder bag full of knitting. "Purple?" she indicated the yarn.

"Perfect, yes."

With a brisk nod of her own, Angelina settled into an older woman's shuffle, calling out, "Buon giorno, Signorina!" as she entered.

Upstairs, in the command room, two guards watched the monitors, inside and out. All according to plan.

"And now?" Riccardo asked.

"Carry on." He started for the stairs. Instructions had already been sent.

"What will you be doing?" Riccardo called after him.

"Research." Moishe continued down, and out through the main door, which automatically locked behind him.

The door popped open again almost immediately and Riccardo strode through, pausing to be sure it closed again. He scowled. "Moishe. You can't just go off like that, like you have done in the past. You can't be opaque all the time. Our investors will want more."

"They are getting it."

The other man flapped his hand toward the building. "Yes, we have a painting, it seems convincing, certainly it will excite everyone, but it's still just a painting. You must let me, at least, know what's inside your head. Give me something."

Moishe notched his eyebrows upward, and Riccard swallowed, adjusting his tie. "I am not saying I don't trust you, or that I don't believe they trust you. You are, after all the reason we're all here."

For a moment, they stared at each other across the paved courtyard. Finally, Moishe said, "And?" He lifted his gaze toward the building at Riccardo's back.

The man sighed. "Yes, and. And you told us about the painting, and now you've found it. Brought it here, even, and we secured a qualified professional to examine it. They'll want more. They'll want action. Information, at least."

Of course they would. Why did the man keep speaking? The only thing the investors had to offer Moishe was the financial means to his eternal end. At times, he considered whether life would be easier if he were the sort of person who continued speaking when the conclusions seemed obvious. If he were the sort of person who explained, justified... sympathized. "You are delaying me from those things."

"Well, I can send them a photo, at least? I can have Stella write up the art restorer. We could even do an interview." Riccardo's eyes lit. "I think she'd like that, don't you?"

Moishe considered smiling. "Yes."

"Good. Great! I'll get going on that, then." He gave a cheery wave, and headed back to his own office, springing up the steps and tapping the numerical code to enter the door.

Riccardo's entire job was to keep people happy. The restorer. The investors. Happiness was not part of Moishe's make-up.

While Jacinta began her work, his was to confirm any detail or additional source of information. To scour the historical record (again) for anything that might be of help in completing the great project. Just like a proper investigation, he would begin with the last people who had seen the missing item.

Aside from the Biblical instructions for its creation, and some early Rabbinic sources, only two records remained from those who had seen the Menorah. The historian Josephus, who witnessed the Temple's destruction around 70 CE, wrote his account of the Jewish War, providing one version.

As for the second, the successful Roman legions carried home booty from Jerusalem, and paraded their treasures through the streets before depositing them in various temples in tribute to their gods. To commemorate the event, a huge stone arch had been constructed, incorporating scenes from the parade.

Moishe knew exactly where to go next to confirm the Menorah's structure: The Arch of Titus.

Chapter Twenty-Three

With her soundtrack streaming to her ears from the high-powered computer they'd set up for her, Jacinta stepped from behind the viewing wall back to the x-ray closet while the latest images processed and uploaded. Given the state-of-the-art equipment, she definitely hadn't asked for enough money. Nessun problema. She could simply increase her rate for the actual restoration work. She'd want to do at least a basic cleaning along with the photographic analysis though.

She unlocked the wheels of the rolling table and carefully wheeled it back into the studio. È vero, just looking at the work still gave her chills. She would have begged for the opportunity to work on something like this at the museum, and would have been turned away in favor of someone else, someone older, with better family connections. Given the job she was on at the moment, she might have some new family connections to claim...eccetto...these men didn't feel like Mafia, and she would know.

Angelica glanced up from a comfortable chair by the windows, raising her eyebrows. Her hands kept working, a lovely purple yarn twining between her needles to become another row in the shawl.

Already, the woman's quiet presence and the clicking of her needles faded into the landscape.

Jacinta lay out her tool kit on the side table, locating a small pair of pliers with a curved tip, and a slender palette knife.

Thanks to her family's position, she knew any number of mafiosi from her years in Naples and visits to Sicily and beyond. Some of them took care to resemble the stereotype, enjoying the effect of their slick hair and dark suits—or copying their look from that American television show. Others worked hard against those images, spending too much on casual clothing, and only wearing suit coats when they needed to conceal their weapons. Dom's American friends had a similar impact, though without spending much money. Probabile, that fact had smoothed their way a few times during their time in Italy as people made assumptions and behaved with respect that wasn't due.

Well. She took up the palette knife and started to work around the edge of the frame, gently probing with her grip and the rounded blade to loosen the gilt woodwork from the canvas.

Certo, they were due respect but not as Made Men. This team she worked with now, Riccardo struck her as a salesman, Moishe as his muscle, a combination of bodyguard and errand boy. Eccetto...his entire understated affect suggested something else, something she'd yet to—

"Buon Giorno."

The knife clattered from her hand and she swung about, plucking an earbud to find Riccardo standing close by.

"Accept my apologies, I didn't mean to startle you." He offered a smile. "I saw the x-ray warning light go out, and thought I'd check in with you. I have an office just upstairs."

Jacinta chuckled. "Va bene. I get wrapped up in my work, and don't notice the doors. It's good you're here. I can use the help to remove the frame. È Moishe qui? I think he does this without, eh, breaking a sweat —that is the phrase, sì?"

He gave a chuckle as well. "It is indeed. He's gone out for now, but I think we can manage between us." He slipped off his jacket, as if to show himself unarmed, and unbuttoned his cuffs to roll them up a few times. "How should we proceed?"

"Gloves first." She pointed.

He plucked a pair of rubber gloves from the large box provided, snapping them on with practiced ease, then awaited instructions. Together, they spanned the frame, carefully separating the frame from the canvas, calling for help from Angelica when it stuck at one corner. At last, the frame stood against the wall, leaving a waft of dust and the accumulation of centuries. The piece had clearly been on display at some point, but likely centuries back, before being relegated to this crate.

Angelica wrinkled her nose and hustled to bring in the vacuum, taking care of the floor immediately, then resuming her place near the largest window. Her knitting needles started clicking again immediately. How the woman kept track of her place, Jacinta had no idea.

"Grazie for the help to remove the frame," Jacinta said. "Much better to get the full view. I'll take more pictures of course, but it's a little risky all of this handling, so best to capture at every stage."

"Very wise." Riccardo examined the painting. In verità, he studied the Menorah almost exclusively, as if the fact it was a Caravaggio had no meaning for him at all. "This subject matter is unusual, isn't it, for this artist?"

She turned her hand one way and the other. "He paints many of the religious themes, yes? But mostly the more popular: St. John, the Virgin, specialmente the apostles in their conversions." She warmed to the subject. "But these things are common to so many artists of the period. This is how they are paid, like photographers now take weddings, portraits, pets. Caravaggio can do these well—St. John is a favorite--and also has made some portraits, but two things he does that people remember."

"Oh? What are those?"

She held up her fingers. "First, the self-portraits. So many times, the person is him. He is Bacchus, he is Goliath, he witnesses the burial of Santa Lucia, and the killing of St. Paul."

"Seventeenth century selfies." He pointed at the angel, then Zacariah. "Is he one of these?"

She shook her head. "I don't think so, but the pentimenti may show otherwise. Pentimenti, these are the signs of underpainting, things the artist paints over. The change of a hand, the expression of a face, like this."

Riccardo's smile looked a bit rigid, the smile of a man who's losing interest, and she hurried on, "The other thing for which he's known, though, and sometimes there are more selfies. Caravaggio paints beheadings. All the time, especially after he flees the murder charge, and is under this threat of his own death."

Riccardo's fingers brushed over his throat. "He was beheaded?"

"No, no, but it is the punishment if they catch him for this murder. He leaves Rome and hides in the mountains, then in Naples. Trouble follows him even there, and to Malta to join the knights." She dropped her voice a little lower, as she did when telling children and tourists the next part. "Already he has twice painted Judith removing the head of Holofernes, and several times the David, then also Medusa. His master work, *the Execution of St. John,* in the co-cathedral at Velleta on Malta, this is the only work he has signed, and he did so in the painted blood that pools from the saint's throat."

Riccardo looked frozen in horror, but Jacinta completed the tale. "What is most interesting, so many of these are examples also of the first thing. They are selfies. He paints himself as the victim, his own head being removed. His final *David and Goliath,* he is the corpse, and also the executioner."

With a little shudder, Riccardo crossed himself. "He seems rather a disturbed individual."

"È vero." Jacinta added, "Some hypothesize that this two-times self-portrait shows his remorse and rebirth, the pious young David having overthrown his darker, more monstrous self."

"Hunh." Riccardo considered that. "Reborn in Christ. Like so many of us, our sins redeemed in blood." he murmured.

He hadn't displayed so much religious feeling when they first met.

Perhaps she shouldn't have told him all of this? But it established her credibility as a Caravaggista, even more so than the talk they'd had when they met up in the cafe that morning. She gazed at the red-brown darkness of the painting before her, then the desperate face of the priest, dismayed by the angel before him. What depths would be revealed when she began her cleaning, stripping away layers of accumulated soot to view the true painting.

"Thank you for the introduction," Riccardo said. "I'm rather glad not to have him paint me."

They shared a laugh, then she said, "I am happy always to speak of him, but this is not what you come for, I think."

Riccardo took his eyes from the canvas. "Oh, yes, yes. Ah...it's a little delicate." He sidled toward her, beckoning her closer as well. "Moishe...he wants everything played very close to the chest, if you see what I mean, but we're here on behalf of a consortium of investors, you see. Investors who may need some incentive to increase their support for the project."

Jacinta nodded as if she understood all of this. Under any other circumstance it would make sense: a group of speculators share ownership of a number of works in the hopes of profiting from a future auction if something in the collection turns out to be valuable, though she knew for a fact that wasn't the case here. Nonetheless, this man, or his investors, were paying her well, treating her well, and giving her everything she wanted. So, she would be diplomaticamente.

She ventured the most obvious explanation. "These people supported the initial purchase, and all of this." She gestured toward the compact, high-tech laboratory. "In exchange for the chance of future profit."

He brightened. "You do understand. We've already spent rather a lot, and proper security, not to mention your own skills, require additional funding. But Moishe...well. I feel that we need to provide our backers with some hint that the project is making Bing progress, perhaps some preliminary images from your study? Some reassurance that the risks they are taking are worthwhile."

Risks. Like Moishe engaging with Dom's rather dangerous friends. "What do you have to mind?"

"Ideally, if you're willing, a little recorded presentation, something to help them understand the magnitude of the work, its importance, and your own expertise."

"Sì, certo. I can use the camera and also add some of the images, maybe ten minutes or less?"

He clasped her hands eagerly. "Precisely. I'm so glad to have you on board." He released her as quickly as he'd touched her and backed off a step. "Oh, sorry. I need to respect your space. Anyhow, when do you think you might have something ready?"

He looked so excited, and his spontaneous touch had been unexpected, but not unpleasant. Jacinta thought this over, and said, "Late tonight, I think, if there is video software on the computer? For the editing and compilation?"

"Yes, of course. If you can put it on one of the flash drives from the drawer, Angelica can bring it over. I shouldn't like to bother you again. You've got work to do!" He was backing away, with a wave of his fingers, then a pause and a slight furrow of his brow. "I don't expect Moishe to be back for some time, but if he should drop by, could you keep this between us?" His gesture between them linked her with him in an intimate group. "I don't worry about Angelica—she's on my side."

The maid glanced up with a warm smile.

"All right." Jacinta waved as he departed.

Not Mafia. What was the relationship between them? She thought Riccardo was the capo, the head, and Moishe just a hired man. Now Riccardo's desire for secrecy, from Moishe, of all people, and the introduction of these mysterious backers complicated that picture, on top of what she already knew. What he hadn't mentioned: that the painting had been highjacked from a Nazi stash, one discovered by her own friend and his American treasure hunters.

On the table, the painted Menorah gleamed bright as real gold, beckoning her back to work. What, actually, had she involved herself with? Aside from the most thrilling experience of her career, confirming a genuine Caravaggio—a pinnacle she was unlikely ever to achieve again. When she assembled her video, she need not mention her own theory that the artist had seen the Menorah himself. That was a reward for their risk that the unknown investors could not even imagine.

In her chair, Angelina knitted away. Her maid, her cook—her minder. Jacinta swallowed the tension in her throat. Back to work. Whatever she had agreed to, the work came first, before any other concern.

She reached to replace her earbuds, hesitated, and stuck them back in their case. No need for her excitement to overwhelm caution. One thing for Riccardo, the salesman, to sneak up on her, hoping for a favor. Imagine how she would feel to be startled from her work and find looming over her, the immobile darkness of Moishe himself.

Chapter Twenty-Four

Autumn in the Owl Mountains of Poland meant a chance of snow, but down south in Rome, it delivered a fair, breezy day with light clouds. Before emerging from the car, Grant sorted out a fresh shirt from the items Chadad secured out of their old transport, and threw on a windbreaker. Hard to be full-on tourist without a shopping trip, but this would do for now. Maybe he'd pick up a *Buon Giorno a Roma* t-shirt, or some Gladiator thing from one of the souvenir shops that filled in every tiny storefront.

The enormous brick and marble bowl of the Colosseum towered at the center of the traffic circle where Nick let him off, tourists prowling the lower arches, but Grant reluctantly turned his back. The Arch of Titus stood close by—as he approached, he could even see it down a short promenade beyond the fence that surrounded the Forum. Meant he'd have to buy a ticket and cruise through half of the Roman Forum just to go see the one panel he needed to examine. Oh, gee. Rough work.

Half the glory of Rome still lay buried, not only the remains of the buildings once at street level, but some of their great engineering works like sewers and water pipes, not to mention the occasional Mithraeum where the Persian god Mithras performed his sacrifice in subterranean gloom for the benefit of a newly risen warrior cult. Grant was literally surrounded by wonders.

His pace picked up as he moved through the crowds toward the entrance. He still ached from the beating he'd taken over the last few days. Bruises shadowed his stomach and chest where Moishe's fists hit their mark, and he wore a fresh bandage on his wrist.

Right now, none of that mattered. He could take the pain, the risk, the international complications, so long as he also got the reward. Sometimes, that came in the form of lives saved, lost treasures recovered and restored to their rightful owners, not to mention traveling to sites he'd only seen in magazines, and some he'd never heard of before. Trouble was, half the places he visited were stained with blood before he left and he was lucky if it wasn't his own.

How long could he justify spending at the Forum? Didn't have anyplace else to go, until D.A. reported back on her hotel search and they reconvened to go over their next moves. Meantime...he offered a credit card at the gate and walked through the metal detectors into a wonderland of Roman ruins crammed together with lawns, pools and landscaping, more of the ubiquitous umbrella trees shading the pathways.

Steps and ramps led down among the ranked columns of the original Basilica. To his left, the Temple of Romulus, founder of Rome, famously suckled by a wolf whose image adorned much of Rome's brand marketing. To his right the Temple of Vesta and the House of the Vestal Virgins, keepers of the sacred fire who could be expelled if they lay with a man. A rather narrow view of the loss of virginity, as the Romans well knew. Every book he'd ever read about Rome, every afternoon spent leafing through the pages of his mother's books or in the university library in the time before he'd been a soldier—they unfolded in his mind, suddenly made real.

Keep moving, keep moving. Objective first, then take a look around. He slowed a little as the view opened to the towering, domed arches of the Basilica Maximus, then pushed himself onward, weaving around tour groups being led in Mandarin, Japanese, German, English and a few other languages. A number of frustrated tourists posed with selfie sticks, trying to deliver some sense of their surroundings on five-inch screens with their own faces in the middle.

The Arch of Titus rose close to fifty feet tall and nearly that wide, framing a partial view of the Colosseum along with more milling bodies. In warm beige stone, elaborately carved with columns, it dwarfed the handful of people standing it its shadow. The lower portions inside the arch showed smooth stone, with deep relief carvings on the next layer up, well over Grant's head.

A recently installed placard showed the what the carvings would have looked like almost two thousand years ago, fully painted, with a vivid blue background, white togas on the parade of Roman citizens, and bright gold on the spoglia, the spoils of war they toted through the streets of Rome. At least six men held the poles that carried the Menorah, suggesting the immense weight of the gold. In front of them, another group of bearers carried the golden offering table with its vessels, and a pair of horns.

The actual carving showed the damage of the centuries between, with a few figures nearly obliterated, but the Menorah itself remained intact. Seven arms curved upward, embellished with petal-like shapes at their joints and pinnacles. Two thick layers formed a hexagonal base down below. All it needed was the kneeling priest and the angel to complete the image of Caravaggio's work.

Didn't mean the artist had seen the real thing, did it?

Much of the Forum had been buried during that time, with visible parts of the columns and brickwork taken away as building material. Grant cast about for more signage. In the long afternoon sun, shadows of tourists stretched toward him, merging into clumps and separating again. No, that large, dark shadow moved with single-minded efficiency.

Grant darted behind the arch, his pulse racing in a different way. Moishe.

Chapter Twenty-Five

Moishe stopped short of his objective. From here, he had a partial view of the frieze showing the Jewish artifacts, but his peripheral vision had caught movement too brisk for the average tourist, unless that person wished to take an especially vigorous selfie.

In deference to site security, he'd left behind his guns and most of his other weapons. No need to spend all of his accrued goodwill with the Carabinieri by asking them to release him from a weapons charge in this era of heightened terrorist concern. So far as he knew, he wasn't on anybody's watch list. He should be.

Besides, this had been purely a research mission. Until now. Perhaps it still was. Moishe, after all, was a patient man.

He took a few more steps, to the side this time, where his view of the carving improved, and a signboard showed the before and after images of the digital restoration approach. Interesting. He took this in with flickers of his glance. The sign, the arch, the sign, the narrow avenue leading to and from the arch. A ruined wall to one side, with stairs beyond it. On the other side, walls and fences that guided people to stay on the paths. Always, in Rome, they wished to keep people on the straight and narrow.

His target, if he had one, could chose to move to the left toward the stairs, where he'd shortly be visible. Toward the right, to be herded by the fences and lawns, but still visible. Or straight back, though that direction promised only more obstacles and fewer places to hide. He might simply remain where he was, behind the monument, trying to out-wait Moishe. Assuming Moishe had seen anyone worth seeing at all.

Tourists streamed around, mostly in groups, mostly following the proscribed routes around the Forum. Moishe walked a little back from the sign, placing just enough distance between it, and him. He stood at an angle to the arch, completing a line of obstruction that shifted the flow of the tourist stream, forcing them out and around him to the right. No need to watch the upstream result of his stance. Instead, he watched them reach the far corner of the arch, where his enemy was, or was not. His enemy, hiding with the stone, would make another such break in the flow. Trying to merge himself with the arch, he would become a smaller stone, an eddy.

A woman in a red coat held a phone away from herself, filming a tour of the place. A useful marker in the stream.

She walked steadily around the right side, just as Moishe intended. Then, she took a step to the side, widening her path. Her face registered a brief annoyance.

While Moishe waited, the position of the sun had shifted enough to align his own shadow with that of the arch. A large tour group arrived, encouraged by an upright man with a blue umbrella hoisted aloft. With a glance at Moishe, he gathered up his mob onto the right-hand side, effectively barricading that route. Moishe's adversary had only two paths open to him now: the open stairs of the left, or the dead end behind him. The tour guide brought out a megaphone and began his narrative. Josephus, the Roman occupation of Jerusalem. All very old news.

Moishe walked straight forward, ignoring the scattered tourists, letting them stop or step aside for him. He marched under the monument, the woman in the red jacket now aiming her annoyance at him. Moishe shook out his hands, limbs loose and ready, then he lunged around the side, his long arm snatching.

Chapter Twenty-Six

A child's astonished face, the girl shrinking back toward her father, alerted Grant that something was about to happen. He bolted forward, away from the Arch as a big hand stretched around the corner, Moishe in mid-lunge.

He extended like a fencer snatching Grant's jacket, and the girl screamed. Grant ducked low, swinging his arms up to get free of the jacket, but the Fist was already pivoting toward him, his other hand hurtling forward.

Moishe yanked the jacket back down, entangling Grant's hands, and slammed a fist into his gut. The breath rushed out of him, and Grant staggered, dropping to one knee as he slipped his jacket at last.

Another fist aimed for his head. Grant flung up an arm, pushing off from the ground to drive his own fist under Moishe's ribcage. The jolt of impact shivered up his arm.

Moishe's hand grabbed for his throat, and Grant dropped low, rolling aside to find his opponent already lining up a kick sure to launch Grant into the next millennium.

With a wild leap, Grant evaded the blow. Tourists shouted, some of them withdrawing while others swiveled their attention to watch the excitement. The last thing Grant wanted was for Moishe to send him viral—again.

At least they'd both had to pass through the metal detectors on the way in. No guns, small blades maybe.

He started right, then spun back from the astonished faces of an entire bus-load of visitors. Moishe came up fast, skidding on purpose, sending a spray of gravel to pepper Grant's legs.

Grant dodged his landing, scanning for the quickest way out of this place. Toward the Colosseum looked like a dead end, unless you could scale an eight-foot fence. But it was designed to keep people out, not in, and the metal support structure criss-crossed the side facing him.

Moishe lunged again and Grant ducked, sliding further right. A man with a selfie stick shouted in Japanese, narrating the action, as far as Grant could tell. Grant swiped the stick, giving the guy a nice close-up of Grant's hand on the phone. He thrust the handle toward Moishe's face.

The big man twisted, and Grant followed up with a slashing blow that drove him further. He delivered a smack to Moishe's cheek, then jabbed for his eye. Moishe's hand closed over the shaft, bending the aluminum. Grant released his hold.

He cut in front of Moishe, dashing toward the barricade.

His single-minded opponent followed, hard and fast.

Thirty yards of gravel path and grassy verge, the bulk of the Colosseum growing in his view. He'd been a track and field star in high school. How long had it been since his last high jump?

Twenty yards to cover. Ten.

Gravel scraped as Moishe surged forward.

Grant pushed to his limit. He launched hard and grabbed the top bar of the fence, hurling himself over the top.

Moishe's hand wrapped Grant's ankle, hauling back.

Grant's chest scraped the top of the fence. He kicked down slamming Moishe's arm with his foot. The man's grip shifted, and Grant broke free. He worked his feet up, rolling sidelong, then dropping down on the other side. His knees bent to absorb the impact, breathless, the fresh scrapes and bruises throbbing, fingers spread against the road surface on the outside. Superhero pose had its uses. A few people behind him cheered or shouted.

From beyond the fence, a chuckle echoed from the great stone arch. Grant half-rose, poised for what might happen next. No guns, no ranged weapons. Didn't necessarily make him safe. Moishe was faster and more agile than his size would suggest. The tourists on both sides stood well back from them, uncertain what this explosive action could mean.

Near the arch, Moishe hulked into the shadows of the enclosing wall, as if thinking he, too, could make the leap. Moishe the Fist, they called him. Should've called him the mountain—but Grant knew the impact of those fists all too well. Grant was lighter, faster. He could take off right now and be gone, or Grant could catch his breath, maybe catch some intel, get this guy to give up any clue what he was after.

"What do you want?"

The man's face flickered. On another person, it might be a smile. On him, a fissure in the stone. "Nothing."

"Bullshit. You don't chase me across four countries for nothing."

Little knots of tourists close by, startled by the initial intrusion, loosened up like the first ice breaking off the surface of a pond, willing to race downstream. One guy tried to film Moishe, earning a swivel of that head and a hard stare. Half a step toward him, and the guy took off running, his phone clutched in his hand. The others shuffled quickly off about their own business, and somewhere a stentorian voice demanded caution.

"Oh, you mean right now. Here." Moishe's voice rolled across the path like the rumble of a distant train. Or an avalanche.

"Sure. Start with that."

Again, Moishe's lips parted. "Nothing."

Grant spread his hands and let them fall. He stepped back. Maybe ten yards to the end of the pathway by the street. Another ten to disappear in the winding streets of Rome.

"You don't believe me," Moishe called. "Come back. Let's talk."

Grant laughed. "About what, nothing?"

"If you like." Moishe shrugged. "Wasn't there some great American television show about that, nothing?"

Already getting tired of hearing him say the word. "Are we talking the vacuum of space, big, fat empty kind of nothing, or the small talk about sports and the weather kind of nothing?"

"I think we're not men for small talk."

Grant conceded that with a tip of his head. "Cosmic then."

"Now you understand me." Moishe's head rocked a little. "We are men of life and death, being and nothingness. To make small talk is to waste what matters."

"Okay, so what matters to you?" Grant realized his mistake, even as Moishe's lips formed the word, and he put up his hand. "Don't say it. Nothing."

Back to Intel 101. Sometimes the easiest way to deceive was to tell an unbelievable truth. In short, to confuse, misdirect, piss off, or disappoint your interrogator so much they forget you even told them. What if this was a man who'd literally fight, kill, hunt, destroy property and ruin lives for...nothing?

"Why?"

"Because my evil is so great, only complete annihilation will do."

An unwitting tourist had backed closer to the fence, trying to frame the Arch, but her eyes flared white and she took a few quick steps away.

Grant said, "If I offered you that, would you take it?"

Moishe regarded him almost condescendingly, head slightly cocked. "I'm not the only one so fallen. We are both wolves and shepherds, Mr. Casey, are we not? But you fight for preservation. You kill for your flock. You take on the darkness to guide others to the light. What sort of shepherd would I be if I let you kill me? If you gave me the gift of nothing, while so many others struggle on in the darkness. How is that right, that I should have freedom, and you, and them, and every one of the others must go on suffering?" Moishe gestured toward the people around him. "I'm a patient man. I do my part so God does the rest, and we all are taken to our just reward."

Traffic honked and snarled around the Colosseum circle, building up in advance of the rush hour, drawing tourists away, eager for escape from these two strangers, wolves or shepherds.

Grant struggled to process what he was hearing, to bind the man's words to his actions. "You're serious. Kill them all and let God sort them out?"

Moishe's fingers worked through his exercises, limbering up for the next blow, whenever it would fall. Behind him, a security officer received pointed directions and a rapid-fire explanation from a couple of tourists, and Grant was glad they didn't all speak English. Or was he? Would the authorities know how seriously to take Moishe's resolve? They'd just as likely hear Grant's words as the threat, detaining him while Moishe walked away, especially given that the man had a proven connection with the Carabinieri while Grant's only link to the police was his own arrest for murder.

How was Grant supposed to defeat someone who literally cared about nothing? Moishe studied him through the metal mesh of the security fence. Cold, sharp, fast and deliberate. The most dangerous kind of enemy. And Moishe didn't care who went down on his quest for oblivion.

For an instant, Grant thought to race back through and take him down, right now, before anyone else could get hurt. Might be worth the prison time to stop it, even if he couldn't say what "it" really was. Didn't know how he'd take him out, but he'd find a way.

He started forward, but Moishe receded as the crowds resumed their motion. His adversary vanished into the Forum as completely as the nothing that he craved.

Chapter Twenty-Seven

While the computer processed the inordinate number of photos Jacinta had already taken, she perused the bookshelf for any resources she didn't own herself or borrow at the museum's archive. One item stuffed in among the general materials appeared to be a bound printout. She pounced, hoping for an pre-publication thesis of some kind, some new research that might illuminate the latest knowledge. Instead, she found a scientific paper about the plague, annotated with strong markings that appeared to be Hebrew. She filed that with the other plague references, and found a few texts of stronger interest, making a little stack to read at bed time.

For now, she turned her attention to the cleaning. A jar of her special blend solvent stood readily to hand—though not so readily that it might spill where she didn't want it. Earlier, she had cleaned a tiny swatch of a dark corner, to make sure there was no adverse reaction, and it looked fine. To continue the process, she used long cotton-tipped swabs to gently remove the centuries of grime. She wore magnifying lenses equipped with a localized light, viewing every square centimeter of the canvas. This close, the image became just a pattern of brush strokes in darkness and light—mostly darkness. She made out some incisioni, the so-called "incisions" Caravaggio made with the back of his paintbrush, generally to align the major portions of an image so that his models could relax from time to time, but resume the same, sometimes awkward, position when they returned.

At every moment, she grew more convinced the painting was genuine. Caravaggio transported the technique of incisioni from his apprenticeship painting frescoes where a drawing could be transfered to the wet plaster using such marks. They were a hallmark of his own work.

Curiously, these incisioni appeared in the dark area in the upper left of the canvas—far from the figures of Zacariah or the angel. Maybe he'd originally placed the angel up there, then changed his mind about the layout. She'd see when she got further into the occupied portion of the canvas. When she viewed the processed images—when she needed a break from the close and time-consuming work of cleaning—she would look for pentimenti in this area, indicating an older version of the work on the same canvas.

Removing her magnifying rig, she took a short break, using an oblique light to bring out the markings for a few more photographs, then add those to the ever-growing file.

Ah! The little movie she'd made for Riccardo had finished converting. She transferred it to a flash drive as requested, then used another flash drive to back up the images so far and stuck it in her pocket. Without her usual cloud back-up, she worried something might happen to corrupt the files or crash the machine. It took only one such disaster in graduate school for her to become even more methodical.

The smell of fresh coffee overwhelmed that of solvent alcohol and Jacinta rose, stretching her back. Used to be, she'd call Dominic over her coffee, or he'd call her. She reached to her pocket. No phone. Ma forse, he might still be in the air. Late last night, before her own plans were finalized, he'd sent a message with his flight back to Rome. She looked to the translucent windows. What time was it, actually?

She walked to the kitchen where Angelica placed a little cream pitcher on a tray alongside a few other things.

"Ah, signorina. I think you could use a snack." She indicated the plate of biscotti.

"Sì, grazie. Also, I made the film for Riccardo. It seemed better to do it early." Jacinta held out the flash drive, and the other woman slipped it into a pocket of her old-fashioned apron.

"He'll be so pleased." Angelica's smile matched her name, broad and beatific.

"I hope so. Could you bring my phone from the locker, please? I should check in with my family." Jacinta matched the smile.

Angelica patted her pocket. "Let me deliver this and I'll take care of it. Here, the coffee. Where do you want this?"

"I can—"Jacinta started, but the maid had already hefted the tray and marched with it toward Jacinta's workspace.

"There you go." Angelica put down the tray, then paused, gazing at the painting. She crossed herself. "Just look at it. Look at it! That angel, and the candles."

"It's coming out well, yes." The painting drew her own reverence because she knew the artist, but this sounded more fervent than an ordinary artistic enthusiasm.

With a bob of her head, the older woman hustled out the door. Jacinta sipped her coffee for a moment, looking at the portion she'd already cleaned, with its strange incisioni and overall...not so dark as it had been, not at all. With her face up close to the painting, the magnifiers in front of her eyes, she saw something like the pixels of the work. From here, she could see another scene emerging, faint, but now discernible. *The Ecstasy of St. Francis* had something like that, another scene hidden in the background, purported to be a group of shepherds as they marvel at the glow of the seraph who appeared to the saint.

Jacinta leaned in, trying to make out what she saw. A face, perhaps, save that people saw faces in trees, faces in clouds. Setting down her coffee cup, she took up another cleaning swab and went over the areas adjacent to the image.

Decisamente, something was there. Someone.

Sip the coffee, swab the painting. Before too long, the cup was empty, and the painting a little more clear. A face indeed, distraught, as so many of Caravaggio's faces were, but this one remained almost entirely dark, composed of slight variations in the ground color, the shade so distinctive that some claimed he'd made it with his own blood. Wait until she told— Jacinta frowned, noticing the click of knitting needles. She looked to the sitting area where Angelica worked.

The woman glanced up immediately, as if acutely aware of Jacinta's gaze. "Do you need more coffee, Signorina?"

"Grazie, no. You said you could bring my phone?"

"Ah, so I did. I got to talking with Signore Riccardo, and it slipped my mind. He is so happy with the video you made he wants to share it with the backers right away."

"That's great."

Angelica smiled. Jacinta smiled. "My phone?"

With a trill of laughter, Angelica tapped her forehead. "Touched, as my mother always said." She set aside her knitting and shuffled to the door. Jacinta followed her onto the landing, and Angelica glanced back swiftly, a fleeting expression darkening her face.

"Just a few texts, that's all. We can stay out here if you like, so I don't show the painting at all."

"Or speak of it."

"Or speak of it, of course." Faint music came from somewhere. Riccardo's office, perhaps?

A numerical lock controlled the chemical locker, built into the blank wall opposite the stairs. Angelica shuffled over, and squatted in a way that made it impossible to look over her shoulder.

Several times now, Jacinta's situation tingled the base of her skull, as if some long-gone peasant ancestor urged her to run, to run away and not look back. Why, because an old woman had trouble to open a locker? How many times had Jacinta had the same thing at the gym or at school? Because they took her phone to begin with, or because they'd stolen the painting from some very dangerous people?

"Mi dispiace," Angelica began, and Jacinta braced to be told that she couldn't open the locker at all, that she'd forgotten the code or some other menzogna. Instead, Angelica rose stiffly and held it out to her with an encouraging push. "Yes, if you don't mind, we'll stay here? That way I can leave the locker open. And you must tell me what you like for dinner, sì?"

Just an old woman, trying to do her job and keep an eye on Jacinta as well as providing for her. "Pasta or fish? I don't eat much meat." Already, Jacinta had unlocked her phone, seeing a half-dozen messages from Dom, and a few other messages from various people. Her boss protesting her sudden vacation, a potential client reaching out.

Used to hearing from her promptly, regardless of the time, Dom commanded her attention first. He texted when boarding, texted when he landed. Texted to tell her he was at his apartment, that Tony was staying with him for now. Texted to say he missed her. Texted to say he was worried he hadn't heard from her. She cradled the phone in her hand, gazing at his little portrait beside the message. There had been no declarations between them, though she thought it might happen, and soon, before all that had befallen him. Perhaps sooner, now, if it had caused him to think harder of what really mattered.

:Miss you too! I am in Rome also. Sorry I didn't say sooner!: She added a few emoji to indicate her apology and her enthusiasm.

She replied to another message, but Dom's face popped up with his response. *:Rome? Will you come see me? Hurts to travel.:*

He'd looked awful in the hospital bed, worn out and bandaged. He needed to sleep, not worry about her. *:Sending hugs!! Get some rest. Maybe we can meet soon?:*

:How long are you here? Where are you staying?:

Her thumbs hovered over the screen, then she wrote, *:I don't know:* How much did she dare say to him? But the questions she didn't answer would tell him things she didn't mean to say. *:The client has put me up. V. Comfortable.:*

:You've earned it!:

:Not yet, but I will.:

Down the stairs, a door opened, almost slammed closed and ponderous footsteps rose. Moishe's head appeared then he emerged onto the landing. His glance flicked from one woman to the other, and his lips molded into a smile. "Must be time to get back to work."

Riccardo pattered down from the floor above. Did they own the whole building?

"Moishe! Good to see you. I wasn't sure we'd see you for supper." Riccardo's smile carried some warmth, too much so, as if to make up for Moishe's lack.

"Just let me say good-bye," Jacinta told them, though her fingers felt numb, the phone suddenly slick in her hands. She flicked on her Bluetooth and felt the answering buzz of the earbuds in her pocket, then tapped the recorder she used during lectures. It would eat battery, but if these two men had more to say without her, she wanted to know what it was. Shutting down the screen, she held out the phone to Angelica, but Moishe's hand intervened, and he slid the phone from her hand.

"Some rough characters downstairs. Be a shame if they broke in, looking for drugs, and found this."

"Grazie. Good thinking." She waved her now empty hand and started toward her studio. She tried to imagine a character so rough they'd loiter near a building they saw Moishe enter.

"Ravioli for supper, Signorina?" Angelica called, and Jacinta assented as she returned to the studio. The maid bustled after her, closing the door as she got busy in the kitchen.

Jacinta hurried back to her easel, and fumbled one of the earbuds in as she opened up her cleaning solution, swabbing vigorously at another section of the darkness as she listened.

Chapter Twenty-Eight

Once Angelica returned to the kitchen, clanging pots and turning on the tap, Moishe faced Riccardo. "Casey's in Rome. The Nazi sympathizer. He would kill me if he could."

"This is the man who killed the priest? But you left him in Poland. Still alive, apparently. How would he know to come here?"

"I can think of a few ways." He pulled the art restorer's phone out of his pocket and bent it between his hands until the screen cracked and the internals distorted. "You'll get her a new one. Help her with the set-up. Or not. They'd only taken the lid from the crate, so it's unlikely the crate itself or the painting was tagged in some way."

"So he probably doesn't know where we are, but clearly you saw each other." Riccardo started up the stairs toward his office and the security center, Moishe joining him step for step.

"We did, though he could not have followed me. He might also have other evidence, or he might have received some from my former employers."

"The mafioso, you mean? The one whose archive led you to the painting?"

Riccardo wasn't an idiot, per se, but he had not been hired for his ability to make creative leaps. Moishe explained, "That particular employer is no longer in a position to share information with anyone but a forensic analyst." A necessity to prevent the mobster himself from pursuing his claim to the artwork his ancestor lost during the war.

Riccardo blinked as he absorbed this truth, then he tipped his head. "I have been offering prayers of gratitude that you found the information you did, through that unsavory connection. I shall add a prayer for his soul. Your prior employers perhaps, the Mossad. What do you think they might know?"

Moishe shrugged. "It's hard to say. They almost always know more than it seems. If I don't interfere with them, they're not interested." He worked his fingers. "Usually."

"Time to call in our people, then. I thought we'd have more time before we had to deal with outside interests." They paused outside his office and Riccardo offered him the door, deferentially, but Moishe paused. The opposite door led to his operational headquarters, including the security camera monitoring.

"I assume she's been working steadily, your art restorer?"

Riccardo chuckled, his voice warming, perhaps a little too much? "Oh, yes, Angelica says it's hard to get her to take a break, even for coffee. She got right back to work."

"Sounds like you made a good choice." Throw the show dog a little bone.

"Thank you, I believe I have."

"I should join her for supper and learn more. She may have ideas on where to look."

Riccardo's eyes flinched. "I'm sure you don't mean to let her in on the truth, what we're really looking for." His voice dropped low as he spoke, even here inside their secure building.

"She doesn't need to know why."

They regarded each other warily, then Riccardo said, "She prepared a sort of executive summary for me of the day's work. Perhaps you'd like to view that?"

Interesting. Riccardo had taken some initiative. Or preferred that Moishe not interact with the woman face to face. Why? "Better to hear it directly." Moishe allowed himself to smile. "You doubt my ability to charm. To earn trust."

With a spread of his hands, Riccardo shrugged. "Isn't that why you hired me?"

"Have you never considered you don't know me as well as you believe?"

Riccardo stilled, his lips compressed, but he didn't speak.

Moishe held the man's gaze a breath too long, then he turned to go. "Bring in the others. Send teams to the key locations for both the artist and the artifact. I don't want another surprise." At Riccardo's nod, Moishe added, "Locate the Bone Guard and get hold of their evidence, whatever it may be. By whatever means necessary." He started down the stairs, but Riccardo's voice stopped him.

"What about the woman? Sadie."

He should never have shared even her name. Moishe's foot hovered over the next step, not quite ready to take it. "The countdown starts with her," he said. "If there's no other way."

His foot landed and he moved on.

Chapter Twenty-Nine

When he got D.A.'s message, the location of the hotel, Grant left the piazza where he'd been studying postcards. He took his gelato with him. Kinda wished he could spread it across his bruised chest where the cold might provide some relief to the sting. No more sign of Moishe, thank goodness, but the incident left him hyper-vigilant as he made his way to the new base.

Built into an old palace in the Jewish quarter, the hotel bragged about its modernity, and he stepped through a towering double-door into a sleek lobby, moving quickly to the stair. The mirrors he passed suggested he had escaped the fight looking mostly respectable, even if he didn't feel that way.

D.A. opened the door and ushered him in. She swept him with an experienced glance. "Moishe?"

"Affirmative. Where's that first aid kit?"

She pointed toward a table where her laptop already took pride of place. "I've been plotting locations. The cardinal's main home, Palazzo Madama, is a no-go, it's now the seat of the Italian senate."

Grant stripped off his shirt and dropped into a chair, availing himself of a few alcohol swabs.

Approaching with a cup of coffee, D.A. glanced to his chest and winced. "That's from just now?"

"I used to be better at fencing." Coffee had just the right balance of bitter and sweet. "Dead end, then?"

"Not hardly. Take a look." She turned her computer, taking the seat next to him. "Del Monte had a villa in the city as well, and our boy did some work there, including this crazy big mural. It's called the Casino dell Aurora. The Dawn house."

The map on her screen highlighted an irregular section of town north of their location, near the Villa Borghese. "Sounds like the right target. I read about Del Monte's alchemical studio, with the gods painted on the ceiling. That's gotta be where he wrote the letter."

"Gets better. During the excavations to expand the villa, a number of Roman-era statues and fragments came to light, including the 'Dying Gaul,' you know that one?"

"The letter refers to workers who might be spreading the word, even though Del Monte wanted it kept silent. If he found the Menorah, it might've been during that work." He considered his own research on the ride over, getting to know the artist. "Some of the art world thinks Caravaggio was among the first to see that statue, the 'Dying Gaul', that it might have influenced his work." He drained his cup. "How do we get in?"

"Call up the owner, apparently. It's on the market, so there's no telling what response we get. Could try B & E, but I'll bet this place has security up the whazoo."

"See what you can do." Grant pulled the letter closer as D.A. made the call. The cardinal had also supported Galileo's optical research against the Church itself. The more Grant learned about Del Monte, the more he liked him. As for the rest, Naples...the artist's other patron...

D.A.'s conversation grew abruptly animated, then she hung, the phone held to her chest. "We're not the only ones asking for a tour. She'll do it, if we can come tonight, with these other people. Eight o'clock."

Grant alerted immediately. "I don't like the sound of that. Too many coincidences."

"Not really." D.A. plopped into the seat again. "We're working the same map from different directions. If he's done the same research we're doing, we're bound to run into each other."

"Let's just say I'm not crazy about the impact."

"Maybe it's not him, the other visitor."

Grant raised an eyebrow. "The owner. How old? Married?"

"Middle-aged. Widowed. Literal princess." D.A. tapped another tab on her screen. "I think I see where you're going with this, so you'll appreciate this part." She turned the screen again, revealing an elegant woman with long blond hair. "The princess is a former Playboy model."

Grant ruffled his hair. "Do you think I have a shot with somebody like that?"

"You'll need a better outfit."

"Nick's gonna love this shopping trip." He held out his cup. "If I'm pulling this off, I definitely need another cup."

Chapter Thirty

Jacinta heard only two exchanges before her phone abruptly died, but that was enough to set her teeth on edge. The man Dom and his friends were so keen on was a Nazi sympathizer. He'd killed a priest, and apparently tried to kill Moishe not long ago. Was that the 'rough character' the big man alluded to?

Angelica bustled around the kitchen, humming, while Jacinta swabbed the surface of the painting, uncovering what looked like an animal's snout. A soft knock summoned Angelica to the door, then she approached, and Jacinta looked up. "Moishe is here. Will it bother you if he stays for supper?"

"It's alright to say no," Moishe added from the doorway.

As if she would turn away her employer's right-hand man. "Certo, it's fine." She wiped off her hands and replaced the lid on the jar as Moishe approached. Buffo. A little while ago, she wondered how frightening it would be to turn and find Moishe beside her, but he had the courtesy to knock and request her attention. As she turned on her stool, starting to rise, he waved her back again.

"Please, don't allow me to disturb you." His shoulders hunched a little, his head bowed, then he took something from the pocket of his shapeless jacket. "I hope you can forgive me. Sometimes I get so clumsy. I was going up the stairs with Riccardo, and your phone slipped. I broke it before I could stop myself." On his over-sized palm rested her cracked cellphone. Moishe gave a deflating sigh. "I thought I would protect it, but I've only done worse to it."

Jacinta took it from him, her nails catching on the shattered glass.

"We can try to have it repaired?" he suggested. "Or I can have another one delivered. Whatever model you want."

His face, so impassive before, crumpled with concern or contrition, not too different from the faces of Caravaggio's unknown models, taken from the streets. She set the phone gently aside. "Thank you for telling me."

"I try to do the right thing. Clumsy as I am." He shrugged, then said, "May I watch you work?"

Not creepy at all. She swallowed, and nodded, then reached for her solvent jar. "I'm only cleaning the surface, still. The chairs are—"

He waved this away. With a little grunt of discomfort, Moishe folded his legs and sat on the floor beside her stool, his head now below hers, his posture reminding her of the bright-eyed children who came to her museum talks. As he adjusted his position, she noticed a bruise across his cheek, a raised welt as if he'd been whipped across the face and the overheard snippet of conversation lingered in her mind.

When he lifted his face to the artwork, he breathed deeply as if he could draw Caravaggio into his lungs and send particles of the master-piece out into every cell of his body. His expression had gone again, as if it formed only when he willed it so, but he gazed up at the golden Menorah, his hands gripping his knees.

"I am Jewish," he said softly, and cut her a glance, then swallowed, one corner of his mouth lifting, his shoulder, too. "I don't speak much of this. There is so much prejudice."

With a soft breath of her own, Jacinta said, "E vero." She'd known that before she let her true self be seen.

His glance fell, almost bashful. "It is too personal. Forgive me again." Gesturing toward the painting, he said, "Tell me what you see."

"It's hard to say." She touched a swab to the surface, widening the area over the animal's face, the soft tip of the swab growing red-brown with the grime of ages. "These small images are coming from the darkness."

Moishe's laugh rumbled. "When I brought it up here, I thought that was all black, but you're right, there are faces."

"At least a man and an animal. I think a ram, perhaps. That would prefigure the ram who is shown with Giovan Battista—John the Baptist —in later paintings. Caravaggio has done many works of him."

His eyebrows twitched upward. "The man who baptized Jesus, who lost his head to that girl."

Jacinta laughed out loud. "I have not heard it said that way, but yes, that is him." As she cleaned, though, the horn that emerged near the head wasn't ridged and curled like a ram's horn, but rather smooth and gently curved.

"You are certain this is Caravaggio, then."

"Si, certo. I have no doubt. The color of the ground—it's not really black, that is the patina, only—gives it early period, maybe 1590's, but the quality of the brush strokes suggest a later date, with an effort to adopt his earlier mode. The angel shows similar to his St.Francis of that period, his first known religious painting. Also these marks—"she indicated another area of the painting—"they are incisioni, an artifact of his process, and not so many painters would use this."

"Very convincing." His gaze returned to the Menorah. "Why this, then? Why should a Christian commission a Menorah?"

She rolled the swab between her fingers and finally said, "For a chapel to the Baptist, perhaps? For his early life?"

"Like the paintings of St. Matthew, where he shows him before he is a saint, all the way to his death."

Startled, she inadvertently flicked a drop of her cleaning solution, then said, "Apologia. I should not be surprised you have seen these, if you have an interest."

He shrank a little bit, murmuring, "It is a little strange to be in a church, but the artwork is there, and so I must go. Is it not so that he always paints from life, from models or from props? So somebody has given him a menorah for this. Somebody trusted him, in spite of his reputation."

Their eyes met, his deep brown under his furrowed brow. From his position on the floor, he had to look up at her, almost beseeching.

"Cardinal Del Monte might have procured it," she said. "Or la famiglia Colonna." His observation coincided with her own conclusion, and the desire to share that confidence to have someone believe in her insight, burned sharply at her breast. Dom's friends turned down her offer, but with what she now knew about their leader, she might be just as glad. She focused again on the painting. That animal. Not a goat, a bull.

Moishe leaned in beside her. "You noticed something, what was it? What caught your eye?"

She tried to shrug it away, but his earnest expression, the longing in his voice..."It's not a ram, it's a bull. Taurus, perhaps? He has painted the signs of the zodiac—"

"On the ceiling at Del Monte's villa!" The big man's grin flared.

"You have seen this?" The Aurora chamber, Caravaggio's only mural, remained in the same family for centuries, though the owner sometimes gave tours. Jacinta had been there once, years ago. With the villa now on the market, who knew what would happen to it, or if access would still be available.

His head shook, and his hands drew together in his lap. "If I could go there, would you come? My Italian is not so good, and also you could explain all of this. What we should see."

The swab hesitated on the rim of the jar as she allowed the excess liquid to drip back inside. "You have the knowledge."

"Not as you do." He spread his large hands, then knotted his fingers together in his lap. "But if you don't wish to come with me, I—"

"Oh, no, non è quello!" What an idiot she was. How often had she wished for company, only to be turned away for what she looked like, for who she was.

Imagine being built like Moishe, tall and large-boned, his intellect and curiosity underestimated, even by her. If she found it hard to make friends, hard to overcome the reactions of strangers, how much harder must it be for him. "If Riccardo is all right for me to go. It's only..." her chuckle turned nervous.

"You worry about leaving your work." He cocked his head. "And...I think you feel a prisoner. No phone, no windows. That's me, I'm afraid. I try to make everything secure. Everyone. And maybe I go too far. Again, I ask you to forgive me."

To protect a masterpiece like this? A secret treasure—and maybe another treasure besides, one, if possible, even greater? What could be too far? Jacinta put out her hand. "Va bene. We'll go together."

He grasped her hand with careful pressure, one of few hands that could dwarf her own. The bruise on his face urged her to ask more, to dig deeper, and she flicked her eyes away, but he said, "It barely hurts. I've been hit so often I hardly notice." He released her hand. "A man attacked me today. It happens more than you'd think to look at me."

"Attacked you?" she said, trying to make her voice sound normal. She turned her attention back to the work.

"They feel threatened, or they want to prove how big they are." A snort. "Is it so hard to let a person just live their life, just follow their dream?" He seemed to compose himself, then said, "Again, too personal." He shook his head. "But here, I can smell the sauce. It must be time for supper, eh? I should go wash up."

He started to rise, getting as far as one knee, their heads close to level as he murmured, "You are a good listener. Thank you. Don't worry over me. Truly."

He pushed up the rest of the way, leaving her speechless in his wake.

Chapter Thirty-One

When they arrived outside the gate a little before seven, a door-keeper scowled at them, but her glance kept returning to Grant, newly decked out in Italian leather shoes, a pair of khaki trousers that cost more than some of his cars with a creamy silk shirt, sleeves buttoned, collar open, and a watch that would pass for a Rolex as long as you didn't look too closely. He missed the silver cuff bracelets his grandfather had given him, but they'd be too ethnic for this situation, this persona he was claiming.

Removing his imitation Bentley sunglasses, he offered his most rueful smile. "I am so sorry, but the tides wait for no man. If I'm going to make it to Crete for my sister's wedding, we need to sail by eight-thirty at the latest." He paused while D.A. translated for him, standing a half-step behind, like an accessory that could be otherwise forgotten.

The housekeeper's frown deepened.

Grant leaned his arm against the old stone wall, meeting the woman's eye. "We did call, but I've heard about la principessa's plight, the fact that she might be evicted—it's really awful. I'm just afraid that if I miss this chance, there might not be another one. I'm willing to pay, of course." He offered a folded bill between his fingers.

With a sudden movement, the housekeeper snatched the bill and tucked it into her blouse, finally flashing him a shy smile. "Va bene. This way, Signore." She led the way through the gate, past the glower of another servant, and up a set of stairs. "You wait in the gallery. I see what can be done."

She glanced back at him again, then hurried away, leaving them in a long corridor lined with art.

"Seems like the makeover did its job so far. Nick'll be pleased."

"He'd be more pleased if he weren't left doing the research." Grant maintained his casual air, becoming the sort of man who owned a yacht, whose sister would hold a wedding on one of the—no-doubt many—family properties.

Paintings crowded the walls, top to bottom, end to end, turning the gallery into a space of gilt and gloom. Most of the subjects were religious, no surprise there: saints being shot with arrows or strung upon the rack, Christ in various stations of the cross—things Grant vaguely remembered from a few church visits with Teo back in the old days—and a life-sized depiction of the Last Supper, Jesus gazing beatifically up, Judas at the front, eyes downcast, the pouch of silver already in his hand. Low light befit the valuable nature of the collection, protecting the family's legacy of Old Masters, and casting the whole scene into a chiaroscuro worthy of Caravaggio himself.

"There's gotta be some place else we can wait," D.A. muttered.

"It's the Italian baroque period. It's pretty much all like this."

"Can't believe people just live with this stuff." D.A. waved a hand at the gruesome martyrs all around them. "I think it would turn my stomach, having somebody dying while I'm trying to eat, somebody else bleeding all over the library. It's like these dour, deathly faces staring down at you all the time."

"Reminding you how to behave," Grant murmured.

He leaned in closer to one of the paintings, well-executed, but lacking in vision. He tipped his head, trying to work out what set it apart from the Caravaggios. Darkness? Check. Powerful streaming light? Check. Dramatically posed figures? Check. No beheadings, of course. Nobody chopped heads like Caravaggio. "I take it the synagogue's not like this."

"Ya, no. We're not meant to need all these other people to tell us what's right, or encourage us to make sacrifices. There's no intermediaries, no intercessors." She glanced at him sidelong. "Were you ever religious?"

He shook his head. "Teo is. Took me to church a few times. My grandmother was, in her own way, but not all saints and martyrs." He flashed a smile. "Up until now, I've spent more time in mosques than churches."

"Seems like there's plenty of bloodshed in real life, especially back then." Her gaze flicked across the Last Supper, over to Saint Stephen and away again. D.A. swung around, her posture tense, and Grant straightened. Nobody there but the saints and martyrs. But he didn't think that's what she saw.

"What's up?"

Her hair tossed. She walked a few paces along the hall, arms folded. "There's not a single empty inch, is there? It's a little much." Her glance darted back toward him and away again. The way she'd been watching him for days. Since they talked about faith and doubt in a parking lot back in Poland? No, before that. Since Lake Como.

Grant caught up with her as she paused by a stained glass window, vivid blue, red and gold light washing over her face.

"See, here's a space without torture."

She snorted, then recoiled, waving a hand at him. "So you say: looks like you're bleeding."

Crimson light washed down his chest. "You want me to do a dramatic death scene?"

"No!" She jerked away from him, back into the gloom. "For f—no, Chief, I don't."

Apparently, provoking her wasn't the way.

Her pointing finger thrust back into the light. "And don't tell me it wasn't my fault."

Grant sidestepped away from the window, his eyes adjusting, finding her haunted face. "It was."

She flinched, and her chin dropped. "At least you're honest."

"Wasn't the first time I nearly died. Won't be the last." He rolled his arm, palm up, his tattoos peeking out of his shirt cuff, every one of them a record of his death.

"Better be the last time I was responsible." Her shoulders hunched. "The only time."

"What happened to me was an operational hazard, one you couldn't have accounted for." He looked for the right words to pinpoint what really weighed her down. "When do I get to forgive you?"

"Maybe some things are unforgivable." She swallowed. "At least you're still around for my atonement."

She broke away, walking further, still looking for a place that wasn't hung with martyrs. "Even if you can forgive me for that, I broke faith with you. How can you ever trust me? I gotta rescind my own clearance."

Yeah, it might be a while before he really trusted her again. If ever. But that wasn't all there was between them. "D.A."

Her steps paused.

"I'm not going anywhere."

She flipped a thumbs up, and he added softly, "Neither are you."

Chapter Thirty-Two

Heels clicked down the hall, and Grant slipped on his persona like a comfortable suit. Look at the paintings a moment longer, turn smoothly, nonchalant, not like a guy with a hair-trigger who vaulted the fence at the Forum two hours ago. He let his eyes crinkle with his smile, putting his hand out, palm up, the opposite of a power move. "Principessa?"

The tall, blond woman swept him with a glance, and returned a smile of her own as she took his hand. "Pity I haven't adopted the Italian traditional greeting."

"Beso a beso?" Grant chuckled. "Never too late to start."

"My housekeeper tells me you're on a tight schedule." She drew back her hand, he let his hover a moment longer with an air of regret.

"It's true. When I realized the villa was for sale, I was afraid I'd left the visit too late. I cannot imagine having to leave your home under those circumstances."

"Step-children, inheritance disputes, I'm sure you know how it goes." She flicked her perfectly manicured hand, and he gave an understanding nod.

"If I were in the market, I'd ask for a proper tour. I'm looking forward to seeing the mural, though. I've been wanting to for a while." He shrugged. "You know how people never see the sights in their own city? I have a place on the Capitoline, but it's not this...grand."

Her bright laughter echoed among the saints and martyrs. "That's one word for it, but anyhow, I shouldn't keep you. I'm afraid I really do have a dinner engagement, so Lise will have to show you the mural." Her gaze tracked over his face and she shrugged a little. "I'm sorry you couldn't join the later party."

"Well, I really appreciate your being flexible on timing." He held her eye. "Maybe when I get back from Greece I'll reach out."

"You do that." She turned, and strolled away, taking her time, putting on a show with her high heels and model's instincts. For the sake of the housekeeper, Grant kept watching. When she'd gone out the far door, he cut his gaze away and found D.A. staring at him.

She sighed and shook her head.

"Signore." Lise, the housekeeper, indicated that they should accompany her through another door and up an arched staircase. "This room is the cardinal's study. There is another half the house which has been destroyed and turned into the park." She carried on, narrating as she went.

D.A. translated some of it, clearly listening more than she spoke, synthesizing the information rather than deliver the raw data. Should be able to trust her to pick the right things.

At the top of the grand stair the housekeeper unlocked a tall, narrow double door and ushered them through. Inside, ornate plaster frames and pillars embellished the walls, and a few glass cases held smaller items, mostly antique scientific instruments and a few personal items of a similar era. Dark wooden chairs with embroidered cushions occupied the corners. The real attraction arched overhead.

"Wow. Okay, then," D.A. said as they gazed upward.

After his crash-course on Caravaggio, Grant had known what they would see, but the reality of the work in living color startled the eye. Against a backdrop of clouds and blue sky, a pale globe represented the cosmos with a band of astrological symbols girding the painted sphere.

The arc of the zodiac showed Pisces, Aries, Taurus and the Gemini. At one end, the god Jupiter, seated on a painfully small eagle, touched the globe in recognition of his domination of the known worlds. At the other end stood Neptune, god of the sea, with his trident and a hippocampus, a fierce-looking horse with fins for swimming. Beside him, as if in conversation, stood Pluto, god of the underworld, accompanied by the wild-eyed three-headed dog, Cerberus.

Painted as if seen from below, the gods stood in full-fleshed glory. Completely naked.

Jupiter's eagle seemed placed for modesty, while a cloth draped the loins of the sea-god. Fabric draped Pluto as well, but only flicked over his shoulder and wrapped one leg, leaving his manhood absolutely unquestionable.

"And it's a self-portrait," D.A. remarked as Lise, the housekeeper, continued her stream of patter, the speech she'd likely given a thousand times to those curious enough to seek out the work. "The perspective allowed Caravaggio to reveal...great skill with, uh," D.A. paused, turning her hand as she looked for the right word. "Foreshortening. Right. Anyway, each of the figures also has alchemical meanings. Jupiter represents the element of air, Neptune is water and Pluto is earth."

"Fascinating," Grant said. They'd have to add alchemy to the research queue. Assuming that the cardinal's letter pointed them here, what had he meant for them to see?

In the meantime, D.A. pulled out her phone, taking plenty of photos, zooming in on every part, even when she shook her head at what she was viewing. "This was his alchemy lab. The cardinal's, that is. That's why some of the equipment is here."

The cardinal said his studies would lead the way. "Is the stuff original?" Grant took his eye off the painting and scanned the cases, prowling in front of them.

D.A. relayed the question, and translated as the housekeeper walked over to where Grant stood by the case. "She says that some of the equipment was found here, but nobody looks at that, just the painting, even though the telescope was a gift from Galileo, along with a treatise. Apparently our man was a patron of science as well as art."

Grant quickened at that. Galileo hadn't invented the telescope, but he had trained it on the sky, and first seen moons around the planet Jupiter. *The mirror of moons...*only telescopes of this era, so far as Grant knew, contained only a pair of lenses, one at the eyepiece and a larger one at the viewing end. The god overhead, and now this. "May I see it? The telescope?"

Grant leaned closer, and the woman produced another key, opening the front of the case with a smile, her other hand hovering nearby. He obligingly filled it with another large bill. Galileo's telescope sat on the bare glass. A pattern of gold-tooled stars and lines wrapped a green-beige leather cylinder as long as his arm.

The telescope carried a line of Latin, and he puzzled over that for a moment. Perhaps the master's apprentice had made the inscription, mistaking a few words in the reference to Biblical justice. "An ear for an eye and a tooth for a tooth..." wasn't quite right, though he could see why Galileo might think of justice and Del Monte in the same moment if the cardinal had been instrumental in supporting him against the pitiless church.

He squatted down, looking into the near end, and finding his reflection looking back, as if the long-dead astronomer could see him now. One of the founders of modern science, not to mention a pioneer of the very methods of science, made this telescope with his own hands. Probably ground the lenses and fitted the tube. Grant's mouth felt dry. Might never get a better chance.

He indicated the telescope. "May I?"

Lise frowned a little, her hands tapping in the pockets of her apron. One of those pockets held the equivalent of three hundred dollars of his money already.

He turned up the charm with a rueful smile and a little shake of his head. "Apologia. Of course not. Please, forgive me. I shouldn't have asked." He drew back a little, letting his gaze stroke over the antique instrument almost the same way he'd tracked its current owner not long ago.

"With a cloth, only," the housekeeper said. "Spetta." She marched to a little side table and pulled out some linens, then returned to him, thrusting out the cloth napkins.

"Mille grazie! Thank you so much. You have no idea how much this means to me. My cousin is an astronomer. She'll be so jealous." He took the napkins, one over each hand as he lifted the scope, and turned it for D.A.'s camera, then lifted it to his eye, posing for the camera, feeling as though he, now, reached back through time to unite with a genius. He looked through the scope and saw...nothing. Shouldn't be surprised, maybe, after so long, but still...

As he lowered it, examining the tube, something shifted at the larger end. Of course he couldn't see: a silver-backed mirror blocked the lenses. The mirror of moons indeed.

Catching D.A.'s eye as she lowered her phone, Grant made a subtle tip of his head, away. She caught that signal, too.

Gesturing toward the mural again, D.A. launched into a lengthy question, her movements bringing Lise's attention upward.

Grant turned his body toward the case, preparing to replace the scope. He tipped the tube and rolled it against his thigh, his hand over the viewing end. The smooth weight of the mirror rolled out into his palm, thence to his pocket. He still reflected in the end, but faintly against the blackness within. The ghost of Galileo saw the truth as Grant stole the cardinal's secret.

Chapter Thirty-Three

Moishe asked questions, listened deeply, expressed himself unsurprised that Jacinta rushed dinner to make their promised excursion. Her nervousness showed in perhaps talking too much, the clatter of flatware, and little darting glances. Still uncertain of him. To be expected, in spite of his efforts.

"You are still nervous," he observed, and she chuckled, spinning her glass of wine in her hand. A nice red, not too expensive, but enough to show. "Here, let's play a game."

She gave him a quizzical glance. "We need to go soon, no? For the villa."

"Of course, yes, but this is not long. It's called two truths and a lie. You tell them to the other person, and they have to guess which is the lie—you've heard of this?"

"The kids play. In school, like a dare." She set down the glass.

"Ah, okay. I think it's to get to know each other, but maybe it's just for kids." He patted a napkin across his lips.

"No, if you want to play, this is all right." Eager to please him, as her employer's representative, if nothing else. "I agree, it's maybe a way to know someone, if the things you speak are interesting."

Moishe leaned back in his chair and spread his hand. "This may let me out then. I am not so interesting."

She scoffed. "I don't believe this. Here, try. You've been thinking about it, yes? Tell me and I will try to guess."

Scrubbing a hand over his chin, he said, "Do you know how to tell if someone lies?"

"They look away, I think. Up or down. Sometimes they hold their breath."

"Then you are perhaps too good at this, but here, I'll try." He held up his fist, then produced one finger. "I have no living family." A second finger. "Uh...I have seen my best friend die." A third finger, he flicked his eyes away, the slightest thing as he breathed out. "One time, I escaped from a burning car."

Her smile shifted, her eyebrows pinching as she listened, her sympathy tweaked by his truth. "I think you've never escaped the car."

Moishe laughed and raised his glass to her. "It's true."

He had never escaped. The smell of burning flesh still lingered in his mind. "I told you, you are too good. It is your eyes, I think." He squinted at her, looking her in the eye. "You are used to studying details." He drained his glass. "Now you."

Jacinta kept her face perfectly smooth. Or so she must believe. "I am a championship football player." She adopted his habit of showing one finger. "I once ruined a Renoir. And!" She waved the three fingers together, "I adore Federico Fellini."

The pulse twitched at her throat, and her lips made a tiny movement, so small, she likely had no idea she did it. Moishe studied her for a long moment. "Tell me again."

"One, I am a champion football player. Soccer, maybe you call it. Two, I have ruined a Renoir, and three, I adore Federico Fellini."

"I think you're trying to fool me with the Renoir," he declared boldly. "So I say, you can't play soccer."

Genuine laughter pealed across the table and her eyes sparkled. "I was new on the job, and it wasn't a very great Renoir. My boss was able to save it. Mostly. No, I hate Fellini. I know, I am an artist, and he's the greatest Italian director—"she waved her hand in a grand gesture, then turned it to dismissal. "He bores me. My friend—I have a good friend who always wants me to watch with him, who tries to fool me to watch with him."

Moishe showed himself mystified. "Who doesn't love Fellini?"

"Not you, too!" She lightly slapped his arm, then let the touch linger a moment longer, her sympathy returning. "If you ever want to talk about your friend...or your family, I am a good listener. I can work on the art, and not even look at you. Sometimes that helps."

He let his face grow solemn, closer to his customary expression than he'd been all evening. "Sometimes, it does." Then he drew back. "But we should go, really. Thank you, Angelica. Everything was perfect," he said as he rose, then turned to his companion. "How would you say this? Chi perfecto?" he flubbed the word, and she waved that away.

"Nell'italiano? Era perfetto! But you are very close."

"Language is not a gift of mine." Not far from the truth: he had to brute-force every language he spoke. Fortunately, as Avram once put it, Moishe had enough brute to go around. "Would you like to drive? I think you know the streets here better than I."

She brightened. "Sì, grazie. That sounds good." She stuck a hand in her pocket, betraying slight puzzlement, then retrieved a cardigan and displayed the keys from that garment.

At every moment, he ceded power to her. At every moment, she grew more assured, more embedded within his domain.

Moishe held the door and followed her down. "Where have you parked?"

From the driver's seat of the purple car, she leaned over and worked the lever to push the passenger seat all the way back before he got in. "I'm tall, but you are taller. I hope it won't be uncomfortable."

"No, it's fine." He held his coat as he climbed in, ensuring that his twin pistols remained concealed. One benefit of his size was his ability to add bulk at any moment without most people noticing. Pistols, documents, knives, small electronics. Avram had—

Moishe fixed his eye on the exit signs. No surprise that Avram arose in his memory now, after seeing Sadie again. What would it be like to speak to her, after all these years? Might not happen. He'd already given orders, after all.

For now, he gave directions. She knew the general area of their facility. With access to gps, she would pinpoint it quickly enough, he had no doubt. But she had no such access, and so she took his directions at face value. The headlights cutting ahead deepened the gloom of twilight, adding a useful level of difficulty.

"Turn here—here, the left," Moishe called, and she hurried to obey, surging her little car into a gap in traffic as he groaned. "Oh, sorry. It should be the next one. Here, take this right. We'll come back around." And so they did, in a series of careful not-circles that even an experience operative would struggle to retrace.

"Are you sure you have the address correct?" she asked after the third such turn.

"I do, I do, but I think the screen is too small, or I should have my eyes checked." He shook his head at his own folly, holding the phone too close to his face, preventing her from seeing the screen. "I am too proud for glasses, though."

"Ha. My—a good friend of mine, he wears glasses. They look intelligent, I think." She compressed her lips, then added, "If you want people to think past your size, maybe it's a good idea."

"I haven't considered that. Turn at this column, yes—don't worry, I'm sure this time." He offered a little shrug. "Is this why your friend wears them? To be seen more intelligent?"

She shook her head, her ponytail tossing. "Oh, no. He is, as the Americans might say, a huge nerd. Already too smart."

"Your boyfriend?" he asked lightly.

She shrugged, sighed, fidgeted on the next turn. Telegraphing her feelings all too well. Jacinta pointed out his window. "Here is the crypt of the Capuchin monks. Have you seen this? It is all bones in stacks and patterns! Human bones. I think it is, ah..."

Her language failed for a moment, and he supplied, "Disturbing?"

"Sì! But also it means we're close."

He had seen enough bones during his lifetime to find them rather ordinary. They were merely the scaffold of a body, of a man, and fell apart without him. "Yes. Anywhere you can park is good, I think."

As they turned down the Via Lombardia, he spotted one of his men, loitering with a cigarette on a corner opposite the villa. Nice to see his orders being followed. They must have arrived not long ago.

"Ah!" Jacinta spotted a car backing out on the next block, and bided her time, staring down the driver of another car that seemed likely to take the place away from them. Moishe observed, complacent, from the passenger seat.

She turned off the car. "We are early. Is it a problem?"

"We'll go find out. If so, we stroll on the block. It used to be a much bigger house, and I wonder if one can see the old foundation, the way the streets still show where the city wall has been."

"It's a palimpsest. The city. Do you know this word?" She climbed out, waiting for him to exit, then tapping the button that locked the car. "For a manuscript, it is when the parchment is used again. The scribe will scrape away the words and make it smooth, but the old words, they show through."

"Like the marks you showed me on the painting. What are they called?'

"Incisioni. Sì—perfetto!" She grinned at him. "With underpainting, too. It is like a palimpsest."

He was the star pupil. Whenever he needed to be. Together, they walked the sidewalk toward the gate that would lead them inside.

Chapter Thirty-Four

"Mille Grazie. I really appreciate you accommodating us a little earlier," Grant told the housekeeper as she escorted them back down the stairs. "And please give the principessa my regards."

"Sì, certo." As they came back to the long gallery of paintings, knocking echoed through the corridor, and the housekeeper frowned, then glanced at her wristwatch. "Troppo presto," she muttered, then shrugged.

D.A. shot Grant a look. The mysterious eight pm guests stood on the threshold. Grant indicated a side door that led to a brick-paved path between formal plantings. Small lights illuminated the way with a taller lamppost visible in the distance. "Would it be all right if we took a look at the garden? Just a quick stroll through then we can let ourselves out."

The woman frowned through D.A.'s translation, already shaking her head, then answering sharply and pointing toward the door. As if she had summoned it, another round of knocking began, the brass knocker rapping against the wooden door.

Grant shrugged off the refusal, then D.A. leaned in closer to the woman and whispered something, making a gesture around her abdomen.

"But only a moment!" the housekeeper admonished.

"Female troubles," D.A. said. "I'll try to be quick. I know we need to be at the marina pretty soon."

"I'll meet you outside." Grant indicated the small antechamber where they'd originally entered. Something like a guard room in the original structure, no doubt. A great archway led up the stairs they emerged from, a smaller door to the side, probably the servants' passage or other belowstairs storage. The exterior door stood opposite the archway, with an alcove space occupying the remaining wall. A brocade curtain drooped partway over that, revealing a few crates and a closet bar with empty hangers.

"Un momento!" the housekeeper called over her shoulder as she shuffled into the servants' corridor, beckoning D.A. along to attend to her theoretical troubles.

Grant listened for a moment, breath held. A throaty, feminine voice said, "It's because we are early," her English accented with Italian.

"We can be patient," a man answered, his voice deep. Patient like a rock, or an avalanche waiting to fall. Moishe. No idea who was with him, but maybe Grant could find out since he had no intention of engaging the man here if he could help it.

Grant ducked into the alcove, moving quietly. He slid behind the curtain, careful to disturb nothing, leaving nothing out of place to draw the housekeeper's eye. Stay quiet, let them pass by along the same route he and D.A. had taken earlier, then he'd be more than happy to show himself out.

After a moment, the housekeeper's distinctive shuffle returned, and the metal inside latch ground back against its plate. "Troppo presto!" she said.

"Mi dispiace tanto," said the woman outside. "Vuoi che aspettiamo fuori?"

The housekeeper grumbled something else in Italian, and the other person explained, "There was another visitor who didn't want to wait and come with us, so her schedule is already off."

Moishe didn't reply to this, but Grant felt he could almost hear the man thinking, adding things up. No coincidence, D.A. pointed out, if the two of them were following the same map. Should've gotten out of the whole affair when the getting was good—and before he stole part of Galileo's telescope. Could come in useful, actually. Grant slipped the mirror from his pocket and held it a little in front of him, aligned with a tear in the curtain. He glimpsed a slice of the open door and the housekeeper's back as she held it.

"Viene, viene." The housekeeper carried on a little longer, and two more people entered the antechamber, both of them ducking the small, arched opening.

Leading the way was a striking auburn-haired woman dressed in russet and green, her face alight as she took in the room and the stairs ahead. And behind her, Moishe, in his charcoal-grey suit, the drape of the coat likely hid his guns from just about everyone. He, too, glanced around, but in a series of methodical arcs, back and forth, up and down. Threat assessment. Grant held his breath.

They walked toward the stairs, the housekeeper complaining, the other woman making appropriate noises of sympathy and apology. Moishe making no noise at all. They passed beyond the mirror, then beyond the curtain, their backs visible as they mounted the first steps, the tall woman's boot heels clicking. Moishe set one foot down, his head slightly inclined.

Then he turned sharply, shouting, "Watch out!" as he hurled himself toward Grant's hiding place.

Chapter Thirty-Five

Moishe could hardly have planned it better: his enemy, lying in wait behind a curtain. His enemy bursting out of hiding as Jacinta screamed and the housekeeper shouted. His enemy raced out the door, Moishe behind by centimeters.

Moishe caught the fleeing man's arm and hurled him against the wall. The guy twisted away, staggered, and pulled a slim pistol from the concealed holster at his waist.

Leaping back again, Moishe flung his arm in front of Jacinta. "Stay back, he's armed!"

"Duck!" she told him. "He's after you!" Then she half-turned, hearing the Italian woman on the inside. "No, run—there is another still inside!"

She gave Moishe a shove just as Casey pulled the trigger. The bullet cracked stone behind Moishe's head. An admirable shot. Moishe missed his own demise by a few centimeters and the span of a woman's trust.

Casey bolted down the sidewalk.

"Jacinta, go," said Moishe. "Don't worry about me!"

He raced after Casey. His fingers twitched to take his own guns in hand, but he refrained. No need to disturb his ally. Besides, he had more allies than one, and he could have this one back whenever he wished to. She cared too much about the painting to be severed from them so abruptly. His adversary bounded around the corner, turned sharply, and dodged into the street. Across the way, a convex mirror meant as a traffic aid showed Jacinta running the opposite direction, toward her car, and a curly-haired woman emerging from the villa gate, promptly flung closed behind her. Sadie.

Moishe didn't stop. Jacinta wouldn't see him now, and had no way to know what he would do. Sadie...she already knew what he was capable of.

She raced across the street, paralleling her employer's course.

Casey darted past a bus pulling from the curb, between parked cars and Moishe pounded after him. His own associate sped down the block, gun held low.

Ahead, the street looked clear, its twilight peace unbroken by a running figure. Moishe spun on the sidewalk, reaching into his coat, cool metal in his grip. Down the sidewalk, his own man paused as well, pivoting, and a few old ladies hunched together under a streetlight. The bus.

Distracted by his concern over Jacinta, Moishe missed one of the oldest tricks. His adversary must have boarded the bus just as it was leaving. He released the grip of his weapon, and his associate vanished his own pistol immediately.

"Moishe." Sadie's voice, stern and familiar.

He expected she held a gun on him, even now. Instead, she stood far back, near a busy tobacco shop, her hands empty.

"Stop this. Whatever it is you're doing. Leave us alone."

Sadie. After so many years. Sometimes, a man didn't know what his brother saw in his chosen mate, but Avram had been blessed to find an equal. Moishe breathed a heavy sigh, and raised his hands a little, in token of their emptiness. His man would be finding a new path, and Moishe was patient.

"There is no other work but this. No greater work." He took a few paces closer, getting out of the way of customers heading to the trattorias, of dog-walkers coming home from the park. Sad souls trying to make their way through another broken place. "You know what Reb Nachman of Breslov said. If a person won't be better tomorrow, then what need have they of tomorrow?" He took another step, and she withdrew, though there must be twenty meters yet between them.

Her eyes narrowed, and she shook her head.

"Does it not then follow, if the world will be no better tomorrow..." he turned his upturned hands into a shrug.

"That's ridiculous."

A traffic light changed down the street, and his confederate crossed over with the crowd. Another moved along the wall, ambling as if to head to the tobacconist for a cigarette. And why not? How much longer did he want to live in any case? They formed a triangle, with Sadie, all unknowing, at the short side. Getting shorter by the moment. Far off, he spotted the distinctive purple car driving furiously away. He might need her to gain access to the villa, if the owner would even permit anyone to visit after this.

"Do you think so?" Moishe nodded, rocking on his feet. He moved no closer yet. "But you weren't there when he died."

Her eyes flashed in the sudden stillness of her face, her whole being focused on him, in that instant. "Were you?"

"I was his brother, Sadie, I wouldn't leave him."

Her cheeks flushed slightly. "I was on assignment, Moishe. You know how they were."

Never letting the husband and wife serve together. He knew. Just as he knew how guilty it made her feel. "We should talk, just the two of us." Or maybe the four of them.

She ducked, twisted and sprinted toward the villa as the first man came up behind her. The second stepped into her path, weapon drawn.

She didn't pause, but sprang into a kick that knocked the operative back against a car. His gun fired into the air. Then a commanding voice behind him said, "Let her go."

Chapter Thirty-Six

Jacinta's sweaty palms slid on the steering wheel as she peeled out of the parking place and roared down the street. Horns blared around her, and she had trouble swallowing.

It was true. Everything Moishe told her, the Nazi sympathizer who tried to kill him, over and over. Don't worry about him, he said, but the man had a gun. She shouldn't have left him! The man looked every inch a cold-blooded killer: handsome and athletic, impeccably dressed, his eyes concealed behind dark glasses as he turned with absolute calm and squeezed the trigger. Yet he ran instead of firing again.

She missed something. Her analysis lacked the evidence, and she envisioned Professore Carbone chiding her for insufficiency of sources.

Her tires squealed as a light turned red in front of her, and she nibbled on her fingernail. Who was he? Who were either of them? She gulped a breath, and the light turned.

Jacinta stamped on the pedal, jolting through the intersection. Could she even get back to the lab? Already, she had missed a turn. She took the next one. Wait—was it the one after? She must calm down.

Somehow, she must find her center and focus on her driving. Or on where she was going.

Jacinta entered a roundabout and came out the wrong direction, heading into the park. The long curve ahead of her, lined with trees on one side and medieval brickwork on the other, looked ordinary and inviting, just as it had for a hundred years or more.

What had she said to Dom, not that long ago, when the chance for adventure came to him—and she feared for his life? What would he tell her? But after his adventure, he couldn't even speak. Thinking of him, she eased her shoulders away from her ears and made the next turn.

Twenty minutes later, she nosed into an illegal parking space not far from the three-story, Italian Republic-era building where Dom lived. Even if he couldn't speak, he could answer her questions. He could tell her what had happened. He could tell her whom to trust.

She pressed the buzzer. The bell gave a bleat, then the intercom grumbled with static. Before Dom could try to speak, she said, "C'e Jacinta."

With a whir and a clunk, the magnetic lock released, and Jacinta pulled open the door, trotting up the stairs. At the end of the hall, his door swung open. She fled the rest of the way and flung herself into Dom's arms. He absorbed her presence with the stiffening of surprise, then relaxed his arms around her, drawing her into his hallway with a few shuffling steps to let the door close.

Dressed in an old hooded sweatshirt, his throat bandaged, he clung to her. His breathing hitched at first, then evened out. Hers did the same. He smelled of antiseptic over sweat, with a hint of coffee. She missed the savor of the antique shop, with its notes of dust and furniture polish. His head bowed, his face nestled close to her throat. The frames of his eyeglasses dug into her neck.

"You can't speak, I know, but we will find a way. It's all right." She stroked his hair.

His fists pressed her back, then his hands slowly relaxed, stroking gently.

She heard a clatter from elsewhere in the apartment, a pan precariously set, perhaps? She didn't care. Finally, she drew back from him, looking him in the eye. He freed a hand, pushing the glasses up on his nose, then he gave a little smile and a wave.

"You're surprised to see me, I know." She took his hand in both of hers, and he gave a slight nod, wincing at the same time. "I couldn't call, I don't have my phone." She hadn't even thought of it in her rush to be with him.

At his puzzled expression, she said, "I can explain, but there are some things I need to know from you. These people you got involved with, that you went to Germany with. Who are they? What do they really want?"

A crease appeared between his brows. He glanced away from her, down the short corridor leading to the apartment proper. Posters from World War II lined the walls, along with photos, advertisements, old newspapers in frames showing headlines from key battles and pivotal moments.

"You think you can trust them. I don't know if it's true."

His frown deepened, and he shook his head, the slightest movement creased his face with pain. He tugged her toward the apartment.

"I have heard some things from other sources." She moved after him, clipping her long strides. "This chief, the man who leads them. I've heard he is a Nazi sympathizer, that he killed a priest."

They entered the main room, and she stopped short. Another man leaned against the wall between the two windows, arms folded, face bruised—and not just shadowed because of the dim light. "I'm not trying to eavesdrop, honest to God, I was trying to give you some privacy, and of course, Dom couldn't say a word."

Dom lifted his free hand in a half-shrug, gesturing toward the other man. His friend, or so he thought.

Tony, that was the man's name. She'd met him at Dom's grandparents' farm outside of Naples, where his lightning reactions and powerful presence made her instantly on edge. Broad-shouldered, green eyed, hair growing out from a buzz-cut. Hard to mistake for anything but law enforcement.

He straightened away from the wall and turned to face her, arms still folded. His face in the light revealed a black eye, the white of his eye still faintly streaked pink. "That first thing, being a Nazi sympathizer. That's bullshit. Absolute and total bullshit. Yes, he worked for a Nazi. Because a Jew asked him to. He saved the woman's life because that's what you do. Objective achieved, contract terminated. Period, end of story."

Jacinta lifted her chin. "And the second? The priest?"

Tony cut a glance over to Dom, as if looking for permission. "Yeah, he killed the guy. I would've done it myself, but my job was to keep the Mossad from getting in his way. By getting in theirs. Where'd you hear about it?"

Dom moved toward the sofa, and Jacinta let him go rather than cede the space to this man. "Aren't you on the side of law? And the Mossad too? So how are you on opposite sides, if what you say is true?"

Sinking onto his old sofa, Dom reached over and picked up his laptop. He tapped the case, drawing her attention. He made a gesture she couldn't immediately place.

"It's your story, Dom," Tony said. "You want me to tell her, I will."

Dom replied with another sign, as if they were using another language, one that shut her out. Jacinta's gaze flicked from one to the other.

Tony nodded, and gave a faint smile. "You're a quick study." To Jacinta, he said, "ASL: American Sign Language. My daughter's deaf, so I'm used to working with non-speakers. I taught him a few signs to make it easier to get us this far."

A quick study, certo. "Since we are children he learns fast."

With one hand, Dom beckoned her closer, then patted the cushion beside him, and she reluctantly sat down, turned so she could see them both.

"I'll give you the brief version. Dom's got the book rights, so he'll spell it all out later. What you need to know is this. We were hired to locate a Nazi stash, one that included this Jewish library stolen from Rome. You know the Gladio was after us?"

"Meaning you and the Nazis."

Dom poked her in the side, as if they were children again, and she held her tongue.

Glowering, Tony said, "Sure, put it that way. Whatever. We tracked the clues to this church in Poland, only the Gladio got there first. Their leader was a priest, pretty far up in the hierarchy, I think. During the fire-fight, Mossad intervened along with the German authorities, trying to take down the Nazi group. They took us prisoner, Dom, too, holding us in the church office while they mopped up the combatants. When this Italian priest showed up who knew Dom's name, the Mossad turned him over. They didn't know the guy wasn't a friend."

Under his thick eyelashes, Dom blinked rapidly, his eyes gleaming, and Jacinta snaked out her hand to grip his knee.

"I didn't know what was happening at first, just that they were letting Dom go. I thought maybe he'd finally be out of danger." Tony aimed a stern expression at her friend, then he went on, "But the guy was armed with a blade. He took Dom ...brought him into the crypt."

The crypt? Jacinta swallowed. Dom flattened out his hand and pressed his fingertips up, toward his injured chin, mimicking the weapon that cut him. Then he lifted his laptop against his chest, revealing the puncture through the case, holding it against his heart for a moment before lowering it back to his lap. The puncture went straight through to the other side. He touched his chest.

"The priest tried to kill you, to stab you."

A nod, then he made another gesture, a sign, she realized.

"When they got the chief and brought him in with the rest of us, he connected the dots, figured out who the priest was and what he want-ed," Tony continued. "I was the distraction, Chief went after Dom. I would've gone in a heartbeat. So would Nick. Dom saved my life a couple of times. The priest got what was coming to him, capsice?"

"Oh, Domenico!" Jacinta stroked his face, and he leaned a little into her touch.

Pushing aside the ruined laptop, he pulled over a tablet and wrote, *"Chief saved my life, in the dark."*

Uncertainty blossomed through Jacinta's core. If the priest had been served justice, and the Nazi was just his boss, just for a little while—

A phone rang, and Tony answered, then his head jerked up. "What the Hell?" He aimed the phone at Jacinta. "How'd you learn about the priest? Who have you been listening to?"

Chapter Thirty-Seven

Grant ran out of parked cars to use for cover at the corner, but Moishe had stopped, D.A. answering him from somewhere ahead. Ten yards further, dark shoes moved into view, stealthy, and Grant slid from beneath the last car. His creamy silk shirt might never recover. "Let her go."

Gun extended, Moishe's head in view. Would the big man even buckle to a threat, if he didn't care who lived or died?

D.A. slipped the second man's arms. The first dug his hand into her hair. She dropped low. Had to hurt. The guy raised his other arm, something in his hand blocked from view. His arm plunged downward.

Grant pivoted and fired, taking her captor in the side. The man staggered and jerked. D.A. rolled forward, out of his grasp as he collapsed.

Tense from head to toe, Grant expected D.A. to stay down in a pool of her own blood. Her assailant had landed only one blow, maybe not enough to kill her.

When she staggered to her feet, Grant's spirit surged.

In his peripheral vision, Moishe shifted, his coat billowing. Grant vaulted forward, onto the next car, up the hood and over the roof.

Bystanders were shouting, filming, two of them running forward to the downed man as D.A. fled down hill. Moishe fired.

Glass shattered under Grant's feet and he stumbled, shards of the windshield gouging into his leg.

He went down head-first, his momentum sliding him over the hood to sprawl onto the ground. Moishe's second ally lunged toward him, and Grant fired, then scrambled up, shoving the injured man out of his way.

Grant raced along the line of parked cars, between them and the press of evening rush hour. A messenger on a Vespa pulled up to the curb.

"Mi dispiace," Grant said as he shouldered the woman out of his way and leapt onto her captured moped, cutting immediately into traffic.

Horns blared and Italian curses scattered the wind of his passing. A sharp whistle to his left. Grant turned sharply, racing up hill. Running footsteps fell in beside him. He put out his arm, and D.A. caught his bicep, accepting the boost as she scrambled onto the Vespa behind him. The engine protested and she leaned into his ear. "You think this thing can handle both of us?"

"Nope!" Grant revved the little bike and tore down an alley, putting distance between them and the villa as D.A. clung to his waist.

Silent and grim, they raced away from the conflict, Grant choosing turns more or less at random—whatever was easy and gained them cover as he steered the Vespa away from their encounter, dodging pedestrians and cars alike. Finally, satisfied they weren't pursued, at least for now, he slowed to a more reasonable pace, one less likely to attract attention.

D.A.'s breath at his back, her arm around his chest faltered, and he slowed a little further. "Sitrep?"

"Your leg's bleeding," she muttered.

"Copy that. You okay? Thought he was stabbing you back there."

"Yeah, I'm good. Just." She drew a sharper breath. "Gimme a minute."

Listening intently, he didn't reply. Sounded like she'd been more affected by the fight than she thought.

Her head dipped, her forehead touching his shoulder, then she pulled back. "Sorry."

Her voice caught. Her breathing should have leveled out now that she wasn't running any more. It didn't.

"You sure you're not injured? Something hidden, maybe?" Maybe internal, but he didn't voice that. Neither of them needed that kind of stress.

"Bruises—"she gasped. "Maybe." She clutched him almost convulsively. "Some of these turns are a little much."

"Dizzy?"

Another ragged breath, and she said, "Guess so."

He found a straightaway, or what passed for one in downtown Rome, scanning ahead, glancing in the little round mirrors to make sure nobody was following. "Better?"

Her head shook against his back. "Hell, Chief. I'm sorry."

"Enough apologies, D.A., talk to me."

"Ah—"she panted. "Might vomit."

He gunned the engine and bumped them up onto a sidewalk, cutting across a stone piazza to a mass of parked Vespas just like theirs, then cut the engine.

She stumbled getting off the bike, and Grant caught her around the waist. "Trashcan. Three paces. Let's go."

"I can," she started to say, but she swayed heavily.

Grant pulled her arm over his shoulder, the height differential not helping, and got her as far as the trashcan. She gripped the side, doubled over and retching.

Keeping one hand on her back, Grant turned away giving her a little privacy. "Jeez, D.A., it's not like Gooney was driving."

Each ragged breath jerked beneath his palm. She retched again, then fell silent, just breathing, her sweaty shirt clinging. Her body flared with heat. What the hell was going on?

"Easy, easy," he murmured. Not much different from soothing a horse. Maintaining the contact, he turned, staying close as he looked her over. "You want to sit down? How about some water?"

"Don't know."

"Come on." He assisted her to sit on the stone curb, her back against the trashcan. Pulled off and stowed his sunglasses, then took a knee in front of her. He took her wrist, finding her jumping pulse. Her face looked blotchy and pale, blue eyes watery.

"I'm sorry," she said again, her other arm crossed over her gut.

"Female troubles?" He smiled a little. "You didn't mention feeling sick. Can you tell me what happened?"

"Came on suddenly." Her voice stayed low, subdued. She swallowed repeatedly. "During the drive. Dizzy, my stomach is doing flip-flops. Can't focus."

Rapid onset illness, after an encounter with undercover agents. "Did you feel anything else? Just before this, before you got on the bike?" He shifted back, scanning her for any sign of injury, her arms clutched over her stomach. When she didn't answer, he ran his hands along both arms, along her sides, performing an injury assessment, looking for anything broken, displaced, swollen or sore. His hands reached her shoulders, then shifted her hair. She flinched.

At the nape of her neck, under her hair on the left hand side, he found a few drops of blood, a tiny puncture wound. She had, indeed, been stabbed—by something more dangerous than a blade.

"I'm sorry," she whispered as she slumped against him, head bowed, breathless, then she went limp in his arms.

Chapter Thirty-Eight

Jacinta flinched from the American's tone and his sudden ferocity. Even if this Chief were not the enemy, that didn't make Moishe completely wrong. Did it?

Dom wrote something, then showed the screen to both of them. "She said she had a job, in town."

"Big time," Tony said. Then, into the phone. "Yeah, Nick, she's here." Pause. "I don't know yet, but you can bet I'm gonna find out." He stared at her, the bruise around his eye giving him a particularly brooding quality as he held the phone to his chest. "Chief's not answering his phone. Neither is D.A. What the hell do you know, lady, and how do you know it?"

Writing again, his face stormy, Dom thrust forward the tablet. Italian this time. "Your big job, it's the painting, isn't it? The one that I showed you?"

She blinked a little, then said, "Si."

Dom flung his tablet against the back cushions, the tumble of his dark hair obscuring his face, and she felt herself shrinking.

"It was such an opportunity. Not once in a lifetime is there such a chance. You know how hard it's been for me, always."

He scrubbed his face with his hands, but didn't look up.

"How did you get the work?" Tony held his phone out now, the line still open, letting Nick listen in.

"The dark web. There are places for illicit art exchange. I made a profile and I got lucky that they would need someone like me, that they chose me."

"You knew they stole it, right? That they took it from us? The bastard tried to throw me under a bus, Jacinta. I got called out of the fucking hospital to chase that guy. Hit by a fucking car." He stalked a few steps into the center of the room, clearly stiff, from his injuries, then he pivoted. "Did you drive here?"

"Sì, certo. I was—I didn't know where to go, and I thought that Dom —" What had she thought? That he wouldn't mind if she betrayed his friends and put herself in danger for a job? But if his friends weren't the people he thought, then was she wrong?

Dom slid back his hair, regarding her solemnly.

"Did they have access to your car, the people who hired you?" Tony demanded.

Jacinta shook her head. "It was parked, by the lab." She shrugged. "Why would they want my car?"

He tossed the phone onto the couch. "Tell her about it, Nick." Snapping his fingers at her, he said, "Car keys. Fast."

Dom's eyes went almost comically round, and he caught her shoulder, his face frantic, pointing at Tony and gesturing for her compliance.

"I'm not gonna trash it or ditch it somewhere. You can pick it up later—Dom, airport or train station? Sorry. aspetta, aspetta." Tony put up his palm. "Airport?"

Dom gave a thumbs down, then up to the train station.

"I'll be back with the keys. Hand 'em over."

On the phone, a disembodied voice said, "Your car may be compromised. Marked with a tracking device. He'd like to move the car before—"

"Before they come here, to Dominic?" Jacinta fumbled out the car keys and tossed them over as if they'd bite. He snatched them mid-air, and was already turning to go, racing down the hall with a grunt of pain. Then the door slammed behind him.

On the phone, Nick cleared his throat. Dom picked up the phone and handed it over to Jacinta. She swallowed, then spoke to the other American. "Sì?"

"Hello, Jacinta. How are you doing?" He had a deep, comforting voice, the kind of voice that encouraged trust. If she knew anything about it, but perhaps she didn't.

She suppressed an urge to giggle. "Va bene. I have the best job ever, but then my employer is attacked when he takes me to see an artwork, and he tells me to run." She found Dom watching her. He hadn't run, had he? Only into danger, not away from it.

"You were going to the Villa Ludovisi—in your car, I take it, with Moishe the Fist?"

She flinched from the phone. "Moishe, si, but I don't know this other name. Why does Tony think he has put a bug to track my car?"

"He's Mossad. Ex-Mossad, I should say. If he let you have access to your car, that's because he can find you any time he wants. Nobody, not you, not me, and certainly not Tony, wants Dom involved any more than he already is, am I right? Think of this as a precautionary measure. If we're just being paranoid, you pick up your car at the station later, and nobody gets hurt. We'll pay for the cab."

"Grazie," she murmured.

Dom shifted at her side, then rose, walking into the kitchen. She heard him fussing with a kettle.

"Great. Thanks for understanding," Nick said. "You mentioned your employer was attacked. What happened?"

Burying her hand in her pocket, slumped into the sofa, she told him what she'd seen at the villa and what Moishe had said, still trying to reconcile the humble, sympathetic man who had invited her to the villa with somebody called "the Fist." Nick asked a few more questions, almost as sympathetic himself. Her fingers closed around something in her pocket, then she blurted, "They are looking for the Menorah, aren't they? Are you?"

"The original plan was, we're staying out of trouble. Getting Dom and the Land Rover home, then heading home ourselves." He sighed. "Doesn't seem to be working out that way."

"Aspetta, aspetta! How did you know I was involved? When Tony picks up the phone, he tells you I am here, but you must have asked."

Nick chuckled. "I can see why you and Dom make a good match. While D.A. and the Chief are playing tourist, I'm back at the base, doing the research. D.A. set up an image search, in case the painting showed up anywhere on line, and we got a match, a video that's got your voice on it."

"You know my voice?" Talking with these people felt surreal: they were always a few steps ahead of her.

"My dad was a musician. I've got a good ear. Did you know what the video was for?"

She swallowed, cringing a little as she suspected she wouldn't like the answer. "Sì? For investors, backers, he says."

"Could say that." Nick's chuckle this time was a good deal less pleasant. "Dom still have that tablet?"

"Sì, he does."

"Okay. I'm sharing a link. You've been looking at the dark web. Everything we've got out here, they have in there."

She picked up the tablet as the link appeared, and tapped it open, trying to take it all in. At the top of the page, Riccardo spoke animatedly across a series of scrolling headlines that highlighted all the bad things happening in the world in recent years—but good news! Thanks to last year's successful campaign, after learning of the existence of the original Temple fittings, they had already built a replica of the Temple to receive them. Now, Riccardo enthused, the items were within reach. An expert investigator had uncovered compelling evidence, bringing in top people in the field to confirm the authenticity of the evidence.

The video—her video—the images of the Menorah highlighted in pullouts, with measurements and Biblical quotations, came up next on the page. Apparently she, Jacinta Scipiano, was a "top person in the field." Her thrill shriveled as the sidebar information began to sink in.

Icons of the Menorah appeared alongside various levels of buy-in, stated in Bitcoin, with titles like "Pious Sinner" or "Righteous One"—entitling the donors to an inscribed brick in the Temple foyer—through "Disciple" and "Apostle" all the way to "Zealot." At these higher levels, the "rewards" included things like witnessing the opening of one of the Seven Seals, or the blowing of one of the sacred horns—all with dates another year in the future. "Your place in Heaven is assured by YOUR faith!" the site declared. "Now you can bear EXCLUSIVE witness as the events so long foretold come to pass—with your financial support!"

Backers, indeed. These people were crowdfunding the apocalypse.

Chapter Thirty-Nine

oishe walked briskly away from the excitement as others worked over the downed men and sirens wailed closer by the moment. Italian sirens this time, with their shrill bleat of fear. The man Casey shot, the first one, didn't have a gun in his hand at all, but something smaller. It had begun, with Sadie. Moishe walked with that truth.

He walked up the hill. When he'd passed the upper end of the villa gardens, with the larger public garden stretching out to the other side, he returned to the villa side of the street and looked for his point of entry. The housekeeper would not answer the door now, not with police and ambulances converging across the street. But still, he would very much like to speak with her, and to see the mural, of course. The trouble was, what he needed lay inside of their heads now. He needed to know what they knew, what, if anything, the mural had shown them. Part of the wall lay swathed in caution signs, barricaded with temporary fencing. Moishe shifted the sand-filled base of the post nearest the wall and edged inside, then shifted the post back again.

A few tools later, he stood on the landing, stairs down to the vestibule on his right. Up to more interesting places on the left. A long corridor filled with paintings, a few doors leading off. One had voices beyond. He ignored it and walked on, a servant emerged from another door, carrying a covered plate.

The man stopped short, gaping.

Moishe flashed his wallet open and closed. "I am with Interpol," he said in Italian. "I need to speak with the housekeeper, the woman who led a tour earlier."

The man's startled expression shifted to wary. "We did not hear the door."

"Because of the sirens. You must know that someone's been killed." A guess, but likely accurate given the placement of the shot.

The servant blanched. "I will fetch her, Signore. Just a moment."

And so, a moment, and another, he stood beneath Caravaggio's genitalia, along with some other things, as the housekeeper's glance darted repeatedly to the case in the corner. "You showed them the painting. Anything else? Anything in particular that interested them?"

She shook her head, too fiercely.

"My associate and I have been tracking this man. That is what brought us to your door, knowing he would come here. Now, she must deal with the deaths that he caused. The Carabinieri detained him not long ago, for a woman's murder, but he escaped them." Moishe shook his head, then regarded the woman with a low glance. Moishe made an educated guess. "If he gave you any money, you may wish to donate to the church. It was tainted by the crimes he's committed. " She had no reason for loyalty to that other stranger, beyond the adoration given to the beautiful. How long would the effect of the man's presence last?

The woman's fists clenched inside of her apron pockets. "The telescope," she blurted. "They wish to see it, he is especially interested. Galileo's telescope." Her chin jerked to indicate the artifact. Tears shimmered in her eyes. So much pain. She thought the money would help to alleviate her pain, only to find it was the source of yet more anguish.

"I see, thank you." He strolled in that direction, examining the case.

He hadn't the tools he would need to study the artifact properly, but its presence, and Casey's interest, indicated something. "I'll need to take it for evidence."

"What? No, of course not. It's priceless."

He nodded. "True, true. I am so sorry. I'll give you a receipt, of course, and return it immediately when we've had the chance to analyze it. It may have the killer's fingerprints," he confided.

The woman crossed herself, then fumbled her way through opening the lock, reaching toward the telescope—"Ah! Don't touch. A cloth, please. And a bag to receive it."

On a folded card from his wallet, Moishe wrote out a receipt and signed with a flourish, taking the telescope under his arm as he departed. She showed him to the door, of course, but he believed the furor across the way would prevent any potential witnesses from putting the finger on him as he stepped outside. His phone vibrated in his pocket, and he waited a little to answer it, putting some distance between himself and all of this.

"Riccardo."

"The car is moving again, and I have reports of police activity near the villa. I take it you're away?"

"Not really."

A pair of first responders loaded a covered bed into the back of an ambulance. Blood stained the street.

"Let me know where the car stops. She won't be able to find her way back."

"It did stop for a while, then got moving again."

"Watch the hospitals. We need to know when Sadie gets admitted. I think the delivery mechanism might be too efficient. The lab will need to know how the illness progresses. If the target sickens too fast, it won't spread."

Riccardo hesitated. "This won't interfere with your work, will it? Your attachment to this woman?"

Had Moishe revealed something he didn't mean to? And yet, his reasoning was perfectly sound. "Attachment is suffering, Riccardo. There will soon be an end to suffering."

"Right. But first, a whole boatload of money." Riccardo added, "I know, money is suffering, as well, but I might as well suffer comfortably before the end."

Chapter Forty

Grant paced the hall while his "wife" was brought in for examination, his demeanor alternating between pleading for the service D.A. needed, and the sort of quiet menace that sometimes provided the extra nudge. D.A., always so intense, even when she was just sitting still, lay on a gurney, eyes closed, an oxygen tube breathing for her. And he had no idea what hit her.

He'd taken the precaution, on the short trip to the hospital, of swapping their cell phones. At least he'd have the images captured at the villa, and she would still be able to reach out to him if she—when she—woke up. Don't, don't, don't fall into that mindset.

Sunglasses tucked through his shirt collar, Grant tried the numbers again. Nick's phone remained busy. So was Gooney's. Probably talking to each other, though he could see D.A.'s phone had missed calls from both of them. The team fell apart around him. What the hell else did he have?

A name. And a few old friends in high places. Grant called a certain number, the kind that didn't get flashed around. When a silent someone answered, Grant said, "This is Grant Casey. I need to hear from Dafne Chadad of the Mossad."

"Living still, I presume?"

"So far, so good. Can you help?"

A long pause, then his contact said, "Mossad is...difficult."

"Give her this number, tell her I have her car keys."

His contact sighed. "I'll do my best."

"Thanks. I owe you."

"Someday, I will collect." The line went dead.

A doctor approached, regarding him through a face shield over a mask and goggles. "Americano, si? You prefer English, yes?" At Grant's nod, the woman continued, "We have stabilized her, I think, for now, but the testing will take some time." She gestured toward his leg where blood flecked the khaki pants, showing the scrapes from the windshield Moishe shot out trying to stop him. "This injury, when did this happen?"

"Tripped over the curb, getting her to the trash can to vomit. Do you have any idea what's wrong? Some kind of poison or drug?"

"I don't have enough information yet. But the fever is...unusual. I'm afraid we must isolate her, in case this is communicable."

"She was hit with a hypodermic needle. How would that be communicable?" Did they even believe him about the puncture? Surely they had checked.

The doctor attempted a smile. "It is a precaution, signore, that's all. I need you also to submit to quarantine, until we can determine the level of contagion."

Oh, Hell, no.

The woman's gaze flicked over his shoulder, her face shield reflecting the movement of a few large people in their direction. "I'm afraid all of your clothing will have to be destroyed." She gestured him toward a corridor off the mall hall. "You say she was attacked?"

He gave a nod. Complying. For now. Give them everything he possibly could without giving up himself. "There were three men working together, I think. This big guy, really big, started shouting at her, and she stopped, then when she tried to come join me, two other men went after her. One of them grabbed her hair. I thought he

stabbed her. There were shots fired. I panicked and got us out of there."
Ninety percent truth. Hadn't panicked then, but maybe he was starting
to.

"This was by the Villa Ludovisi?" She waved him to keep walking.

He moved ahead of her through a swinging door, untucking his
shirt, more to provide extra cover for the concealed holster at his waist
than for anything else. "When I was taking care of her, after she started
vomiting, I found the injection site, the bruise." He tapped the side of
his own neck. "You must've seen it."

"Mmm. Does she have any history of drug use? You understand I
must ask these questions." She pointed toward a private room. One of
the orderlies crossed behind her, taking up a position next to the door
on that side. "There is a bathroom attached. I suggest that you shower.
There is an anti-biotic soap. We should also see to your leg. And is it a
bandage at your wrist?"

The woman seemed very concerned about his own injuries. Just in
her medical training, or something more?

"No drugs. Absolutely not. And my wrist is pretty much healed."
The last thing he wanted was for her to see the injury. If she had any
level of experience with law enforcement or criminal justice, it'd be
hard to mistake the scrape for anything but a handcuff injury. Maybe
he could convince her that he and his "wife" were kinky that way.
Could he even afford to permit an exam?

Grant's core tightened. Make a scene in the hospital, freak out the
patients in the emergency room outside, maybe hurt some people who
didn't mean any harm. Submit to the order, no idea when he'd get out
or who'd come for after him in the meantime. Moishe had allies. What
the hell had they injected her with? What were the chances it really
was communicable and not just something pharmaceutical?

Two urges warred within him. He needed to give the hospital all
cooperation to track down what had stricken D.A. and get her well
again. He needed to get the Hell out of there and figure out how to stop
their adversary before much worse happened.

Hesitating by the threshold, Grant made himself smaller, weaker, more worried. "At least tell me there's a window. I'm not crazy about being cooped up, especially with Sadie being so sick."

The doctor's smile gentled, growing more genuine. "The windows don't open, and there's no view, but you will have some light, certo. And there is television. Internet, even."

The orderly still behind him pushed open the door, revealing a small private room with a window at the far end looking onto a battered wall punctuated by similar windows, metal-framed, industrial. From the window across the way, a child's wan face stared back at them. The room wasn't much but he could work with it.

"Thanks." Grant stepped inside. A folded johnnie lay on the plastic-coated bed.

"Take a shower and get changed. Your clothes can go in the hazardous waste. Sunglasses, phone and wallet, and anything else you carry, in the little tray." She indicated the bathroom and the bins as if he needed a tour of a place that would fit inside their hotel room with space to spare. "Knock on the door when you're ready, and we can begin your examination. Also, we will reach the Carabinieri about this incident. They will want a report from you, everything you can remember."

Wonderful. Even if the Mossad had worked some wonder and gotten him off the Italian national police's "Most Wanted" list, they wouldn't forget their last encounter with him had been an arrest warrant for murder.

"Yeah, that makes sense." Grant rifled his fingers into his hair, the image of a distraught spouse. "I'll do my best."

The doctor stepped back into the doorway. "I'm sure it's nothing to worry about. Maybe some kind of dating drug, you know the kind? Ti assiccuro, we will ensure that Sadie gets the best treatment possible."

"Thank you." Grant met her eye. "Whatever else happens, I really appreciate that." Maybe she'd remember his sincerity when the cops arrived.

Another nod, then the door closed. An orderly stood to either side in the corridor. Grant pulled the curtain that curved across the doorway, blocking the view from the corridor. He swiftly crossed to the bathroom and started up the shower, full blast, then snatched the pillow off the bed. At the window opposite, the young witness blinked and straightened. Peering to the left revealed a featureless wall. To the right, a slot open into the night. Down, a drop of only one floor to a concrete alley maybe two meters wide, leading toward open air.

Catching the kid's eye, Grant smiled and waved. Hesitantly, the kid waved back.

With a scooting motion, he urged the kid away. The kid frowned, and Grant delivered a commanding gesture, down and back. When he pulled his gun, the kid scrambled away, mouth wide.

Wrapping the pillow over his gun to muffle the sound as much as possible, Grant fired three times into the window at an oblique angle, making sure the bullets would go no further than the cinder block end wall of the narrow alley.

The window cracked and Grant punched through with the pillow, clearing the shards, then clambered onto the sill. Tuck and roll to the cement below. He bounded up again, hearing the call of a voice beyond the door, asking was everything all right. Not really, no. Across the way, the kid peeked out at him, eyes huge. Grant winked, and ran.

Chapter Forty-One

Numbly, Jacinta addressed the phone. "I have found the site. Surely this is for the money. They don't actually do these things."

"What, like make the rivers run with blood?" Nick said. "I don't know. Maybe it's all for the money. They get rich off some religious nuts, then disappear with their millions. I also don't know how many people get hurt before that happens."

"Vedo." She swallowed. The job was strange, yes. The people awkward, but eager. They reminded her of Dominic...or of herself. That didn't make them dangerous. They'd shown no sign of that with her. They took her phone, è vero, and did not allow her own laptop. But for privacy, security, just as Moishe said. Especially if people like these Americans would read danger into anything they did. And the crypto currency made it easier for them to be paid and to vanish. Perhaps the sort of people who wished to witness the apocalypse deserved to lose their money.

Dom stepped out of the kitchen, a teacup in one hand, and his phone in the other. Setting the cup beside her, he held out the phone, pointing to the screen, then to the phone in her hand.

She glanced down to a news feed. Shots fired at Villa Ludovisi. Suspect at large. One man dead, one in critical condition. Her chest tightened. Moishe? Where did he fit on that list—a suspect, or a corpse? She had thought they were filming a movie, a young woman told a reporter. A man raced over a car, shots being fired, as he fell. Then her Vespa was stolen by the movie star, dark and handsome, compete with sunglasses.

"Jacinta? You still there?" Nick asked

Gripping her shoulder, Dom pointed again at the other phone.

"Ah...There is news coming through. I think Dom wishes me to tell you?" She raised her eyebrows, and Dom gave a thumbs-up. "Your Chief, he is handsome? Dark haired, dressing well?"

Nick's voice warmed. "He is today."

"He has shot two men and killed one of them, then stolen a Vespa."

A muffled curse on the other end, then Nick said, "I gotta clear the line. Shit—you have Gooney's phone! Look. If it rings don't answer, okay? Doesn't matter how many times. If somebody needs you, we'll call on Dom's phone and you answer."

His change of tone startled her to silence, and he demanded, "Capisce? Don't answer. He needs to get through to one of us."

"Sì, capisco." She tapped the phone off, but the line was already dead. "I don't think much of these friends of yours."

Dom's lips parted, then he clamped them shut and grabbed his tablet from her hand, sliding back to the blank screen. "You don't know them. You don't know what they've been through or what they can do."

"This is exactly it. I do know. Today, one of them has shot two people—"

He was already erasing his screen, scribbling again, his hand shaking. "He saved my life."

The cup of chamomile tea he'd brewed for her steamed by her elbow on the little end table. "You weren't always so sure of them, were you? He saved the life of the Nazi woman, too. Tony said so." She reached out, and Dom flinched away, his expression stormy. "You barely know him," she said. "Any of them."

He paced in front of her for a moment, glancing up at his antique headlines and posters, then pausing to rest his forehead against the high shelf stacked with history books. Finally, he turned back to her, and wrote, "Does it matter? Your boss, my friends, they're looking for the same thing." He drew the Menorah.

"You think this is just another adventure? A quest to find something lost? But also a matter of life and death." And more, if that crowd-funding campaign could be believed. A matter of shadowy people trying to end the world.

She finally took a sip of the tea, looking at the simple drawing he'd made, then at his earnest face. He gestured toward the posters around him, images showing the Third Reich and their attempt to take over Europe...and to utterly destroy the Jewish people. He pointed again to the Menorah, and their eyes met.

"You're right," she said. "Not just a thing, a symbol, the heart of a nation. I am an art restorer, Dominic. What do I know of use to men like these?"

He picked up a copy of his first book, with its ugly cover—why had he been so eager to publish, he never even asked for her help? What did he know of use to men like those? He was an author, an expert in a few, very specific things, just as she was an expert in--

"Caravaggio may have been the last person to see it." The implications rushed over her, and Jacinta bolted to her feet, upsetting the tea cup. "Caravaggio! He was murdered."

Chapter Forty-Two

Moishe paused a moment on a corner with good data connectivity and downloaded the app to track Jacinta's car. The screen circled, then showed a target dot quite close to his own location. Could it be accurate? No reason to believe it was not: central Rome remained as compact as the original Roman walls decreed. The dot moved slowly around the Stazione Termini, Rome's largest train station. Perhaps Jacinta wanted to go back to Naples but didn't feel capable of driving.

Moishe could help. He started in that direction, rapidly. His size and demeanor cleared sidewalks and stopped traffic. His phone rang, and he tapped in a Bluetooth earpiece.

"Moishe. There's been some developments in Poland." Dafne Chadad. "I'd like to talk with you. Do you have a moment?"

"I am taking a walk. I may lose signal."

"Oh, really? Seems a bit late for a stroll. What's the weather like?"

Fishing for information, some hint of his location. "Autumnal. Is this about Casey?" She was not the only one with a fishing license.

"Everything's about Casey these days, it seems. I don't suppose you've seen him?"

"Does he have something you want?" On the screen, he converged rapidly with the location of Jacinta's car. He should get off the phone soon.

"He might have taken something from me."

Ah, now that was interesting. "So he's a thief and a sympathizer."

Moishe slowed behind a utility pole. The sky darkened above, but light poured from streetlights and doorways. It pulsed from signs and beamed from headlights. In two more steps, he allowed himself to merge with a corner, watching as another set of headlights turned, and a purple vehicle slid through the patch of light across the intersection, turning into a parking lot. It drove smoothly, quickly, with a pattern of acceleration unfamiliar to him.

"He's probably not, you know. A Nazi sympathizer. If he were, in truth, I find it hard to believe that Sadie would keep company for long."

Moishe's neck prickled. He tried to focus on the purple car as it nosed along the spaces, hunting. "If you say so. How is Sadie these days?"

He heard the silence, listened to it with an intensity he should not feel, trying to hear what Dafne knew, what had precipitated her call. "I don't know," she said. Truth. Probably she was not dead.

The lights before him blurred as if his vision itself decayed to nothing.

"She seems to enjoy her work," Dafne told him. Present tense, and utterly bland. Either she didn't know what had happened, or she wanted him to fill the silence.

Moishe excelled at silence. But the pattern of dark and light made him think he and his people had acted rashly. Better to have the item in hand before they broke the seals. Once he had it in sight—the seven candlesticks foretold by the Christian Bible, the greatest treasure ever stolen from his own people—then, the fires could begin.

"Speaking of work," Dafne went on, "I'm a little concerned that your current line may violate the terms of our exit interview."

Not to stir up trouble the Mossad would prefer not to deal with.

Not to work with persons or organizations antithetical to the Israeli cause. Not to embarrass the nation of Israel as a former intelligence agent is made an example of before the world.

"Rest assured, dear lady, that what I do, I do for all of us."

"Oh, Moishe. That's no assurance at all. These people, Sadie and her cohort. They're well-respected, gaining prominence. Also American, and we'd like to maintain that relationship on friendly terms." She let that settle for a moment, then said, "Have you spoken with Sadie at all?"

"Not much."

Dafne cleared her throat, her personal attention signal when she feared someone wasn't listening. But Moishe was. He just didn't care what she said. "I'll tell you directly, Moishe. Don't kill these people. We're not letting that Italian kid get all the credit when the Mossad could get a little positive note for once. Sadie brought it to us, and when the PR department gets through, she'll be the hero, for the entire Jewish diaspora. It won't look good if her friends are dead."

What if she were? For a moment, he imagined being the hero himself, finding something much more valuable, much more meaningful to the Jewish nation. Would he terminate his mission for that? For fame or recognition? But he was always listening, so he heard the threat beneath the words. If the Mossad came down on him, his great work came undone. "Okay, bubbe, I won't kill them." *Bubbe.* Grandmother

The purple car parked at last, and his suspicion was confirmed. A man emerged from the vehicle, tall and broad-shouldered, flicking his jacket smooth. Concealing a gun? Probable. That pricking sensation returned, needles at Moishe's spine. What had this man done to Jacinta? How had he claimed her car? The car's lights blinked as he locked it.

The man limped slightly, revealing himself in a pool of light as he moved back toward the train station. Casey's ally. Moishe had thrown that man into the street to make good his seizure of the painting.

"I have to go." He hung up on Dafne's protest and pulled the earpiece. They had Jacinta. Why? How? Moishe would find out. Because this man was going to tell him.

Chapter Forty-Three

By the time Grant fled the tangle of smaller streets surrounding the hospital, sirens approached the front. Had to get out of these clothes, ideally, change his demeanor entirely and/or get off the street. And get in touch with his team, if only to find out why the two men had been talking on the phone for the last twenty minutes. D.A. needed them. Maybe so did he.

The cuts on his leg stung. Doc was right about that: should've cleaned it.

Blood borne contagion. That's what she worried about. Should he? Little late now. Given how fast it hit D.A., if he'd been infected, wouldn't it come on just as fast?

Grant turned down a busy street lined with shops and restaurants. This close to the Forum, tourists from all over clumped together, reading menus. One shop caught his eye, selling colorful imported clothing.

Ducking inside, Grant purchased a few things, then cut down an access road and transformed himself. With a tunic, a sash, and a long scarf, Grant changed his nationality and religion. Still remembered how to wrap a turban even a few years out of Afghanistan.

His stomach growled, and he decided to appease it while he made contact with his team. A few more turns from the major tourist routes, the smaller trattorias weren't as busy, though they did eye him with a little concern. He found a Middle Eastern restaurant where the maitre'd grinned at him like he was a long-lost brother.

At an outdoor table beneath a colorful draped awning, Grant sat and tried to relax.

Water arrived, along with a menu. He settled on a Halal platter with one of everything. Just looking at the listings brought him right back to Afghanistan. Hadn't all been bad memories.

The phone in his pocket buzzed. Grant found the slit side of his tunic and plucked it out, finding Gooney's number on the display. Tapping to answer, he said, in Arabic, "Your mother was a camel, and your father smells of elderberries."

For a moment, nothing, then, "Hello?" hesitant, Italian accent.

Suddenly, the smells from the kitchen seemed much less enticing. Who had Gooney's phone and why. Shouldn't have opened with Arabic, or with a joke. Even he was subject to nerves. "Sorry," he said. "Who's calling?"

"I am, uh." The caller drew a deep breath, then said, "I am looking for a woman called D.A.? Or maybe this is the Chief? C'e Jacinta Scipione."

Nope, didn't like that at all. He smiled broadly and nodded at the waiter who brought him a full tray of their house special meal served in a half-dozen little silver bowls. The art restorer was meant to be well out of this. "Is Tony there?"

"No, he takes to park my car, and he leaves me the phone to talk with Nick."

Explained why both of their lines had been busy, and meant that Gooney was ears-off, with no way to communicate. Shit. Before he could answer, she plunged into a jumbled version of what had happened, her work with the painting, with Moishe, her flight from the mess at the Villa Ludovisi, finding Gooney at Dom's place. Should've known that any friend of Dom's wouldn't be shut out of a find like this so easily.

Grant stared at the meal before him, a mosaic of color and texture, and imagined D.A. waking up in the hospital, alone, eating bland hospital food, or forbidden anything but an IV. He focused on imagining her waking up at all. Kickstarting the apocalypse and unleashing the plagues of Revelations. Oh, Hell.

"Hold on," he told the phone, then to the waiter, "Mi dispiace. Can you wrap this please? I need to go."

Had he been exposed to something? Hadn't taken the doctor's fear nearly seriously enough.

"He was going to the station, you said?"

"Sì, sì. Ma..." She broke off, as if she worked over what to say.

"Why did you call me?" he prompted, handing the waiter a credit card as he accepted his meal in a take-out sack. Outdoor seating. Good. No close contacts so far. Should take advantage of the restaurant's facilities to wash his wound and discard the clothing beneath his tunic. Anything that might be tainted. He wasn't far from the station now—he'd seen the signs on his walk over.

"I need to know what is the truth. I think if this, what we're looking for, if it is real and Caravaggio has painted it, that maybe its why he died."

Slipped the credit card back into his wallet with another smile and started walking again, stomach growling. The station would have benches where he could eat, and keep an eye out for Gooney, if he didn't get heckled over his apparent religion.

His own brief research into the artist gave him an overview; might as well take advantage of an expert while he had her on the line, and at a distance. "Lay it on me, Jacinta. What do I need to know about the life and death of Caravaggio?"

Chapter Forty-Four

With Galileo's telescope tucked under his arm, Moishe made all haste to parallel the stranger's route. Man seemed to be looking for a bus, he paused at a schedule posted near a covered stand, then he moved on, closer to the station. Moishe moved faster, choosing an angle that kept him behind cars or barricades, matching pace with a bus coming to a halt. Definitely the man went for the station now. Had Moishe been spotted? Or did the man really want to get out of town, after however he'd gotten to Jacinta, whatever he'd done to her?

Moishe approached a news stand and walked swiftly along the side. He tucked the bundled telescope under the risers for the outside display. Should be safe there for a little while, and he would want both hands.

Definitely the man had a slight limp from his impact with the car back in Poland, and his face was bruised. Also Moishe's doing? Hard to say. In any case, he was not at his best, but the vastness of Termini station would be a fine place to get lost, and Moishe had no intention of losing him.

Huge, bright and modern, the station encompassed ranks of shops, masses of commuters arriving home or departing for it and tourists preparing for the night trains to distant places. The crowds thinned somewhat at this time of evening. The odors of French fries and pizza from the food court drifted along with diesel and steam. Ranks of kiosks sold tickets, and his target approached one, tapping the screen, presenting a card...presenting Moishe the chance to get closer.

Security gates prevented further access to the tracks without a ticket. Moishe should have his own.

In front of the nearest kiosk, a woman with a stroller and another child fumbled to replace her wallet after tapping to print her ticket.

Angling toward the machine as if to slide between her and the device, Moishe paused, palming a few coins from his pocket. He tossed them with a quick movement to his left, then pointed. "Signora! You've lost some change."

She looked up, startled, then confused, softening a bit to Moishe's smile as he bent to collect the coins, handing them to her with his left.

"Grazie mille," she told him, with a distracted smile, her children staring at him with big, round eyes.

His right hand slipped the fresh ticket from the window at the bottom of the kiosk, then he was on his way.

Target moved more briskly now, likely aiming for a train about to depart. Moishe swept the departure board with a glance. What was the soonest? What, the latest?

His target swiped his ticket through a gate at track seven, passing through a metal detector. Either he had a plastic weapon, or he was unarmed. Interesting. Would the man regret telegraphing this fact?

Moishe's ticket would not win him through as easily as he wished. Instead, he pulled his wallet out, flashing a meaningless badge at a few people in the queue and readily moving ahead of them, not bothering to slow. He flashed the badge again at the security officer as he passed through the metal detector and said, "Affari ufficiali," as the machine blared at him.

Adding a flare of his eyebrows, he aimed a gesture of command at the man, then the machine. "Turn this off before people panic."

The man nodded several times as he hurried to comply. Down the line of gates, other security men looked up, but his man waved them off.

Trouble was, they were not the only ones alerted by the sound.

Moishe stood at the top of the ramps leading to the actual trains and scanned for breaks in the pattern. Next departure, track seven, a minor eddy. He strode in that direction. Those who'd seen him set off the metal detector parted like the Red Sea, fearing whatever official business such a man might be up to, discretely armed, unlike the Carabinieri with their big guns.

Pivoting around a pillar, Moishe wrapped his hand around it and hoisted himself to the low protective rim meant to fend off luggage carts. He rarely needed more height, but today, he appreciated the lift. The eddy he noticed ceased partway down the train. Either the man already boarded or...

Moishe scanned the other direction, not where he'd come from, but toward the far end of the platform. A man in a cap with a fast, slightly irregular pace angled away from the train at platform nine, insinuating himself into the crowd debarking from that fresh arrival. A little behind him, another man brushed his head, glancing back toward the train, the ground.

With a little jump, Moishe propelled himself from the barrier. He didn't run, not yet, but he cut toward his quarry like a border collie after a sheep. Shepherds and wolves again. Sometimes, the wolf was the shepherd.

The group of passengers moved up the ramp, the hat suddenly gone. Moishe plunged toward them. A railing divided the ramp from the next track.

He swung wide around the end, scanning the shadowed area beneath. Something slammed into the back of his knee, tossing him toward the railing, buckled sideways.

Moishe half-turned as he fell, letting his head get below the level of the rail as the enormous wrench clanged off of it instead of striking his skull. His target immediately spun from an overhead swing to baseball to golf, the wrench coming down low. Sharp green eyes, a determined set to his square jaw, another man's hat tumbling from his head.

Dodging to the inside, Moishe took the blow across his thigh. He slipped one hand under his coat for a pistol.

The target swung his foot up, kicking back Moishe's arm, but placing himself off balance. Moishe drove upwards, taking a knee and pushing into the man's space.

The man stumbled to regain his balance, his injured leg wobbly. Moishe slammed a fist into that thigh, outside.

With the suck of his breath through clenched teeth, the man staggered. Nonetheless, he came about with his wrench, knocking it low against Moishe's jaw. Pain surged through Moishe's head. A familiar friend.

Moishe snatched the wrench, twisting it free. With a howl of brakes and a grind of metal, the nearest track received its next train.

His target fled, clearly in pain himself, his teeth caught in a grimace as he pushed toward his limits. Did he know what those were? They would find out together.

The target leapt from the platform just in front of the train and raced around the engine. Clever to use a train as cover. Foolish to give up the solid ground of the concrete platform for the gravel of the track itself.

Back on his feet, Moishe raced down the concrete header that joined the platforms like the spine of a comb. Sighting along the incoming train, he spotted movement in the shadows between tracks. Another train prepared for departure. A few voices shouted meaningless protests from that direction.

At the next track, Moishe shouted himself. "That man is a criminal! Don't let him board!" He aimed his finger toward the target with every bit of authority he possessed. His voice, his figure, his all-black suit conveyed exactly what he intended.

A small group of people looked up, then toward the target. One of them flagged down a conductor.

The target lurched onward, herded though he knew it not. How far could he run in this condition?

Matching his target's direction, Moishe kept to the header. The next track was empty. At the next, warnings buzzed and lights flashed for the train was about to depart. His target jumped between cars, landed with a grunt of pain. Moishe passed the engine as it started to chug into motion.

He paused. Light flickered between the cars as the train slowly ground from its platform. Flicker. Flicker. Flick—the train picked up speed, and his target couldn't match that pace.

Moishe stalked forward down the platform. He took a knee behind an array of trashcans and drew his pistol. God willing, the man would fall away from the train. Else Moishe would have violated Dafne's precept.

Taking advantage of the grind and howl of iron all around him to cover the sound of his shot, Moishe aimed and fired.

Chapter Forty-Five

Jacinta briefed this mysterious "Chief" about Caravaggio's early life, the loss of much of his family to plague, his various quarrels and patrons, the number of times he was arrested for wearing a sword against the laws of Rome, and, of course, the day in 1606 when he slew a man and had to flee the city.

"Quite a character," Chief observed. He'd entered a busier area, with traffic noise filling in around his voice, when he spoke, which was rarely.

"Since then, he seeks a way to return to the city, hoping for Del Monte or another of the Cardinals to help him win a pardon. For a long time, he's at Napoli—"she glanced up and smiled as Dom brought her a fresh cup of tea, this time in a travel mug with a lid. "This is where I am from, and Dominic, too. From there, he wins the invitation of the Knights of Malta and goes to make some of his great masterpieces."

"The Beheading of St. John. His only signed work, as I recall."

"Sì, esatamente. But even there, after he is knighted, he still fights, and so he's imprisoned—"

"Wait a minute, he was imprisoned on Malta? I hadn't read that far." His voice quickened as it had when she mentioned the plague earlier.

"In a bell-dungeon. A room carved into stone with only a grate at the top for entry and food. Don't worry, though, he escapes this, perhaps with help from a relative of his patron in Napoli. He is in Sicily for a while, but when he returns to Napoli, everyone remarks he is scared, and this is one reason I think maybe someone knows. Someone hunts him for the Menorah."

Chief was silent a moment. "Maybe."

Dom brought her a blanket, draping her legs as she sat curled on his couch, then his own phone rang, and he went to retrieve it.

"At a bar, maybe a gay bar you would say, he is ambushed and badly injured. Still he makes a few more paintings, and finally, we think, he has word of the pardon, but on the way back to Rome, he is detained and his boat sails without him. He tries to chase it, but falls ill and dies at Porto Ercole. That is in July, 1610..."she trailed off as Dom returned from the kitchen, his phone clutched in his hand. He thrust it toward her.

"Listen," he rasped, then winced with the pain. "Please."

"Dom needs me, I have to—"

He shook his head violently, his off-hand clutching at his wounded throat. "Don't. Hang. Up."

"What's going on?" Chief asked.

She reached for Dom, drawing him onto the sofa beside her. "I don't know. He's taken a call and he wants me to listen, but also not to hang up."

"I'll hold. But I have to get off soon. Still haven't reached Nick."

"Sì, sì." She pressed Dom's phone to her other ear, lowering the borrowed one. "Prego?"

"Jacinta, it's Nick."

"È vero? I have the chief, we are talking about—"

"I need you to listen fast and do what I say. Can you do that? Tell him it's me, tell him there's an emergency."

"Ma, forse, you just talk to—"

"I'm sorry," he cut in even sharper than before. "I don't have time for that, and it's you that I need. Hold the phones close, and he can hear at the same time. You ready?"

These men. So commanding. She thought of rolling her eyes, but Dom's expression stopped her, and she brought up the other phone. "Chief. It's Nick. He asks us to listen."

Nick continued, hard and fast. "We've got until twenty-one thirty. Moishe needs to meet with you, Jacinta, to see that you're okay. There's a letter that he wants, and he's asking you to bring it to him. I'll pick you up—I'm in the car already, but I need Dom's address."

Jacinta felt dizzy. She wanted to talk to the Chief, to keep a place for the art, the artist, the artifact, if they could find it, in their dangerous game, but she wasn't ready for this next play. Moishe worried about her.

"The letter from Del Monte," Chief stated, and Jacinta lost her breath for a moment. "What's the drop plan?"

"Servian Wall by the station. Nobody but her. Do you hear me, Chief?" Nick's voice cut like a wire through clay.

"Loud and clear. Call me." Chief rang off.

"I'm on my way, Jacinta. I've got the letter right here, and I know you'll be curious about it, right?" Nick sounded brittle, as if he tried to find his former good cheer, but had forgotten how to smile.

"Si, è vero." She wet her lips. Just give him the address.

"I don't think Moishe means you any harm. Did you ever fear for your life when you were with him?"

"No, mai." Never. But every word that Nick spoke terrified her, underscored by whatever made Dom speak over his own pain.

Dom had found his tablet and held it up for her to see. "If ever you loved me, Jacinta, please bring him the letter." *Please* was underlined three times.

If ever? She did love him. Right now. She wrapped her fingers through his.

"We're in Tuscolano; it's not far from the station," she told Nick. "I'll meet you outside." She relayed the address, and he gave her an estimated arrival that shave ten minutes off her best time from anywhere. Twenty-one thirty was barely enough time, if he arrived promptly. Why the arbitrary deadline? Art restoration, academic research, these things might take forever, with deadline after deadline sliding by if the work required more time for its proper completion.

"See you then." Nick severed the connection.

She tapped off the phone, and held it out to at Dom in the sudden silence. "I guess it's good the tea will travel," she said, managing a smile.

Dom set down his tablet, set aside the phone she handed over, and made another of those signs. Maybe Tony had taught him, or maybe, like her, he had picked it up from so much American media: the one word in American Sign Language that everybody must know.

"Sì," she whispered. "I love you, too."

He wrapped his arms around her, her face pressed to his shoulder, and she set her lips to the desperate racing of his pulse.

Chapter Forty-Six

The moment his phone rang, Grant answer, ditching the protocols. "Talk to me, Nick." Couldn't trust himself to say more. He handed off his dinner to a ragged woman sitting near the curb and moved on an oblique line away from the bulk of the crowds.

"He got to Gooney. I don't know how. He knew this number, knew about the letter." Nick paused, then said, "He'll give us instructions for the retrieval as long as we don't tell her what's happening."

"That Gooney's life is in danger." Grant paced to the shadow of a closed store front, every muscle and tendon straining to do something. Anything. But what the hell could he do? "Retrieval," a euphemism to elide the fact that someone they both cared about was hostage to a madman. As long as it didn't turn into "recovery," as in corpse.

"Yep. I'm en route to collect Jacinta now. I told her nothing. I told Dom we had a problem, and he got it, he got her compliance. This guy —Jesus, Chief. Where's D.A.? Why're you on her phone?"

"In the hospital. They hit her with a needle."

"Shit." Quiet pounding as Nick beat the steering wheel.

"He's got allies. Be careful."

"Copy that."

"Jacinta said Gooney was parking her car, bringing it to the station. I'm there now."

"If he sees you, Gooney's dead."

Grant's chest tightened. "Copy that."

"I asked for proof of life. He said my name. He sounded half-dead already, Chief."

"What else, what did you hear?"

Nick blew out a breath, probably, like Grant, fighting down his emotions to do his job. "Chief—the soundtrack. Big space, bad acoustics. Some kind of noise started up, rumbling, but Moishe cut the call, set the meet with a text."

Grant's eyes drifted briefly shut as he tried to master himself. "I've got solid cover and a persona he won't expect. Gooney's around here somewhere, right? Gotta be. The meet location is maybe a few hundred yards, so Moishe's staying close."

Only one place where you could find and subdue a man, then keep him secret until—Grant's heart stopped, his mouth as dry as Afghanistan.

Eleven minutes. Nick would have to drive like a maniac to pull this off. "Why that deadline? Did he say?"

"Just that if we don't meet it, it's out of his hands." The sound of a turn signal clicked on the line, and Nick said, "I see her. Over and out."

"On it. Go." Grant rang off and confronted the truth. Roma Termini, a vast structure with a hundred departures a day or more. His friend was somewhere inside, imprisoned or incapacitated, subject to a deadline that was out of their control.

The light at the end of the tunnel was an oncoming train.

Chapter Forty-Seven

Moishe took his time departing the station. No need to rush. On the contrary, better for him to be sure no one on the other team entered the building or saw where he came from. How many did they have? Not many, so far as he knew.

From his position near a bustling coffee shop, his figure almost invisible in the overlapping, undulating shadows.

A dark sedan pulled up to the drop-off across a plaza from the front of the station, and a familiar figure emerged from the passenger side. Jacinta, her auburn hair tossing as she looked around, then crossed toward the ancient Roman wall. Moishe began his stroll. With each breath, each step, he allowed himself to become visible, but not with the menace or insistence he earlier commanded. No. So far, they were in compliance with his orders. Remained to be seen if they provided all that he asked.

The dark sedan pulled into traffic, readily moved away by the flow of cars, buses, motorbikes and pedestrians around the station. An emerging bus forced the car to follow the rules, shunted down a street in a line with the tracks, but moving the opposite direction.

Jacinta hugged herself, still wearing only the cardigan despite the evening's chill. Moishe might offer his coat.

He kept to the crumbling Roman wall, then came to the gap between the two sections. Jacinta prowled up the second section on the far side, then turned as he paused there. He raised his hand in a gentle wave.

She startled, then squared her shoulders and marched toward him. "What is going on?" she blurted, then scowled with a shake of her head, as if that weren't at all what she meant to say.

"I'm glad to see you're all right. You are, aren't you?"

"Of course I'm fine! I went to see—"she wet her lips. "I went to a friend's house."

"A friend of some people we both know. Apparently." He sank his shoulders and kept his hands visible, making little gestures, helpless things. "They are my rivals to find the painting, but you must know that." He smiled.

"I don't know anything, really." Another blurt. Trying to protect herself from him? To prove she had nothing worth—what?

"You haven't produced any findings yet, after all. You didn't tell them anything, your friend and these men?"

"No," she said. "I haven't said anything to anyone." Her lips made a little flinch he'd seen once before...when they played a game that taught him how she lied.

Moishe gave no sign that he'd seen. No, she told him, she hadn't spoken to the others—true. But she had spoken to someone. Who?

"You know a lot about art," he said. "It's why we wanted to work with you. Your knowledge. The rest of this? It's like...a pissing contest, and I'm sorry if it frightens you."

She shrugged one shoulder, restrained compared with the usual Roman shrug. "Si, it frightens me. Rather a lot." She finally pulled her right hand from under her arm, revealing a thick sheaf of parchment. "This is what you wanted, si?"

"Could be." He let himself show pleasure. "Have you looked at it? Do you think it's genuine?"

She turned it in her hand. "Just a glance. Manuscript is not my specialty, ma...I have see the Cardinal's writing other times. I think it may be."

Moishe held out his palm, open and easy. She placed the parchment in his hand, the thick letter still warm from her touch. "Thank you, Jacinta. For this, and for all of your help. I'm sorry we didn't get to visit the Villa together." She frowned, and he continued. "It sounds as if I'm, how would you say it politely. Making you redundant, doesn't it?"

Warily, she nodded. "You don't want that I should finish the painting?"

"Jacinta, I would love for you to finish the work, and I think you, too, would like that. But tonight, all of this excitement. I know it's not what you're used to, or what you signed on for. I don't know any more what you're willing to do."

He tapped the page in his palm, stepping back from her a little. "I didn't mean for you to be scared. In fact, I—"he shook his head, tilting it a little, like a dog. "No, this is foolish. It is a figment of my mind, that's all."

"What?" she said, moving a little toward him.

"I was scared for you." He met her eye, tracing the soft concern, the curiosity in her face. "That's why I asked for you to bring me the letter."

He allowed a beat, like an actor in a play. "I came this way, after we were ambushed at the Villa, I can take the bus or a taxi, I thought. Instead, I saw your car. At first, I was happy, thinking we again could ride together. But a man got out, a man I know to be dangerous. I pursued him, to find out where you were. He tried to put me off, talking about this—"he held up the letter—"But I insisted, and he gave me a way to reach you."

Moishe smiled, but only a little. His smile could be fearsome, and he didn't want that now. "So I thought of how to have both, to see you and know you are safe, and also learn more about this painting we share. But I have those things. So. If you want to work, you can reach out for Riccardo, okay?"

He stepped back again, signaling reluctance to leave her, then he brightened. "Oh, now you do think me a fool. Here."

He pulled out her keys and handed them over, letting his palm linger over hers, at arm's length. "Your car is in the lot up on the corner. Be careful, all right? These people, they're serious as life and death." He tipped an imaginary hat, then briskly moved away through the gap in the wall.

An alert buzzed on the phone in his pocket, and Moishe checked. Track fifteen would be arriving early. How unfortunate. Apologies, Bubbe. Some promises were very hard to keep. But then, his gunshot hadn't actually killed the man. What happened next, well...

Godspeed to the blessed darkness, now comes the engine of your deliverance.

Chapter Forty-Eight

When a delivery van backed carefully into the pedestrian area and lowered a ramp, Grant took his chance. He walked briskly beside the heap of items being loaded onto dollies, re-stocking one of the shops. If it were him— if Moishe did as Grant believed he had— Moishe would already be gone, leaving his mess for someone else to clean up. He wouldn't risk circling back to ensure the safety of a hostage under these circumstances. If he even cared.

Once inside, Grant moved deliberately, scanning as he passed the shops. A good place to wait or watch, a bad place to stash your victim. He sped up. A giant overhead digital display showed arrivals and departures. Which was it? He forced his hands open. At the top of the screen, times converged with the station clock. Twenty-one twenty-seven. Firenze express, arriving Track Fifteen, ahead of schedule... by three minutes. Oh, Hell.

Cut quickly across the big waiting hall, spotted the signage pointing toward the various tracks. Between him and the ramps stood a rank of queues with metal detectors and automated ticket-readers. Stationed every few booths, security guards with sidearms. Patrolling on both sides of security, a handful of Carabinieri with their flak vests and long rifles.

Well. Some point soon, Grant was gonna need back-up.

He angled for the last gate, closest to the goal, trying to hit the timing right. Too soon, they stopped him, blocked him, shot him, and he would arrive too late.

He headed for the queue like a man on a schedule, not yet a man on a mission. The nearest guard flicked him a glance, then looked away.

Grant bolted. He dodged the line and vaulted the gate, skirting the metal detector entirely.

Somebody called out, but in a startled civilian way. See something, say something. Go for it, buddy. Grant ran for all he was worth. Let his fists bunch now, arms pumping, feet pounding the pavement. Fastest he'd ever run in his life. God, let it be fast enough.

He raced down the header like he could see the Boston Marathon finish line just ahead, down the platform at Track Fifteen. Had to be far enough from the main that the body—the man, the victim—wouldn't be seen right away. A few porters lingered with carts, waiting to unload the coming train, and Grant burst through their midst, swinging the turn onto the platform.

Now, the official shouting began, along with an alarm of some kind. Come on, come and get him. Guy in a turban and a crazy tunic, dodging security? Oh, yeah.

Pillars marked the center line of the platform, supporting the vast roof overhead. To his right, trains rumbled as the idled. They ground as they braked and squealed as they jolted into motion. The cars rattled, and even if somebody screamed, would they even be heard?

Up ahead, he ran out of platform, the lights for passengers replaced by distant yellow bulbs under the lowering gloom. At the far end of a covered yard long enough for dozens of train cars, a headlight grew steadily larger. It would be slowing, coming in to rest.

Signs with tiny lightning bolts warned him about the electrified rail below that ran along side. Least of his worries. Grant jumped to the gravel below. He cupped his mouth and shouted, "Gooney!"

Running again, stumbling over the concrete ties between the tracks. "Arrete!" A bullhorn behind him. Wish he had one of those.

"Gooney! Goddamn it, where are you?"

Up ahead, on the dim track, movement, a darker shape shifting against the low rails. Grant pushed himself harder, his palms sweaty, his breath caught in his teeth, his eyes trying to adjust to the drop in light.

Stopped so suddenly, he nearly fell.

Arms spread, one leg kicking up in a feeble rhythm, Gooney lay between the tracks, a cloth stuffed in his mouth. Blood darkened his right side. Cuffs at his wrists chained each hand to some part of the tracks—Grant remembered those handcuffs, or two sets just like them. Moishe must be a fetish guy.

"Gooney." Grant dropped beside him, touching his throat and finding his bounding pulse. He pulled the cloth that stopped Gooney's throat and tossed it aside. "We've got to stop meeting like this."

Gooney's eyes flared open. "Key. On my chest. He left it. Can't—"

"It's okay, I know." Grant stroked both hands over his friend's chest, sweat-streaked, heart pounding, his breath coming in little gulps.

Now came the moment. Had Moishe ever intended for them to release his victim? Had he told Gooney he left the key just to taunt him with hope until the last moment?

Grant traced the buttons down Gooney's chest, spreading his hands in quick gestures outward, on his knees on the tracks. Praying.

Small and hard, the key dug into his palm. Relief hit him like a wave. He remembered a key just like it from his own entrapment.

The shouting from behind grew more insistent, then the train whistled, a blaring horn that made the both of them flinch. Key in his grasp.

"Get away from me. Get off, get out," Gooney chanted, breathless.

The rail hummed against Grant's knee. Left hand first, ready to get him away from the third rail. Slow is smooth, and smooth is fast—and not nearly fast enough. Cradle the captive hand in his own, trace the cuff with his other hand to find the lock. Key in the lock and turn.

"There's no time! Go away!" Practically sobbing now. Gooney's freed hand shoved at him, desperate to push him away, to get one of them off the track before the train arrived.

The horn blared again, gravel shifting and bouncing, the hot grease smell of the engine bearing down on them.

Sudden illumination from the train's headlight showed Gooney's pale, sweat-streaked face and the second handcuff glinting at his wrist, carving a wound to match Grant's own as Gooney tried to get himself free.

Gratitude rushed through Grant for the gift of light—gratitude for a light that could be the death of them both.

Grant shoved the key into the lock, pulled Gooney's right hand to his chest, finally free. Gooney struggled to roll, to heave himself over the rail.

Grant wrapped his arm around his friend's back and hauled them both, his back against the vibrating rail, then his side hitting the gravel. A painful jab to his elbow as he kept his weight off his injured friend, ending on top as he finished the roll.

They sprawled beside the rail, Gooney's left arm slung around his middle. Gooney's fist clenched into his shirt and Gooney's face pressed to his chest, gasping, as the train growled home.

Chapter Forty-Nine

Grant eased Gooney to the rough ground. Light flashed in patches from the windows of the passing train, the two of them invisible on the ground below. Gooney's eyes gleamed. Sparks scattered from the brakes, spreading the smell of hot metal, and Grant shielded their faces with his arm.

"I'm sorry," Gooney whispered.

"Don't say it." His hand traced down Gooney's side to the spreading stain of his blood, trying to ascertain the extent of his injury.

Gooney gasped as Grant probed his back, finding the exit wound. Through-and-through over the right hip, missing his spine by a couple of inches.

"All I said was...I can't pay the rent." Gooney laughed raggedly, shoulders shaking. Crying maybe. Why not both? He was alive. They both were, but if Gooney were playing the damsel-in-distress, tied to a train track in this melodrama, what did that make Grant?

Grant stripped off his turban. "Other injuries?"

"Sure," Gooney panted. "Head, shoulders, knees and toes." He gulped. "Knees and toes."

When D.A. collapsed on him, she did it silently, slipping from horror to unconsciousness with her usual efficiency. Gooney, of course, half-delirious with pain and fear, wouldn't stop talking.

Keep talking, Gooney. Don't ever fall silent.

"I'm wrapping the wound," Grant told him. "When this train clears, there's gonna be cops everywhere. Tell them everything, whatever you have to, okay?"

Grant propped Gooney's head and shoulders against his own thigh, making space to bind the gunshot with his turban. Gooney stifled a cry as Grant snugged the cloth. Wasn't the ideal bandage, but anything he could do to slow the bleeding could make the difference between life and death. Gooney's blood slicked his hands already, and the train groaned to a halt at its stand.

"You're going after him," Gooney breathed.

"You better believe it."

Flashlights bounced along the far side of the building, and the bull-horn shouted orders he had no intention of following. "Gotta go."

"Gave up the letter. I'm sorry," Gooney whispered through blood-flecked lips.

"You made the right call. I'd rather lose the letter than you." Grant finished the wrap and tied it off with his sash.

"Might still." Gooney flashed a grin. "Sorry I won't be there. With you."

Grant clasped his hand. "You kidding? I can't do a damn thing in this job without hearing your voice." For a moment, he touched his forehead to Gooney's and whispered, "Stay alive."

He let go, crouching into the shadow of the train, racing down the side.

"Hey!" Gooney's voice, ragged, but louder now. "Carabinieri! Need a medic over here! Hey you!"

Maybe using his last breath to set up a smokescreen for Grant's escape.

At the joint between a pair of cars, Grant dropped lower and pulled himself between the wheels. Drew up his legs, dodging the third rail, and rolled back to his feet, moving fast, keeping low.

From behind, a ragged song pursued him. "Wheels on the train go round and round," gasp, "round and round," gasp, "round and round..."

Gooney's voice grew faint on the other side of the train. Grant was almost out of cars, almost to the yard outside, where he'd have little cover but the darkness.

"Ahi! Quest'uomo è ferito!" One of the officers shouted. "Chiami un'ambulanza!"

Grant paused, his throat burning. He'd be okay. Had to believe that. Who else could be such a thorn in your side, even when he was meant to be dying.

Grant slipped out into the night.

Chapter Fifty

Jacinta stared at the keys in her hand. Moishe met Tony, then he...negotiated? He came out with Nick's phone number, knowledge of the letter, leverage to reach Jacinta herself by way of Nick and Dom. Something that made Dom turn pale then plead that she do what they asked of her.

She started toward the car park. Get her car and get back to Napoli, to her little garret. Or reach out to Riccardo and ask for directions back to the lab. The first time, he hadn't bothered to give her the address, just climbed in the passenger seat and told her the turns, and that wasn't suspicious at all, was it, Jacinta?

Holding her sweater closed against the autumn chill, she hustled to her car and started it up, winding her way out of the parking stripes. Should turn right, but emergency vehicles converged on the station from several directions.

Chief might be angry at Tony for giving up the letter, for sharing so much information. She imagined the big American right now being escoriato by his boss. Except that Jacinta still had Tony's phone.

Driving out of the parking lot, she turned left onto the road that went down the side of the station. It followed the tracks to the south until they narrowed enough for bridges. Phone in her hand, she tapped a number.

It rang a few times, then the Chief answered. "If that's you, Moishe, I will not rest until I stop you."

The words startled her like a slap to the face. He sounded different, all business now, cold, calm in a way that Moishe himself had never been, and she knew for certain Moishe spoke the truth about this: they were dangerous men. *Serious as life and death.*

"C'e Jacinta. He's not here."

For a moment, he just breathed, and gravel crunched, every sound echoing strangely. "What do you want?"

Possibly, both sides were wrong, bad or evil, with all the killing and the hurt. Or possibly, one side was true, and striving for the right. They could not both be right, they couldn't.

More emergency lights rushed from the other direction to the front of the station. "Tony. Is he all right?"

The quality of his breathing changed. "Can't say."

She wet her lips, her throat feeling dry as she crept her car along the tracks, leaving the station behind her. "You can't say, or you won't say?"

"I'm unable to quantify how he is, right now," the Chief said in a hard tone almost clinical. "If that's an ambulance we're both hearing, I hope to god he's in it."

He paused, then told her, "Moishe shot him in the gut and chained him to the tracks of an oncoming train."

Jacinta's lips parted, but no sound emerged. What on earth was he telling her?

Chief's voice hitched, and he continued, "A man with a perforated intestine or possible ruptured appendix needs immediate medical intervention before he goes septic. That's like an infection in your blood." Another pause. "When we parted, he was in good spirits." His voice warmed a little, and he added, "Last I heard, he was singing a song."

Either her grasp of English was not so good as she thought, or his story made a few leaps that she couldn't follow. He claimed Moishe had done this terrible thing, then he, the Chief, had found Tony on the tracks, and freed him. Found him medical help, and now? Walked the tracks alone, or hid some place nearby.

Moishe told her that he'd gotten some information along with her car keys. For her own safety.

Both sides could not be right.

"I'm hanging up now. Thanks for asking." Chief blew out a breath. "And I'm glad you're safe."

"Spetta, spetta!" She swallowed. "Do you need a ride?"

Something like a laugh, a single, low "ha." The sound of the ambulance receded, and a clang echoed on his end of the call, the automated switch of a track from one line to another. "That's very thoughtful, Jacinta, but I can't get in your car."

"You don't trust me." In tutto onesta, should he?

"That's not it." A breath, then he said, "You're a civilian, and not even a conspiracy nut like Dom. You don't really understand this stuff. Trust is beside the point. There's two reasons I can't get in your car. One. That's how Moishe got Tony, by tracking your car." He paused, then said, "Two. There's the blood."

How he found Tony? How long ago had Tony demanded her car keys, Dom urging her to give in, so Tony could drive to the station...to be shot and left there to a horrible death. So they wouldn't find Dominic. So they wouldn't find her. Her stomach churned. *Two*, he said calmly, *there's the blood*.

"I might be sick," she whispered, pulling over into a crumbling parking area outside a boarded-up shop.

"Can't say I blame you." Another breath. "You want to believe him. Moishe. His people gave you the chance of a lifetime when I refused. He brought you to the Villa to see the mural, right? Let me guess. He praises your skills, admires your work and can't wait to learn more about what you're doing. He's been kind, considerate, vulnerable when he talks to you. He reveals a little too much, he tells you things about himself and his feelings, then he draws back."

She remembered the things he said over dinner, his two truths and how her own paled by comparison. The phone pressed her ear as if it could keep her heart from racing, and return her stomach to calm.

Chief's voice continued, growing more cool and clear with every word. "When you get worried or suspicious, he gives you something, some reward that proves your independence and shows you that you're in charge, really. You get to make the choices. Somehow you end up making the choices he wants. Every time. He makes you feel important, worthy, a valued colleague. You worry about what you're doing when you're apart, but when you're together, you're a radiant, composed, brilliant professional, collaborating on a project nobody else should know about."

The lights beyond her car blurred as she listened to this total stranger, this man who hated Moishe, so far as she could tell, and had never seen them together. Somehow, he laid bare everything Moishe said and did. Jacinta's mouth felt dry, her eyes frozen too wide. "Come potevi saperlo?"

"We're in the same business, or at least, we were. Intelligence professionals. Human intelligence. Our whole job is to get to know people, to insinuate ourselves into their lives and make them want to help. We manipulate people into giving us what we want. We have a thousand tools in the kit so we can apply the tool we need to the right target. He manipulated both you and Gooney—Tony—but he used different tools. Because he knew what would work on each of you."

As if shooting a man and arranging his death were a tool, just as sharing a meal and admiring a painting—She shook it off, anger welling up with her fear. "You are the same, you say. Then how should I believe you? Anything you tell me? Even what you say has happened to Tony could be a lie."

The chain link fence beside her car rattled with sudden impact, and she whirled sharply, staring out the window.

Beyond the fence in the murky light stood an apparition from a horror film.

A man gripped the fence with one hand, a cell phone held to his ear with the other. Darkness rimmed his fingernails. Darkness stained the tunic that hung to his knees over khaki pants and expensive shoes. She swept him with a glance, then quickly looked back to his face. Movie-star handsome, streaked with grease and more blood. His eyes held hers.

"That's what I want from you, Jacinta." His voice rang in her ear and echoed from the darkness outside. "From now on. I want you to assume that every single one of us who talks to you is lying."

Chapter Fifty-One

The burst of anger that had propelled Grant to the fence dissipated in an instant. No need to give the woman a heart attack. He flicked off the phone and said, "We used to work in the same industry, Moishe and I. Tony, D.A., Nick. That's where the resemblance ends. God forbid I ever grow more like him."

No trains had passed since his departure, all traffic frozen by the dramatic events unfolding, by his turbaned self dodging security to get to the tracks, by the discovery of the wounded man. He was leaving the tracks behind, leaving the scene, and still feeling Gooney's pulse against him, the vibration of the rails thrumming in his body. Still smelling the hot metal of the train's brakes, and the spray of sparks that singed his hand as he guarded Gooney's eyes. Adrenaline jitters still flooded his veins.

Jacinta gaped at him, her borrowed phone still pressed to her face. The phone that might've changed everything, if it had been in Gooney's hands, instead of hers.

Not her fault. His men did all they could to defend her and Dominic both.

Still couldn't help spinning his wheels a little on this one. If Grant could've been there, if he could've known before the shot was fired. If he could've barreled into Moishe like a freight train and ended it right there, Moishe on the tracks instead of his friend.

What did it mean to destroy your opponent without becoming him?

He straightened away from the fence. Moishe's destruction had become an objective, a fact he'd rather not confront just now.

A few feet away, masked by overgrowth of the roadside weeds, the bottom of the fence bent inward. He widened the gap, then shifted underneath. Shedding the ruined tunic, he added it to the wind-blown litter heaped along the fence. His white shirt beneath looked sweaty and rumpled, but at least the thick tunic had absorbed most of the blood. Too much goddamn blood.

Not so long ago, he knelt by a dying enemy and mailed her last letter, so her husband would know what happened.

Grant glanced back. Jacinta remained in her car, watching him. She should be worried. Should be scared to death, and if he had to be the object of her fear, so be it, as long as she applied that caution to the other side. A few cars whipped by or pulled into the businesses across the street. If anyone noticed them, they likely assumed a lover's quarrel, the man walking away, leaving the woman in tears.

He slipped out his phone. Voicemail and a few texts from Nick while he was in there. *:M says track 15*: Nick reported. Their enemy had at least enough honor to follow through on his bargain, even if he must've known they had no way to reach his captive in time, not if they had waited to hear from him. Had Moishe been imagining Grant's arrival to witness the spectacle of Gooney's death?

:G to hospital: Grant told Nick. Then, *:D.A. too, sudden illness. Couldn't reach you. Rendezvous @ my location*: Grant tapped out, then he jabbed a different number.

Jacinta remained in her car, shell-shocked, apparently. Better put some distance between him and Moishe's mark.

He started walking, letting the phone ring twice. Hung up, rang it again. What time was it in Arizona? No answer. Left no message.

Gooney nearly died. He still might. How did you say that on a voice mail?

"Chief, vi prego!" Jacinta ran after him.

"If you wait there, he'll be along for you shortly." Grant was being uncharitable, donning his armor as if it would help anyone but him. Stupid, and mean. Donning his armor too late to defend him.

The vibration of a text felt like a reminder of the on-coming train. Jamie: *At a hearing. That you, Tony?*:

:It's Casey. Call me.:

"I'm sorry." Jacinta stepped closer. "For what I said about Tony. Can I tell Dom? He's worried."

Get Gooney a friend at the hospital, an advocate who could speak —well, at least, understand—the language. "Please. And thank you. Tony would appreciate knowing you guys care."

From the gloom of the road alongside her stopped car, a dark familiar sedan emerged with a man at the wheel. That was fast. Grant had just texted Nick moments ago—the sedan rushed suddenly forward and Grant jumped back as it pulled across toward the fence. He put out his arm to shift Jacinta from the path of the car, and she gave a cry of dismay.

As the driver killed the engine, Dafne Chadad emerged from the back seat. "We need to talk."

Grant's hand went to his gun and sent Jacinta a warning look. "More of the same. Intelligence people."

She nodded swiftly and pressed her lips shut.

With a rapid check-list Grant dismissed most ways the Mossad could've known where he was, and reached an interesting conclusion. "The tracker on the purple car, it's Mossad issue, isn't it?"

Chadad's eyes crinkled. "Very good. He must've requisitioned some before leaving. We looked for any anomalous activity, anything off the books. I didn't expect to find you as a result, but given the lockdown at Roma Termini, I shouldn't be surprised to find you're involved." Her tone grated on his last nerve.

Grant took a step forward, into the light and displayed his hand, wiped partly clean on the discarded tunic, but every line edged with Gooney's blood. "I'm not in the mood for Mossad humor."

She took in his appearance, and her demeanor shifted. Her lips parted to speak, then his phone rang and she scowled instead.

Once, twice, silent. Then it rang again, and he took in the screen. Jamie. To Chadad, he said, "I need to take this."

"Right now? Really. There's nothing more important going on." She folded her arms, addressing him as if he were a petulant child. Dearly tempted to knock her into the next parking lot.

"Absolutely nothing is more important than this." He picked up the call, drawing a deep breath, and putting on a layer of calm. "Jamie, it's Grant."

Her voice sounded distant, and tense. "I made my excuses. What's going on?"

"At least half what you're afraid of, but mitigated to the best of my ability." He kept his eye on the Mossad agent as he lay out, in brief, what had happened to Gooney, concluding with, "If you can get to Italy, I'll cover the fare. First class, last minute, whatever it takes."

She was silent a moment, then said, "That bad, huh."

"I sure hope not. Best case scenario, you're here when he wakes up, and he's the happiest man alive." Alive. The word reverberated in his skull. No need to mention the worst-case. She had already had Gooney die on her once.

"What about the perp?"

"Still at large. I'm working on that."

Chadad's face, pinched with annoyance when he took the call, had gone smooth as he described what happened. Then the corners of her lips turned down.

"Shit on a shingle, Casey," Jamie said on the phone. "I know he loves working with you, but seriously—"

"He's one of the best, Jamie. When he gets off medical leave, I'll give him a desk job."

"He'll hate it."

Grant almost smiled, imagining the stream of complaints they'd both have to deal with. If there were any justice in the universe, they'd have that to look forward to . "Copy that. Just get over here."

"Get the bastard."

"On it." He rang off.

Slipping the phone away, he returned his attention completely to the Mossad agent before him. "Were you the one who made the call when Avram went down? Who had to tell D.A. what happened?"

Her nostrils flared, her lips shifting as if a decision lurked behind them. Nailed it.

Finally, she said, "You didn't have to call a widow."

"I hope to God that's still true in the morning." He tipped his head toward the car, her partner still inside. "You still like this model? I'm thinking of trading ours in."

Chadad pivoted, offering a hand to Jacinta. "I don't believe we've met."

Both hands tucked under her arms, Jacinta replied, "Sono solo un' amica di un amico." A friend of a friend. Like her friend Dominic, she learned fast when the lesson was vital.

The agent's hand hovered and withdrew. "Would you please tell me what this is about? Why you and Moishe have locked in this fight?"

Vengeance.

Grant dismissed the word as soon as he thought it. Smacked of a dangerous lack of objectivity. "We have reason to believe that he's hunting for the Menorah, the one stolen from the Second Temple by the Romans."

Chadad sighed heavily and pinched the bridge of her nose. "And melted down by these same Romans, or maybe by whoever stole it next. It's ancient history, in the most literal sense. I don't believe in folktales, Mr. Casey. Why do you?"

So much for hoping they'd be willing to rein in their boy. "Oh, I am all in with ancient history. So's Moishe. When he finds it, he and his backers plan to start the apocalypse," he told her, watching her face turn stony. "Here's the next lesson. D.A.'s in the hospital, too. Sadie Silverberg, to you. Does your man have any laboratory connections? Anybody who can whip up a few plagues? Maybe a river of blood?"

A second, identical black sedan slid by as if looking for an address. Grant inclined his head, but made no other sign. The car drove on and pulled into a restaurant lot up ahead, coming around so the driver could watch him. Grant's team was down by half, but he still had someone on his side.

Jacinta jerked as if he'd struck her and suddenly clutched his arm. "La Morte Nera! The Black Death. At the studio, there is a paper, a new one, about this plague. It's not historical, this paper, but with the history things."

"Because of Caravaggio's family," Grant surmised. "Do you have reason to believe Moishe knew about this? That the document was his?"

She glanced uncertainly toward the Mossad agent. "There are notes in Hebrew."

Oh, Hell. Grant had been half-joking when he brought up the notion of the plague, but now it seemed too solid to dismiss. "I need to call the hospital."

"Are they any more likely to believe you than I am?" Chadad asked.

"Moishe's men may have infected Sadie with the plague, Agent. I don't care if they think I'm insane as long as they do something to help her."

She regarded him, her lips twisting one way, then the other. "Moishe did say he was seeking the end of days," Chadad remarked at last. "Let me take care of Sadie. I think you will trust me at least that much, to know she's in the best hands?"

Grant gripped the phone, uncertain, and their eyes met.

Chadad reached into her jacket, and he slid one foot back to a ready stance. She acknowledged his movement with a half-smile. "You must be feeling especially hunted these days, Mr. Casey. Is the hospital after you as well?"

Very carefully, she opened her jacket to reveal the expected shoulder holster, then, instead of drawing her weapon, she deliberately reached into a slender inside pocket.

Pulling out a thumb drive, she held it up. "Mossad doesn't have an official stance on the matter of Moishe the Fist. That may change." She revealed a hint of steel he remembered from their fight in the museum. For once, it wasn't aimed at him. "Moishe's Carabinieri contact is a corrupt local capo with a few supporters. I'm turning over what we found to the Italians. The Institute would like us to step back and return to the office, letting the local authorities handle this matter."

"Yeah, right." He added a thin smile. "I'm sure they'll do their best, but they have no idea what they're up against."

She acknowledged that with a shift of her head.

"So what's that?" He eyed the flash drive.

"A dossier. Confidential." She darted a glance at Jacinta. "More than confidential, Mr. Casey. Illegal and classified. Information you shouldn't have. If you ever reveal a source for this, we will smear you in the press in every known language."

To Jacinta, he said, "That's no lie." She managed a faint smile.

"His connections, his movements, everything I could find for the last few years, but I haven't had time to read it all. I absolutely did not give you this." She dropped the drive, and he snatched it mid-air. As she walked back to the car, she said, "I've written off the other car. Total loss. The cost of doing business." She opened the door and asked, "Which hospital?"

"The Red Cross. Isolation ward. I couldn't be sure what hit her, but I knew it was bad." The thumb drive pressed into his hand, like the grip of a new weapon.

"That's why you tried to reach me."

Grant gave a nod. "D.A. has faith in you. It seemed mutual. If it really is the plague, it's already bloodborne." Had he been exposed through his own open wounds, he would likely be showing symptoms by now, given how quickly D.A. had been hit.

Looking him over again, Chadad nodded in turn. "She will have every advantage my government can confer." The agent paused. "It would be impolitic to wish ill to a former colleague, so instead I will say good luck, Mr. Casey. Happy hunting."

She climbed inside, and the car made a hard u-turn, back toward the heart of town, leaving Grant and Jacinta by the side of the road.

He slid the drive into his pocket, and started walking. "You can still go back to him and finish your work."

In a few strides, she caught up. "No, I can't." Then she murmured, "Can't. Or won't. You have lost your friends, Ch—Mr. Casey. Let me help you."

He started to speak, to tell her to stay behind, no matter how short-handed he was, how much he needed what she knew and what she could do.

Instead, he said, "Yes."

Chapter Fifty-Two

Carrying Galileo's telescope like a beacon, Moishe let himself back into the studio. Angelica startled awake from one of the overstuffed chairs. "Signora Jacinta?"

"We may have lost her." He flicked on all the lights, and the maid squinted, rubbing her face. He sat in the other big chair and—being careful of the red seal--unfolded the letter, reading it closely, smiling to himself. *The mirror of moons.* No wonder Casey examined the telescope, but he didn't have it and Moishe did. The painting, the letter, the telescope. Everything he needed to be well underway.

The doorbell rang, then Riccardo entered, his shirt untucked, and cuffs unrolling, a striking disarray for such a man. "Both of our men have gone to their reward, Moishe. What of their killer?"

"We'll find him. Two of his are dead or dying."

"What good to cut off the limbs if the head remains?"

Moishe lowered the letter. "I told you. We will find him."

"Of course, he might have fallen into despair already."

"I don't think so. In the meantime, get this packed up, the painting, the computer, anything we might need."

"Moving south?" Riccardo started getting his own appearance in order, tucking in his shirt and shaking down his cuffs.

"We finally know where to go."

"Back to your old stomping ground, as it were. Do you still have friends there?"

Moishe tipped his head. "I know some people."

With a flash of his salesman smile, Riccardo said, "Excellent!" Then he eyed Moishe more critically. "Do you need medical attention?"

Moishe shook his head, though the question implied he should look in a mirror. His jaw throbbed, and the other bruises from the target's assault made themselves known.

The man had not gone down as easily as Moishe intended. Even when he lay bleeding out on the rails, the man seized a handful of gravel, smashing it into Moishe's face when he came close to transport him further down the track. The target aimed for the eyes and missed only because Moishe gave him a jab to his injured side. That ended his rebellion.

Moishe had run out of handcuffs. He added this to his mental list of supplies for their excursion.

"Well. Don't bleed on the painting. Seems to be one of the few Caravaggios that hasn't got blood on it already."

"We'll need nails, for the crate to protect it in transit."

"Will do." Riccardo turned away, and Moishe said, "Another moment."

The salesman hesitated. "Yes?"

"What did Jacinta do for you?" He spoke mildly, facing his hireling, recalling the twitch of Jacinta's lips as she denied saying anything to anyone. She'd shared something but not with the Bone Guard. Only one logical possibility remained.

"What do you mean?"

Question for question. Riccardo's favorite tactic. "I know she gave you something else," Moishe said. "Told you something about her work."

Riccardo's hand rose to the slender gold cross he wore, and he straightened as if he'd found his spine. "It was none of her doing,

Moishe. I asked her for some information to share with the backers, to show them we're on the right track."

"To share with them...on the website." Moishe moved his fingers through a series of exercises. Too long since he'd had a good bout.

Riccardo's head bobbed. "Of course. We've gotten great results from the video already, a big increase in contributions. I'm very pleased, actually!" When Moishe remained silent, Riccardo hurried on, "It's behind the paywall, Moishe. People have to—"

"Since the very beginning, I've told you there would be others once our purpose became known. Adversaries. That they would have the same capabilities I do."

With a dismissive wave, Riccardo said, "Don't be so humble. Who could really match you?"

Flattery. A tool he used on others. Not one he succumbed to himself. "Remove it. Now."

Riccardo's throat bobbed, and he backed away a few steps. "Right. Sorry. I just wanted to—it doesn't matter. I'll do it." He snapped his fingers, pointing. "And nails. To secure the crate." He hustled out of the room, calling orders, bestirring Angelica to help.

It would be difficult to replace Riccardo at this point, but not impossible. And Riccardo knew better than most the terms of their retirement plan.

Slipping a handkerchief from his pocket, Moishe wiped it over his face, feeling the sting of the gravel scrapes. The cloth came away flecked with dirt and smeared with blood. Well. He needed his body to last a while longer. He should take better care of it. Sorting through Jacinta's work table, he found a bottle of rubbing alcohol and swished some onto a clean part of the cloth, then patted it over his injuries, ignoring the sting.

From the portion of the painting she'd been cleaning, faces emerged: the bull, the figure near it. Other images lurked in the background. More figures? Did they relate to the Zodiac as she guessed?

Moishe dropped the cloth onto the table and took up one of the long cotton swabs she'd been using. He perched on the stool before the easel and unscrewed the lid of her cleaning mixture, then began methodically swiping away at the region beyond the revealed forms. The dark red-brown receded and faint strokes of other colors emerged. He leaned in, the scent of the cleaner filling his senses. What would come out of this?

Jacinta should be here, tending to the work she so clearly loved. He weighed the odds that she would ever return, or speak to Riccardo again. What had Casey's people told her? They didn't reveal Moishe's threat, but still, she was no fool to be persuaded of his goodness forever. Nobody was fooled for long. Nobody but Avram.

Summoned from their other work, the guards from the nearby posts moved briskly through the room to pack up the computer and camera equipment. The IR and X-ray could remain for now.

Something drew his eye a little further down in the frame, and he took a new swab, moving his focus. A person? Someone pale and leaning? A woman, perhaps, or a statue. Moishe sank into the painting as if he could see through the layers and become part of the void. Yet even this void contained forms and figures. Would the nothing that he craved be similarly populated?

Riccardo returned to Moishe's elbow, a hammer and a box of nails in hand. "Pardon the interruption, but we're ready to pack it up."

Moishe's gaze returned to the canvas, to his tiny contribution to the great work.

The pale brush strokes resolved around an inner darkness, like the gaping mouth of some hideous creature. The artist painted nothing from his mind, much less his nightmares. Even his angels were boys with wings.

Moishe's focus revealed not a statue nor a woman but a tree with a warped trunk. Landscaping. Caravaggio taunted him from beyond the grave, as if something, indeed, persisted beyond the flesh, rewarding Jacinta's patience and punishing his own.

Moishe tossed down the swab. "Let's go."

Chapter Fifty-Three

Jacinta followed after Casey, feeling as if she'd passed some test she wasn't aware of beginning, perhaps when she had refused to give her name to the other woman—another intelligence agent, clearly. Mossad, she thought, from Dominic's earlier confidences.

Remembering to tap the lock button on her keys, she left her car behind. Its presence gave these new agents opportunity to find out what they wanted to know about her, if it were so important. What felt important was, as ever in academics, the application of her new learning, like Casey's insistence that she assume they all were lying.

"I think you tell the truth at least as much as you lie," she asserted.

He hesitated a half-step, letting her reach his side. She had a few centimeters over him. "Truth is a tool, maybe one I use more than others do."

He fell silent again, and she prompted, "Why?"

A slight shrug. "Every agent has tools they prefer, and ones they're especially good at. Not that I'm good at the truth, but use enough of it, it tends to obscure the lies. Did you ever lie to Moishe?"

She started to shake her head, then blurted, "Two truths and a lie. He wished to play at dinner."

Casey tossed his head back as if that were the funniest thing he'd heard in a long time. "A former Mossad agent got you to lie to him, when he knew you were doing it." He rubbed his temples. "I gotta remember that bit. That means he knows how you look when you lie. He knows your tells."

"And I know for him," she declared, but Casey's dark gaze suggested otherwise. Jacinta folded her arms sharply. It was a game, they played at dinner, a way that people learned about each other. How could she know what use it might be put to?

"What about—what he did to Tony? Another tool, you said." She swallowed. "Do you—?" she broke off, not sure how to ask without offense. Not sure what would happen if she offended him, at least, more than when she implied that Tony had never been hurt at all.

"Violence is a tool, absolutely. A blunt weapon, if you'll pardon the phrase. Do I know how to use it? Yes. Can I? Absolutely. Would I?" They reached the edge of the parking lot, his demeanor sharpening as his glance flicked over the place. "When I need to. There's too many ways it can go wrong. The cost is too high."

"Oh," she said, trying to absorb the implications of that statement.

"Vulnerability is a tool." No comment about his preference there, she noticed. He added, "Trust is a tool."

"I don't like that idea."

Again, he nearly laughed. "Neither do I. Doesn't mean I can't use it." He cast her a glance. "Thanks for coming on board."

"You don't like it."

A shake of the head.

Since their encounter with the other agents, or maybe since his own experience in the train station, he grew silent with a preternatural still-ness that put her a little on edge. "But you need it. Me. You need someone like me."

"A local expert, and a data analyst, you're not wrong."

Up ahead, Nick stepped out of the car to meet them. Tall Black man leaning slightly on the open car door. "D.A., too?"

This query earned him a nod, and no more.

"Not your fault, Chief. Neither one of them." Nick's voice modulated at every turn, and she recalled what he had told her about his musical background. Nick's voice was one of his tools.

Was Casey using the tool of vulnerability? Manipulating her by his silence? He must be feeling hunted, the other agent observed. If he had been through all of that today, how much power did he really have over what he revealed? Or was his presentation now, like the pentimenti on Caravaggio's canvas, evidence of what came before showing through his attempts to conceal it?

Nick closed the gap, seizing Casey's shoulder in a fierce grip, their eyes locked together, as if they were the only people in the world. "Not. Your. Fault."

Casey shook his head. "Nick." His voice hitched a little, reminding her of Dom's agony, as if the Chief, too, carried a wound. 'If you're gonna die on me today, do me a favor." He drew a deeper breath and some of the strain eased. "Don't apologize."

"Count on me, Chief. God willing and the creek don't rise, I am not dying on you any day soon. And neither is anybody else." He glanced back, acknowledging Jacinta with a smile and a shift of his eyebrows. "Hey. Welcome aboard."

"Grazie. I think."

"Valid." His expression grew more serious. "You get the same rules as Dom did. We match his pay scale and bonus level, take you on as a contractor. Any time you want out, you say the word and we send you home, no questions asked, no hard time."

Through it all, he kept his grip on his boss. His friend. Casey's shoulders drew down, his posture squared, as if Nick's touch eased away the hurt. Nick shifted his attention back. "What'd'you need, Chief?"

"A shower, a meal, a change of clothes. Not necessarily in that order. Laptops, maybe two." He glanced at Jacinta. "And passage to Malta."

Chapter Fifty-Four

Gliding under the commercial flights and promptly out toward the Tyrrhenian Sea, the small jet departed from Leonardo da Vinci Airport, with four passengers and little cargo. Even in Caravaggio's time, the earlier painters had been recognized for their brilliance, and now even this most contemporary transport hub honored the Old Masters.

Moishe's own masterpiece would follow by land, accompanied by a significant escort of his men. Another of those men piloted their aircraft over the blackness of water, and Moishe let his gaze slide over it, spotting the occasional ship by its lights while Riccardo, in the opposite seat watched the coastline disappear behind them. "Her car seems to have been abandoned not far from the tracks. Do you think she's switched sides?"

Jacinta would be useful to his adversary, though he believed his own work in cultivating her would be harder to overcome than even she believed.

Riccardo chuckled. "Don't tell me that another woman has managed to crack your facade, my friend."

Moishe turned to his companion. Riccardo tried a little too hard, since their brief confrontation earlier, to prove his companionship. "When I am cracked, you will know it."

Riccardo's grin went a little crooked. "Merely a jest, Moishe. I know you worked hard today, I should expect you to be thoughtful." As if Moishe were usually so gregarious. Why else had he hired Riccardo? Perhaps realizing that he was digging himself further in, Riccardo said, "That other woman though, the one who became the first martyr, you don't think her loss will slow your adversary?"

So far as Moishe knew, Sadie clung to life, and he breathed carefully. Riccardo knew she meant something to Moishe. Riccardo did not know what. On any other day, under any other circumstance, Moishe himself would have been the end of her killer. He did not imagine her present employer to be any less attached. "If anything, what's happened today will inspire him. This is not a person who gives up." He had never been more convinced of a truth, not since he met the boy who became his brother.

This was a person who had literally gone down with the ship, chained to its structure, only to rise again. He conquered his enemies after appearing to conquer death itself. A flame that Moishe thought long expired flared to life at the back of his chest. They would meet again, him and Casey. Would he conquer death then, or would the Bone Guard's last duty be his death in battle?

Somewhere down below, Sadie lingered in a hospital, or lay in its morgue, her body unclaimed, for who would go to her now? Did this qualify as a regret?

Riccardo's phone jingled and he slipped it out with a smile. "Buona notte! Oh, sorry, no, I don't speak Maltese." He paused, and gave Moishe a thumbs up. The man was half-American, and it showed. Riccardo went on, "I very much appreciate your taking our call, and your support for our efforts." He listened a long moment, then said, "May I have you speak with my associate? He's the one who handles logistics." He held out the phone to Moishe.

Taking the call, Moishe said, "We will need access to the prison, the place of Caravaggio's confinement."

The person on the other end cleared his throat. "I'm not accustomed to taking orders, sir, most especially not from those unknown to me."

Gripping the telescope on his lap, Moishe schooled himself to patience. Where had it gone, these last few hours? "Forgive me, sir. It's only that I am eager to bring holy writ again to life."

Riccardo's eyebrows notched upward, and he gave another thumbs up, doubtless congratulating himself for the contagion of his interpersonal talent.

"We all are, sir, or we wouldn't be speaking. When do you expect to arrive?"

Moishe flicked back his cuff to reveal his watch. "Forty-five minutes."

The other man cleared his throat the way a lesser man would have cursed. "I will have a car meet you at the landing strip. I believe I can clear the way, despite the...unreasonable hour."

"Thank you, sir. You are assured of your place in Heaven." He flicked the phone off, handing it over to Riccardo who stared at him.

"No," said Moishe, "I have not changed my faith." Nor had he Riccardo to teach him how to say what others most wanted to hear, at least when it mattered.

When their wheels touched down, a sleek official car awaited them, the driver holding open the door. The Knights of Malta—technically, the Sovereign and Military Order of the Knights Hospitaller of St. John —no longer wore armor or black tabards bearing a white cross with dual-pointed ends and equal arms. A small pin bearing the seal marked the driver's lapel, and he bowed his head to Moishe and Riccardo as he ushered them into the vehicle. "The Grand Master looks forward to welcoming you at the co-cathedral." He had a clear, firm voice, with an accent a little off from Italy and not quite Greek.

Moishe flicked Riccardo a glance, and the salesman said, "That's marvelous. We very much appreciate the white glove treatment, but perhaps we could view the fort, and meet with the Grand Master a little later?"

"Before praying for the Lord's blessing on the venture? Surely not." The driver looked mystified, still holding the door with one hand, his other hand issuing them into the car.

Riccardo turned to Moishe, hands spread, and Moishe sank into the back seat, still carrying the telescope. "It contains the Beheading of St. John, this co-cathedral."

"Indeed." The driver waited a moment longer, until Riccardo slid into the leather seat as well, then the door clicked shut, and they wound along hills densely lined with medieval houses, before arcing around one of the deep bays that defined the harbor at Valletta. The great gates slid open for them by the hands of a pair of security guards. When they stepped out a little later to stroll the last few meters, no hint of daylight remained, and a few strong spotlights illuminated the facade of the co-cathedral, a white stone structure with two square towers. Modest by Catholic standards.

"Would you like me to make your excuses? For the prayer?" Riccardo murmured as an armed guard escorted them inside.

Moishe shook his head. He could feign prayer to this god as well as any other. He had long ago shed the illusion that any ear in heaven attended to those on earth.

At times, it surprised him that others, in spite of everything, still fervently believed. Better to say, perhaps, that they fervently hoped. They hoped they were wrong about the dark and empty void. Why fear nothing more than one feared something, some definite and horrible end? Yet without these believers, the money dried up and Moishe would lose his ability to deliver the great nothing on the widest scale possible. Riccardo's offer should be taken as a kindness, if one believed in such things. "Thank you," Moishe told him.

Within, the church remained partially lit, their footfalls echoing among the gilded decorations. Burgundy, white and black dominated in dense geometric patterns across the floor and up the walls, punctuated by white marble inlays of the Maltese Cross.

"Did you look for a falcon?" Avram's voice whispered through his memory, a jest spoken to a fellow agent who had cause to visit the

island. The man, unfamiliar with American crime novels or films, looked confused while Avram tried, and failed to explain. And that, more than the joke, had been hilarious. Curious that such things surfaced now. That he remembered his friend's voice, and even knew that he, Moishe, had once been known for the depth of his laugh.

They turned into a rectangular space, and their guide announced, "The Oratory."

Caravaggio's *Beheading of St. John*, a massive canvas almost four meters tall and over five meters long, hung flush with the end wall. In the gloomy light, the figures emerged as if Moishe looked through a window into a courtyard beyond. In that liminal space, the executioner leaned over the fallen saint, his neck already spurting blood. The man drew a small knife to finish the job his sword had begun. Salome and her maidservant awaited their gruesome delivery. From a barred window, two prisoners looked on.

"It does captivate, does it not?" A robust older man rose from his knees on the carpeted step before the altar that barricaded the way to Caravaggio's masterpiece. He crossed himself and put out his hand. Each of them accepted. He glanced around. "I had hoped to meet your Caravaggista. She sounds very knowledgeable."

"I wish she had been able to join us," Moishe said. "She would love to be here." He indicated the painting.

"Here, let me show you the artist's only known signature." He drew aside one of the red curtains framing the over-sized altar, and they drew closer to the painting, hanging at head height. From his pocket, the Grand Master drew a laser pointer, using it to circle the blood spilling from the throat of the downed. "You see? F. MichelAng, a shortened form of MichelAngelo, his given name. Fra, as in brother. It refers to his admission to the order due to his great works." The man's face rumpled with sadness. "It did not last. As I'm sure you know, he again fought, this time with his brother knights. He fled the prison cell before he could be properly tried, and so Grand Master Alof de Wignacourt expelled him from the order in front of this very painting, his masterpiece." The present Grand Master shook his head. "I suppose an artist must always have a trace of madness."

"Tragic," Riccardo murmured, gazing up at the great work, his eyes softening to see the martyrdom of the saint.

"Let us pray for the success of our endeavors." All of the men bowed their heads, Moishe held prisoner by these antique traditions as much as Caravaggio had been held by their bars. Soon, he, too, would be free.

Chapter Fifty-Five

With Jacinta resting in the back seat, Grant fired up one of the new laptops, ran every scan he and Nick could think of on the thumb drive, then opened the folio Dafne provided. He sifted through the files, but one date caught his eye. How would D. A. feel knowing he had this in his hand? It wasn't that she refused to talk about her husband's death, but it never seemed quite appropriate to broach the topic of circumstances. He trusted, if it were relevant, she'd notify him. "Trust" became a fragile word these days.

Nothing for it, but to read. He could always ask forgiveness, or present as if he never knew what he was about to find out. Under a few layers of official provenance, including the designation of the translator, Grant found the meat of the report. Unfortunate phrase, under the circumstances.

* * *

Isfahan, Iran

Summary report:

17:42 M and S arrived to resume surveillance duties. At this time, it is unknown how their identities were revealed, or even if both covers had been broken. The timing and placement of the device strongly suggests one or both had been, and that the surveillance vehicle had been targeted with extreme prejudice, not merely as part of the on-going terror campaign.

M and S were both agents of long standing and [REDACTED] clearance status. After the incident in Dubai, the two agents had requested, and been granted, joint reassignment out of the target zone for the duration of the UAE official investigation. Their surveillance, at the start of the Sabbath, may have been observed, but was not uncommon. This location had been chosen for its large number of live-parked vehicles, drivers waiting for high-status clients or employers. Given the timing of sunset, their arrival should not have been conspicuous. It is the opinion of this analyst that such revelation may have preceded the placement of the device.

Grant took a sip from his water bottle, mentally translating the official language. Sounded to him like the analyst believed they'd been spotted as Jewish, and likely Mossad, because of the timing of the changeover. Either that or somebody made them—identified the two men prior to that moment. With some digging, he could find out what Mossad had been up to in Dubai prior to the date, what danger the two agents avoided that had led them into this. The danger that, perhaps, had caused it.

Given the presence of the file, and Dafne's reactions earlier, "M" must be Moishe. Apparently, like Madonna, he was a one-name super-star. Which meant "S" was Avram Silverberg, D.A.'s husband.

* * *

18:29 *Subject appears at cafe opposite. S moves to intercept, proceeding with* [REDACTED]*—so much for knowing what*

Avram was doing. Not germane to the moment, but Dafne wanted Grant to know she'd done it, to know that even this unauthorized access was abbreviated.

18:37 S accompanies subject toward alley NW corner.

18:39 delivery van arrives, parking between alley and surveillance vehicle, presenting obscured view.

18:45 M, in concern for S, exits the vehicle and crosses to cafe, where he orders coffee. At the sound of a scuffle in the alley, M proceeds to investigate, with the intention of urinating in the alley as cover. S is found to have tripped. Subject departs at M's appearance. Van continues to obscure line of sight.

(Device presumed to have been installed at this time.)

18: 48 (register receipt verified from local investigation) M retrieves coffee order. M and S return to surveillance vehicle. M places coffeecup on roof to open doors. M enters the vehicle, followed by S, who closes passenger-side door.

M starts the vehicle.

M shifts position, reaching to retrieve his coffee. The device detonates. M is thrown out of his open door. S appears to have been trapped by the flames, or to have been killed by the intial explosion. M tries to return to the vehicle, but is prevented by a secondary explosion. M circles the vehicle, sustaining second and third degree burns during subsequent efforts.

Bystanders work to remove M from the vehicle during official response. Three bystanders sustain minor injuries and cease their intervention. Two police officers responding to the scene

also sustain injuries, but succeed in subduing M. Medical
personal administer non-consensual treatment.

M. exfiltrated for further treatment and recovery. Retrieval
team requests medical transport, with restraints and additional
security personnel.

Grant traced the words of the report. Straightforward enough. Two
agents are enticed from their vehicle while a bomb gets planted,
possibly with the complicity of the subject of their inquiry. Grant
suspected the subject was someone they were cultivating as a source.
One of them survived, the other one, Avram, was trapped, possibly
killed immediately. Moishe tried so hard to rescue him that he had to be
removed by force, injuring five other people in the act. They forced him
to accept help for his own injuries. When the Mossad extracted him
back to Israel, he had to be restrained during transport.

If those Carabinieri had caught up to Grant in the train station, if
they had dragged him away while Gooney lay chained on the tracks,
how many of them would Grant have injured to get back to his man, his
friend? Would he still have been fighting when the ambulance got
there for him—too late for Gooney? How much would it have hurt to
watch him die?

On some level, the past didn't matter. Moishe's loss, his guilt,
couldn't justify the fact that he'd been prepared to wound Grant the
same way he, himself, had been wounded.

"You okay?" Nick asked, his voice gone very low.

"Found out what happened to D.A.'s husband."

"Pretty grim?"

"Big time. Moishe was there and he couldn't stop it."

"Ouch."

Grant nodded. He flicked through a few other things and paused,
then said, "Jacinta—that folio, can you open it up?"

She lifted the old leather satchel from the floor near her feet, the
one he'd fought for back in Apice Vecchio. "Si, what do I look for?"

"A deposition from a mobster's house cleaner. The villa was raided by Nazis who made off with the artwork."

She shuffled pages around, then paused and pulled out a sheaf of typewritten onionskin, yellowed with age. "I think I have it. Properties of Signor Livio Giordano." Under her breath, she muttered, "I know this name."

Not surprising if the guy had a rep around Naples. Livio Giordano: the name also showed up in Moishe's file, his last known employer, now deceased. "That's the connection. Moishe worked for the man, apparently in his dotage. Looks like the mobster died a few years back, left Moishe the house he's lived in ever since, in Sicily. Moishe must've learned about the painting from Giordano or someone associated with the estate, then he came out of the woodwork when we started looking for the Nazi stash." And Grant was willing to bet Moishe's old friends at the Institute had tipped him off about the stash, whether they meant to or not. Chadad delivering this dossier felt like an apology. He thought of D.A. and Gooney, both lying in the hospital, their health precarious. Chadad's apology was too little, too late.

"Got us a reservation for tonight," Nick remarked. "Across the street from Caravaggio's favorite bar."

"Still a gay bar?" Grant caught the brief flash of Nick's grin. "It's also where he took the blow that probably killed him."

Nick shrugged. "Don't worry, Chief, still not planning to die on you."

"Load off my mind."

"Better be."

"That blow, when he was attacked at the taverna," Jacinta said from the back seat. "I am thinking, if someone knew that Caravaggio had seen the Menorah, that he had painted it, they may have come after him. His contemporary biographers have said that he moves in fear, after Malta. That he seems..."

"Hunted," Grant supplied.

"Si." Her eyes rested on him for a moment, then flicked away. "I begin to think that all of these accidents, these fights he gets in, the fact he carries a sword, all the time—maybe this is not, how do you say, paranoia?"

"So we gotta assume that Moishe knows what we do. He's got the letter now, and the painting," Nick observed. He slowed the vehicle as they approached the city, the darkness of farmland and distant villages giving way to apartments and shops. "Wish I could take you to visit Dom's nonna—she's a fine cook."

Jacinta laughed. "E vero."

"Maybe when we're done here." Had to be better than the fast food he'd eaten off his lap waiting for Nick to get out of the electronics store, the last customer before they closed up. "He's got the painting, but we've got the expert."

"Also this." She produced a thumb drive of her own. "It is every photo I have taken as I worked. Not so good as the real painting, but we have also x-ray and infrared which I have not yet viewed."

"Woot!" Nick smacked his hand against the ceiling. "Bravo!"

"It is my habit from graduate school. There should always be a backup. I think this computer for me is good, but I have also the desktop at my apartment, if we—"

"Sorry," Grant told her. "We have to assume Moishe already knows where you live." As she slumped a little, he added, "If we need something else, we'll get access, don't worry. The point is, we've both got the same map as of a little while ago. If we work this thing, we get there first."

The car slowed again as a stream of pedestrians went by, and Nick regarded him. His voice dropped low, and a little less mellow. "Are we scooping the prize, or laying an ambush?"

"Tell you when we get there."

Chapter Fifty-Six

When the obligatory period of respect for a dead or distant god had passed, Moishe cleared his throat and got them all moving again, out into the darkness. They followed the Grand Master down to the waterfront where a motor launch awaited to take them across the bay to Fort Sant' Angelo. Wind battered at them with a late Autumn chill and Riccardo's thin, pale face sharpened with the cold. The twin forts guarded a deep bay, prized for its strategic value by Templars, the Knights of St. John, the Ottoman Empire—everyone through the second World War. Powerful lights accentuated the towering promontory opposite with the fort rising up as if carved from the living stone.

Moishe like to imagine these places when Mankind had gone. Quiet, empty. Dark when the sun fell, gradually lit again by the dawn as sea birds launched themselves from the walls where cannons and anti-aircraft weapons once roared their cry of destruction. Even now, other boats muttered through the darkness and they must navigate past super yachts to find their berth beneath the fort. Artworks of the Black Death showed skeletons leading all people to the afterlife, rich and poor alike. Those yachts, emptied of their privileged inhabitants, might float for decades before storms drove them under the sea.

"May I ask what you carry?" The Grand Master inquired as they stepped onto the stone jetty and started up the ramp.

"A tool required to determine the next steps." Moishe attempted a smile. "Not a weapon, not a gun, if that is what you fear."

"The curator is very strict about that. His assistant will meet us tonight. I'm sure he will ask."

This private avenue of approach likely avoided the metal detectors that would notice his other "tools."

Another man stood glowering at the arch that accessed the fort itself. The assistant curator, Moishe presumed.

"Grand Master," the assistant curator said stiffly, then launched into a brief tirade in his own language.

Riccardo slid forward, his face screwed up in concern. "My dear sir, you have no idea how grateful we are for this access. Truly, you have no idea what this will mean to us, and to the world."

The assistant pivoted to this new confrontation, sweeping him with a sharp glance as if he could flay him alive. "National or international security. I do not believe this, no matter what you say." He flicked a dismissive gesture. "If this were so, we should hear about it from other places."

The Grand Master patted the air, speaking in a soothing voice, first in Maltese, then saying in English. "I understand, and we do apologize for rousing you with these requirements. I hope that the Knights' own long-standing friendship with the museum will persuade you to cooperate."

Another delay. Casey would be coming. He could be here soon, depending on how they traveled. For now, Moishe believed they had arrived first and he wished to retain that advantage. Casey was not an adversary to underestimate. "I am not sure you understand the urgency of our task."

The assistant's glare aimed at him. "Then tell me. Explain what you wish and what you will find and how this has anything to do with security. Along with my superiors and my inferiors, I am tasked to defend this site and also its visitors. Allowing you to visit the prison, of all things, in the middle of the night, is not in keeping with my own mission."

Moishe strolled a little closer, holding the wrapped telescope on his palm. "Here, let us step aside, and I will show you something of interest."

Riccardo's lips parted, his hand rising as if to express some doubt, then he transformed his gesture into an invitation. "There's more light around the corner, I think."

The Grand Master stood stiffly, still smiling, as Moishe accompanied the assistant toward a little booth likely meant to shelter knights or guardians defending the gate from sea attack. He guessed the curator had been waiting inside for them: a bright lamp shone down on the high narrow desk and single tall chair. Even without the furniture, the booth would be hardly large enough for the two of them. A sort of vertical coffin.

"Let's take a look." Moishe placed his bundle on the desk top and invited the man's gaze in that direction, stepping aside so the assistant curator stood within the booth in the little space afforded someone to rise from his seat. "Go ahead, unwrap it. I assure you it is perfectly safe, though the Catholic Church once thought its maker to be a terrible threat."

His curiosity aroused, the man eyed him, then turned his attention to the item.

Leaning forward, reaching as if to help, Moishe clamped a hand over the man's mouth. Even as the man stiffened and tried to struggle, Moishe wrapped the other hand to the back of his skull. Pressing his chest to the man's shoulder in sudden intimacy, he pinned the man against the wall and gave a twist of his hands. He held on for a moment longer, lifting the man by his wobbly head, letting the twitching stop. "So you see, it's really very simple," he said aloud. "Don't worry, we can show ourselves up."

Moishe settled the body onto the chair, retrieving his bundle as the assistant curator slumped into the corner. Already, the man's face eased from his earlier aggravation, through his instant of terror, to peace. Taking the keys from the man's belt, he arranged one loose arm over the assistant's face, as if he blocked the light to get a nap.

Stepping back outside, Moishe remained before the booth, displaying the keys. "He seems agreeable, but tired. Shall we go?"

"Please, Grand Master, would you show the way?" Riccardo offered a grand gesture, and the knight marched ahead, either truly unaware, or willfully ignoring what happened to the curator as he kept his eye on his own holy mission.

Moishe calculated that the Grand Master wouldn't reveal the truth of his visitors, for fear of revealing his own complicity. By the time someone more invested in the assistant's life discovered his death, Moishe and Riccardo would have moved on, leaving the mess as someone else's problem. Like the next suspicious character to arrive at the Fort, seeking access to something he shouldn't see.

A key for the gate. A key for the turnstile beyond. And finally, they reached the courtyard beside the Chapel of Santa Maria, where the top grips of a metal ladder protruded from a metal grate leading downward. Moishe squatted and had to put down the telescope to unlock the grill and lift it open on its hinges. "We'll need more light."

"Very well." The Grand Master moved away, and Riccardo held his phone over the hole, flashlight function beaming along the treads.

About twelve feet down, the fixed ladder ended on a stone floor. The bell-shaped oubliette rose up around Moishe now. For as high as an average man could reach, most of the surface showed deep incisions and carvings: coats-of-arms, crude faces, names and prayers in Latin, the Maltese Cross given up by the men imprisoned here, awaiting their death or expulsion. Moishe unrolled the wrapping to reveal the telescope. He rolled it in his hand, pausing at the flawed inscription confusing ears for eyes, as if he should listen to the telescope.

"Is that Galilean?" the Grand Master asked, beaming a large lamp down into the hole.

The powerful light swept away shadow and Moishe began to study the walls through the scope, methodically peering at the inscriptions. "Do you know if any of these are Caravaggio's work?"

"I can not be sure. There's little documentation of the prison prior to the modern period."

Moishe shifted his position, bumping into the ladder, wondering if its installation had damaged whatever he was meant to see. He stepped closer to it, studying the structure and where it entered the hole above. A layer of concrete mounted the metal grate to the piazza surface above, leaving the original round hole intact. At its rim...

Moishe climbed the ladder a few feet, bringing his head almost to ground level. Just below the addition of the concrete the old stone showed a series of notches, probably to support the earlier grate that closed the entrance. One of them failed to align with that installation. An indent perhaps ten centimeters, and partially round. Hooking his elbow through the ladder, Moishe brought up the telescope.

"What are you doing?" the Grand Master inquired.

When Moishe didn't respond, Riccardo murmured, "It's best to let him work in silence."

Clever, that one. The inner diameter of the telescope tube closely matched the circular notch. Moishe brought the leather rim to his mouth and gripped it with his teeth, tearing it open far enough to displace the larger lens. He shook it into his hand and tossed the ruined telescope out of the hole, then set the lens into the notch. It fit perfectly.

"The light," he ordered. "Shine it through."

The Grand Master shifted his aim, bringing the flashlight up, trying to align with the lens by creeping around the outside of the hole. Difficulties were twofold. One, the focus of this light failed to replicate anything available to Caravaggio or his patron. Two. This strongly implied the need for the sun. Three:

"I can't," the Grand Master reported. "The structure for the grate blocks me. I cannot bring the light to where it can shine through the lens."

Obviously. Moishe looked up, leaning back from the ladder so he could peer through the lens from the other direction. Even if the new concrete and metal didn't block access for the light, could the sun's rays ever reach from this angle? The chapel, which had been there for centuries, appeared to eclipse the opening.

"Riccardo? What were the words?"

"The mirror of the moons," Riccardo said. "And my other pursuits will show the way, something like that. That was all."

"Well, of course, that telescope doesn't have any mirror," the Grand Master pointed out, in a tone that briefly made Moishe consider ramming what remained of it down his throat.

Could the reference be metaphorical, then? Clearly, this was the place of Caravaggio's confinement. He had been imprisoned briefly in other places, but nothing of significance compared with his imprisonment here and his daring escape. The cardinal's other pursuits included optics—which should also apply to the telescope, should it not?--mathematics, and the sophisticated construction of unusual sundials... sundials that required a mirror.

Moishe had no mirror, but he had a strong suspicion who did.

Chapter Fifty-Seven

In a small, private dining room over the Locanda, the tavern where an assault and injury led to Caravaggio's death, Jacinta and Nick watched photo after photo populate the screen. Scents of garlic, tomato and seafood drifted from the kitchen, and the clatter of plates and diners filtered up from the main dining room downstairs and down a narrow hall.

"I know this must be normal for you, being in places where famous people were a few hundred years ago," Nick remarked, gazing up at the timbered ceiling, "but for me, it's a bit surreal."

"Do you not have where George Washington slept?" She was starting to understand why Dom had liked these men, why he had become so loyal to them by the end of their shared adventure. "Chief" Casey showered at their hotel and would join them a little later for a better meal. In the meantime...

"Here, this is the face and the bull that I saw better with the cleaning." She indicated the screen, and Nick brought his gaze back, head cocked.

"Looks like there's more to be uncovered over here, but I can't make out the shapes." He traced the bull's neck with one finger. "What's this guy doing? Is he riding the bull?"

"Could be. I have thought it was Taurus, and perhaps another astrological sign, but now I am not so sure." The camera's eye picked up things in a different way, highlighting details she'd been less aware of on the actual painting. Framing smaller portions of the whole made it easier to focus on them rather than be swept away by the mood and intensity of Caravaggio's work. "I wish I had seen the murals. I wished to check the pose against that of the gods, to see if there's a semblance to tell us anything."

"Gimme a minute." Nick tapped a code into his phone, then said, "There—you should have D.A.'s photos from the villa. Check the secure folder."

"Si," she muttered, opening up the new images, not only complete views and details of the ceiling, but also a few shots of the Chief holding an antique telescope.

"What are you hoping to find?"

"Sometimes, Caravaggio uses the same motifs. The same models, the same props, the same tree, even, but it's hard to know if this means anything. We've always assumed this was expedience, what is easy for him, and the models are often his friends or his lovers." She set up the relevant images side by side, zooming in, and flicking her gaze from one to the other.

The exaggerated poses of the gods, while they might be echoed by Zacariah's surprise and awe in the painting, didn't match so well, and Jacinta dropped that line of inquiry with a sigh. No sense in spending time chasing shadows. "Perhaps it is the alchemy we should notice? This image, the ceiling, it is also an allegory of how lead may be transmuted to gold."

Nick chuckled. "It can't though."

"No—"Jacinta took a sip of her wine—"but everybody believes so back then, and they keep trying. Each of these figures has a meaning, a mineral that is meant to be used in the process."

"This guy, Cardinal Del Monte, clearly wasn't hurting for wealth, but even he wanted more gold."

"Si. But I think not so much that he will melt down or sell the Menorah, Grazie Dio."

They fell silent as the server returned with a platter of fried artichokes. They had carefully set up their screen facing away from the room's single door set into a thick frame of timbers dating from before Caravaggio's time.

"Grazie," Nick said with a smile, and the server smiled back, maybe a little too long, departing with a swagger.

"I think he likes you," Jacinta observed.

"Too bad I'm working." Nick popped one of the artichokes and crunched it down, leaning closer to study the gallery of images. "Incisioni, that means cuts, right?"

She turned her hand one way, then the other. "It can, but for this, it's not like a knife." She brought up the first of the images with that tag. "These are marks made with the edge of a palette knife. We think it's a trick he learns from when he makes frescoes. Because he is painting from life, the models can't hold a pose for so long as it takes to make the picture, si? These marks show where they should sit or stand, how to hold their arms, like that."

"Okay, but not these ones." He scrolled to click open another image. "They're pretty far away from the figure, right? Unless he had someone else here, but decided not to include them."

Jacinta nodded, bringing up the X-ray imaging of the same section. This made the incisioni stand out, and made it very clear there was no figure, and no sign of pentimenti where such an earlier figure had been painted over. Also, they were too many, and they looked more regular than his usual framing. "These are something else, but I cannot say what. They seem not to belong to this picture. They don't reveal a deeper structure."

"Or maybe they do, just not one in the painting. To me, it looks like a map. Streets, or alleys." He shrugged. "Trouble is, there's no way to orient. I'd assume north, south, east, west, based on the painting, but where would you begin? How would you know where to look? And what if it's all gone now? It's been four hundred years and a couple extra decades."

She zoomed into the marks. "Si, si, ma..." Something about the image stirred her memory. "The streets here, they don't change so fast. Even when the bombs fall, even when the buildings are taken down and new ones made, the foundations remain. On a map of Rome, you can find the city wall, even where it's gone, because of how they build. Nick!" She grabbed his arm, pointing at the screen. "I know this shape!"

"Fantastico! What is it?"

"Spetta, spetta." She dropped windows, slid things this way and that to bring up a mapping site, giving it half the screen while the incisioni occupied the other half. She scrolled and zoomed, then leaned back, displaying her work. The curve at one edge of the pattern of marks nearly matched the coastline just up the bay from Naples, not far from the home of Constanza Colonna, Caravaggio's long-time patron and defender.

"Yes!" Together, they studied the image, and Jacinta's heart sank as if on the ebbing tide. She almost hoped he wouldn't notice the truth, but he was too smart, too attentive for that.

"Hate to say this, Jacinta," Nick said softly. "But the rest of the lines...they don't match."

"Lo so. I can see that." She folded her arms, blinking too hard as she stared at the plastered wall.

"Well. Should see what's up with the Chief. Said he was starving, but he hasn't shown up." Nick turned from her despair, but Jacinta began to feel her true hunger would never be satisfied.

Chapter Fifty-Eight

Grant took way too long in the shower, washing off Gooney's blood, feeling the whole time like it was too late, like the blood had seeped under his skin. Maybe he should stop with the tattoos for his own deaths and start inking those of his friends. Hadn't seemed like a talisman the first time, the Persian winged lion that embellished the scars at his throat where he'd almost lost his head. But he'd been doing it ever since, and, as he'd told D.A., hadn't died yet.

As if inking his friends' survival could somehow ensure that it happened.

He shut off the water, dried briskly in spite of his scrapes and bruises. He took the time to finally wrap the cuts on his calf, then dressed in dark clothing. Left off the bandage from his wrist. Gooney would have a matching set of his own.

From the window of the room, if he looked sideways down the narrow street, he could see the signs for Locanda del Cerriglio, the historic tavern where two of those friends now waited. Assuming he could count Jacinta on his side. Hard to tell. But he had yet to mention the mirror he'd stolen from the Villa, so there you go. Frankly, he was just pleased the thing survived for this long, through everything he'd been doing since then.

Thicker than a modern piece, it looked dark, the silver tarnishing with age. He wrapped it gently in spare bandages and flicked the lights off. His stomach growled. In the darkened room, he returned to the window where he'd left the curtains slightly parted, and peered down both ways again. This late in the season, this late at night, only a few people moved in the streets. So close to the historic heart of Naples, the place would have been crowded a month back.

That made it harder for the man lurking across the street to conceal his presence. He'd likely moved only because the lights went off. If he'd seen Nick and Jacinta depart half an hour back, or seen them enter the restaurant, he'd likely expect Grant to join them.

They hadn't been followed, no way. Somehow, they'd been anticipated instead. Classic Mossad tactics.

Grant check the mag on his small pistol, then tucked it back into the holster at his waist. Almost missed the classy khakis Nick had chosen for him. The pleating covered, as his grandmother would've said, a multitude of sins. She had no idea.

Leaving the room, Grant took the stairs toward the lobby, changing course on the next floor down and waiting. If they went full Mossad on him, they'd have booked one of the rooms nearby as well, watching for his departure. He pulled off his shoes and sped down the second floor corridor to the back stairs, a cramped and crooked staircase left over from the fourteenth century and meant for servants. Stay close to the wall and slip down to ground level. Back on with the shoes. He caught his breath, listening. Nothing.

Grant stepped outside into an alley at the back of the block. The shops closed an hour ago. A few skinny trash cans occupied the space around the door. Taking hold of one, Grant wheeled it out toward Cerriglio Street with him, slumping a little, taking the role. Wasn't so long ago, a group of men pretending to be trash collectors abducted his client from her hotel room. Good ruse.

The trash can rattled, just like all the rest of them. How to become invisible on an empty street, by looking like something else. At the corner back toward the lobby, the concealed man glanced back and away again. Grant crossed the street toward his position and kept moving toward the main street where traffic still flowed, honking and braking. As he walked past the building providing the guy's cover, he rattled the can a little extra as he "disappeared" with it.

Parking the can near a post, Grant edged back to his own corner, checking distance and placement. Racing on his toes, Grant doubled back and charged along the short block. He caught the guy's right arm, twisting it back as he pressed his gun to the guy's throat.

"Buon Giorno. Don't make any—"

Before he could say it, the guy did it, wrenching away by dropping down, then immediately sweeping out his foot. Grant dropped him, aiming a kick to the man's back. With another twist and a surge, the man was back on his feet, charging in grim silence, a knife glinting in his grip.

Grant seized his wrist, controlling the knife away. The man's off-hand slammed into his kidney. Neither of them wanted the attention of a gunshot. Pulling the man's arm upward, Grant rammed his shoulder into the man's chest.

They slammed into the building, his opponent taking the force of the impact with a grunt. He brought a knee up, and Grant deflected. He scraped the man's hand down the old stone and the knife shook free. At the man's throat, a gold cross glinted. Not Mossad, then, unless he was deep cover.

The guy punched hard and fast, landing a rain of blows wherever he could: Grant's cheek, his throat, his shoulder and rib cage.

Grant slammed him again, harder, and the guy slumped. Grant's grip on the man's wrist told a different story: not unconscious, just a tactic.

Thinking fast, Grant bent a knee as his opponent came suddenly awake again. Grant flipped the man over his back into the street.

Something in the man's arm snapped, and he cried out. Dropping to pin him, Grant brought his pistol back into the fight, pressing against the man's throat. "Where's Moishe?"

The man's throat worked as he choked down each breath, trying to control his pain. Lying there in the dark, injured and trapped—no. Grant rejected the image. Nobody had shot him and left him to bleed out, chained to the track of an oncoming train.

"He wants to end the world, you know that, right?"

The man gave a cackle. "To start the new world, the kingdom of the lord." A reedy voice, cracked with pain, heavily accented.

"Once a third of the world is dead—and you're okay with that?"

Jerking, trying to kick loose, the man said, "Kill me. Kill me. Do it now. Kill me." His uninjured hand slapped at Grant's arm, then tried to grab the weapon. Grant pulled back, in two quick steps out of reach. It went against everything he knew, everything he believed, to shoot a man who could not effectively fight back.

The assailant lurched to his feet and stumbled out of Cerriglio into the main boulevard. Horns blared and brakes squealed. Bone cracked and Grant flicked his glance away as the body tossed skyward, slid down the hood, and tumbled back to earth.

No going back.

Chapter Fifty-Nine

Jacinta could not change the map—it had apparently changed so much already that the markings meant nothing, or meant that she'd been wrong about that curve of the coastline. Va bene. They did not give up, neither did she. She wished she had the painting in her little garret not far away, to pore over its details at her leisure, examining every centimeter and making absolutely sure of what she saw. Instead, she opened a document and started adding to her notes.

At his elbow, Nick's phone rang twice, but he ignored it in favor of another artichoke, and it fell silent. He swallowed hard, glancing at the phone. A moment later, it rang again, just as the sound of sirens wailed up toward them.

Jacinta straightened, taking her fingers from the keyboard as Nick answered the phone without a word. He gestured to Jacinta to wrap up her work as he frowned at whatever he was hearing.

"Chief, you're running on fumes and adrenaline. Have been for hours. You gotta rest."

Nick listened again, then he stood abruptly and went to the door. "Carlo?"

He'd remembered the server's name. No surprise, perhaps, given the way they'd been eying each other. Jacinta saved and started closing down her workspace.

"Carlo, grazie. Our friend has an emergency and we have to go. I know, I'm sorry, too. Is there anything you can pack us to eat in five minutes or less?" Nick leaned against the door with a wistful smile, the phone tucked under his arm. "I'll give you a massive tip. Wish I could stay to make it worth your while."

In the corridor, Carlo laughed lightly, then his footsteps retreated.

"What," Nick said into the phone, "you're the only one who gets ahead by flirting? Don't worry, we'll leave out the back." He rang off.

"What happened?" Jacinta asked

Crossing to the windows at the front of their room, Nick peered outside. "Guess we're hoofing it. The car's aren't moving out there right now." He turned away and faced her. "Jacinta. We talked about the fact it's not safe for you to go home. Is there any place else, anywhere they wouldn't track you, that you could stay for a while?"

Her family's palazzo rose in her memory, imposing and grand and closed to her. She pictured her brother turning away. "A friend, maybe? Are you trying to leave me?" The laptop screen shut down and she folded it shut.

He regarded her solemnly. "There's a man dead in the street down there, one of Moishe's people. You know that two of our own are in the hospital, fighting for their lives. You know what happened to Dom."

She drew the laptop close. "Moishe's not a threat to me."

His brow furrowed. "Meaning you don't feel threatened by him, or meaning you don't think he would threaten you?"

"Either. Both."

He was already shaking his head. "The man wants to end human life as we know it, Jacinta. That's not about you, that's about everybody."

"I know this. But also, it's not personal."

"I don't think he wanted to kill—" Nick broke off just before someone rapped on the door. His hand hovered at his back, beneath his jacket, as he brought out his smile. "That you, Carlo?"

"Si, signore. I have the antipasta, and also a box for li carciofi." The server added a laugh, or at least, Jacinta assumed it was.

Nick froze, then his head turned, slow and careful. He waved Jacinta away from the table, and she took the laptop with her. "Gimme a minute, Carlo."

"Vi prego, Signore," Carlo said, his voice near breaking now. "If you could open the door?"

With his hand, Nick directed her behind him and down, then he whispered. "My mark, you open, capisce?"

Jacinta squatted behind the door, nodding. No idea what had gone wrong with Carlo, or what made the Black man suddenly so strange. Every instinct made her wish for a place to hide.

Gliding across the door, almost without sound, Nick pushed a chair into the table with an audible scrape. He pressed his back to the wall beside the door, behind the thick old wood of the frame, and a gun appeared in his hand. "Come on in," he called, almost jovially, with a gesture to Jacinta.

Pulling the door open, Jacinta kept back behind it.

Carlo stepped across the threshold and Nick seized him around the waist, pulling him away. His other arm extended and he fired a single shot. Something fell heavily against the door as a bullet from the other side cracked through the wood up high, raining splinters down on her.

The dead man sprawled as Jacinta jerked away from the door. A gun tumbled from his grip as his hand relaxed, an open, raw-boned gesture not unlike the paintings of so many martyrs. Blood seeped along the uneven floor boards.

Across the way, the server huddled into Nick's shoulder, gasping for breath, nearly sobbing. She didn't blame him.

"He came in the kitchen and asked for the private room," Carlo choked out. "I thought maybe it was your friend, but I think I should ask you first, and when I tried to put him off, he, he—"

"He pulled a gun on you," Nick finished. He cradled the young man's head. "It's okay. They're not after you. Once we get out of here, they don't care about you any more. You're gonna be fine."

Nick gently separated from Carlo. "We've gotta go, now. Which door did he come through?"

"The back, bottom of the stairs." Carlo pointed the way, then he offered the paper bag hanging forgotten from his other hand. "Antipasta. And a few cannoli."

With a broad smile, Nick said, "You're the best. Really appreciate it." He pulled a handful of large bills from his pocket and dropped them on the table as he took the bag from Carlo's hand. "That should cover the meal and the tip, if not the clean-up."

He gestured Jacinta toward the door and she stepped over the body, then out to the landing.

"Mio eroe," Carlo said. He popped onto his toes and kissed Nick's cheek, then the big man hustled Jacinta down the stairs and the two of them ran out into the night.

Chapter Sixty

Leaving the main street swiftly behind, Grant wrapped the block and found a club, open to the night, with music and dancers spilling out. He snapped a picture of the sign and sent it to Nick. Didn't have to wait long before a tall, fast-moving couple approached, the man moving with a distinctive stride.

Nick flashed a grin. "Not dead yet. You?"

Grant stepped into the light, and caught Nick's wince as his friend glanced over his face. "You should see the other guy." He gave Jacinta a nod. "Glad to see you're okay."

"I think there's maybe blood on my shoe." She clutched a laptop to her chest, reminding him all too much of Dom and how he'd been saved by a hard drive when his enemy tried to stab him. She managed a smile. "Look at your dark clothes. This is one of the reasons Caravaggio raises so much suspicion. He wears the black all the time, and carries his weapon, even against the police orders."

Apparently Grant had a lot in common with this guy—more than just having a fight outside the same tavern. A fight that ended in death. "Where can we bring you?"

She shook her head, auburn hair tossing loose from its band. "You come, too."

"For now. We get you to safety, then we need to get out of here."

"To Malta, in the morning, si?"

He started walking, the three of them drawing together as the left the noisy club behind. "They're using Mossad strategies, that means he's got enough people to set up in advance. They didn't follow us, they staked out Locanda. They've probably got a team at every significant location in Caravaggio's life. If Moishe's not already at Malta, his people are."

"And we still need a place to bed down tonight," Nick added. He handed over a paper bag, freeing up his off-hand. "Brought you something, but it won't be easy to eat on the run."

"Never is." As they walked, Grant scanned ahead and to either side. Nick walked a pace behind, guarding their back. Second nature.

Jacinta drew a ragged breath, and blew it out, then drew another. "I have a place."

"We can't go to your place."

"Lo so!" She stalked a few steps ahead. "Mi dispiace. I should make my words clear. I know we can't go to my home. There's maybe another."

The light from a pharmacy sign colored her too pale, and too red. "It's dangerous, though," Grant suggested. "This other place."

She tipped her head, lifted her shoulder. "Not for you."

Grant closed the distance between them. "If you think you can offer us safety by risking yourself, forget it. Not happening."

Her eyes flared. "Do you give up then? You go home and let him do this, this crowd-funded apocalypse?"

"I didn't say that."

"Possibility we gotta consider." Nick set himself up with his back toward them, forming a triangle with Grant and the wall that let him keep scanning. "He's better prepped, he's got enough operatives to set up a half-dozen ambushes."

"He doesn't care about them," Grant added. "Doesn't care what happens to them. Worse yet, they don't care either. The guy I fought not only wouldn't talk to me, he threw himself into traffic rather than face the hospital or police."

"Yeesh." Nick favored his leg a little. Grant wasn't the only one who needed the downtime.

Moishe's philosophy felt so alien that Grant might have stepped into an alternate universe, one where human life meant nothing. *Honor the dead, fight for the living.* That was his grandfather's mantra, and now one of his own. He couldn't leave. He couldn't risk Moishe finding the Menorah and bringing his plans to their terrible end.

Through the whole exchange, Jacinta's glance flicked to him, away, to the sky, to the city streets.

"No," Grant said, "I'm not leaving. There's no obligation for either of you, though."

Nick snorted. "As if."

"Then if you do not fly home," Jacinta said, "I know a place. Forse. Maybe."

"Either way," Nick said, "We should get moving."

"Lead on, Jacinta, but tell us what we're walking into. Why it makes you nervous."

Jacinta squared her shoulders and shook back her hair, then set out resolutely to the North-west. "My father's house, at the back, there is a garden house, for the entertaining, si? I know where is the key. Or, where it used to be."

"I take it you're not on good relations with the family," Nick remarked.

For a few more paces, she didn't speak, then she said, "Non mi accetta."

"He doesn't accept you."

A nod. "But we are apart long enough now that nobody thinks to see me there, or to look for you. Even we have different surnames now."

"Sounds like a B&E—breaking and entering—followed up by family drama. It's perfect," Nick said. "What could possibly go wrong?"

She shrugged. "E possibile there's nobody home. O e possibile there is no key. If it is gone, we do not B and E. There is too much security."

Too much security? Grant tensed as a police car sped by, siren wailing, then said, "The more you say, Jacinta, the less inclined I am to go along with this."

She laughed then, a high-pitched, mirthless sound. "And I have not said the best." She turned back to face them, but kept walking backward, gesturing toward the grand manor house coming up on their left. "There it is, signori. The main house. We go around the back."

With a shake of his head, Grant said, "First you tell us the rest."

"My father," she said. "He's a Made Man. You know what this is?"

Grant stopped walking.

Nick supplied the answer. "Sure," he said. "He's mafia. Your family's in the mob."

Chapter Sixty-One

Motion detector lights flicked on as Jacinta approached the overgrown fence at the back of the palazzo gardens. The two men stayed with her, vowing only to bring her that far, though their expressions told her more, the sort of grim anticipation of the soldiers at the Crucifixion. She wanted to laugh at herself, at her grandiosity. She wanted to call Dom and have him reassure her. Neither of those things would help.

"My brother and I, we have played here all the time, at the cottage," she told the men.

Dense foliage poked through and obscured the little gate, wrought iron in a stone wall topped with more iron. Nick and Casey watched both directions, closing together as she groped for the latch with one hand, still clutching the laptop with the other. Eccola! Rust flaked into her palm as she located the latch. It lifted with a groan of old metal.

Both men reached for their guns, then hesitated as Casey gave a quick gesture of negation.

"Could be more Gothic, you think?" Nick muttered.

"Only with gravestones," Casey replied.

"C'è una cappella, a chapel for the family, but we don't go there at night." She gave a dramatic shiver. Not since her brother had dared her and Dom to sleep there, then her brother and some of his friends had pranked them with a silk robe and a lantern that snuffed itself. She had screamed and leapt into Dom's arms. He startled, but rallied, defending his friend with an old candlestick. Maybe he'd always been more the hero. Va bene. None of this mattered.

A narrow trail led along the fence beneath overhanging boughs to the cottage at the back. A smoking lounge for her grandfather, a romantic retreat for her father and his numerous mistresses, then a hiding place for her and her brother, a refuge from adult things. And where she'd come out to him, years before she told anyone else.

Nick chuckled. "You're kidding me. That's your playhouse?"

She glanced back at him, taking in the elevation of his eyebrows, the tilt of his head as he studied the facade. A close grouping of Doric columns supported the roof, and gave admittance to the two rooms and the loft within. Moss clung to the marble steps, and a fountain with a naked cherub stood to one side, its scallop-shell bowls filled with old leaves. "Si. The temple of Eros. What else?"

His face shadowed by bruises, Casey moved up alongside. "What else?" he echoed. "I've spotted four cameras since we breached the fence, two more right here. If anybody's looking, we're gonna get company. You'd better be right about being safe here, or there's gonna be a graveyard after all."

"They don't want me," she answered. "This does not mean they want me dead." Unless her brother had opted for their father's role after all. She hoped not.

"Where do we find the key?" Nick asked. Jacinta crossed to the fountain, and another motion-sensor light flickered on, dim with cobwebs and collected leaves.

"One of these dolphins." She knelt and Nick slipped the laptop from her grasp, not joining her on the ground. His limp had become more pronounced as they approached the house.

Jacinta felt inside the open mouth of the carved stone dolphin on the fountain's base. Not the first one...

Casey stalked across the small clearing and squatted, looking toward the main house. "No movement."

"Maybe we get lucky," Nick murmured. "Assuming the key's still there."

Not the second one. Two more to check! Had she forgotten? Since they arrived, the men's voices had dropped to bare whispers, clear and low. Her palms sweat, and she nearly fumbled the key. "Le chiave!"

She smiled, but they did not look reassured, even as the key slid into the lock and the door released. Jacinta entered, immediately moving to pull the blinds across all the windows. Dropping his meal on the table, Casey passed her, moving fast, searching the main room and the bedroom. He paused at the door under the stairs, finding it locked. "What's in here?"

"Wine cellar."

"In the cottage. Of course." He trotted up the stairs to the loft. "Clear." His voice drifted down, then he followed up with, "No cameras?"

"Not inside, no."

Voices echoed a little from the stone roof high above. Jacinta moved for the floor lamp in the corner.

"Sorry, Jacinta. No lights," Casey said.

"It's hardly any. The shade is thick." She jerked the chain, staring up at him. A minimal glow warmed a small arc by the table and a couple of chairs.

Nick sighed heavily in the doorway. "Either they spotted us on the cams and they're coming, or they're not home. At this point, it's hard to see a forty-watt bulb making a difference."

Forearms resting on the railing above, Casey bowed his head.

"Chief. Eat something, I'm on duty," Nick said as he retreated to the porch with the giant columns.

"Copy that." Casey descended from the loft. In the kitchen corner, he dropped into a seat and dug into the contents of the bag. "If I've got this right, Jacinta, your family cut you off when you came out to them. How were relations before that?"

"With my brother? We were close, and then...it hurt him, not to be who we were. For the rest?" She tipped her hand one way, then the other. "Polite. Everything about the families is very polite. At least, everything they allow children to witness."

"You never planned for the family trade?"

With a swift shake of her head, she said, "My father did not want this for me, nor for my brother, I think. He supports me to go to university, at least...before. We have cousins who are being groomed for this, to take his part."

Pausing over the cannoli box, Casey regarded her coolly. "I've been led to believe it's not that easy."

Her face warmed, and she crossed to the small refrigerator, the light inviting against so much gloom. "Okay, so it's not. I'm out of it. I don't know about them, what they do. I work very, very hard not to know." A plastic-wrapped platter of cheese and a bowl of grapes occupied the shelves along with some chilled wine. Someone must have been planning to visit, or had recently been here. She banged the refrigerator door shut and dropped into one of the chairs. "They have disowned me, e tutto via. Why should they wish for me to know anything of who they are or what they do?"

Casey offered a more sympathetic nod. "My family's not too keen on me, either."

Taking one of the cannolis, he crossed to the open doorway and offered the box. "Leave the gun," he said, and Nick replied, "Take the cannoli." The men tapped their desserts as if making a toast. Casey bit down on his, and Nick froze, straightening.

The Black man's entire demeanor shifted. She'd seen that happen once, just before a man died. "What is it?"

Casey chomped the rest of his dessert and set the box on the table, very gently, his other hand emerging with his gun held low.

"Arrete!" Someone shouted from outside.

Nick swiveled hard, taking a knee, gun extended in both hands. Jacinta pushed to her feet just as the cellar door slammed open and a rifle thrust inside.

Chapter Sixty-Two

The vibration underfoot alerted Grant an instant before three men raced through the door at the back of the cottage, long guns extended. "Wine cellar" indeed. He placed his back to the wall by the door, gun ready, not raised. They were severely out gunned, if not completely surprised. "Nick, how many?"

"Two, and a dog."

"Three here."

Jacinta's chair toppled when she flew to her feet, hitting the counter, then the floor. "Massimo!"

"Chi e—" The lead man, Massimo, presumably, stood dismayed.

He opened with belligerence, then cut himself off immediately. Massimo carried no visible weapon but the air of command. His companions' rifles served notice, as did their well-cut suits and startling appearance. Maybe thirty, broad shouldered, with a thick wave of hair across his forehead...and something familiar about his eyes and the shape of his face. Her brother. And everything Grant could see convinced him she'd been wrong about one thing: Massimo was absolutely Mafia.

The last thing Grant needed, the very last thing on the face of the planet, was to mess with the mob. Should've done what they planned: deliver her to safety, however she chose to define that, and get the Hell out. But the idea of bringing her home, to the family that expelled her, then walking way...just didn't sit well.

One thing he knew about the Mafia, they valued respect and family. They had better guns and more of them. Time to break out some other tools.

Controlling his breathing, watching and listening with all that he had, Grant kept his gun low, present, but non-threatening, making it a symbol of their peer status. He inclined his head toward the intruders. "Buona Serra, signori. Jacinta, perhaps you can introduce us."

She swallowed and her lips twitched toward a smile, but didn't quite make it. "Va bene. C'è Grant Casey, e Nick..."

Grant caught the sudden arch of eyebrows for one of Massimo's retainers, and the glance he shot toward the other one at the sound of Grant's name. Interesting. They'd heard of him before now, and he had a good idea of how.

She hesitated, then plunged onward, "Sono amici di Domenico. Anch'io." Drawing a deep breath, she gestured toward Massimo. "My brother, Massimo Sforza."

"Pleased to meet you." Grant felt sure the man didn't need translation, but he paused, and Jacinta supplied his words in Italian. "We're so sorry to intrude. There's been some trouble with a client of Jacinta's, and Nick and I wanted to bring her to safety, in case it goes south."

This took a little longer to translate, but the fact that Massimo was already frowning in his sister's direction signaled that Grant guessed correctly about his grasp of the language.

One of his retainers, a thick-set man with graying hair, chuckled, leering at Jacinta. "A client? What, are you a prostitute now?"

"Basta," Massimo said, with a sharp gesture. The two men straightened up, all trace of humor vanishing. Jacinta flushed, and her fists clenched.

Before she said anything in hurt and anger, Grant continued, "She's an art restorer. World class. That's why we're here." He shifted his own stance, a little less casual, a little more power. Kick the table over, fire over the top, taking out the silent retainer, the one more poised for action, prep to take down the other. Don't take out Massimo unless he wanted to trigger a vendetta.

If he had to, he knew what he'd do. Aside from hoping it wouldn't come to that.

"We couldn't be sure her apartment would be secure, so, when I asked where else she might feel safe, she thought of you." Grant indicated their surroundings. "Sounds like you two have some good memories here."

Massimo's brow furrowed more deeply and he spoke in heavily accented English. "So you have, what now, body guards?"

She eased out her hands. "Si. When I need them."

At the very least, she was good at picking up the cues.

"We're just looking to spend the night," Grant said. "If we're not wanted here, Signore Sforza, I'm happy to escort your sister elsewhere." Underscoring the family bond.

"I never had a sister." He kept his eyes on her. They pinched a little at the corners, his lips compressed.

"Or you always did, and you just haven't really met until now," Nick said, picking up Grant's thread. "How long's it been since you two met up?"

"Ten years," she said, at the same time Massimo said, "Nine years."

She nearly smiled, and Massimo's frown deepened as Jacinta explained, "It was the holidays, New Years, so how do you count?"

"Long time." Nick might appear relaxed—to anyone who didn't know a sniper's instincts.

From the outside, a dog growled.

"I should kill you all right now, and not have this embarrassment on the family." Massimo gestured toward one of his men, and the guy offered a rifle.

"She's already changed her name, changed her life. How many people even know she's family?" Grant observed. Take him now, all three of them. Get it done. Nick's face went smooth, as if he were thinking the same thing.

Massimo twitched toward the gun, mastered himself, and snatched it, baring his teeth. His eyes glinted. How wounded had he been not to have known his sibling, not to have understood? "I know!" Massimo shouted. "That she is family. I know it."

Jacinta pulled back, huddling into herself as if singed. Grant shifted closer to her, ready to cover her if need be, but he held up his hand, palm outward in a plea for peace. "We certainly don't want anyone to die, not when we're just looking for one night's rest."

"As if I should care what you want," Massimo snapped. The older retainer nodded, as if all were right in his world, that his boss should end the life of the Black Sheep. Right to put the interlopers in their place, especially if that were the grave.

Grant could enact his plan, right now, trust Nick to take down the men outside, the dog, too, if he had to. Grant was, as Dafne Chadad observed, a hunted man. Not, as of yet, hunted by this particular enemy. "You've already heard of me, am I right? If you kill us, it'll be a big mess, international. Call a lot of attention to your organization. So, don't kill us.

"Here, I've got a better idea." He reached slowly forward—no sudden moves—and placed his pistol on the table.

Opening his hand to Massimo in invitation, he said, "Arm-wrestle me."

Chapter Sixty-Three

"I know what I told you before," Riccardo said into the phone. "The plan has changed, that's all you need to know." He scowled and rolled his eyes. "That's right. Thanks." He tapped the phone off. "They're...confused, Moishe."

No doubt. The new orders were nearly opposite what he'd been telling them about how to handle the Americans. Half of them now believed he'd gone soft because of the woman, because she was now traveling with his enemy, apparently of her own free will. Moishe strolled the length of the chapel for the seventh time. Small, vaulted, with a dozen chairs and an altar embedded in the end wall. Vivid blue paint marked the nave, nearly invisible now that the main lights were out. A yellow emergency bulb turned the paint more green and made the Virgin's icon look jaundiced. A set of old wooden double-doors gave onto the piazza, alongside his window.

"They can't get here until morning, at least. Do you think we could —" Riccardo's hands fiddled with the words he didn't say.

"If you require your beauty sleep, Riccardo, carry on. I will be here." Two of his men in Naples stopped answering, after reporting Casey's arrival. Who spotted who no longer mattered: his men had been removed. Casey might take a flight in the morning. So far as Moishe knew, the man might simply fly over now on the strength of his legend alone.

Riccardo scrubbed his hands through his hair. "Well, it's a pity there aren't any pews, or I could take a proper nap." He cast about and settled for lying across a few of the wooden chairs. "Wake me if you need me."

Moishe made another circuit. Orange cones defended the door from outside, along with a sign warning off visitors. He peered through the window again. The Grand Master should be well away by now, back to his own comforts.

Letting himself out of the chapel, Moishe retraced his steps down the ramp to the little guard house where the assistant curator still slumped. For his new plan to work, there must be no disruption to service tomorrow. The museum must open as usual. Everything must happen precisely as usual.

He rifled the dead man's pockets. Moishe preferred the idea of allowing Casey to take the suspicion for the man's death, but it couldn't be helped, and he wasn't the sort to dwell on lost causes. Finding the curator's cell phone, Moishe unlocked it with the dead man's thumb. It took a moment to find the right thread, then the right words, but the dutiful assistant sent a message to his boss about his sudden illness. Out of an excess of caution, he felt he shouldn't come to work the next day. He would need the rest. Eternal rest, that is.

This done, Moishe replaced the phone, and scanned the harborside for a moment. Whatever arrangement the Grand Master had established for their privacy remained in force and no security guards were present on this side of the fort. Satisfied that they were alone, he escorted the corpse down toward the harbor. Super yachts lined up to one side, by the formal quay and parking area. Ignoring these, he moved toward the rocky beach alongside where they had landed earlier. As he walked, he gathered stones, slipping them into the pockets of the man tucked under his arm. Jacket pockets, shirt pockets, many pockets in the utility trousers he wore. The man grew heavier, and Moishe contemplated the Jewish practice of leaving visitation stones for the dead.

Typically, an observant Jew might leave a stone on the grave of their beloved dead in remembrance of their life. Likely the man was not Jewish. For the most part, neither was Moishe, but tonight, they shared this ritual placing of stones. It would become the man's grave site, after all. Moishe hauled him out on a promontory where the water deepened, then sent him down to his final resting place

He retraced his steps, ensuring that nothing had fallen to mark the way, then he returned to the chapel for his vigil. Hopefully, Casey would not keep him waiting.

Chapter Sixty-Four

"What?" Nick demanded, incredulous, and the two retainers laughed while Massimo's eye turned on Casey.

Jacinta had been listening closely, ready to translate if she must, but still she wasn't sure she'd heard him right. "Arm wrestle?"

"Sure." Casey unbuttoned his cuffs and started rolling his sleeves back. Inch by inch, he revealed a band of scraped flesh around his wrist, then a series of colorful tattoos tracking his lean, strong arm.

"Non sei serio," Massimo said. You're not serious.

Jacinta didn't even know what to think. Her brother, the person she loved most in the world after Dom, held a very large rifle, looking perfectly at ease with it. He spoke of killing her, removing her stain from his family honor, and her heart nearly stopped to hear him say it. His eyes hadn't changed, deep and liquid, dangerous and sly. He hadn't told their father, when she first came out to him. He gave her time to change her mind, or so he said. She changed her body instead.

"Sono serio." Casey matter-of-factly completed the rolling of his sleeves, the cloth bunching a little over his biceps as he moved. Scars marked some of the designs, though some of them had been drawn over and around old wounds, making a palimpsest of his skin, layer over layer of his personal story.

Her brother's senior retainer stared at the band of recent injury around Casey's wrist.

"Lake Como," Casey prompted. "You've seen the video."

"You sure you're up to this, Chief?" Nick murmured.

Casey kept his attention on Massimo. "Have you seen it?"

The second retainer cleared his throat, and said, in Italian, "We made good money betting he'd live."

"The man who went down with the ship? The chained man, that was you." Massimo regarded her companions more critically.

"The same." Casey pulled out his chair and sat down, propping his elbow on the table, holding up his hand in the classic posture. "Let's do this."

Massimo shook himself like a dog out of a river. "Your man is pazzo."

Jacinta was beginning to wonder that herself. "Forse." But Casey's nonchalance seemed contagious. "We were a little crazy back then, too," she said, her voice very low.

"If I win, we stay the night, undisturbed," Casey said. "We're gone in the morning. You don't have to see any of us again if you don't want to."

"And if you lose?" Massimo growled.

"If I lose, you kick my ass down those steps and get it on video. Anybody with a gun could kill me," Casey said, then smiled. "Maybe. Maybe not. I know the kind of things they're saying about me."

His eyes gleamed. "But you—you'll have the bragging rights. Your victory. My humiliation. We get out of here now, tonight. And you never have to see us again."

Her brother studied her face, swept her figure again with his glance, then back to her face. He stepped closer, and she stiffened, but didn't retreat. Casey's left hand hovered by the table, very close to his gun. Body guards, when she wanted them.

"You left me first," Massimo whispered.

Turning sharply, he slammed his rifle down on the table and snatched the chair opposite Casey, his much larger weapon casting a deep shadow over the pistol lying near Casey's side. The negative space between them filled with shadows, too. "Va bene. We do this thing." He aimed a finger at one of his retainers. "Be ready to film, when I kick his ass."

Massimo peeled back the sleeve from his beefy forearm, revealing a weight-lifter's power. Likely he outweighed Casey by twenty or thirty kilos, and she began to suspect all of that was muscle, partially building up the strength to do what he had to, what La Famiglia required of him, and partially to stay a little ahead of his men. She knew this much, that the capo might not be twice the man of any of his retainers, but he must at least appear to be.

Jacinta tried not to hold her breath as the men set up, their hands clasping. Casey, in spite of his confidence, in spite of his tattoos, looked like a light-weight.

"You got this, Chief," Nick said. His face softened, the terrifying rigor of his deadly truth once more concealed, and she suddenly knew what had happened.

Casey offered up his reputation—because he'd already saved their lives.

Chapter Sixty-Five

Malta

"Would've hurt," Nick said as he shouldered the computer case, their most important luggage, and Grant took up the other bags. Nick tipped his head to scope out Grant, then added, "That's all I'm gonna say. Your ass is pretty skinny. Nice. But skinny."

"Good thing he didn't need to kick it, then." Grant watched Jacinta emerge from the Ladies' room, dressed in a new outfit that coordinated with Nick's transformation into a budget tourist, complete with the sort of flowing, colorful scarf she clearly enjoyed.

All three of them slept well the night before, in spite of everything, thanks to Mafioso luxury bedding then had a large meal at the airport in Naples. They'd taken everything in shifts, allowing Grant to accumulate their new clothes and a few other things he hoped would get them through the next few hours. For the moment, he, too, matched the tourist look. No black, with apologies to Caravaggio.

"Still don't know how you managed to pull that off. You looked pretty beat last night."

"Ah, does he now reveal the secret?" Jacinta asked lightly. In spite of the sleep, she looked pale and distracted since their sojourn at her old hide-out. "My brother has been working out, and he has the strength of anger. How do you beat him?"

Grant indicated for her to lead the way out of the airport into the warm sunlight draping the island. "Not really my secret to tell, but since you asked."

He scanned carefully. Air travel meant leaving their weapons behind—the obvious ones, anyhow, and Nick's custom job took time to assemble, not to mention the conspicuous act of pulling rifle parts from his prosthetic leg. No sign of Moishe or his men. No doubt they were here.

He and Nick shared a rapid agreement, and proceeded, avoiding the taxi queue in favor of the rental cars. "Your brother let me win."

Jacinta stopped short, turning on him with flared eyes. "No, I don't believe this. Since we are very small, he cannot abide to lose."

"Maybe so. But this time he lost to the unkillable, the revenant, the man who rose from the dead. He lost to Lazarus, and you better believe he's gonna be telling that story down at the pub tonight."

She was already shaking her head as they fell into step, heading for Vittoriosa. Nick cuffed Grant's shoulder. "You out-foxed him. Nice."

"It's an honor-cult. You just have to make sure nobody loses face."

Nick went to collect the rental car, leaving Grant as look-out.

"I do not understand," Jacinta declared, "and no, still, I don't think I believe this that he allows you to win. Of course you can win without his help."

"Believe what you want, Jacinta, but here's what I think: after all those years, you came to your brother for safety. He'd have to be heartless not to respond, but his position constrained his options for helping, with his men watching. I gave him the chance to help you, without losing face in front of his men." He met her eye. "Whatever he might say when other people are around, he still cares."

The museum wouldn't open for a couple of hours. Just as well, he had work to do, along with a bunch of other folks.

Nick drove them all into town, readily adjusting to new street signs, or the lack thereof. He got expertly "lost" in an area not open to the public near the bridge and causeway that provided access to the for itself. By the time the car drove off again, Grant slouched toward the staff entrance of the fort, dressed in a nondescript coverall and carrying a basic toolkit, all of it carefully removed from the airport. A few other people moved ahead of him in the early light, scanning badges. Dang. He'd been hoping to slip inside as one of the anonymous workers who kept these places running.

The risks mounted. Would he be permitted inside? Given the access he needed? Would he live long enough to work out where Moishe laid his trap? The area around the prison hole stood mostly empty, a piazza formed by the Chapel of the Virgin's Nativity, and a space apparently used as a cafe. Welcome to history, tourist-style.

Grant joined the little group, reaching the point where a security guard waved at him, indicating that he should swipe his badge. Grant glanced around, as if looking for someone. The guard said something in Maltese, and Grant shook his head.

"He's supposed to meet me here, about the engineering review? What was his name, ah—" he braced his forehead. "About the safety review?"

Appearing mystified, the guard raised his palms helplessly. He didn't speak English. Perfect.

Grant pointed to his wrist, as if to a watch, then toward the building, then mimed looking for someone. "The man should meet me." He pointed to himself, then toward the building again. "To let me in." He displayed his tool case.

The guard frowned at him, then said, "Luca Cassar?"

"Is that his name? I'm so sorry, the office didn't copy me on everything." Grant smiled in relief.

Either Luca would be easier to convince, or Grant would have to use plan B. Once he knew what that was.

The guard shook his head, talking into his radio for a moment. When he spoke again, he raised his voice, enunciating clearly a number of words that Grant couldn't understand regardless of their volume or clarity. But he understood the gestures that went along. Luca called in sick—the guard feigned vomiting, and Grant winced in sympathy, then shook his head, glancing back, and to his kit.

The guard said something else, then, in Italian, "La cappella?"

The chapel. It was about the chapel? Of course it was. "Yes! Si."

Sinking back to his stool, the guard buzzed a hidden button and waved Grant through for his inspection of the chapel. Didn't recall any mention on the website of a chapel being closed, and there was the matter of Luca Cassar's illness. Intelligence work gave him a healthy dose of skepticism about coincidence. The guard produced a clipboard with a sign-in sheet, which Grant filled out in a rapid scrawl. Much easier now that he knew both the name of the person he was to meet, and the reason they were meeting.

"Le chiavi? The keys?" Grant mimed unlocking a door, and the guard shook his head, grumbling something that involved Luca and some words that didn't sound very nice in any language. He reached into a drawer, and handed over a bundle of keys with a stern admonishment, that Grant emphatically agreed to.

Grant moved briskly up the ramp. Fortunately, both chapels were in the same direction from here, and he had no intention of visiting either until the sun rose higher over the fortress wall. In the meantime, he had a ring full of keys, and an excuse to be where he didn't belong. For a guy who dropped out of a history major, so tempting.

He briefly slipped out his phone: *I'm in*

Nick replied with a "thumbs up."

Maintaining a brisk pace, Grant gave himself a tour of the facility, heading upward as often as possible. At this hour, only his fellow staffers and a few security guards occupied the grounds. He nodded to them, they nodded back. Cleaning crew worked to get ready for the coming tourists, polishing display cases and scooping up bits of litter. Arches opened to the sea and to the city of Valletta on the opposite promontory. Cannons still aimed over the harbor, ready to destroy the enemy. Grant ascended yet again, this time to the roof from a ladder clearly marked as forbidden. A pile of tarps and tools rested in one corner, evidence of recent or on-going repairs. Some of the original roofs had been covered with contemporary metal roofing while others remained stone.

Grant walked about authoritatively—nothing raised more suspicion than people skulking on rooftops. He spotted the entrance to the prison, presumably opened by one of the magic keys in his pocket. Opposite that access point, the Nativity Chapel comprised one wall of the piazza, its facade nearly flush with the wall save for a triangular cap thrusting at the front over an oval window. Glass doors protected the wooden doors within, and a single window with a metal grill pierced the wall adjacent, the only viewpoint into the piazza from there.

From the vantage point of the upper roof, he noted the orange cones outside guarding the door of his presumed destination. No better place to lie in wait. Implied either that Moishe hadn't gotten what he wanted, and counted on Grant to do it for him, or that he had, and he now waited to take care of his enemy.

Grant hated the fact that he needed to literally climb into a hole in the ground. Only one way in or out. He'd be the proverbial fish in a barrel. If he had a weapon of his own, the chapel, with its single door and barred window, would be no more than another barrel.

Most places, acquiring a gun wasn't so hard if you knew the sort of people to ask, but on a small island where none of his team knew the language, the challenges mounted. Grant was armed with nothing but a few tools, a mirror, and freedom of movement, at least for now. And the sun was rising.

Grant considered his options, then reached for his favorite tool: the truth.

Chapter Sixty-Six

At intervals, while Riccardo snored softly, Moishe rose and peered out the windows again, moving his fingers through his warm-up exercises, just to keep limber. As ten o'clock slipped away and the first visitors would enter, he positioned himself where he could overlook the entrance to the prison. Very soon now—

Riccardo twitched sharply and nearly fell from his chair-bed. Sitting abruptly, he yanked his phone from his pocket, frowning, then his brows rose, and he approached Moishe's position.

Not taking his eyes from the prison entrance, Moishe said softly, "What is it?"

"A text, claiming to be from Jacinta." He displayed the message.

Moishe absorbed that. "Ask her what was my lie."

Riccardo looked skeptical, but shrugged, and his thumbs tapped over the screen, then he held up the phone again.

J: *You escaped from a burning car.*

Moishe took the phone. :*Why are you contacting me?*

J: *We're here, in Malta. They want to kill you.*

His lips curled of their own accord. Of course they did. The feeling was mutual. :*Thank you for the warning. If I go there, I'll be careful.*

J: *He thinks you are here. Nick is a sniper, he has a gun.*

Your concern surprises me.

For a moment, no reply, then :*Me, too. I guess I do care.*

Moishe felt a breath of laughter. :*I think you want to see the painting, to keep working on it.*

That, too.

They had, indeed, gotten to know each other over that game. One of them better than the other. :*Are you safe?*

They trust me.

They must have something else, some other information than just the letter.

A longer hesitation, then :*I don't know. I think they don't trust me that much.*

Interesting. That rang true for operators like Casey. Did they ever really trust anyone, even each other? A sad failing in mankind. One of many.

"Moishe!" Riccardo's hiss drew him back from the phone. The salesman pressed himself to the wall between the door and the window. He pushed at the air, as if to shove Moishe out of the way. "I saw a muzzle flash. On the roof."

Immediately, Moishe flung himself away from the window. Jacinta's information was good. An oversight, not claiming the roof for himself, but there were too many ways it could be seen. Brazen of his opponent to make use of it anyhow. He must be about to make his move on the prison. How had they circumvented the metal detectors at the gate? Perhaps, like Moishe, they had special access.

He slipped out one of his pistols.

"What do we do?" Riccardo demanded.

Already, Moishe's thumb slid over the screen, summoning his two men inside the fort, warning them of the danger on the roof. If Casey entered the piazza, though, he could still—

Sudden darkness plunged over the window and his view vanished, replaced by an indistinct glow. In an instant, he and his companion went from predators to prey.

Chapter Sixty-Seven

Once he had released the tarp over the window, Grant raced lightly to the near end of the chapel. A few tourists down below looked up as he clambered down the old stone wall to drop into the piazza proper. No telling how long Moishe would be pinned, or believe himself to be.

Grant moved briskly through the shade to the front of the chapel—careful not to reveal himself in silhouette on the covered window. With the turn of a key, he locked the glass doors enclosing the chapel. Best to secure the facility. Given the presumed occupant, it was most certainly unsafe.

Grant nodded to the handful of tourists and crossed quickly to the metal grate, squatting down and scanning the lock. Before he opened anything, he pulled a vial of machine oil from his tool kit, with a silent apology to the technician he'd swiped it from. He oiled the lock and hinges, just in case.

He flicked through his keys to try one. Fail. Try another—it fit, the lock turned, and he lifted the grate. It sighed open. A shaft of sunlight spilled down into the hole. A metal ladder led inside, its rungs mostly illuminated.

With a forbidding stare and a shake of his finger at a tourist who edged closer, Grant descended, scanning quickly. He'd like to close the grate behind him, but that would interfere with the light he needed. He'd have to risk the curious tourists—thankfully, few, and most of them not daring enough to climb into a prison cell.

Medieval and later graffiti cut into the walls, Latin inscriptions and knightly emblems of the prisoners who'd been here.

He pulled the mirror from his pocket. The angle of light couldn't change much down here: the hole itself would receive light only from that opening, and even then, large parts of the hole would never be directly lit. *The Mirror of Moons.* Nothing here that looked like a moon, or any celestial icon. No place down at the bottom to set the mirror, at least, nothing obvious. He started climbing back up. It was possible the emplacement had been destroyed by the work to set the—

He spotted a semi-circular depression to one side of the metal grate, below the level of the original entrance, but not by much. The mirror fit perfectly, resting against the stone, directing the sun toward an area of the cell not otherwise strongly lit.

Grant scrambled down again, squatting to avoid blocking the beam. Among the carvings stood a pagan figure in profile, with a laurel wreath, a drape of cloth, and a goblet. The beam rested on the figure's ear like a sniper's red dot, about to take aim at the mythic man. He took a few pictures, burst mode.

J: *What do you see?*

Grant sent her a photo. :*what else to look for?*

It's Bacchus! A favorite subject of C. Even he paints a self-portrait this way.

Grant could practically feel her excitement. :*Back to the art?*

Si! Va bene.

He slipped the phone away, then turned as the grate slammed shut.

The mirror bounced free and cracked against the metal ladder, falling in two pieces to the ground as Grant leapt out of the line of sight. Caravaggio had escaped this prison. Grant might well die there.

Chapter Sixty-Eight

From the shaded portico, Jacinta watched the piazza where Casey had disappeared into the hole. Her veins felt alive as if she'd drunk a double espresso: Bacchus! What could it mean? She wanted to race straight back to her studio and find out.

Moishe hadn't answered her text since Casey dropped a curtain over the window. That should be good, a sign he took the threat seriously, a sign that Casey was right.

An imposing figure dressed in the traditional tabard of the Knights of St. John swept into view, and the tourists gasped, immediately turning to snap photos. A sword hung at his side, and he might have stepped directly from a portrait Caravaggio painted during his tenure. His sudden appearance came like a sign from above, and Jacinta wanted to cheer this apparition from the past.

The man marched toward the prison, and Jacinta held her breath. Instead of calling down the hole, or apparently noticing anyone, he kicked the grate closed with one booted foot. The clang echoed from the stone walls around them. With a twirl of his cape, the man proceeded to stand atop the cell door, arms spread. He declaimed first in Maltese, then in English, "Welcome, visitors, to the enclave of my brethren. That's right! I am the Grand Master of the order of the Knights of St. John, and I assure you—"his voice grew louder—"that you have nothing to fear!"

Other than blocking Casey's exit, what was he doing? Was this truly the Grand Master?

Across the piazza, not far from where the re-enactor had appeared, the wooden inner door of the chapel eased open.

The Grand Master flung his arm wide. "We knights are guided by honor and faith." His hand pointed directly toward the so-called "sniper's nest" Casey indicated on his earlier photo.

She'd been watching for Moishe's men, the kind of people he stationed to look for them in Naples, she wasn't expecting this, but what could she do about it? Nick wouldn't risk the lives of tourists, would he?

But Moishe would. If Casey could be believed, Moishe and his men had no respect for lives, save that their plans ceased if they were captured for something like murder or terrorism. Stood to reason, then, that they preferred for the tourists to move on.

The Grand Master said something else in Maltese, and gestured again, toward the high arch leading away. "Please, carry on with your tour."

If Jacinta didn't act soon, their protection would wander away, while Moishe's confederate held Casey in a hole, ready for execution. No no no.

She tossed back her hair and marched out with a cheerful wave. "Welcome and thank you, ladies and gentlemen, to our living history day. If you gather here, I would like to tell you about the most famous knight of St. John, and their most famous prisoner! A murderer, a madman, and one of the greatest artists of all time!"

The tourists, already excited by the knight's arrival, followed her directive, filling in close to the chapel.

"If you please, Sir knight, will you translate for the Maltese." She summoned him closer. "Please, so that I don't need to shout."

Flustered, the man stared at her over the heads of her new audience. From the corner of her eye, she glimpsed Riccardo behind the door. Moishe was near.

Movement on the roof near the sniper's nest, and a stranger scowled over the edge, gripping a shiny wrench as he scanned the piazza.

Jacinta waited expectantly, then said to her audience, "Please, applause for the Grand Master." She started clapping, breaking off to wave him closer again. Some of the audience beckoned also, eager to bring together two singular figures, the knight, and the idea of this famous prisoner.

Scowling fiercely, the knight marched toward her. "What are you doing? Are you a docent here?"

"Va bene," she said, "we begin. How many of you have already visited the Co-cathedral, in Valletta?" She raised a hand to indicate how they should reply, and a number of hands rose. "Then you have seen the dramatic painting there of—"

"You can't come here to look for tips," the knight said, but he glanced back to the grate, over to the chapel, his awkward expressions caught at every moment by the eager tourists all around them.

The glass doors rattled, Moishe on the inside, jerking on the handle. Half of the tourists startled, while a few swiveled their cameras that way, for a glimpse inside the closed chapel.

Moishe stood to his full height, his glance sliding away from her.

A dark form parted from the corner opposite, and she tensed, then recognized Nick as he dropped swiftly to open the grate. Casey appeared at the top of the ladder, keeping low.

The glass doors shattered.

Chapter Sixty-Nine

Moishe surged through the broken door. He'd concealed his gun, but still, tourists screamed and stumbled.

Jacinta called out, "This way, this way!" trying to turn them toward the big arch, the fastest exit.

Her strong presence and insistent voice called them onward, rallying the tourists and shepherding them, keeping them safe. They raced around her, trained by so many dangers, so many terrible things, to fear anything sudden and seek an authority to direct and guide them. Sheep again, between the wolves.

The Grand Master turned about, flustered by the speed and urgency of everything that happened around him. A man of faith, who attempted to help by trapping their enemy, but not really a man of action.

Casey and his man sprang from the prison door and split up immediately. The Black man ran down the ramp toward the main entrance. One of Moishe's men would be there. The other, on the roof held the evidence of the decoy "sniper" that had distracted them. That man flashed his gun, a question. But Moishe needed what Casey had. He ran toward his adversary.

Moishe needed his mind or his evidence. Apart from his ability to think and to speak, Casey's bodily integrity was of no matter. The man needn't pass through this encounter intact.

Lunging for a windowsill, Casey leaped upward, angling for the low roofline over the portico. Moishe lunged as well, grabbing his foot and hauling down. The man's hands slipped and he fell backward. Moishe wrapped an arm around his core, trying to control his center of balance.

Changing tactics in an instant, Casey kicked off from the structure, tipping them both.

They landed hard atop the metal grill closing the prison. Moishe doggedly clung to his target, rapping him against the flag stones. Casey gasped.

With a roll, Moishe pinned him down. "What did you find? Quickly, if you want to live."

Dark eyes met his. The man flailed at the ground—no, he grabbed something lying nearby.

Moishe flung up his arm up, partially blocking the blow. A heavy canvas tool kit slammed into him. Knocking this aside, Moishe grabbed the man's arm, digging in his powerful fingers, preventing a repeat blow.

Left-handed, Casey wielded a slice of shimmering darkness. He carved across Moishe's jaw toward his throat, aiming for a vein with a broken mirror.

Moishe twisted away, grinding his knee into the man's gut. Again, the mirror came at him, this time gouging his ankle.

Moishe heaved himself up to avoid losing a tendon. He kept his grip on Casey's right arm, dragging him to his feet. Instead of pulling away, Casey rushed toward him. Blood already streamed from Moishe's face. He pivoted, trying to gain leverage to pop the man's shoulder. Instead, Casey curled into Moishe's chest in a move Moishe had seen before only on a dance floor.

Moishe groped for the man's throat, then glass sliced into his wrist, laying it open. His hand jerked, and Casey pulled free, slamming the tool kit across his temple to make good his escape.

Staggered and bloody, Moishe threw open his coat and drew his gun.

He should have known Casey would give up nothing. That word again. Ironic. Before Moishe could squeeze his trigger, a bullet punched through his coat not far from his chest.

Only his uncontrolled movement saved him from stepping into the shot. He assumed Casey's partner had gone for the exit. Again, he'd been mistaken. Moishe's assumptions today might be the death of him.

Moishe let himself drop, then dove toward the arch. From the roof above, his man shot back, forcing the sniper to divide his attention.

The gashes on Moishe's face and arm stung with cold fire. Too much blood.

Chapter Seventy

Jacinta stumbled in the wake of the fleeing tourists as they ran through the arch toward safety, or at least, away from danger. She heard the slam, scuffle and desperate breaths of a fight behind her. Casey and Moishe, it must be.

Aside from a few moments on the football field, Jacinta's experience of brawling was mostly external: high school battles or the sort of liquor-fueled beatings that sometimes broke out in the streets of Naples. When kids and drunks fought, they shouted, grunted, cursed and sometimes taunted, a vocal performance as much as a physical one. This fight had no soundtrack but the impact of bodies against stone and each other, save when Moishe demanded to know what he'd found.

Distract Moishe with the warning, then stay alert, those had been her only instructions, so she, too, raced for safety. When they evacuated, she, too, could be gone among them and reunite—

"Signora!" With a swirl of his cape, the knight appeared before her, sword in hand.

Jacinta flung up her own hands, empty, and jumped back from the blade. "What are you doing?"

They stood in the shaded passage between the piazza and a broad patio for gun emplacements. The last of the real tourists, accumulating others as they moved, rushed the stairs and interior doors to vanish.

"What have you done? You do not work here, I would know it."

"I'm an art historian," she blurted. "I give lectures, lead tours, that's all!" She never planned to use her skill to save a man's life.

The Grand Master pressed closer, and she bumped into the stone wall as his sword-tip aimed at her throat. "Not here. Not for the Fort Sant'Angelo, nor for Malta, I think."

"You're with them, aren't you," she whispered, as if dropping her voice would save her from a skewering.

"The question, Jacinta, is who are you with?" Riccardo strolled into view, his clothes rumpled, but his eyes keen. He carried a small pistol, but aimed at the ground.

"Grazie a Dio you're here," she said. "This man is crazy."

The Grand Master twitched his gaze toward Riccardo. "I live in service to my faith. That is all."

Behind them, gunshots echoed from the stone. All three ducked their heads, and Riccardo caught both of the others around the waist. "Move, move!"

With little need for his urging, they ran down the slope and around the corner from the piazza. Tables and chairs rolled on the paving in the wake of the tourists' speedy departure, and Riccardo immediately commandeered one of the tables, propping it to face the arch, and tugging Jacinta toward it. Should she go back? How could she now extricate herself from these men to return to the Americans?

"We should see—" the Grand Master began, still standing. He broke off, his beard parting with a gasp, then he crossed himself.

Jacinta popped her head from behind the cover, glancing up in the direction they'd come.

A bloody apparition stumbled down the slope. Moishe clutched his left arm tight to his chest, wrapping and supporting it with his right. Blood streamed down the side of his face. When his coat flapped open in his hurried descent, it showed a clean, round hole straight through.

"Moishe!" Riccardo held his gun at the ready, scanning the roof and arch behind.

The big man angled toward them, weaving like one of those drunks. How much blood had he already lost? Was he shot? He looked, for once, not distant or strong, but haggard and humble. He had no living family, he said. He'd seen his best friend die.

Jacinta pushed up from her hiding place and ran toward him. She pulled the scarf from her neck. "Where are you hurt? Are you hit? The bullet?"

His eyes grew wide at the sight of her, then he swayed. His knees buckled and she caught his elbow, easing him toward the ground. As his arms parted, she saw the blood oozing into his palm, his shirt and jacket cuffs already saturated. "Your coat. Take it off. We have to see to your arm."

He shook his head, blood sprinkling from his gouged jaw. "I can't. My guns. The guards are coming."

His voice came in little pants of breath.

"Then we have to get out of here," Riccardo insisted. He emerged from the table, standing over them with his gun held close, a guardian.

The Grand Master's cape fluttered as he joined them. "We can go the same way as before. I have the key."

"He can't go anywhere like this, and if he loses more blood, we can't carry him," Jacinta snapped. She guided his arm toward her and started wrapping it tightly with her scarf. "We must do better."

"We," he murmured, their heads close together as she worked. "Twice now, you said, 'we.'" He swallowed, his breath heating her face. "Are you returning then?" Another gasp, then, "please."

"You are just after what I know." She took the elastic headband from her hair and wound it twice, slipping it over his large hand and down to hold the makeshift bandage.

He laughed, a soft, deep chuckle of warmth. "Should a man not want you for your mind?"

She twitched back from him, and his eyes flickered shut and open again, damp and dark. "Forgive me," he said. "It is not the time of humor."

Sirens rose in the distance, and the loudspeakers at the corner of the building barked instructions in a language she didn't understand.

"Come, come," the Grand Master urged, his sword replaced, his gloved hand beckoning.

"Can you rise?" Riccardo already gripped Moishe's elbow, tugging on him, but he was not so easy to steer as Jacinta had been, like a tugboat at harbor trying to steer a cargo vessel to a sound berth.

"It's all right," Moishe said, working to get his feet under him. "I know things, too." His foot skewed, and he nearly fell beside her.

Jacinta caught him around his back, rising, righting him at the same moment. He knew things. Like what? What new evidence might he have that the Americans did not? More than this, he had the painting. He knew she wanted it. Trust was a tool. Truth was a tool. Vulnerability and violence: both were weapons and tools. But she could see the blood welling from his injuries. This was no invention, no mere convenience to get her back on his team.

Keeping close to his side, Jacinta hurried with them through a locked grill in the floor and down a set of stone stairs to a lower level.

The Grand Master brought them to the dockside, waving them onto a small cabin-style motor launch. Riccardo stepped in, and Moishe stumbled after him, Jacinta supporting his arm to stabilize him as he clambered into the boat, then Riccardo took over, his gun out of view, Moishe leaning, reaching back.

The strong light of morning illuminated his figure and his bloody, beseeching hand. Dark clothes and an air of deep emotion. She stood a moment, the viewer to this new tableau, chiaroscuro in the broad daylight.

Taking his hand, she stepped inside.

Chapter Seventy-One

Winded, Grant tapped Nick who kept him covered as they departed from the piazza by the main passage way. Spotting a rest room, he signaled again, and they slipped inside just as heavier treads raced from the other direction. The official response was incoming.

Grant shifted a trash can to barricade the door temporarily as he stripped out of his coverall and stuffed it into the can. Nick crossed to the counter, breaking down his skeleton rifle. A fire alarm started, flashing and wailing. Maybe not the best thing to do if you've got an active shooter situation, but it would work in their favor for sure.

Most of Moishe's blood went with the outfit, but Grant washed his hands and forearms, then his face. Scrapes stung and his ribs felt bruised from Moishe's crushing embrace. Beneath the coverall, he wore a long-sleeved jersey for the Italian National soccer team and a pair of shorts.

"You okay?" Nick met his eye in the mirror.

Grant gave a nod. "You?"

"A-and-O. Last saw Jacinta fleeing with the tourists."

"Hope she's okay. That was some A-plus improv on her part."

More footsteps echoed in the hall, but with less hurry. A voice issued single, brisk commands. Nick snapped the magnetic cover back over his concealed weapon, and sank down to the floor, giving a quick signal as he rested his back against the wall. Victim scenario. Grant could oblige.

Someone banged on the door, then tried to push it open, shouting, "Iftah il-bieb!"

"Who's there?" Grant shouted back, putting a little fear in his voice.

"Polizia," the voice responded.

Figured.

"Thank God! Did you get the guy?" Grant pushed the trash can out of the way and retreated to Nick's side, placing a protective hand on his shoulder.

A large officer in a Kevlar vest, a rifle in his hand stepped through, glancing quickly around and into the stalls, then finally down at Nick and up to Grant. "What did you see?"

"There was a guy with a sword, like some kind of re-enactor, I guess? And then one of the docents started talking about the history of the knights and some guy who was kept in the prison. Is that right?"

"Something like that," Nick confirmed. He was massaging his thigh, wincing, leaving his prosthetic partially exposed at the ankle.

"We were starting to go over there—my friend can't move real fast—then somebody on the roof started shooting. I think he broke the chapel doors, there was glass everywhere."

The police officer nodded absently. In the corridor other voices rumbled. Everything Grant said tracked with the evidence. Thanks to the knight and Jacinta, everybody was looking the other way when Nick had fired his own shots.

"Do you need a doctor?" the officer asked.

Nick sighed. "I don't think so. I just need to head back to the hotel and take this thing off."

The officer nodded again. "Leave your information by the gate, there's a person."

"Thanks," Grant said. "Did anybody get hurt?"

The man's glance flicked away. "I can't say that."

Blood spatter, no bodies. Best outcome for the people on the ground, big headaches for the investigators.

"Well, I hope you get the guy." Grant turned away, helping Nick to his feet as his friend rose with elaborate care. If he wanted to, Nick could've kicked the officer back out the door, run to the entrance and leapt the turnstile, but for now, he played the helpless crip. Sometimes the best escape unfolded slowly.

The two of them made their way to the turnstile, supplying the name of a hotel they'd passed on the way in, telling the woman with the clipboard they'd be staying three days, then Grant pulled the guard's keyring from his pocket.

"I found these in the hall."

She thanked him, placing the keys to one side. A few other people moved down the narrow pedestrian bridge. A small lagoon opened to their right, to the left, the bay enclosed a marina full of small boats. Sunlight danced from the water, dazzling, and Grant pulled out a pair of sunglasses.

When they'd put a little distance between them and the entrance, Grant took out his phone and dialed Jacinta. No answer. Hell.

He left no message. Had he just lost another team member? Was it better to know his friends were critically hurt, but at least in the hospital, or to have no intel either way?

"She'll be okay. Either she's with the tourists and she'll get processed and released with everyone else," Nick said, and Grant finished the thought, "Or she's with them, and they'll want her alive. Question is, was she willing, or not?"

His phone vibrated, and Grant plucked it out. Jacinta was alive and able to respond...but what was he supposed to make of the message? On the screen, she had sent a single word. :*Ear.*

"What does that mean?"

Grant shook his head. It seemed too deliberate to be mis-typed, but too random to carry much meaning. "Maybe she got cut off from responding, and hit send before she finished."

"Could be some kind of auto-correct mistake."

"Given how she stepped up with that tour guide routine, I think it's deliberate." He slipped the phone away as they reached the end of the narrow bridge. A phalanx of emergency responders, gawkers, family members, and a couple of reporters clustered around the end of the bridge.

"Signori! Vi prego!" One of them called out, waving toward Grant and beckoning a cameraman forward.

Another man dodged out of their way, ducking his head as he shuffled back into the crowd.

"That guy was inside," Nick muttered. "Saw him on the way to my position."

"Copy that." Grant continued to "assist" Nick inside the cordon set up by the local police. At the back of the throng, the guy Nick noticed shifted his position.

They proceeded at their careful pace, assuring the attending officers they had signed out with the gate, and giving the same story they'd given to the other team, with the added detail of finding the keys in the hall.

As they departed the museum grounds, Grant made the guy tracking them, catching a glimpse down an alley, then in a shop window. Did they still want him alive? Moishe hadn't been fighting to kill a little while ago.

The city streets had gone silent save for the urgent response at the tip of the peninsula housing the fort, one of several fingers of land separating deep bays. Everyone else hunkered down in fear, or in front of their newsfeed. Made it harder to ditch somebody in a crowd, but the narrow medieval streets could play to their objectives.

"Looking for a double-back, you're the decoy," Grant murmured.

"Copy," Nick replied.

Spotting a corner shop, with entrances on both streets, Grant steered them in that direction. A shopkeeper inside, an older woman with a big smile, gave them a hearty greeting in several languages, and they started down the aisles of fine foods. After a few minutes,

Nick took the carrier bag containing a few items and headed out the opposite door while Grant became very interested in local wines, and finally selected a bottle that fit nicely in his hand. Would've gone for a hardware shop, but those were in short supply in the tourist district.

Close by the door, near a large stack of crated goodies, Grant took a pause, dropping down to check his shoelaces.

A figure moved by the window, walking slow, then continued past and made the turn, scanning the shop. Taking his wine, Grant slipped out the door and followed, moving fast and silent. Just down the side street, the man paused in a covered doorway. Grant caught up, snatching the man's elbow as he slipped a hand into his coat.

"Buon giorno. Nice day for a walk by the harbor."

The guy spun about, a knife sliding into his other hand. He thrust toward Grant's core.

Grant slammed the wine bottle into his face. Staggered, the assailant stumbled back, shaking glass, wine and blood from his face. His nose bled profusely and a gouge marred his cheek.

Jabbing toward his arm with the broken bottle, Grant pressed forward, forcing the man to dodge another nasty cut. Grant kicked the back of the man's knee, tipping him sidelong.

With a twist and a lunge, the man broke away. He stumbled a few steps, then whirled, reaching again for his gun, but Grant was already on him, ramming a shoulder into his chest that sent him sprawling to the street.

"Hey, hey!" the shopkeeper leaned out her door.

"He has a gun!" Grant shouted back, and the woman retreated.

Grant kicked the guy in the ribs. The man slashed toward him with his knife, and fumbled the gun from its holster. Grant stomped his wrist as the door behind them opened again with a cheery jingle. The downed man's eyes flared as the shopkeeper emerged with a shotgun, both barrels aimed at the assailant's head.

Grant averted his gaze as the guy swiped his knife across his own throat.

The shopkeeper paled and drew back. Her weapon slipped as she covered her mouth with one hand.

Grant dropped his wine bottle, and caught the woman before she fainted. She accepted his help to sit on the bench outside her shop, easing the shotgun to rest beside her as the fallen man bled out in the street. No way Grant got used to that.

Nick should've been there by now, at the end of the side street at least. Where the Hell was he?

"I have to find my friend," he told her, earning a bob of the head.

He backed away from her, then skirted the body and raced down the street. Visions of another friend bleeding out, or falling ill, of Nick convulsing in the street or dying in the darkness of some blind alley.

Sunlight dazzled his eyes at the end of the street, and he heard Nick's voice say, "I'm sorry."

Chapter Seventy-Two

Moishe regarded Jacinta across the narrow aisle of the small plane. "You might have saved my life, Jacinta."

She smiled nervously, glancing out the window again. "Where are we going?"

"To the painting. It's not safe to be on Malta for now. By any chance, do you know what he found down there? In the prison?"

She wet her lips, and her eyes narrowed just a little. He could almost read the considerations on her face. Would she lie? What did she fear more? She had intervened, first for Casey, then for himself. Conflicted loyalties caused so much pain.

"Bacchus," she said, facing him fully. "You know this name? He is one of Caravaggio's favorite subjects I think."

"Ah, yes." Moishe let his face soften. He cradled his bandaged arm in his lap. They had paused at the airport long enough to peel back the blood-soaked sleeves and stitch up the gash, wrapping it with clean bandages and consigning Jacinta's scarf to the garbage. When it healed, he would be left with the classic suicide scar. His second of the kind.

His arm throbbed. His face, too, burned with pain every time he moved or smiled. Fortunately, this wasn't often, but he let it happen.

He gave his body freedom to reveal its hurt, and every time won the reward of Jacinta's sympathy. Butterfly bandages held that wound. Not adequate for the best healing, but then, could his face be more forbidding? Soon enough, he would be done with it.

"I've seen his sick self-portrait, as the god. It was among the first of his works I've seen." Moishe blew out a breath, shifting as if in discomfort. "What was your first Caravaggio, do you recall?"

"Ha! Certo. It was the *Seven Acts of Mercy*, at the Misericordia in Naples. I was a child and with my family." She grew briefly wistful, then plunged ahead, "Such a very strange work."

"But you were captivated."

From his position sprawled across the joined seats behind them, Riccardo snored softly. Or at least, he seemed to.

"There was a woman's breast and a dead man's feet. Angels might fall from the sky. What child could be unmoved by these things?"

"But not all of them would pursue Caravaggio as their career, I think. Have you seen his works at Messina?"

She shook her head, then brightened as the plane banked and began to descend. She looked to the window. "We're going to Sicily?"

"I have a place there. Not so well organized as the workshop in Rome, but good enough, I hope. There is only one room suitable for your task, but we will manage. Look, can you see the airport yet?" He leaned with her, moving into her space only as she leaned to the window. His hand shifted to rest on the edge of her seat, supporting himself, restraining his presence—or so it would seem. She flicked him barely a glance, moving a little closer to the window.

"It looks terribly dry, doesn't it. The groves, and all," he murmured.

His hand slipped into her cardigan pocket and out with her phone. At least, the phone she had been using. Riccardo's hand reached Moishe's to receive it, then he retreated back to his seat.

"You've been to Sicily, of course, Jacinta?"

"Not for a long time." She kept her gaze out the window, her voice dropping a little. Did she know she did that?

"Whereabouts? Palermo? Catania? Syracuse? Maybe you've

already been to Messina?" He spoke slowly, unspooling the names of the cities, watching the pulse at her throat. Much easier without the scarf. Syracuse got the most reaction.

"It was a tour, with the museum."

"It's a pity about the *Nativity*, eh? The one from Palermo."

"Tragic."

"I saw it once. Very impressive." He leaned back in his chair, gazing skyward.

"Perdonami, but you don't seem old enough to have seen this." She sounded brittle all of a sudden. Nestling her back toward the window, she watched him keenly now. "The painting is stolen in 1969."

By the man he used to work for. Had he given himself away? Pity he couldn't trust her, or she could see it, too. Moishe let his eyes slide shut, furrowing his brow. "Perhaps I have confused it with something else. Forgive me. The pain."

"You shouldn't talk so much," she told him.

"It's true." For a moment, he kept silent, then let his eyes flicker open again. "Caravaggio was in Syracuse, wasn't he. After he escaped the prison at Malta."

"He had friends there." She folded her arms, her face unnaturally still. Ah, Jacinta, even when she wished to keep things from him, she only revealed more. Perhaps she, too, thought she would have friends there.

As the plane came in for a landing, something slid on the floor, and Jacinta startled into motion, reaching. "Il telefono!"

"Here." Moishe stuck out his foot as the phone slid back, and it lodged against his shoe, where she quickly snatched it up again and pulled it to her chest.

"Must have fallen out when we banked," Moishe said. "It's not damaged, I hope?" He tried a faint smile. "I still owe you a replacement, I know."

"It's fine." She tucked it back into her cardigan pocket, but didn't let go this time.

Pity that women's clothes always lacked enough pockets. Sadie had a penchant for wearing men's trousers for that very reason, despite the difficulties of finding them in her diminutive size. Moishe suddenly recalled a trip to the commissary where he had complained of the opposite trouble, and Avram, so perfectly proportioned he might have been the model from which the display dummies were made, only laughed at them both.

"Moishe," Jacinta said. "You look sad."

He allowed himself to relax too much. "I thought of my own friends."

"Well, you do have us," Riccardo said warmly from the back seat. "Have I missed anything?"

The wheels touched down, bouncing a little and settling to taxi down the small airstrip.

After they parked, the pilot came to assist Jacinta down from the plane, and Riccardo leaned forward to Moishe, whispering, "The message was ear. That was all. Following a photo he sent of the Bacchus carving from the prison."

Bacchus. She told the truth about that. But why 'ear'? "Syracuse," said Moishe. "Whatever it is, we'll find it there."

"And if our men haven't stopped him, we'll find Casey."

Chapter Seventy-Three

Grant felt the apology like a blow, the words he'd made Nick swear he wouldn't say—if Nick found that he was dying.

His pulse thundered at his ears and every sense grew instantly acute, hearing the man who came out beside him, smelling his sweat. Ready to send his friend's assailant to an early grave if he had to use his bare hands to do it.

Spinning sharply, tensed for battle, Grant instead found himself swept up into Nick's hard, fast embrace.

"I'm sorry I'm sorry I'm sorry. I was not tweaking you, Chief. All I meant to say was that I'm sorry I was late that's it, that's all."

Back on his own feet, Grant braced his fingers on his friend's chest, looking into the face of stricken sincerity. "Got it. When I can breathe again, I'm gonna beat the hell out of you, missing leg or no, you hear me?"

Nick spread his hands, shoulder height as if ready for Grant to make good on the threat. "Absolutely. I earned that one. I didn't even think about it. No way I would joke like that with you."

Then he cracked a grin, in spite of the scraped chin and scuffed clothes that showed he'd been fighting. "Your face, though. Wish Gooney coulda seen it."

Grant breathed a laugh. "Me, too. You ever imagine, when I first joined the Unit, that either of us would miss him?"

"Absolutely not." Nick posed as if sighting down a rifle. "More than once I might've taken that shot if he happened into my sights."

Grant cuffed him lightly. Sirens behind. Both men started moving.

"Car's this way," Nick said. They walked down toward the next cross street, and Nick indicated a dark patch of liquid along the sea wall. Surf crashed down below. "You were right. Two of them."

Grant glanced over and saw the body hung up on the rocks two stories down, out of reach of the waves. "Your man went overboard."

A nod. "He had some help. Yours?"

"Dead drunk. I picked up a bottle of wine that didn't agree with him."

They hesitated as a police car raced down the main road and stopped at the junction, then they sprinted across the gap before the police started looking for witnesses. Good news was, two shooters reported at the museum, and two bodies about to be discovered, both of them armed. Open and shut case...unless they questioned the ballistic evidence or tried to figure out a motive for the Fort Sant' Angelo assault and how its aftermath left only the shooters dead.

Squeezed into the public car park, their rental awaited with Jacinta's laptop still inside along with their meager belongings. Some day, they'd have to do a full re-stock.

"Airport?" Nick inquired, and Grant affirmed, already pulling up the documents on Jacinta's machine. What did they have? A carving of Bacchus in the prison, illuminated by Del Monte's mirror. Jacinta's single word, "ear."

He uploaded the pictures he'd taken at the fort. Still had part of the mirror he'd retrieved from the prison floor and subsequently used to fend off Moishe's attack. Nothing obvious in the pictures, though the beam of light did, indeed seem to pinpoint the ear of the odd carving.

He pulled up a browser, and almost immediately found a hit. The Ear of Dionysus. "How do you feel about Sicily?"

"Makes me sorry we don't know Jacinta's family a little better."

"Maybe it's better if we don't." Opening a second tab, Grant searched for flights and calculated the odds they'd have a welcoming committee on the other end.

Chapter Seventy-Four

Sicily

Jacinta's heart rose at the thought of seeing the painting again. Moishe owned a vintage farmhouse in the hills above Catania, not so far from the airport, or so he said. Ancient olive groves and ranks of orange trees spread through the arid landscape marked by sandstone buildings and tumble-down stone walls and fences. An automatic gate guarded the end of the driveway, and their silent driver made the turn smoothly.

Passing through the fence topped with razor wire echoed with a few days from her childhood, visits paid to distant relatives on the island, being sent to play with the cousins while her father conducted business, as she now knew. A pleasant family getaway, she and her brother hiding among the trees and ruins, learning to shoot by targeting empty bottles on a stone wall, a skill she'd never employed since, but suddenly knew might be needed. Did her brother still love her, as Casey implied? And, on a different concern, would Casey understand her message?

In front of the building, their sedan parked alongside a farm truck still loaded with a jumble of farm tools, and Angelica emerged from the door with a broad smile as they got out of the car. "Buon giorno! It's good to see you again. Here, the painting is settled, and waiting for you." Exactly as if they'd known she would come.

"Grazie."

Angelica's gaze rose to Moishe's face and she went rigid, then crossed herself. "Do you need a doctor?"

"No, thank you." He strode past both of them into the house, and Jacinta followed, curious now, to see the place that such a man called home.

Whitewashed walls and spare furnishings greeted her. Updated windows held in the chill of air conditioning, an uncommon luxury. Those echoes from her youth grew louder, especially as she looked out the picture window over the sofa and saw the avenue of trees leading to a grand house. She turned to ask Moishe about the neighbors, a light-hearted question that might still give some insight. He'd already vanished to some other part of the interior. No crosses, nor any other religious artifacts embellished the walls or tables.

"This way, Signorina. You'll want to see the work," Angelica prompted.

"Go ahead," Riccardo echoed. "We'll likely head out for lunch soon, but I know you want to get re-acquainted."

His manner seemed stiff, too cheerful, but she obeyed, following the maid down a short hall. One room suitable, Moishe had told her. A bedroom, as it transpired, where Moishe worked to remove a few items to a suitcase. His bedroom, it must be, just as sparely furnished as the rest, save for the over-sized bed. Well, over-sized for one person, but likely what he required. The easel and covered painting already stood in the middle of the room, making it harder for him to maneuver as he packed what he needed.

"Me dispiace," Angelica said. "We should have waited."

Moishe shook his head, though it must hurt.

A single framed photograph hung on the wall where someone lying in bed could see it, but the painting now dominated along with a few boxes of tools and chemicals for her trade. Jacinta stepped out of the way against the window, giving herself a view of the photograph as Moishe moved by. Her throat felt dry, as if this were a clandestine act, spying on the sole personal item in his entire house.

The photo showed three people, all of them grinning, the two men wearing Jewish skullcaps. The man on one end squatted to bring his head in line with the others, while the woman at the far end stood on tip-toe. In the middle, a handsome young man with vivid blue eyes. From their clothing, she guessed it had been a wedding. Moishe, with his friends—and one of them she'd seen before, in one of the follow-up photos of Dom's Nazi cache. Sadie, wasn't it. Or D.A. as they called her, but much younger. Happier. Moishe looked happy, too, an idea Jacinta found incongruous.

"Excuse me." Moishe reached out to remove the photo and tuck it face-down on top of the clothes as he clicked the case shut.

"This should not kick you from your room," Jacinta protested. "I can work only when you aren't—"

"It's fine. I'll use a spare room. I'll see you for lunch." He tucked the case under his arm, almost cradling it as he departed.

Lunch took on an ominous tone, for reasons she could not quite name. Left alone once more with the painting—her painting, she couldn't help but think.

Jacinta moved a few items, clearing her stool, and starting to arrange the space as it should be, though the work table here was much smaller. As he said, it would do. How long would she even be here? Long enough to find out what else he knew, what other clues they possessed which might point the way to the hidden Menorah. Curious that he pursued it for reasons other than his own faith, and almost all the people he worked with, from what she could tell, were Christians. Va bene. That was not her mystery.

After adjusting the blinds to prevent sunlight from streaming in on the masterpiece, Jacinta drew back the cover from the painting, revealing its full glory once more. Her hand twitched to cross herself. Their brief parting made the work all the more amazing.

"Ciao, Zacariah! Ciao, Gabriel!" She assumed the name of the angel, God's messenger.

Finding her cleaning solution and cotton swabs, Jacinta settled in front of the work, preparing to—a small section of the work caught her eye, a section she hadn't been working on. In that area, the patina of age had already been removed. Her gut tightened and her jaw clenched. Who dared, without proper training or supervision?

Then the image itself drew her closer. From the red-brown ground of the painting—it looked even more like dried blood to her after the morning's events—a pale shape emerged, with a distinctive darkness at its heart. A tree loomed, silvery wood gaping around a strangely shaped black hollow. Unmistakable. Caravaggio painted this tree before, at least four times. Her had shook as she cleaned around it, widening the area, revealing more, and nothing at all. The tree stood among ordinary vegetation, as if it were just part of the landscape in a distant vision of the past or the future.

That tree meant everything, but how on earth could they find a single olive tree in a nation renowned for its olives? She knew exactly what it looked like, and had no idea what to do next.

Chapter Seventy-Five

"She sent a picture," Riccardo reported. "An image of that section of the painting you worked on. Looks like she's expanding the restoration from there."

"She gave them no location, no conversation?"

"Nothing so far."

So she updated the Americans on the progress she was making, and the fact she said nothing suggested a furtive quality to her contact, just as the previous contact consisted of the single word.

Moishe nodded, but focused on the work in front of him. He used a fine tissue to repair the tear he'd made in Galileo's telescope, the lens back in place.

"Ready for the word?" Riccardo asked. "This is fascinating."

Holding the tissue down with the butt of a knife, Moishe waited for the glue to dry. Fascinating. "Go on."

Riccardo began to read from the screen in front of him, summarizing his research. The Orecchio di Dionisio, the Ear of Dionysius, stood in the archeology park at Syracuse, among the more famous Greek ruins, the amphitheater and nymphaeum, all of those familiar elements of so-called civilization quarried from local stone. The Ear stood testament to that effort, a tall cave hollowed from the quarry itself and named for its shape by none other than Caravaggio himself on a visit to the area with a scholar-friend following his flight from Malta. The tale didn't end with the naming, however.

If this article could be believed, the acoustics of the place meant that voices deep within the cave could be heard clearly on the outside, and some claimed that the governor Dionysius kept his prisoners inside, either so that he could hear their whispers and learn valuable information, or so that their tortured screams echoed to the surrounding countryside as a warning to others. The story appeared to be apocryphal, the Baroque-era equivalent of an urban legend also created by Caravaggio, in one of his well-known dramatic outbursts.

Moishe would not have liked the man at all. Too wild, too fierce and uncontrolled of action. He'd been like that once. Literally, once.

"Apparently," Riccardo finished, "Caravaggio liked the site well enough that he used it as the backdrop in his Burial of Santa Lucia. Look."

A glance at the screen showed a gloomy atmosphere consistent with the artist's other work, and a crowd of mourners and on-lookers gathered to watch the young martyr laid in her grave. "That one's Caravaggio, his self-portrait." Riccardo pointed to a troubled face looking away.

Satisfied the repair had taken, Moishe looked again at the strange inscription on the telescope. Here, then, they would view another ear. The telescope may yet yield something. He re-wrapped it. At this point, he would take any advantage over Casey. Rising, Moishe said, "Position our advance party."

He withdrew from the little office Riccardo occupied and walked through the living room, waving Angelica to peace when she moved as if to inquire something.

Down the short, dark hall to his bedroom, her work room. His men placed the painting according to his instructions, with the easel facing the hall, and he stood now at a distance, able to see over her shoulder. Indeed, she worked to clean the area between his small patch, the forest or grove, and the work she had previously done, the man and the bull. Given their placement, he began to wonder if it weren't a minotaur reference and not astrological at all.

"Was my work acceptable?"

She flinched and plucked an earbud free, tapping off the phone in her pocket. At last, having covered for her instant fear, she faced him with a smile. Brave girl. "I should have known this was you, your work. Si, you've done well."

"Only because I watched you work that time, and you provided the solution—" he noticed her eyes flare, just a tiny bit—"the cleaning solution, that is."

She chuckled awkwardly.

"I realize it's a bit early for lunch, but we have a stop to make before then. Are you ready?"

"Si,certo." She screwed the lid back on her cleaning solution and rose. "Where are we going?"

"Syracuse," he said, then, very gently, "I believe you know where."

She fumbled the earbuds and one of them rolled to bump against his foot. When he bent to pick it up, their fingers brushed, and she flinched away, on her knees now, gazing up at him. Her expression so closely mirrored the trepidation and amazement on the painted Zacariah that Moishe wondered if he might sprout wings.

With a shake of her head, she tucked the earbuds away. "I am not sure what you mean."

Moishe smiled and offered his hand, the motion burning along the line of sutures. He showed the wince. "But Jacinta, you gave the clue when you mentioned Bacchus. You thought the answer might be found in his paintings. Our research suggests otherwise." He moved his fingers in a beckoning gesture.

With a longing gaze at the painting, she took his hand and rose to her feet, brushing off her slacks. "The Ear of Dionysius." Her voice sounded bleak and distant. "I thought of this. I should have said."

He offered a benedictory nod. "Next time you have such an insight, I suggest that you share it. " With a careful turn, he showed her to the door. "Last time you had to choose between us, you moved to save me. Your compassion does you credit." What would she do the next time the choice came?

He did not ask. She walked ahead of him, back straight as if walking to her execution.

Chapter Seventy-Six

Syracuse, Sicily

Keeping his shoulders bowed, his back bent, Grant shuffled around the antique pathways. He paused from time to time, picking up litter with the extended grabber he carried as he worked closer to the Ear. He deposited the scraps of wrappers and empty drink containers into a bag hanging from his waist. His own ear now included a Blue tooth clip, hidden by his work cap. Tourists strolled the area, gazing down into the Greek theater and reading the posted list of upcoming events.

For a moment, he yearned to be one of them, with nothing better to do than hear a concert in a theater built two thousand years ago. Maybe one day when he wasn't trying to prevent the apocalypse.

"Hard to say," Nick muttered in his ear as Grant approached his destination. "One guy sleeping on a bench, newspaper on his face, your nine. Couple in flashy gear holding up a camera, not taking any pictures. Could be more."

"Copy." Grant spotted the ones Nick made. "Principals?"

"No sign."

"Might not be. Maybe got smarter."

"Copy that." Nick cleared his throat. "Jamie says stable condition, out of surgery. May need another one."

"Thanks." Still hadn't fulfilled his promise to his fallen man. Maybe today, maybe in the next hour, Moishe, too, would fall, never to rise again.

Grant descended to the lower part of the site, where trees and cacti sprouted among stone spires and caverns left over from the quarrying. Low fences of wooden bars divided the landscaping from the trails. Tourists here lingered in the shade, grateful for the green. Jacinta sent him a picture of a tree or a landscape, buried in the background of the religious scene. Couldn't see the forest for the trees, or maybe vice versa. Shade chilled the sweat along his neck, and he paused to mop his brow and throat, scanning. Nick lay concealed above on the lip of stone that began the plateau of ruins. Didn't know exactly where, but counted on his sniper to have clear line of sight on the Ear as well as a good arc around it. Even he couldn't see through the vegetation, though.

Once again, this particular quest required entering an enclosed space with only one exit. Thankfully, not barred by a small grate over a narrow hole, then held shut by a figure who stepped out of time. Still.

When the next clump of tourists ambled toward the entrance, Grant followed along, pinching the odd piece of debris, but moving a little faster.

Voices from within echoed strangely to the cavern's mouth, a jumble of Italian and other languages, interspersed with giggles as people experimented with the acoustics. One of the tourists he'd just followed trotted back to the entrance, hollering to her people inside, then listening as the voices fell low. Grant moved past her toward a bend in the cave, beyond which it opened out again. He carried his grabber casually. A few people walked past him toward the exit, leaving one young couple kissing and giggling.

He glanced back, and the framing, the grand, rough archway overhead and the murky lighting clicked in his memory.

Grant took a few more steps. From here, he imagined the scene before him, the gravediggers looming over the body of a saint, the arch of darkness to the left, mourners gathered around and to the right. From that side, only one figure looked away: a self-portrait of the artist.

This had to be the place. What was he meant to see? Grant studied the opposite wall, as if looking through the imagined figures of the painting, then to the ground, but this had been leveled with a layer of poured concrete. If the clue had been under the saint's body, it had followed her to the grave.

Someone else entered, walking faster, and Grant moved a little deeper, looking toward the ground, his grabber at the ready, scanning for trash. If he had, indeed, stepped into the painting, he now blocked Caravaggio's view. Grant scanned upward. Small, crisp letters carved into the wall at eye level read "Matthew 7:3."

Footsteps stopped somewhere behind him. Took all of his will not to look back. Instead, he continued his slow progress around the walls, subtly dropping a wrapper and reaching to pick it up.

A voice from behind. "I'm in, yes."

Not Moishe, but it had to be one of his people.

No answer. At least, none that Grant could hear. Keep moving, keep in character. Really wanted to vocalize, to tell Nick what he'd seen and hope that Nick's religious up-bringing, or, failing that, his mobile data plan, could provide the answer. Assuming Grant could even transmit from in here. Take it easy, shuffle along. No reason to care where the other guy looked.

The young couple brushed past, heading for the exit, still giggling. Grant was nearly to the bend, somewhere in the background of the painting among the mourners. An ordinary man, just like the rest of Caravaggio's models.

"Floor's been altered," the voice muttered. "Just a—" a scuff of shoes against the floor, and Grant glanced up, not lifting his head all the way, hoping the hat, together with the gloom, would be enough to obscure his face.

"Yes! Matthew, seven three!" The stranger grew animated. "Ah, the mote in your neighbor's eye and the log in your own."

The beam, Grant had heard. He knew that one, but the speaker's translation made more sense. Jacinta sent him a photo of a landscape, with a very distinctive tree—and that Latin inscription suddenly made sense. Everybody knew that verse, too. *"An eye for an eye."* Except that wasn't what the telescope had told him. Not just an ear for an eye, but this "Ear."

Grant took a pause by the entrance, not yet stepping through. If this were the eye where he would find the "log," if the log even remained where it should be. The cave's mouth framed a slice of the quarry floor, with its pathways and careful planting, then up a rugged slope toward Nick's position, covered with dense growth. Amidst the greenery, he spotted the silverly glint of olive leaves. Could be. Could be one of a hundred, or a thousand other trees.

A familiar giggle rang out not far away. Grant lunged to the side as a bullet spit past his ear.

Chapter Seventy-Seven

Grant rolled, his litter bag crunching under his hip. He snapped off the carabiner that held it and whipped the bag sideways at the woman who had drawn on him with a sound-suppressed pistol. Her companion dropped to a brace position beside her, a little slower on the draw.

Thrusting forward his grabber, Grant snatched the gun by its barrel. Didn't expect that to work, but the startled agent twitched the wrong direction, and the trigger guard hooked around Grant's foam "finger." The sound-suppressor made the weapon forward-heavy and the agent fumbled, trying to master his grip.

The agent lurched backward, snatching the tool and Grant ran toward him before he could regain control. He plowed into the agent, knocking him into the stone of the entrance. The man rebounded, fouling his partner's aim. Taking advantage of the chaos, Grant slid beneath the adjacent wooden bar into the leaf mold, letting the slide carry him to the next trail junction.

Back at the cave, a man in a light blue jacket stood, staring at the forested slope through Galileo's telescope. "Are you there?" he called to the air, presumably to his confederate. Tempting to hang around and hear if he delivered instructions. Instead, Grant took off running.

Another bullet ripped the foliage nearby and smacked into a cactus, splattering him with pulp. Grant dodged left, behind the plantings. Twenty yards, he'd be in the trees.

"A-and-O, Chief?" asked Nick's voice in his ear.

"A-and-O. Target acquired." Hand to the wooden rail, Grant jumped the next low fence and his feet hit the gnarled roots of a thousand years of growth. "They've got eyes up. May need coverage for a speedy getaway."

Moishe's people knew where to look and what to look for. Speed was Grant's only advantage.

Ducking branches, jumping roots, he tracked toward the silvery patch of leaves.

"You want eyes on?" Nick asked.

"Negative. Need you on backup." Yeah, he wanted the extra eyes, somebody else to pinpoint the tree and guide him to it, as Moishe's companion apparently was for him—but not as much as he wanted to live.

The report of Nick's rifle echoed across the quarry and somebody cried out. So much for avoiding notice.

A sudden gap of sunshine forced Grant to slow, glancing around for hidden dangers. The taller trees he'd run through petered out at a section of rougher ground. A rocky clearing interrupted the thickets, with a few twisted trunks topped by silver-green leaves. An olive grove, defended for all of these years.

Grant stumbled over the stones toward the target.

Tufts of brittle grass clung to what little ground they could. The olive tree he searched for reared back from craggy roots dug deep into the porous stone. Grant doubted he could span it with both arms. A thick limb split off down low, reaching almost horizontally before pushing back toward the sky while the main trunk greeted him with an old wound, a hole an arm's length tall and a hand's breadth wide. This tree overlooked Caravaggio's *Ecstasy of Saint Francis*, and kept watch over John the Baptist in the wilderness.

Grant climbed up the slope, dropping to one knee at the base of the ancient tree. A few old beer cans, crushed, burrowed into the bottom of the hollow, and Grant pulled them out, sorry he didn't have his litter bag. He groped into the bottom, but no, anything placed there would've been found by any number of drunk wanderers. Lucky he didn't end up with a needle to the palm, actually. Assuming whatever had been placed here remained to be found. Assuming he wasn't meant to look for graffiti again, some symbol carved into the tree, inside or out. Assuming...or hoping.

Slowing his breathing and working methodically, Grant explored the inside with his hand. Punky wood crumbled. A few insects skittered away. In the trees down below, someone thrashed. He was about to have company, and he'd lost even the grabber he'd used to good effect against the agent down below.

He reached the apex of the hollow, his arm nearly inside of it, no hope of seeing inside, then his fingers brushed metal. Grant's hand closed over the last thing he expected to find.

Chapter Seventy-Eight

"He's here!" Riccardo bleated pointlessly in Moishe's ear.

Of course he was, fool, and he had walked right by. The two agents on the entrance leapt into motion. Moishe rose from the ticket booth and flipped the sign to "chiusa," then shoved out the back. Moishe moved fast along the trail. Somewhere above or in the bushes, he knew Casey's second would be waiting. He would address that issue when he could. For the moment, let confusion reign and trust the next shot would not be aimed at him.

They would expect him to head for the tree, for whatever discovery Casey had made. Instead, he went to the ear, just as most of the tourists scurried away, frightened by what they had seen and heard. Inside the booth, Moishe's dark clothes served for a uniform. Out here, they projected a different air, one more serious, and much more dangerous. He suspected he could tell who was Italian by how quickly they cleared his path, even though his hands were empty. But then, who else would move into danger when everyone else was leaving?

Riccardo stood near the entrance, still gripping the telescope, and the female agent waited with him.

"At our ten o'clock," she said. "My partner's gone after him."

"There seems to be a clearing, a few olive trees," Riccardo reported, offering the telescope.

Moishe moved briskly past him. Mindful of the Black man hiding somewhere. His attention, too, should be with his friend, but Moishe could not risk it being otherwise.

Riccardo pivoted, still holding out the telescope, wearing a quizzical frown.

From the shadows of the Ear, Moishe cleared his throat, changed position, and clapped his hands. The sound lacked projection. Once more, a shift of pose, another clap. Outside, the remaining tourists hesitated, a few glancing back, a few picking up their children and running.

Moishe's voice resonated over the landscape. "Grant Casey. Put down your weapons, and you will not be killed." Not immediately, anyhow.

He waved for Riccardo to scan the area where Casey had disappeared into the trees. Riccardo shook his head.

Moishe sighed. He preferred not to do this, but really, the man had closed off so many options. "Jacinta would prefer for us to work together, don't you think?"

He let the words echo for a long moment, then added, "Why not come with me and ask her?" His words hung in the air, then evaporated under the threat he had no need to voice.

Chapter Seventy-Nine

Like a character from the entirely the wrong mythology, Grant wrapped his hand around what was unmistakably the grip of a sword. He wiggled it back and forth, releasing the wedged blade then pulled, bracing for the blade to come free.

It swept from the darkness of the hollow tree to gleam in the brilliant sunlight. Twenty inches or so from tip to hilt, the short sword showed few signs of its age or its long entombment in the wood. A few tendrils of earth and wood clung to the swept hilt and guard that wrapped his hand.

Across the clearing, the male agent scrambled into view, stopping short at the sight of Grant, newly armed. As he brought up the gun in his hand, Grant charged, brandishing his sword.

"Merda!" The agent jumped away, getting off a shot that flew wide, and almost falling on the uneven surface.

Taking advantage of the high ground, Grant slammed a kick into the man's chest and followed up with a slice across his arm.

His attacker grit his teeth and ducked low, reaching for Grant's ankle.

Grant dug in his heel and knocked loose a stone that smacked the agent and sent his feet skidding. Instinctively, the agent tried to balance by flinging out his hands.

Dropping a knee, Grant thrust toward him, skewering the man's gun arm. The blade resisted a bit—it hadn't been sharpened in far too long, and only the dry climate saved it from ruin—but the power in his blow drove the tip through cloth into flesh.

The agent twisted, trying to free his arm and only carved the blade deeper as he struggled. Blood streaked down the blade. The man's face registered panic and the gun shook loose.

His feet slid out from under him. Grant snatched his off-arm, turning them both so the blade slid free as the man sprawled on his back on the rough slope, gasping against the pain. Better that than find he'd carved through the man's hand.

"Under control?" Nick asked in his ear.

"On it," Grant replied. "Hang tight."

"Helluva toothpick you got there. Red alert: Moishe's on the go."

"Is he incoming?"

"Can't get a bead."

Pinning the agent with his knee, Grant brought the blade to the man's throat, then Moishe's message echoed across the landscape. Yield now, and avoid death—in a battle where Grant already had the upper hand. From their experience at the fort, Moishe had to know Grant wasn't alone.

The next line chilled him in spite of the sun. Jacinta. She may have gone with Moishe willingly. That didn't mean he was above turning her into a hostage.

The downed agent tried to muster a sneer, but his face betrayed him, and he lay sobbing, his trembling arm shaking blood across the stones. Maybe the guy would kill himself if he had the means, like the other ones had. Didn't mean Grant had to hurry the process.

"You have a phone? Un telefono?"

The man's glance flicked away, and Grant patted him down, finding the device and holding it to his captive. "Call him."

Blinking back tears, the man took the phone in his shaky left hand. Grant steadied it as he made the call.

"Pronto?"

The agent's brows pinched, his glance flicking back to Grant as if this were the moment of his doom.

Not Moishe's voice. Grant drew back the phone, keeping his blade under control at the ragged pulse of the downed man. "Put him on. It's Casey."

"I see you got the warning," the other man continued, and Grant interrupted.

"I'm not dealing with you. Put. Him. On."

The other man cleared his throat, then something rustled against the phone, likely as he turned the microphone to his clothing. After a moment, Moishe's voice came on. He echoed a little, but did not resonate across the quarry as before. Must've stepped into another part of the cave.

"Good afternoon, Mr. Casey."

"Does she know you're using her like this? Holding her hostage?"

Moishe cared about her; according to her, anyhow, he wouldn't hurt her.

"I suggest you come and find out."

"I'm not meeting at any place of your choosing."

Moishe's breath suggested laughter. "Just as I am unlikely to attend on your suggestion. What have you found, Mr. Casey?"

"Call me back, and put her on the phone. No meeting unless I know she'll be present and unharmed." Grant clicked off, withdrawing the blade in a smooth motion, then adding a sweep upward, and down: a salute. He scooped the man's gun, just in case.

Chapter Eighty

The driver pulled into a shaded parking spot. He smelled of cigarette smoke, and reminded her too much of her childhood in his demeanor. His local accent heightened the effect of his tidy professional appearance. "Va bene?"

Jacinta hugged her elbows, not answering.

Moishe and Riccardo had stepped out of the vehicle half an hour ago, and Moishe leaned back in saying, "The driver will take you to a good place to wait. And Angelica will be there if you need her."

The maid gave a nod, with that same old smile. She was no maid, or at least, not the sort who just cooked and cleaned house. When Angelica had climbed into the back seat, with the tote bag she always carried, Jacinta caught a glimpse of the pistol under her knitting supplies. Casey's demand echoed in her mind: that she trust none of them, not even him.

Angelica fanned herself with her hand. "Grazie. It's a good spot."

Jacinta reached for the door handle, and both Angelica and the driver faced her. "I just want to step out, that's all. The car is stifling."

"I'll go with you." Angelica slid across the seat, emerging from Jacinta's door, giving her no chance to slip away. Would she? Moishe said her compassion did her credit, when she choose to save him. What choice did she have now? She remained in his power. Even if she tried to run, even if these people had orders not to kill her—what then?

She was a virtual prisoner, at the mercy of these terrible strangers who tried to pass themselves off as her friends.

They'd parked on a side road overlooking the sweep of the hills which led down to the bay harbor at Syracuse, the harbor where Roman ships had attacked the Greek city, slaying even the inventor Archimedes. From here, she saw the modern apartments and houses, ancient ruins and clusters of trees, even groves of olives that gave her pangs. Would they find it? If they did, who would lay hands on the next clue and race to the next destination—dare she hope, the final one? Which side was she on? Both sides needed her. Her, and the painting.

A breeze cooled the afternoon heat as they waited. Angelica set her tote bag by her feet to stretch out her arms. After a moment, the driver, too, got out, hitching his pants a little. He, too, carried a gun. He strolled casually toward the trees. Smoke break, it had to be.

Jacinta's gut tightened and her throat felt dry. He shouldn't smoke near the trees. For more reasons than one...

Jacinta strolled in the same direction while Angelica shook back her hair, showing her face to the sun.

The driver reached into a pocket, his hand emerging with a pack of cigarettes and a lighter. He shook out a cigarette. The moment both hands were occupied. Jacinta burst into motion. She rammed her shoulder into his back, hurling him against the trunk of the nearest umbrella pine.

They hit hard, his head rapping the wood, her body shoving him harder. He staggered and she kicked the back of his knees, dropping him to the ground. Cigarette and lighter fell as he tried to recover, reaching for his gun.

She yanked his jacket open with one hand and grabbed his pistol with the other.

"Don't do this!" Angelica shouted, running closer, then turning back toward her tote bag.

They underestimated Jacinta. People always did.

"Leave your bag alone, Angelica. You won't draw that weapon, not at me." Cocking the trigger, she pressed the gun to the base of the man's skull. "Hug the tree. Both arms. Do it."

"Hush, hush, Signorina, piacere." Angelica patted the air, speaking in a soothing tone. "You don't wish to hurt anybody, surely."

The man hesitated and she pressed the muzzle of the gun against his throat, where the pulse jumped. "Would you prefer to bleed out, or a quick death?" She remembered what Casey said of the man he fought in Naples, the man who leapt into traffic, and wondered if these people would even care, then she whispered, "You will die unshriven."

The man's hands—held up, at first—now clasped around the trunk of the tree.

"Get over here. Tie his hands."

"But, Signorina—"

"Do you know who I am!"

Angelica flinched, her supplicating hands now turned to a shrug. "An art restorer?"

"My father is Antonio Sforza. My brother is Massimo Sforza. My grandfather was called the Scythe of Sicily. You want to defy me, do you want to fight them? Do you want them to come for your families?" Jacinta tugged the tie from the man's throat, holding it out.

Angelica's eyes widened, but the man at the tree trunk whimpered, then said, "Do it. Please just do it. Gli Sforze don't have mercy. Please."

At last, the woman stumbled forward, binding the man's hands with his tie.

"Take his phone and his keys." Jacinta tried to project a sinister air, the kind of thing she'd seen on television more than in her own family. Angelica complied, shaking her head the whole time.

"Get in the driver's seat," Jacinta ordered, taking the seat opposite in the back, where she had a clear line with her weapon.

"The airport, signorina?" Angelica tried, and Jacinta laughed. "No. We go home. His home. There's something I need before I leave."

Moishe approved the choice she made last time. Once more, Jacinta had chosen.

Chapter Eighty-One

Exiting the archaeological park just before the authorities arrived, as usual, Moishe waited through Riccardo's apologies. He couldn't see what Casey had done. With the aid of the telescope, he could tell two people moved around up there, he could tell there were olive trees. One man ran on alone. Casey, given his attitude on the phone. Presumably, Moishe's agent was dead. If not, he'd wish that he were.

Casey had the clue, whatever it was, and Moishe had the leverage to retrieve it from him. Va bene, as the Italians would say.

Moishe made the call to summon his driver as he and his companions walked briskly from the scene. No crimes, save the use of a firearm. No reason for the police to be unduly concerned. Unless they heard what had happened in Malta, in which case a rumor of local terrorist attacks would sweep the area faster than a brush fire in the Sicilian heat.

The phone kept ringing. Slapping it off, Moishe swiveled to look at the woman. "Where's your car?"

Riccardo alerted immediately. "What's the matter?"

At one time, offering greater autonomy to specialized people like

Riccardo seemed wise. Now, Moishe considered the options for shutting the man up.

The woman, on the other hand, simply said, "This way, sir." She turned and led them toward a side street jumbled with rubbish tills and parked vehicles, large and small. The agent's car tucked between a few others. She held out the keys, and Moishe accepted. He drove with careful haste to the overlook where he had directed his driver to wait.

As they approached along the road, he noticed the emptiness of the pull-out, then Angelica's knitting bag resting on the ground.

"What on earth?" Riccardo muttered.

He'd wisely been silent for the ride. He might be an extrovert and a fool, but he did know how to read Moishe's moods, subtle as they tended to be.

What did he read now, Moishe wondered, as memory flamed behind his eyes and he swung the car very wide into the dirt parking area, isolating the knitting bag. Calculations rushed through his mind. It was impossible for Casey to have known where to find her, much less to come here so fast. Yes, Moishe trusted her with her phone this time, building trust in turn, but Riccardo's app would show if she'd made any contact.

Something moved near the trees, and Moishe's gun extended immediately. His driver emerged from the trees, hands up, looking disheveled. His tie dangled from one of his hands and a large bruise swelled the side of his face.

"She has taken the car and my weapon," the man said. "She made Angelica drive. She attacked me from behind—"

"Where did she go?" Riccardo demanded, stepping from the car.

The man's head shook. His shoulders heaved in a shrug as he began to lower his hands. "I don't—"

Moishe fired. The single shot pierced the man's forehead with a spit of fire and a crack of blood. The man's knees buckled. Replacing his gun, Moishe said, "Please retrieve the tote bag."

"Yes, sir." The woman slipped from the back seat and hurried over, scanning the area, then taking the bag.

"Is there still a gun inside?"

The woman nodded.

"I doubt she'd go to the police. She'll likely head for the airport, or the ferry," Riccardo said. "She'll want to get away as fast as possible, I imagine."

"Then she wouldn't need Angelica. Get in, let's go." Moishe put the car in gear as the others raced to jump back inside. He accelerated even before the doors had closed.

They pulled up to the gate, and Moishe punched the code, still in a rush. His tires slewed, the vehicle flinching sideways as they ran over a series of rakes and hoes arrayed across the gravel drive. Air hissed from two punctured tires.

Moishe flung open his door, already striding toward the isolated farm house as the others followed along in his wake.

The truck was gone, the stolen car sitting on four flat tires, its windshield shattered—the hammer still embedded.

Angelica emerged to kneel on the doorstep in front, her hands clasped. Tears seeped down her face. "Jacinta says that she will contact you when she is ready, Signore. I do not think she has so much anger." She looked toward the ruined car.

Anger had not propelled this destruction, no. Every act Jacinta performed worked toward the goal of preventing their pursuit.

"You drove her here. Why did you comply?" Moishe extended his gun.

Angelica crossed herself. "Forgive me, Signore." She swallowed and said, "I am, in fact, afraid to die. In spite of the blessings of the Lord, and the kingdom that awaits." She broke down, crumpling onto the step, sobbing inconsolably.

He preferred not to shed blood on his own threshold. Stepping over her, he replaced his gun. He entered his desolate home, knowing already what he would find. Or what he would not.

In Moishe's room stood the empty easel.

Chapter Eighty-Two

Nick found them a cafe with outdoor seating and a broad view in several directions. They waited for their meal, nursing Limoncello, trying not to look dangerous or suspicious, or like they were waiting to hear from a kidnapper about the state of his victim.

The sword, cleaned of blood, remained wrapped in the back seat of their rental car. Nick leaned back in his chair, sun hat on his head, gazing expansively at their surroundings as he scanned for hostiles. Nobody impersonated casual like Nick...as long as his medication level remained steady and he didn't get triggered to the wrong kind of flashback.

"Shouldn't be taking this long." Grant finished his drink, the lemon soda tingling in his dry throat. Couldn't afford to get dehydrated in an environment like this, not knowing what he might be called on to do next. The phone he'd taken off the agent, the one where he'd called Moishe, remained silent on the table in front of him.

Nick eased his leg out in front of him, his eyes crinkling a little in token of the discomfort of wearing his prosthetic for so many hours in a row, especially through the varied circumstances of the last twenty-four hours. "You think that sword belongs to the man himself? Caravaggio?"

"Might explain why he always went armed, even when it was against the law. Maybe he needed it for something other than self-defense."

"Like it's the key to the secret cave or something."

Nothing about the weapon suggested it had any role beyond skewering one's enemies. Every detail accorded with bladesmithing of the late fifteen hundreds, so far as Grant and the internet could tell. Possibly an expert would see more. Nothing about the guard, pommel or handle shifted, shook, revealed any hidden compartment or code. No names, words or strange symbols inscribed the blade, not even a maker's mark. The patches of corrosion from its long concealment were too small or shallow to hide much. After every examination to be performed without access to a lab, Grant concluded the sword was no more, and no less, than that.

The server delivered big platters of pasta and salad, then departed again. Nick set to, and Grant lifted his fork when his pocket vibrated. Not the agent's phone, his own.

Grant slipped it out, and Nick's chewing slowed as he looked over, expectant. "Gooney's number." The phone in Jacinta's possession, last hew knew. "Hello?"

"Mr. Casey, is this you?"

"Jacinta?"

Nick set down his fork already signaling for the check and a box. Grant seemed destined never to get a sit-down meal in all of Italy.

"Si, Mr. Casey. I am not with Moishe."

"Which is precisely what you'd say if you were, but he had a gun to your head."

She laughed, a ringing delight that caught him fully off-guard. "Certo, Mr. Casey, that's true. I don't know what tools to use to persuade you. I don't have so many tools as you."

In the background, a long, distant horn sounded. Grant stood up immediately, mouthing, "binoculars," to Nick, pointing toward the harbor and sweeping his arm North-east.

"If you're really not with him at the moment, you've got more tools than you let on."

She hesitated, then said, "È vero. Tools I never thought to use. Va bene. What you need to know. I am free. I have the painting. I have not yet decided how and when to reveal myself, but first I need to spend a little time with this. For once, when I find the clue, I will be the one to know it, not you and not him." Her voice grew forceful. "I am nobody's tool. Not any more."

Nick returned from the car, binoculars in hand. "What am I looking for?" he whispered.

"Be careful. He'll be tracking you somehow, Jacinta." On the napkin —cloth napkin, now ruined, sorry about that—Grant wrote "ferry."

"No, already I have gotten rid of the car, and the truck, and now I have another way. No, he does not track me."

"Search the painting when you get a chance. The crate, anything else you brought with you that he might have touched."

She made a sound of exasperation. "And also I don't go home, and I don't go back to where we went together."

"Sounds like you've got a solid plan."

"Si, lo so."

Nick indicated a straight line, past Messina to the north where the boot of Italy rose up in green and gold, mountainous glory, ready to kick Sicily into the goal at the Dardanelles.

"Did he kidnap you, in Malta?"

Another hesitation. "I have to go. I will call you when I choose."

A hundred thoughts flashed, a dozen things to say, every one sounding more patronizing than the one before: Stay safe, be careful? She wasn't stupid, and she'd proven herself both resourceful and resilient. "Thanks for the call."

Seabirds chattered in the background, then she said, "I don't want you to lose another team mate, Mr. Casey." She rang off.

"Looks like a big vessel almost at the mainland," Nick reported. "Probably launched from Catania."

The server appeared, carrying take-out containers.

"Grazie, bene," Nick told him.

"Gotta make another call," Grant said. He collected the agent's phone, though he didn't expect to hear from Moishe any time soon. Leaving Nick to finish up at the table, Grant retreated to the shade on the far side of their car.

Dafne Chadad picked up promptly. "You have reached the Institute for—"

"It's Grant Casey."

She made a little sound of interest, then said, "You were right, Mr. Casey. About Sadie's illness, but the Bubonic Plague is no match for modern medicine. She's already much improved."

Grant found it suddenly hard to swallow. He squinted at the distant ferry boat. "Thanks. You still doubt the rest of what I told you?"

Something tapped softly, like a pen against a desk. "Is this why you called me?"

Deep breath. "I need your help."

"Of course you do. I told you, the Institute has no official position on Moishe the Fist."

"Heard you loud and clear, agent. Are you willing to check for tracking devices?"

The tapping stopped. "You must know I am not at liberty to say if there are such things in the area, Mr. Casey. They might be here for any reason, and for no reason that you need to know about."

Time for a careful application of the truth. "The woman with the purple car. I think he's still tracking her. I just need to know if you've got a signal moving out of Catania toward the mainland, or maybe just hitting the toe."

Tap. Tap. Tap.

"You heard about the shots fired at Malta? That was him, his people. You'll hear about shots fired at Syracuse. Also him."

"And you, Mr. Casey. Don't try to pretend you're not part of the problem."

"I'm trying to be the solution." Calm, clear, direct. The truth was his tool. "Agent Chadad, I know you don't believe me, but consider what happens if I'm right. What if he's raised money to end the world? He gets hold of the symbol that will galvanize the average believer, then he just needs the evidence that the end is near. He can scale up the Black Death and let that loose. Buy a plane and some incendiaries—I'd bet he already has the explosives—rain fire down on whoever he chooses, get everybody fighting everybody, pointing to whoever they believe is the Antichrist, and every Abrahamic religion convinced the End Times are here. What if it happens? There's a lot of things messed up in the world right now, how much worse will it be if he can prove the Biblical predictions are true?"

Tap. Pause. Tap.

He gazed at the sky, deep blue and empty. "Revelations doesn't have to be in your world-view for it to ruin your world. How will you feel if it begins, and you know you did nothing to stop it?"

Softer tapping this time, and he wondered if she were even listening.

"Well," he said. "Nice talking with you. I've got work to do."

"Yes," she said abruptly. "Yes, Mr. Casey, there's a signal. And it's moving north." Then she was gone.

Chapter Eighty-Three

Jacinta cranked the gears in her borrowed car as she pushed the vehicle harder up the hills outside Naples. She couldn't go home, and she'd rather not head to anyplace where either side knew to look for her. Some chance that Nick would think of this particular destination, but she thought it a distant possibility. She took the precaution of removing and discarding the crate when she had secured the vehicle, cringing a little both at giving up evidence of the work's provenance and also at leaving it so exposed. Ordinary blankets must do the job though she winced as she wrapped it. Soon, she promised, it would be safe again.

The old art school friend who loaned her the car understood about her need to transport the client's project, nodding sympathetically as she spun a tale about the inaccurate measurements, and her expectation that she'd be able to fly home with the piece—an ugly contemporary work on which a party guest had spilled...something. Reason enough not to reveal the work to her friend. Her museum job provided the excuse for her haste. Every shadow seemed to conceal a man in black. Would it be Casey or Moishe? She might die either way.

Golden light draped the pastoral scene as Jacinta turned past stone walls into the old farm and parked near the farmhouse door. Where Moishe's house on Sicily had been whitewashed and austere, this one showed every decade and century. Some of that, she knew, was a carefully preserved illusion, creating a photogenic backdrop for weddings, reunions and foreign visitors.

A mastiff lolled in the sun near the stoop, peeling itself up and coming over to wag its tail as she stepped out of the vehicle. She imagined Casey and Nick reacting to this "guard dog" who failed even to bark when a strange car pulled in. Would she ever see her own car again? Who knew. She'd been a graduate student when she acquired the purple car, a splurge to celebrate her internship. Today, she became an art smuggler.

Also a kidnapper, an assailant, and, for perhaps the first time ever, her father's daughter. She hoped it never need happen again. How did one celebrate any of that? With dinner at the grandparents', chiaramente!

The door opened onto a noisy scene with the long table full of tourists all chattering and reaching for wine while Bianca stood at the head of the table, up to her elbows in flour. Class time. Enzo looked up from pouring wine and tottered over, his bow-legged stride accentuated by perhaps a few glasses of his own vintage.

"Jacinta! Welcome. Dom's not here. He was injured in recovering Nazi artifacts stolen in the war. You've heard this?" He waggled the bottle at her. "You want some? I'll get you a glass."

She shook her head. "Grazie, Nonno. I was hoping you had a room for me, actually. There is some work I need to do that I can't at my place. It's a big painting. Too many stairs."

His brow, already knotted with age, furrowed deeper.

"C'e Jacinta?" Bianca called from the end of the table, and all the tourists turned to look. Some of them were Asian, a few European, based on their clothing, and a pair of Canadians—or perhaps Americans who wished people to think them Canadian, so they wore maple leaves on everything. "I tell you my grandson is a famous writer, si? This is his friend! Come, we're making pasta!"

"Grazie, Nonna, but I can't do this today. I have my own work."

"It's a big painting, but we don't have a room, we're full up!" Enzo hollered back.

"Oh, are you an artist?" one of the tourists asked.

Jacinta really didn't want to get into any of this, and began to think of where else to go.

"A restorer, for the museum," Bianca said. She kneaded thoughtfully for a moment then said, "Domenico can't be here a little while. You can use his room, if this works for you?"

"Just a few stairs, and we can help with the painting." Enzo set down the bottle with a thunk. "Yoni, Wong! Give her a hand, come come! Don't worry, the lesson will pause for you, and more time for wine, sì?" He winked, and a few of the guests cheered.

Two of the tourists pushed back, ducking herbs and crockery, then the doorway itself.

"No, really, I can—"

"It's no trouble." One of them popped the hatch on the car, and they slid the wrapped painting out of the trunk. Jacinta picked up the box she had directed Angelica to fill with the most vital supplies.

"This way!" Enzo waved his arm, then waved them past through the kitchen with its giant table, and up the stairs to the converted loft. Crooked stairs and drunken men, who had no idea what they carried.

"Piacere," Jacinta cried, lunging toward them. "Really, I can manage!"

One of the men slipped and the stretcher bar hit the doorway with a solid thump. "Sorry!"

They lugged the painting up the last stairs and deposited it triumphantly on Dom's bed, then thundered away again, promising to let her know when dinner was ready. Given the inebriated state of the people meant to be cooking it, Jacinta had her doubts. Depositing the box she carried on Dom's desk, she shut the door behind them, blessedly alone with her masterpiece.

Immediately, she set to unwrapping it, terrified at what she might find. Dio conceda they hadn't damaged the work. A bit of dust and a few flakes of the gesso used to prime the canvas marked the point of impact. She retrieved a soft brush and gently stroked away the bits. The painting appeared unharmed, and she began to relax, if only a little. She couldn't work with the piece like this, lying down. Also, she'd want to rest at some point. She had been traveling so much, and in so many different ways that the whole day made her quite dizzy.

Taking down a few photos of them as children—Dom wouldn't mind, surely—she made room for the painting to lean against the wall next to the door. That way, nobody coming up the stairs could immediately see it. With the space prepared, she shifted the painting carefully, touching only the back rim of the stretcher bars as she pulled it off the bed toward the new spot.

Something clinked to the floor, shaken loose from the blankets, apparently, but she focused on the painting until it rested securely against the wall. The light here would be terrible. How had Dom ever studied here?

Sitting on the floor at the end of the move, Jacinta reached out for the dull object that had fallen. A coin maybe? Something that had slipped from Dom's pocket to the coverlet—save that the blankets on top were still those that wrapped the painting. She brought it closer, peering at it. Thinner than a coin, and imprinted only on one side, with a little loop pierced at the top.

Taking it to the desk, she flicked on the lamp and studied the thing in her hand. A cast lead medallion commemorating San Carlo Borromeo, a familiar figure to many Italian believers, and in Caravaggio's time, a brand-new saint, renowned for his piety in life and his austere governance over church matters. In fact, Cardinal Del Monte, benefactor of Caravaggio and Galileo alike, had commissioned one of the first churches dedicated to the new saint, less than thirty miles from where she sat.

Chapter Eighty-Four

"Sì, signore, your daughter has taken the ferry, couple of hours ago." The woman behind the window looked sympathetic. "Do you want a ticket? It's for everyone in the car." She gestured toward their vehicle.

"I'll have to talk to her mother."

The woman nodded. "I hope you find her."

"Grazie," Riccardo said, returning to where Moishe waited in the driver's seat, his face carefully turned so he didn't reveal the injury. Nothing undermined a good lie so quickly as a disturbing vision like his face. He held the letter in his hand; the telescope rested in a tote on the back seat. With the spare tires from both cars, they had managed to get one of the vehicles drivable, though the undersized spares would make long distances a trial.

"Well?" Riccardo prompted.

Moishe glanced at the phone in its cradle on the dashboard. "It hasn't moved. The location is behind a shop. In a rubbish till, most likely."

"She's met up with Casey, hasn't she."

Moishe shrugged. "She's smart enough to think of such things on her own." He held out the letter. "Del Monte refers to his other pursuits. We found the telescope and used the mirror. But he says 'pursuits,' more than one."

Taking the document, Riccardo frowned over the lines. "Could be anything." He turned it in his hands. "Or just a flick of the pen in the wrong direction. Perhaps we should pray on it."

"Perhaps we should research it. Forget Jacinta, we stay on Casey."

"They've disabled tracking on that phone." Riccardo's hands clenched together in imitation of prayer, or to stop himself strangling Moishe.

"And Casey has twice now gotten past you and our other people."

Riccardo inhaled, about to speak, then gave a hard shake of his head. "You're right."

"They have two options for getting off the island. One is here. The other is the airport. Casey makes himself invisible, so we look for his friend." Moishe brought up the image sent by one of the dead from Malta. The martyrs, Riccardo would say. Tall, Black, with a slight limp. Much more distinctive than the man beside him, who had transformed from a football fan to a trash-picker to a warrior in the span of hours. Moishe would bet on the airport, unless the men had acquired weapons, maybe from the agent who disappeared at the Ear. At this stage of the operation, Moishe couldn't imagine Casey abandoning a weapon.

To the agent, he said, "Taxi to the airport, call me immediately if you spot them, and pursue, but don't engage. They may lead us to her."

With a nod, the woman let herself out, walking toward the taxi queue.

Moishe slid from the seat of the car. "Take the keys, be ready to board the ferry."

One possibility remained, that they would charter a boat of their own, and while he waited, Moishe searched for options. This late in the day, they'd struggle to make contact with someone and establish a contract, unless they could pay in cash, he doubted a local boat owner would give up his craft to the Americans. Slim chance of that. They might steal a boat, but he imagined Casey might be wary of another water-born encounter with law enforcement.

Moishe purchased a ticket for a passenger, then one for a vehicle, confusing the woman behind the window, but not so much that she broached the subject. Her glance lingered on his injured face. Taking their plane would be easier, but where would they take it to?

A few vehicles lined up waiting for their ride. A nearby waiting room and gangway offered space for walk-on passengers, and a few people sat inside or lingered outside with their cigarettes. Moishe walked further, looking harder. Casey had seen Riccardo now, and might identify him, though the vehicle would be suitably anonymous. From an old man begging, Moishe bought a gray fedora, the ubiquitous hat of the Italian and delivered this, along with the auto pass, to Riccardo who eyed it suspiciously. "Wear it low. If you see them, ring my phone. Let it go three times, no more, not less. If I see them, I'll do the same, capisce?"

"Capisco." Riccardo tugged on the hat.

No, just as they scanned for the Black man, Casey would be looking for him, Moishe. He was too big to climb reasonably into a trunk, and his wounded arm precluded that sort of thing in any case. And so, he looked now for a way not to be himself.

When he spotted it, he nearly smiled.

Chapter Eighty-Five

Grant scanned the crowd in the boarding area, and the vehicles lined up to drive onto the ferry. Looming over the scene, Mount Etna looked serene against the vivid blue of the sky, concealing the deadly truth of its fiery heart, a volcano, just waiting to explode. "Anything?"

"Negative."

Down in the car, clad in Moroccan tunic and cap, Nick waited with everyone else. No way they could fly with the sword. Would it be worse if Moishe and his crew took their private plane, arriving at the mainland before them, or if they, too, lurked in this gathering of holiday makers and business people, just trying to get home.

Jacinta had taken the ferry directly across to the toe of Italy, and proceeded on from there. To where? Hard to say, but Grant was betting on Naples, or somewhere close—somewhere familiar to her, where she could get the resources to do her work and have access to numerous escape routes if things went wrong. Couldn't wait to hear the story of how she'd gotten her hands on the painting. That was a twist he hadn't foreseen.

Buses, vans, panel trucks and private cars. Tourists from all nations, nuns and priests, delivery drivers and families, and somewhere among them, his enemy. Wish he'd had time to come up with a better plan, but Moishe already had people on the mainland and had access to the tracker he'd planted, presumably on the painting or the crate. If they had to, they'd ditch the car and proceed without it, snarling up ferry traffic and maybe foiling the enemy for a little bit longer.

The last of the disembarking passengers and vehicles trickled away, and the time came. The rumble of anticipation grew not only in the boarding line above, but among the vehicles shifting into gear for their own turn.

Grant took the handle of his dolly and moved along with the queue on the lower deck, a small group of delivery workers with trays of baked goods and cases of wine to re-stock the onboard snack booths. Grant's contribution consisted of a large plastic bin marked with recycling symbols. His ambiguous skin tone readily placed him among the tanned dock hands and Italian service people. Like the others, he'd passed the time with his phone in hand, randomly scrolling around and poking things on the screen. Nobody got close enough to his bin to see the empty screen. Some places, the increased security since 9-11 remained in full-force, but this wasn't one of them, maybe because some part of the local economy relied on being able to move casually, fully armed, around the Mediterranean.

Too often spy-vs-spy ops like this devolved into second-guessing. Would Moishe, knowing that Grant had been a trash-picker at the last stop, expect him to continue in that vein, or to pick a different way to blend with the crowd? Didn't matter in the end what Grant chose, Moishe would be scanning just as intently as Grant did.

Walking briskly down the ramp with his load, Grant went about his business precisely as if he belonged there, push past the tourists already filtering through the vessel. The engines rumbled through the soles of his shoes, making him think again of the volcano. Grant planted his bin near a similar one. He had already jammed the swing lid shut from the inside and turned it now to make it unappealing as a receptacle compared with its twin.

With a patterned blaring of horns, the ferry roared to life. It nosed along the docks, lumbering like a walrus, then geared smoothly into higher speed when they reached open water. Grant took his dolly and strolled back toward the crew and service area.

"Six private cars with single male-presenting drivers. Four with female," Nick reported in Grant's ear. "Go for stretch?"

"Go." Parking the dolly alongside a tool cabinet, Grant removed the high-visibility vest that marked his status and walked toward the vehicle deck doors. Nondescript pants and shirt, a grubby cap on his head, he could be anyone now.

A few people moved out, heading up the stairs to the upper decks for cigarettes, snacks, or a view. On a trip this short, most drivers would stay with their cars. People with laptops populated the tables immediately, already on their phones. Families vied for places near the windows in spite of the shaded material that cut the dazzling sun. Those in religious habits moved in little clumps among the others, standing out for their clothing, but an ordinary sight across Italy. One of the priests held the doors for a nun who leaned heavily on a walker, head down, focused on every step.

Grant leaned against the windows, letting his upper body be obscured by the father supporting a child with their hands against the pane, pointing and chattering. Grant opened a stick of gum, folded it into his mouth and started chewing.

From this vantage, he saw the nun proceed at a diagonal across the lounge area, between tables, apparently making for the door leading toward the bow.

"Target acquired," Nick murmured. "Man in a hat investigating our vehicle."

"Prime?"

"Negative. The other."

"Pretty sure our man's taken holy orders."

Once the nun had "her" back to Grant's position, he casually moved the other way, back down toward the vehicle deck—moving faster once he was out of sight. "What's my target?"

"Black, late model, five cars back, second column."

"Keep him busy." Grant ducked low into the vehicle deck. Already the ferry slowed for its berth.

Near the big vehicle gate, Nick spoke loudly into his cell phone, trying to be heard over the engine noise, his back to the parked cars. Man with a hat leaned toward him eagerly from the cover of a panel truck. The driver glowered down at him.

Slipping along the shadow of the buses, Grant worked past the target vehicle without slowing. By the time he arrived at the back tire, he slipped a chip from his pocket, stuck it to the gum, and tucked it inside the wheel well, then kept moving. Over the loudspeakers, a voice ordered vehicle passengers back to their vehicles.

Grant hustled out the nearest passenger door and back to his recycle bin—broken open and emptied, with Moishe retreating down the corridor faster than any aged nun ever could.

Chapter Eighty-Six

Carrying the bundle he'd found in the recycle bin, a smelly, canvas-wrapped parcel guaranteed to put off casual examination, Moishe shed his habit the moment he passed out of the ferry terminal. People side-eyed him every moment, first as a very large nun, face obscured by a bandage, and now for his smelly packet and sudden focus.

The dumpster where their tracker still sat occupied a street not far away, and he walked briskly, choosing random paths, and doubling back once to be sure he wasn't followed.

By the time he arrived, Riccardo idled the car outside the nearby cafe. The large crate from the painting rested against the rubbish till, just as he'd expected. There, he tore the packaging from the item he carried. A layer of waxed paper lay beneath the canvas layer, and inside that: a large fish stared at him with dead eyes.

"What is it?" Riccardo called from the car.

Moishe hurled the fish into the rubbish bin, then stalked over to the parking area. "Get out of the car."

"What?"

"They tagged it. They must have. This wasn't a set-up of them, but of us. Get out."

Killing the engine, Riccardo complied.

A red Ferrari roared up, honking at their vehicle's poor positioning.

Moishe turned as the driver shouted something at him in Italian. With a grin that made his wounded face throb, Moishe made a rude gesture.

"Think you can take me?" Moishe asked in the Sicilian dialect. "You're not man enough."

Moishe started to walk back down the alley, rewarded by the slamming of a door behind him, and a stream of Italian curses. "Turn around and face me, Meatbag!" the driver called after him.

When Moishe failed to turn, the driver rushed him. Moishe flung out his arm, sweeping the man off his feet and slamming him to the ground. Gasping, the driver tried to struggle to his feet.

Moishe grabbed him across the mouth, lifted him by the belt and cracked his skull against the edge of the bin. The man went limp.

A quick search and he plucked the keys, wallet and phone from the man's pockets before plunging him, too, into the rubbish. Dead or alive, he wouldn't be sending the police after them for a good long time.

He returned to where Riccardo stood, looking a little more pale as he crossed himself. "The signal. Where is it?"

"Right." Riccardo swallowed, climbing gingerly into the passenger seat of the Ferrari as Moishe shoved his own seat as far back as it would go and peeled out of the parking place.

If the Americans knew they had a tracker as well, they hadn't stopped to deal with it when they departed the ferry, and Moishe now had a car that definitely outclassed their compact rental. Surprising that anybody would rent to those people after everything they'd done. Moishe had two or three identities in his pocket at all times. How many did they?

"Got it: they're taking the E45 north."

No surprise.

Riccardo called out directions as Moishe zipped his new wheels around pedestrians, delivery trucks and parked cars. He kept to the near end of acceptable speeds; having to kill traffic enforcement would only slow him down, and he was done with slow. His hands still smelled of fish.

Finding the on-ramp, Moishe raced onto the highway. "The car?"

"Dark green hatchback. Uh...ten miles or so ahead of us."

They'd had no delay in either picking up passengers or choosing new transportation.

"Eyes up," Moishe said, and he pushed the car into motion. Late afternoon traffic accumulated around them. The local version of rush hour. Horns sounded, fists waved out of windows as Moishe blew past them, cut between cars and slid his performance vehicle through impossible gaps, closing the distance. It was now that his true advantage over the Americans would be revealed.

"Past the big lorry, could be them." Riccardo pointed.

"Buckle up," said Moishe, punching the accelerator.

Chapter Eighty-Seven

"You sure the fish was a good idea, Chief?" Nick steered expertly through the traffic, heading north.

"Had to be done." Grant's gaze flicked to the mirror on his side, to the rearview, to the behavior of drivers around them.

Nick lifted one hand and tipped it this way, then that. "Maybe could've worked without."

Somewhere behind them, horns blared.

"I think we've got incoming."

"How far do we take this?"

Grant dropped his glance to the phone braced at the dash. "There's no exits, the next few miles." No road, in fact, and Grant did a double-take. "Tunnel," he said. "Long one. Aim for Scilla."

The long-hauler to their left and behind braked suddenly and a red Ferrari dove into view in front of it. A gun thrust through the side window, aiming in their direction.

"Hang on." Nick cranked the wheel, scraping the front end of the Ferrari, then racing ahead, peeling past a couple of vehicles, then plunging into the darkness of the tunnel. Little chance for passing, too narrow for a shoulder. If they hit anything, or any one, in here, there'd be a flaming wreck to ruin a bunch of lives.

Grant twisted partway in his seat as the Ferrari screamed after them. A bullet shattered their car's rear window and the back window behind him. He ducked down. Few inches straighter, he'd've been out on that one.

Agent Chadad's words echoed in his head, about how he was part of the problem. So. Shoot back, maybe cause that fiery death?

"How fast can we go?"

In answer, Nick punched the gas and raced around a tour bus. He threaded the needle between the bus and the wall, sparks flying as the guardrail scraped along the side of the car, illuminating the terror on the faces of those around them.

Calculated risk, heading for the highway rather than one of the other roads. Maybe the mountain route would've been fast enough to put some distance between them and any civilian population. And increased the risk they just went over a cliff. Figured that Moishe would suspect a tracking device. Hadn't counted on him stealing a sports car to make up for that.

They burst into the sunlight, but just for a moment. Another tunnel cut the mountain ahead and they rushed back into darkness. Traffic thinned out a bit as they left the port behind and slower vehicles found their cruising speed.

"Exit's on the other side of this one. Can you buy me a few hundred meters?" Nick asked.

"On it."

Grant slid between the seats to crouch on the back, trying not to make himself a target. Moishe said he wouldn't meet at a place of Grant's choosing, but he would, he just didn't know it. Bringing his pistol up to the level of the blown rear window, Grant kept to the shape of the molded headrest. No way to count this one or time it to his racing heart.

"Gimme a beat," Grant said. "In three...two...one."

The car slowed, just a little. The Ferrari raced closer. Grant edged up, aimed and squeezed the trigger. The Ferrari's radiator hissed with a burst of steam. A second shot shattered their windshield. The car lurched aside to throw off his aim, and Nick gunned their own car forward, dodging another bus and slewing sidelong for the exit, cutting off a panel truck that blared its horn.

The exit curved sharply through—oh, joy—another tunnel. They burst into the sun again. More horns suggested the Ferrari had made the turn in spite of everything. Good.

Grant crouched on the back seat.

"What's the call, Chief?"

"Cemetary, right turn, left to parking," Grant called out.

"Copy that." Nick made the turns, whipping the car around in a circle at the far end of the parking lot as Grant checked his ammo. Should do, if he didn't waste any shots.

A streak of red as the Ferrari emerged from the exit tunnel and around the curve. Then Grant's phone rang.

Chapter Eighty-Eight

Moishe swung wide around the turn and stopped short as he realized they'd been led not to another street, but to a dead-end parking lot alongside a cemetery. Ranks of cenotaphs elevated from ground too rocky to dig into formed a blocky landscape to one side. The pierced, cracked windshield fragmented the scene.

At the far end, the Black man sank very low behind his steering wheel. Casey must be in the back seat, unless he'd already slipped out among the bushes or the graves.

Through the hot afternoon air, a phone shrilled. Riccardo flinched, glancing down. "There's a text. Jacinta's asking for a truce."

Moishe glimpsed a hand snaking forward in the other car, withdrawing just as quickly. The ringing phone silenced.

"Try calling her," Moishe suggested, and Riccardo complied.

"Busy."

She reached out to both of them, but called his counterpart, and only texted him. If he had feelings, they might be hurt. Then his phone rang. Riccardo flicked a glance, then answered. "Pronto." After a moment, he held out the phone. "It's her."

"Moishe. How are you?" She sounded tense.

Moishe stared through the damaged windshield toward the other car. "Could be worse." They could have long guns, and already be shooting, for example.

"All three of us want this, and I think each of us had something the others need in order to succeed."

Did he? Moishe wasn't sure this were true, and also knew it didn't matter. "È vero, Jacinta."

"I have told him first, and now I am telling you. If you kill him, you'll get nothing more from me. Is this clear?"

The phone warmed his ear. She called Casey first...to tell him not to kill Moishe? Then all of his work on her was not in vain. "You wish for us not to kill each other. I knew you were an idealist."

Riccardo smiled and tapped his crucifix then pointed skyward in token of his faith.

Faith had nothing to do with preparation, manipulation, and simple psychology.

"You could say this, but I'm not so sure."

"I suppose you're lucky we've not killed each other already." He envisioned how this parking lot encounter might happen, the green car accelerating at them, ramming them or not—his vehicle had more power and sharper turns. Likely they did not have much ammunition. He favored his odds. But she had the painting. "How will you know we don't kill each other?"

"You'll call me. I need to hear your voice every half hour. He'll do the same. You'll drive to Naples and I will give you more instructions."

"What if I kill him anyway, and just find the painting again? I've done it a few times already."

She paused.

Moishe warmed his voice. "Don't tell me you will destroy a master-piece, not you."

"The painting was lost for centuries, Moishe, it can be lost again."

And with it, his best chance to find the Menorah and bring about the peace this world so needed.

"The trouble is, Jacinta. Does each of us want to find it more than he wants the other man dead?" He took a breath, then said, "I do. But I don't know that he does." After Sadie, and the man on the tracks.

"He's promised me," she paused. "I believe him."

"Naples," he said. "We'll talk again soon."

But he wondered if Jacinta, too, had worked out the handle for controlling his adversary. If Moishe raised no weapon, voiced no threat, would Casey kill him anyway? Moishe did not believe this was true. At the very least, Casey would hesitate long enough for Moishe to move. Moishe needed no weapon. He already was one.

He threw the car into reverse, and accelerated back out, around the corner, throwing it into gear and racing away toward Naples and his long-awaited discovery, leaving the Americans in his dust. Ashes to ashes...they would meet again soon. And who, then, would back away?

Chapter Eighty-Nine

Naples, Italy

Jacinta stalked back and forth by the low stone wall, watching, waiting, as the sun rose. Darkness suited the need for stealth, but less so their access to the places they would need to go. Besides, waiting until morning gave each side the time to rest and prepare. Perhaps not such a good idea, really. Jacinta herself had gotten little rest...

The meet location should have clear lines of sight, but offer enough privacy to speak openly, Dom advised her during a furious series of text exchanges. He was mad, he was terrified, he was at the hospital, trying to help this woman, Jamie, who was in love with his friend, Tony. Helping Jacinta choose a location for the meet gave him something else to focus on. And something else to worry about.

It should have multiple avenues of escape, which meant, unfortunately, multiple lines of approach, making it harder for her to scout or watch them all. She should be confident they were in compliance before revealing herself, and certainly before revealing anything she knew. She should have a back-up plan, someone who would expect to hear from her at set intervals, or who would take some action, like calling the police, if she didn't return. Dom couldn't even speak, and she dare not tell him where the painting was, or who she was staying with. Would he be relieved to know she'd found a place with his grandparents, or only the more terrified, now for his aged relatives? She couldn't be sure they wouldn't tell him themselves.

Nearby, the Fountain of Neptune pattered cheerfully, while Napolitani strolled the park on their way to work, or just to get coffee. Her phone buzzed, and she jumped, clutching it to her head and glancing around. "Pronto!"

"Moishe's near the trees by the bus stop. I take it he hasn't called you yet." Casey's voice, cool and self-assured as ever.

She turned to look in that direction, almost immediately chastising herself for making it obvious. But then, she was looking. She was meant to wait for them and the good news was, neither side wanted her dead—she was too valuable to them alive. That made her wonder about Moishe's remark, how he wanted the prize enough to refrain from killing Casey, but he didn't believe the reverse was true. She made the truce, or tried to, if they still wished to kill each other, what more could she do?

Surely she had looked at the bus station a hundred times since she arrived. Still, the sight of Moishe emerging alongside the structure astonished her as if he had materialized from thin air. Dressed in his customary black, he gave a slight wave, then started strolling toward her, the parchment letter in his hand.

"He's coming," she told Casey, then realized of course, he already knew.

About fifty meters away still, Moishe paused and removed his coat, slowly, as if his arm still bothered him. No—not that. First, she could not afford to spend sympathy on him. Second, he only took off the coat to comply with her demands that both men come unarmed. Their seconds, Nick and Riccardo, would be lurking in the background, she knew, as an insurance policy against the other's compliance. Moishe turned, his arms spread away from his body, displaying the fact that he did not wear any guns, at least, nothing obvious. Casey's voice from the past told her not to trust any of them.

"There's something you need to know," Casey said in her ear.

She waved back to Moishe, and he retrieved his coat, draping it over his arm as he strolled toward her.

"Okay, two things. One, if I wanted to pretend I had no guns, I'd have set them down along with the coat, then picked the coat back up again, just like that. Like a magic trick so you think I'm unarmed."

Jacinta still had a gun of her own—and more ammunition. His patronizing attitude began to annoy her, and she schooled herself to patience. She had yet to see any of the terrible things he claimed Moishe to be capable of. "What's the other thing?"

"I've got a sword."

That jolted her, shredding the patience she so recently desired. "Why on earth have you got a sword, Mr. Casey? Do you try to become Caravaggio in truth?"

His voice rang with humor. "I wish I could achieve that level of genius, but I'll have to stick with madness. This might be his sword. He left it for us to find."

"In the tree?"

Moishe, close enough now to hear her words, stopped short again, and she beckoned him closer. "Are you speaking of snipers, now?" he asked. His broad, unreadable face looked the more dangerous for the wound tracking across it. The skin around the cut looked red, possibly infected. He should have gotten better care.

"It's Casey. He can't come unarmed."

Moishe's brow furrowed, and he sighed, but she touched his arm. "It's not bad faith," she told him, "He's brought the clue from the tree, just as you brought the letter, but the clue was a sword."

"Come see," Casey told her, and, as had happened once before, his voice came to both ears at once, from different directions.

Moishe whipped around, and sank a little into his stance as if he would draw a gun against the fountain itself, but his hands remained empty, both coat and letter dropped to the ground at Casey's words.

Casey chuckled, and rang off.

He stood on the far side of the fountain, where the central statue arrangement would have concealed his approach. Arms folded, a long package on the stone wall in front of him. His loose shirt fluttered in the breeze and he wore no jacket, his own demonstration that he was unarmed. She didn't believe him, either, but wherever they concealed their weapons, it would be just that much harder for one of them to kill. He had a concealed holster at his waist in Rome, and the boots he wore, low though they were stood high enough at the ankle to conceal a gun or a knife. If he wanted her to assume everyone lied, then he remained the first person to whom she applied his own caution.

"It is your show, Jacinta," Moishe said pleasantly, with a gesture of invitation. "After you."

Casey lost his smile. "Don't let him get behind you, or within arm's length."

"Va bene," she said, "We'll go together." They paced as if in a ceremony, side by side, with nearly two meters between them, around the fountain to where Casey stood.

Moishe's coat draped his arm, letter in his hand as if he sought a job and brought his references. "Once again," he said, "we are wolves together."

"All three," said Casey, "unless I missed my guess about what happened back on Sicily." His glance toward Jacinta felt less like an appraisal than an acknowledgment.

Did she want men like this to think of her as a peer? How far she had come from who she'd thought she was. How much farther would she have to go to see this through?

Moving with deliberate care, Casey reached to the covered item and drew back part of the cloth, revealing the hilt of a short sword. He flicked to concealment into place again before anyone outside their circle could catch a glimpse, then tucked the bundle under his arm. His left arm, leaving his right hand free. She had begun to study them like works of art: the iconography of dangerous men.

"Like the man says, Jacinta, it's your show. What's the next act?"

"Well. I have already done the breaking and entering. Or at least, the entering." In addition to the shoulder bag containing her laptop, she'd chosen a pair of men's work pants, with plenty of pockets, and revealed a heavy set of keys. "The museum where I work also has ties with many of the churches around, to take care of their artwork."

The two men regarded each other, close enough to lunge or stab, each holding his part of the puzzle, each eager to know what parts she carried.

"Here is how I think. I don't reveal all of what I know. I am sure neither will you give up what you have, so we must work together." She must sound painfully naive. She drew a deeper breath. "Each of us wants to see where this ends, to find what we think is hidden there, è vero? So we go together, all three of us, to the end of the map."

Casey gave a nod. "Then what?"

"Then it is finished," said Moishe. "One way, or the other."

Chapter Ninety

"As long as you don't expect us to shake hands," Grant said evenly. Pretty sure Moishe could break bones with his grip, without even squeezing real hard. Grant was hoping he didn't have to draw the sword in anger, but he wasn't ruling it out.

Jacinta was doing her best, under the circumstances. Now she waved them forward. "It's a couple of blocks."

The three of them strode in silence, Grant scanning to spot Moishe's back-up, as, no doubt, Moishe scanned for his. That challenge leveled up when the came to the church, a rather plain, white and gray building with flat, square columns so typical of 17th century architecture around here.

Another church, just like Poland. How far would the similarities go? A secret crypt, a flaming corpse, a civilian gasping for breath and left for dead? Shake it off, Casey: gotta be at your best for this one, or beyond. He knew what happened when they found the Menorah—if they found it—Moishe would try to kill him, without regard for witnesses, setting, or collateral damage, human or historical.

Bound to be a church. There was a cardinal involved, one with papal aspirations, and a church artist, and Europe was lousy with churches. Graffiti marked the front of this one, along with its relief carvings, suggesting it wasn't considered a high priority.

At a side door in the narrow space between the church and the next building, Jacinta sorted through the keys, trying one and another, then finding one that fit. Again, she waved them to go ahead of her, and the men complied, Moishe as meek as a well-trained dog. Fascinating to see them together, the way he deferred to her, the way she reached for him, treating him like a gentle giant, wounded and misunderstood. Grant understood that all too well.

She was a source, an especially valuable one, a person worth cultivating—and Moishe had gotten there first. It would take an act of murder, or an act of god, for her to be convinced of his truth.

An oval dome covered a church interior large enough for a half-court game of basketball, but just barely. Rows of pews defined aisles but the church lacked the traditional cross-structure, placing its altar and side chapels radially rather than emerging from a central nave. Warm red and orange stone defined the space with degrading frescoes on the ceiling wearing away to the plaster. Large windows pierced the dome, spreading light below. Colorful paintings hung in a few of the chapels, none of them Caravaggio, though a few looked to be of a similar vintage.

"San Carlo alla Arena. Saint Charles of the sands, for what it's built on. San Carlo Borromeo was a new saint at the time of Caravaggio, and one favored by Del Monte." Jacinta's voice rang in the space, and their footsteps echoed.

Grant split left, Moishe moving to the right, each of them scanning as she spoke. Grant's portion of the church featured the large wooden double-doors of the main entrance, a collection box for tourist donations, and an assortment of fliers, religious tracts and tourist information, that might have been there almost as long as the church itself. So far as he could tell, no crypt at all. He glanced over a handout for the church itself. It consisted of little more than he could see from right there.

At the far end, Moishe investigated chambers to either side, a vestry, and another storage area, according to the diagram in the handout.

He glanced up at the dome with its geometric pattern, taking in all of the red. "Moishe. Where's the letter?"

Turning at his name, he held up the letter, and all three came together again, close to the altar. "What are you thinking, Casey?"

With a gesture at the space around them, he said, "It's red and it's round. It's also intact."

Moishe turned the envelope to reveal the seal, still complete, despite the letter itself being open.

With a gasp of excitement, Jacinta brought out a small bag containing a round metal pendant of some kind. She slipped it from the bag, and Moishe steadied the letter while Jacinta confirmed that it fit perfectly into the impression on the old wax. Confirmation, fine, but what next? They needed more information, not just the seal of approval. Walnut ink on prepared sheepskin. When they'd had the letter, they focused on the words, but the object itself could have more to reveal.

"May I?" Grant held out his hand, but Moishe drew back the letter, eying him.

"It's parchment," Grant pointed out. "You can write on it, but it's also translucent. Are there any other marks, punctures—"

"Scribe lines," Jacinta supplied. "Sometimes they use a thin rod or the back of a knife to make lines for the writing." She, too, reached for the letter, but Moishe stepped back and unfolded it the rest of the way, holding it up.

In the bright light spilling through the windows, Del Monte's writing became mere shadow. Thin lines arced through the shadows, intersections marked and fine pinpricks.

"It's astronomical," Grant said, stepping close to Moishe to see better. Both of them stiffened, their breathing hushed and nearly aligned.

"Is it for Taurus again, as on the fresco at the villa?" Jacinta inquired.

He pulled out his cellphone and snapped a photo of the alignment. That cluster had to be the Pleiades, one of the most recognizable of the constellations. "Jacinta, can you get on a historical calendar? I don't think it's gonna be that easy."

While she fired up her laptop, he sat on one of the pews, the bundled sword across his lap as he pulled up an astronomy app.

"Even with a date," Moishe said, "how does that help? How much research will it take to know what it means?"

"Ha. It is in Taurus. May 12, give or take," Grant said, comparing the image of the stars with the faint outlines on the parchment. "Look at Del Monte, or the saint, what else—"

Jacinta's fingers flew over the keys. "The day of Charles Borromeo's beatification."

Moishe stalked away from them, taking up the brochure about the church, then he paused and looked back. "Moments from the life of the saint are carved in the walls outside, around the top." Immediately, he went for the door they'd come through.

Slipping from his seat, sword under his arm, Grant joined Moishe outside, again splitting up to scan the carvings high above. At the side of the church, where a few trees marched along the curving street, Moishe pointed up. "The pope is the one with the strange hat."

Joining his adversary, Grant looked at the sculpture. The pope held a shepherd's crook and raised his hand in blessing. Before him, the figure of Charles Borromeo, with a new round halo.

Moishe glanced at him, and one corner of his mouth twitched up. "We might have worked well together."

If he hadn't already put two of Grant's friends in the hospital. "Any time you want to stop killing people, I'm for it."

Still carrying her laptop outside of its bag, Jacinta hurried over to join them. "This is like the incisioni in the painting I think. They are a map."

"Then I'd guess this is where it begins." From the corner of his eye, Grant noticed a tourist stroll by the trees, pausing on the corner as if looking for something. Familiar stride and stance. Moishe's back-up.

Didn't know where Nick might be, but he trusted him to keep an eye out.

Jacinta folded her laptop to become a tablet, holding it flat in front of her, then she frowned.

On the screen, a grayscale image of the Caravaggio painting showed a series of lines and a couple of circles, the markings unrelated to the paint strokes that overlay them, but they bore only a distant echo of the streets and structures visible.

On his own phone, Moishe marked the location on a map. "It's been a long time, things change."

"He was meant to find a safe place, some thing that wouldn't be affected by politics or weather." Grant placed his back to the church, imagining the place four hundred years ago. Buildings and streets would be in nearly the same locations. People, trees, names, all of those would have changed. What else? A mother with a stroller lifted the front wheels off the curb and into a cobbled gutter scattered with leaves. Metal grates punctuated the gutters, but given the litter, they'd hardly—

"What about the sewers?"

"And the cisterns!" Jacinta pointed to one of the circles on her screen.

Moishe started toward the nearest grate, but Jacinta stopped him. "There's another way. Easier. Come."

She hurried off, no longer caring who was behind her, and Grant hesitated a beat, to keep Moishe in his own sights at least. Sewers and cisterns underground. Like bones and graves.

Chapter Ninety-One

In the little time they'd been inside, more people moved through the streets, shopping and going to work. Horns honked, and Moishe considered the blessed emptiness that would one day conquer all of this. No more stress and hurry. Peace at last, for everyone. Casey need not carry the guilt that propelled him. Jacinta need not fear rejection. That man crumpled by the street corner need not worry for his next meal, or his next dose of the drug that would kill him.

Traffic stopped for Moishe, and the gap between him and Jacinta closed. Let Casey take care of himself—if Casey were hit, Moishe could simply secure the sword for himself. Then the Black man would shoot him in turn. Pity they did not understand there could be an end to all of this strife. Soon. They had no idea how soon.

On the sidewalk, Moishe paused, rubbed his ear, then kept going. Jacinta's chosen time had given him more than enough time to prepare a few things. People. Gear. Signals.

A banner over a gated arch proclaimed, "Napoli Sotteraneo." Naples Underground, but not in the British sense of a train or subway, at least, not that he knew of. The posted sign included opening hours, ticket prices, and a few photos to tantalize the tourists into visiting a place they'd now enter for free.

Stuffing the laptop in her bag, Jacinta sorted frantically through the key chain. Moishe strolled up next to her and looked at the lock, an older padlock. He'd put his coat back on, the letter returned to its inside pocket. Now he produced a small tool from his wallet and thrust it into the lock.

Casey appeared nearby, close enough to react, not close enough to be jabbed with a hypodermic needle, or such, Moishe presumed, was his fear. Fair enough. The man wasn't stupid. He didn't need to know that Moishe didn't carry such a thing himself. He had bigger plans, and enough extra hands to achieve them.

When he no longer required Jacinta's cooperation, Moishe could act. All he needed was to get that sword out of Casey's hands.

Moishe the Fist hoped, when they had found what they were looking for, to once more live up to his name, if only to test for nerve damage after what Casey had done to his arm back in Malta. No doubt Casey still carried the bruises of their first encounter.

Hmm. Was this emotion? He had the brief, astonishing thought, that he and Casey had become brothers in some dark way, bound together by blood and bruises.

Moishe popped the lock and slid it from the loops on the gate, pushing it open.

Jacinta looked up, still checking keys but slowing. They jingled together in her hand, and she glanced at him uncertainly, then slipped the keys back into her pocket and found her smile. "Va bene."

Indeed. All three stepped into the chill of the archway, and Casey closed the gate, preserving the appearance of the barred entry. "Let's go." Casey hung back as before, trying to maintain his position in the line.

Jacinta started past the ticket booth and down the stairs. "There are miles of tunnels beneath the city, sewers and cisterns, si, but also these have been made into bomb shelters for the war, and into storage for the police department. That is mostly to the south and west."

Casey and Moishe matched steps until they had descended below street level. Moishe stopped short, then doubled back fast, trotting up the steps.

"Moishe!" Casey called after him.

"Sorry, I dropped my tool," he called back, racing for the gate as Riccardo slipped inside. He dropped the padlock into his second's hand and palmed the tool as he leaned in. "Lock it and hide. Don't let the man follow us. Tell the others to go to the next gate and come here with the package."

Riccardo crossed himself. "You're sure about the package? You don't think it's too early to deliver?"

"We've waited long enough. I'll mark the way." He ripped the bandage from his arm, letting it tear through a few stitches. Immediately blood oozed from the wound and he flicked a drop against the wall to demonstrate.

"God be with you!" Riccardo called out.

But Moishe had already gone. Was he sure? He had significantly increased the odds in his favor. The odds in favor of Casey's death.

Chapter Ninety-Two

Jacinta scrolled up the brightness on her screen as she paused in the darkness.

"Don't suppose you have a flashlight in that bag?" Casey asked.

Moishe brought out one of his own, one so small it looked like a toy in his hand, but cast a bright beam. "Won't you thank me for bringing the light?"

He sounded happy, maybe a little excited to be close to their mutual objective. Sometimes, he struck her as almost childlike—wary of revealing himself, for fear of being hurt. All right, so he may have hurt Casey's friends. She knew for a fact Casey had injured or killed some of Moishe's men. Did she really know who had started this feud? Did it really matter? Either of them could choose to be the bigger man. Perhaps. Naive again.

"Your cut. It's bleeding." Jacinta pointed to Moishe's wrist where a fresh darkness oozed.

"Mmm." He glanced down. "It doesn't hurt much."

She wasn't sure she should believe him, but perhaps his near-euphoria—at least for Moishe—might be covering the pain.

"This way." Casey indicated a narrow passage to their right. "To get back to the church."

Moishe pivoted in that direction, then said, "He's right."

Skills she did not need to have: underground navigation. A short way down the new passage, a wooden door barred the way, showing rot along the lower portion where it must get wet with some frequency. Before she could even pull out the keys, Moishe slammed his foot into the door alongside the handle. The sound echoed, far too loud in this narrow place, but the wood cracked and the door swung open. He was rough, but efficient. Not surprising he had been employed by someone like her father.

"Whatever we seek must have already been there, when the church was planned," Jacinta said. "Even here there are many ruins from the past, things discovered, built over or built into something else."

"Like the Menorah was found in construction," Moishe supplied.

"Like this, yes."

Moishe had moved closer to her, his flashlight illuminating the smooth floor of the passage. "These bricks don't look modern."

Insects fled the course of the light, and Jacinta's skin twitched. "Nineteenth century, I think. This is not my specialty." She shrugged. She tried to shrug off the damp and smell of slimy darkness as well. She failed.

Moishe stayed close to the wall as they moved, touching it from time to time. Was he less steady than he seemed.

Casey still hung back a little, keeping a prudent distance between himself and Moishe; she saw little more of him than the glint of his eyes, always on her, or her companion whenever she looked his way. She had first met this man when he was covered with blood, and now he walked behind them with a sword.

Jacinta tried a smile. Casey tipped his head, a gesture almost regal, and they got moving again, toward the sound of dripping water.

Eyes glinted suddenly in the darkness beyond the light and she cried out, jumping back.

Moishe clasped his arm around her briefly. "A rat, that's all." He swung the light as the creature scuttled away between a gap in the bricks.

Moishe swung the beam again to the right when they reached a junction, this time a rough arch cut through the brick. Different shades of bricks and the heap of rubble suggested a collapse of some kind forced this diversion. The passage angled, then encountered another passage, running straight and made of stones arched over a trough. Sand sifted along the bottom, leading them to a wider underground chamber with a couple of metal grates in the ceiling where sunlight shot through.

"San Carlo all'Arena," Casey said.

Pulling out his phone, Moishe checked the screen. He gave a little grunt, and his eyes narrowed.

"You don't like it when I'm right."

"It makes no difference who's right, so long as we find what we're looking for."

Their voices echoed, one light and amused, the other low and cool. Their passage continued straight, but another arch led out on the far side. Jacinta checked her screen. Caravaggio's map began here, with a line across and one ahead. Caravaggio's map. The idea thrilled her, even now. "Through the arch," she said.

Moishe paused beneath it, his hand lingering on the medieval stonework.

"Maybe we should be putting down bread crumbs like in the fairy tales," Casey remarked.

"Or have a string, like in the labyrinth," Jacinta said, then thought of the minotaur, and she hoped Moishe didn't have the same thought, even as she knew, she knew from the ghost of his smile, that Casey did. Which of them was the monster at the center of this maze? She cleared her throat. "But I don't think we shall be lost, not with your sense of direction and Moishe's flashlight."

Moishe gestured ahead with the light, and Jacinta started walking again, grateful to be wearing her old trainers and not any nicer footwear. A few puddles remained, and leaves accumulated in rotting little piles where they slipped in from above, then accumulated in the paths of the water. With access to the sun, some weeds sprang up from the muck, and green tracks of algae streaked the wall. Bits of litter and a few coins gleamed in the stripes of sunlight. She walked through the beams as if she could gather their light to take with her into the darkness.

The passages away from the church were mostly stone, and opened suddenly on one side to access a giant cistern, a round excavation where water would fall from the grates above. An old staircase led from it to a door on the surface in a squared-off, modern basement. Even here, at the roots of the city, old and new grew together, one on another, intertwining the past and the present.

Following the map, she made a few more turns, flinching back from the sudden opening of another cistern in the floor. Moishe's light played along its rim. The previous cistern had risen up from the ground to about his shoulder, this one sank down a few meters. Stumps of metal showed where a railing used to protect it, many years ago. From here, a short passage ended in a barrier of stones, and she stopped. The map itself seemed to go a little further, but how could she tell?

Moishe aimed his light upward to a rim of darkness, a gap between the rubble and the ceiling.

"That's Roman stonework, isn't it?" Casey shifted forward at an angle. They wouldn't all three fit in the tunnel together.

"It was, I think." Jacinta took in the awkward space.

"Over the top looks like the only way."

With a low rumble in his throat, Moishe waved them back, and handed the light to Jacinta. He reached out his big arms and scooped an armload of stone.

She and Casey scrambled back as Moishe pulled the stones down toward them with a thunder that vibrated the ground and sent up swirls of dust. A few of the stones showed traces of his blood. He reached and pulled again, leaving a pile waist-high at the center and spirals of dust that tickled her nose and throat.

The beam of light caught an animal's terrified eye, rolling back, its throat stretched, and a dark hand gripping, preparing it for sacrifice.

Chapter Ninety-Three

Jacinta yelped as the dust began to clear, and Moishe again moved to comfort her. Grant took advantage of this compression to slip by them, up the pile of stones and down the other side into the space revealed. Smooth walls, painted with white and red, embellished with images of birds and fruits, all in the distinctive style of Roman murals. The long wall opposite had a stone bench built in across the bottom.

Revealed by the tumbled wall stood the focal point of the place, a bronze statue of a bull, caught in a pose of terror. A sculpted man held the animal with one hand, his other hand raised, partially closed into a fist, but empty. He wore a toga and sandals, one knee pinning the bull in place for what happened next. The joints of the figure looked awkward, poorly sculpted at first glance, but Grant thought otherwise. Someone had modified the figure after its creation. Maybe an artist, a student of anatomy, and the son of a mason.

"What is this?" Moishe clambered over the rubble into the chamber, staring at the statue.

"It's a Mithraeum," Jacinta supplied. She stuff the laptop into its bag and scrambled into the room. "Nearly intact! These were secret temples to the god Mithras, who was not Roman at all, but brought from Persia. He is the god of warriors. Soldiers would meet here to observe the rites, and any fighting man could be invited to the cult, even a slave, even a gladiator." She prowled around the statue. "Almost perfect," she said again.

Grant and Moishe, in the secret cult of warriors. Yep. "I don't see the Menorah though, or any other way out. Maybe we should—"

"No," Moishe said, turning sharply on Grant. The hand he gestured with was empty of anything but threat. "No, you don't speak." His swiveled toward Jacinta. "Nearly intact, you said, Jacinta. What's missing?" Then his face shifted. "The painting, when you began to clean that darkness, it revealed a bull and a man. Like this."

Moishe straightened, his hair nearly brushing the ceiling and Jacinta darted a glance at Grant.

He willed her not to speak. They didn't need Moishe any more, didn't need what he had brought. What happened when Moishe found what he wanted? Grant knew beyond a shadow of doubt what would happen to him. What about her? How far would Moishe's affection go? His discovery of the Menorah led to a chain of events that precipitated, if all went to Moishe's plan, the end of the world.

Clearly, she was reluctant to answer, but there was only so long she could fail to answer, only so long before Moishe worked out the truth.

Grant hugged his bundle to his chest with one arm and braced the other hand on stone. He vaulted the rubble, racing away from Moishe, and taking the blade of sacrifice with him.

Chapter Ninety-Four

With a growl, Moishe swung away from the sculpture and chased after Casey and the sword. That open bronze hand, the grip held just so, the bull's muzzle drawn back for the slaughter: Casey's sword would fit in that ancient hand. Moishe's rough passage scattered more of the stones. He grabbed one in his off-hand, the flashlight's beam bouncing as he moved while Casey ran, fearless, into the dark, in spite of the open cistern that occupied most of the next chamber.

Footfalls echoed, more than just one man. Casey hesitated, just for an instant, hearing the trap.

Turning the corner, Moishe hurled the stone he carried. It struck Casey's chest from behind, staggering him toward the wall.

With a cough, absorbing the impact, Casey spun about, getting his back to the wall. From behind the bundle he carried, his hand rose in a smooth movement and the pistol in his grip spat fire.

The shot struck Moishe's chest, perfectly targeted just to left of center, and a second shot followed as Moishe reeled backward.

The gunshot echoed, and Moishe appreciated that they had moved the venue of their fight to the larger space where his ears throbbed, but did not bleed. Time for that later.

Three of Moishe's people appeared in the other door, while the lingering impact of Casey's shots, following on the assault of the stone against his back made him slow. He spun, they attacked. Had the order to stay his death not been rescinded? Moishe left that to Riccardo. There had been distractions. His chest ached, and he reached to rub the tufted holes in the fabric. Blood on his fingers.

The woman from Sicily had seized Casey's right arm with both hands, pinning it, leaving him exposed to the hard-driven shoulder of the next agent.

Casey swung the bundle in his left hand, landing a hard blow on the agent's head and neck. The third remained a step back, gun drawn. "On target—am I go?" he shouted.

Moishe thought about that for an instant too long.

The woman ground Casey's hand against the wall. Bracing his back, Casey kicked the second agent, sending him back into the gunman.

Taking advantage, of his off-center movement, the woman hauled Casey to the side, forcing him to turn and stumble. He landed on one knee, facing Moishe. The gunman stepped in, thrusting the barrel of his gun to the base of Casey's skull.

On his knees, mastering his breathing, Casey met Moishe's eye.

Moishe rubbed at one of the holes in his shirt, then he tugged at it, tearing between the two holes to reveal the layer of body armor underneath. He sighed. "It still hurts. It's hard to find Kevlar in my size. Anything tactical, really, so when I find a piece I like..."he shrugged. That hurt, too.

The woman wrenched away Casey's gun, and pressed the muzzle to the junction of his shoulder and throat, making it very hard for him to draw that sword.

At Moishe's back, a muffled sob. Jacinta stood on her side of the low barrier, next to the statue, her hands pressed over her mouth. Moishe gestured toward Casey, pinioned and controlled by three of his people.

Two more stood in the tunnel beyond, tactical flashlights and weapons held low and ready.

"We had an arrangement, did we not? We each would bring our part of the puzzle? We three wolves would hunt, for once, together, but Casey turned sheep, didn't he, and tried to run." He indicated his ruined shirt, with Casey's well-placed shots that failed to kill him. "He even brought a gun, against your express wishes. You see what he's done to me. You know what he tried to do."

Moishe balled his fist and stepped up.

Even as Jacinta shouted, "No!" Moishe's fist slammed into Casey's face.

Chapter Ninety-Five

Pain exploded into Grant's skull by way of his left eye and temple. He had turned his head, ducking his chin, tempted to close his eyes rather than witness the inexorable advance of that fist into his field of view. Unable to avoid it.

The impact rattled his teeth and knocked his head back against his captors. Blood streamed into his mouth. Somewhere, Jacinta shouted. Between the lingering echo of the gunshots and the blow, Grant heard and did not understand.

Lights and figures twitched around him, the whole scene jumpy like an old filmstrip caught off the reels but still trying to flow. Still images: Moishe standing tall, hands spread, still claiming himself unarmed; one of his people picking up the bundle Grant guarded for so long; the flash of the sword revealed in the dashes of light.

Somehow, he had to get moving, to get up, find a way to do the next right thing.

Die.

What else could it be?

The hands gripping him hauled him to his feet, a disturbance that rocked his aching head and snapped the moment back into focus.

Moishe's face swam in Grant's limited vision—half the world blurred. His left eye slid closed in spite of his attempts to keep it open.

"You're right, Jacinta, forgive me. He deserves to see the end." Moishe grinned, a cartoon image of a Cheshire Cat. The cat that catches the canary.

When he dragged down a deeper breath, Grant's ribs ached. Something burned inside his chest. Something broken. He shook off some of the hands, maybe. Somehow got his feet under him for the lurching, dizzying trip back to the Mithraeum to witness the god once more given his blade. Too big. Should be a dagger, classically speaking.

Dying in a temple of sacrifice to a warrior god. That was a first. He'd been impaled outside the Great Khan's tomb. Might've been a little like this.

Jacinta stared at him, maybe she spoke. Had to pull himself together somehow. Where was Nick? Someplace where he couldn't apologize.

Grant willed his body to obey his scattered mind. Half expected to see parts of his brain on the plain clothes of his assailants. "I'm sorry, Jacinta." He swallowed blood. "I missed what you said."

She winced. "It's all right. Don't apologize. Here, look." Her hands directed him toward the sculpture.

The act of looking required turning his head too far, bringing his right eye to bear. Two of the agents aimed flashlights to illuminate the actors in the scene. Moishe held up the sword, tilted it to match the angle of the bronze god's grip, then slid the hilt into the still, cold hand. With the added weight, the arm shivered, then groaned downward. Chain rattled within the hollow bronze. One of the painted plaster walls trembled and started to rise, then stuck, plaster dust sifting down as it ground against its hidden rails.

Moishe reached out, his hand bloodied across the knuckles from its impact with Grant's face, and at the palm by the slash on his wrist, the sutures still visible. Why remove his bandage? Grant's memory supplied another series of snapshots, this time marking their route to get here, every time Moishe rested his hand against the wall. Shoving his hand under the stuck panel, Moishe heaved upward. Even for him, it took both hands.

Plaster cracked, and Jacinta said, "Be careful." As if she thought he still cared for any of this, or for anything at all.

But he cared enough for her that Grant still lived, and for that, he should be grateful. Maybe later, he would be.

A wooden panel, warped by the centuries since its installation, formed one section of the temple wall, now open in spite of itself. Moishe stalked beneath the low opening, fallen plaster cracking beneath his feet.

"Do we have it?" one of the agents asked.

Grant and Jacinta stepped forward, staring into the gloom. The revealed chamber was shallow, maybe six feet, just large enough for what it held: a massive Menorah embellished with crude, cup-like blossoms, its seven blunt arms spreading wide over a base of two angled layers, the entire structure thick and dull with the gray glint of lead.

From the chamber echoed a sound Grant assumed he must be hallucinating. The sound of Moishe sobbing.

Chapter Ninety-Six

Moishe had no words. Even this guttural sound he now produced must cease, and he made it so. Had Del Monte known? Had the ever-struggling, half-mad artist disposed of the golden one, melted or sold or gambled it away, replacing it with this replica in case his benefactor came looking? Or had they never really possessed it to begin with, and Caravaggio, who could imagine a boy into an angel, given a pair of fake wings, and make a prostitute into the Virgin Mary, merely painted the likeness of the Menorah in gold?

Could he, Moishe, do the same, presenting this fraud to his backers, embellished with a little paint, or real gold leaf? He, Moishe, made things happen all the time, and he could make this happen, somehow. He could transform this failure into the success he required, the next stage to inspire the masses.

Then where had his grief come from? He had claimed for a decade now that God didn't care, if he even existed. He thought he believed it.

A patch of warmth penetrated his disbelief. Jacinta's hand on his arm. "It's over, then," she said softly. "You can lay down your weapons."

Somehow, he had a friend again. His last friend, his only friend, had been incinerated before his very eyes.

Moishe turned, his arm withdrawn from her touch. "It is not over until everything burns."

Her eyes widened, but her mouth turned in sadness or sympathy. "You did escape the burning car."

"No," he said. "I died there, too."

Chapter Ninety-Seven

Grant managed his pained breathing as Jacinta's hope and Moishe's despair sank in whispers. Had Grant really imagined any other outcome? Any possibility of Moishe's retreat?

Moishe's face went smooth as stone. He brushed past her, shouting, "Where's the package? Bring it on!"

"But, sir," said one of the agents, gesturing toward the false Menorah.

His hand thrust toward Jacinta. She pulled away, but not before he'd grabbed a gun from one of her cargo pockets. "I didn't need to come armed," he muttered. "I knew you would. Both of you."

For any other man, the expression he aimed at Grant would have been a sneer, but Moishe displayed nothing, as if his momentary lapse in the sanctum had taken all the emotion he had.

Already, he moved beyond them, to his own people. "There is no reason," he told them, "that we can't go on. I promised them a Menorah and a sign, that the time was at hand. We will give it to them. Where's the package?"

Oh, that was bad.

"Right here," said a voice from the room beyond. "Where do you take delivery?"

Moishe indicated the side of the Mithraeum past the god with his bull. "And Riccardo?"

"The other American showed up. There's a party of eight to deal with him." The technician placed a metal case on the stone bench and snapped open the lid to reveal lead wires, electronics and a cluster of pale gray bricks. C4.

The other one must be Nick, trying to reach him, confronting eight agents of the enemy. Agents of the devil.

"What is he—"Jacinta began.

Grant caught her wrist lightly, then let her go, dropping his voice to a whisper. "A bomb, Jacinta. They're going to plant a bomb. Any idea what's above us?" he indicated the ceiling.

"Apartments, houses, shops. We're still beneath city center."

Half-mile from the church, and no other exits they knew of. "If you can get out of here, can you get below the church piazza? The grates might give you signal to call for help, or to yell if you have to."

Her glance flicked toward the half-dozen armed people between them and the passage. "But how would I?"

Couldn't do anything about the path beyond the cisterns, but he could gain her some ground. "I'll do my best to clear the way. Get ready to move."

She pulled the strap of her bag over her head, and lowered it to the floor, the two of them briefly ignored as Moishe and his crew arranged their nasty surprise. Time to break out a few more items from the toolkit.

With a sigh and a wince of pain, Grant sank down, shifting toward the back of the statue as if he just couldn't take it. The female agent still covered him with the gun he'd taken from her partner. He cupped his hand over his injured eye. "You don't have an ice pack on you?"

"You won't need ice, Mr. Casey," Moishe boomed. "It will be over soon enough."

Agent with the second case, opening it up, fiddling with whatever lay inside, his back to Grant, his weapon holstered under his arm.

Easing himself against the far wall, playing up his injury, Grant ducked the arm of the statue and swiped back his sword. He thrust it though the female agent and grabbed the man's gun with his other hand. He lunged for the bomb itself, but Moishe's bulletproof bulk intervened and he kicked Grant away before he could line up the headshot.

Staggered, Grant tumbled over the rubble back toward the cistern chamber. He brought the gun up and fired. The shot cracked into stone a little off from his target. He needed his eye, and he couldn't do a damn thing about it. Two jobs: don't die. Get them to clear the narrow path between Jacinta and a call for help. At least one of them could get free.

As if dazed, Grant stumbled toward the back of the cistern, away from the passage. When the agents in the passage rushed forward, taking their stances. Grant fired again, every time a ringing assault on his already battered senses. One of the agents jerked and clutched at his gut. The other returned fire, but Grant's lurching path protected him. That time. He took a knee behind a partial wall and shot back.

More gunshots echoed, someplace far away—or just inside his head, he couldn't tell any more.

"He's one man, and wounded," Moishe said.

Two of the agents sprinted around the far side of the cistern, coming into view. Grant swiveled, taking aim.

Moishe's big hand plunged over the top of the partial wall, grabbing him by the back of the neck. Grant hacked toward him with the sword and Moishe shook it loose from his grip, slamming Grant's hand against the wall. The sword clattered away on Moishe's side of the wall.

Digging in his heels, Grant scrambled up and back, "helping" his captor. He shoved against Moishe and lifted the gun. His shot streaked past Moishe's face, taking Moishe's ear along with it in a spray of blood.

Swinging like a woodsman with an ax, Moishe hurled Grant away from him toward the cistern floor.

Couldn't be more than twenty feet. Arcing a little upward, then sharply down, and yet in Grant's warped perception, the flight was eternal.

He hovered, inverted like Caravaggio's angels in the Acts of Mercy. The sword lay on the ground past Moishe's feet. The agents drew back, or fired anyway. Two worked over their bomb, and Jacinta walked away toward freedom and help.

Freedom might come on impact. Help would come too late.

Chapter Ninety-Eight

Casey's desperate race led them to the cistern chamber. Of course she followed, of course anyone would. Her heart thundered and she gulped for breath. She wasn't running. She dare not draw their eye from the man with the blade, the man with the gun, the man suddenly flying.

Madre di Dio.

He had done this for her, to give her time to get help, for the city and for the world if not for himself.

Calmly she walked toward the agent at the door. Staring at the spectacle before him, he took a step forward, out of her way, then all the way to the rim of the cistern, looking down.

Clamping a hand over her mouth, holding in the wail that threatened to tear free, Jacinta stepped through the door, then fled. Tears stung her eyes. What else could she do? She had nothing, she was nothing in this mad and horrible place.

At the next turning, she pulled out her phone, flicking on the light, moving as fast as she dared in the narrow corridor, her ears ringing. She stumbled to a halt, hearing the echo of gunfire. Were they firing down on him, even now? Bile burned at her throat, then, gagging, she pressed herself to the wall, frozen. The gunshots weren't coming from behind—they came from ahead.

She had an ally, if someone fought back, but on the other side of another firefight.

"Jacinta." Riccardo emerged from the shadowy hall. He, too, held a gun, a pistol, its barrel lengthened by a sound suppressor. "You shouldn't be here."

"Moishe needs help," she blurted.

"With the package?" Riccardo's head cocked, then he caught her elbow, turning them back in the other direction. "Casey fought, didn't he."

"To the last." Her mind raced. They moved the wrong direction. Even if she could attack Riccardo, if she could down him as she had the driver back on Sicily, what then?

"Good girl, coming to find me."

"Who is fighting?" she ventured.

"They'll send him to his reward," Riccardo said. "Don't worry about it." He added a nasty little laugh. "When you made off with the painting, Jacinta, I thought you'd truly left us."

"I've been so confused," she said. Honesty. One of Casey's favorite tools. "I didn't know who to trust."

"That's perfectly understandable, but you've come round at the end, and that's what matters. We're doing God's work, you know. And making a lot of money doing it."

"You are truly blessed," she said, taking a sharp turn for the left.

"It's awfully narrow," Riccardo muttered. "Can you shine the light further."

They'd come to a marginal section of tunnel, off anyone's map. Rubble partially blocked the way and dirt sifted down from the crumbling ceiling. Riccardo frowned.

"Over the top," Jacinta said. "I'll hold the light, then you hold it for me, capisce?" She held the light higher, but still aiming down, as if to guide him over the rough pile.

"Very well," he said, eying her. His gun lifted a bit, aiming toward her as he moved, then he turned sharply on her. "No. I don't believe you." He extended the weapon, and she flicked off the light.

Jacinta lashed out with her foot, connecting with flesh, and Riccardo fired.

Chapter Ninety-Nine

Moishe checked the connections, and cast a final look toward the Menorah that betrayed him. God's final joke on his creation. Well. There would be no one to laugh. Today would be the first blow in the war, but more would follow. When they released the plague, when the rumors began to spread.

"How long?" His technician indicated the readout on the device.

"Seven minutes." The number seven, a figure of power to many. Enough time for them to depart and move on to their next destination, to deliver the message of death and silence.

The technician tapped buttons, turned a key, and the readout sprang to life. He pushed up to his feet, and Moishe gave a nod, sweeping them ahead of him with one gesture.

His people hurried out, away from the god with his sacrifice. Moishe strolled out, considering. His moment with the Menorah, his own moment of dismay, like Zacariah in the painting, made him wonder if it were time. If he stayed right here, he could be among the first to know the power of the end, to relinquish the anguish of living for the eternity of peace.

He kicked the sword aside and took another step forward, shining his flashlight down into the cistern toward the spot where he'd thrown down his enemy. Nothing but a smear of blood. Moishe tracked the blood. His spotlight pinned Casey's foot and tracked upward.

Casey crouched against the wall, one hand reaching up along the wall, the other spread upon the first crumbling step leading out of the cistern. One foot under him as he tried to stand.

His head turned. Blood streaked the left side of his face, his eye now swollen shut. The other eye stared directly at Moishe as if his grim determination could transform the beam of light connecting them into a weapon to fight back.

"You're a hard man to kill, Mr. Casey."

Casey stared back at him, the set of his jaw undeterred by injury or agony. "We all are, Moishe. You should know that by now."

Moishe aligned his pistol with the beam of light. Take him now, or let him die in the cataclysm. Any further delay, and Moishe might join him. It was hard to judge how the shape of the chamber would concentrate the blast.

"You're the sort of man who thinks there's always a choice, aren't you, Mr. Casey, so here's the final one. Would you prefer the swift death of the bullet, or to be crushed beneath the city?"

"I'd prefer to live."

"Pity that's no longer an option. The void is coming, Mr. Casey." He almost smiled. "The end is near."

Chapter One Hundred

Stones crashed and dust filled the tunnel. Riccardo gasped, flailing, but Jacinta danced out of reach as the ceiling smashed down on him. Cracks raced through the old stonework overhead, and she fled as more stones fell, the ground trembling underfoot.

One way and another, people would hear and feel what went on below. They'd know. Already, police would respond, rushing to the entrances, brought by the sound of gunshots or the rumble of this new collapse. They would arrive too late—or just in time to die when Moishe's bomb went off. When would that be?

She raced toward the hall she knew and spotted the back of an agent running past—toward the gunfight, or away from the bomb? Gunmen to her right, ruin to her left.

Back in the hall, Jacinta felt no more hesitation. She turned left.

There must be something she could do. Some way to turn off the bomb, to stop all of this before it began, as if she could roll back her own part in it. If it hadn't been her, some other restorer would have taken the job. If it hadn't been her, would Casey and his team even be involved—fighting and dying to stop armageddon.

Moishe's voice rang out ahead, she rounded the first cistern, and entered the chamber with the second, cistern lit as Moishe beamed his light down below, his gun aligned with the light as he addressed his fallen enemy still, miraculously alive. And what could she do? She had nothing. She was nothing but an art historian.

Her gaze fell to the sword on the stone before her.

Chapter One Hundred One

Grant stared up at his doom, facing it, as he'd always imagined, head on. What strength remained to him, what focus beyond the pain, he employed in that gaze. It wasn't his life that flashed before his eyes—it was a sword.

A hand from the darkness gripped Moishe's hair, tugging his head back. He started to turn, revealing the bloody streak of his missing ear, and the blade slashed across his throat. Moishe tried to speak, his throat and lips spilling with fresh blood.

Moishe's knees wobbled and he slumped backward, his slayer stepping back as the beam of the light pitched upward, illuminating the willful, frightened face of Jacinta behind the blade.

The flashlight tumbled away above. Grant planted his hands more firmly and levered himself up, propping his shoulder against the curved wall. His left leg buckled, and he guided his fall to land, none too gently, on the next step. Right then, he'd do this the hard way.

His back to the stair, place his hands, lever himself up, digging in his right heel to push himself up.

Light traced wildly over the ceiling, then Jacinta came to the edge, lighting the stairs. "You're alive!"

"The bomb!" he said. "What's the time?"

She hesitated. "But you need the light—"

"Just go."

She vanished, leaving him in darkness. He braced his hands. Right hand flared every time he opened his palm, every time he put his weight on it. Something broken, more than just the skin. He imagined his hand print, like those of the ancient cave painters, leaving his mark in the darkness.

Another step, and another.

"Three and fifty!" she called. "What do I do?"

Another step. "Is there a key?"

"It's gone. I can't do this alone, Mr. Casey."

Another step. "Moishe had a lock pick, in his wallet. Get it." Eyes closed, he heaved himself onto the next step, and tried to picture the key. "If you have a hairpin, or an earring."

"His wallet, there's two, and a toothpick."

Praise the man's vanity. Grant's next boost brought his head and shoulders above the level of the floor, and Jacinta hurried over. She wrapped an arm around his shoulders, her handful of picks jabbing him as he got his good leg under him.

They stumbled past the bodies, Grant's targets, Moishe laid out with his head tipped at an odd angle, blood pooling from the wound. At the mound of rubble, Jacinta cursed in Italian, and Grant sat down, swinging his legs over.

"Go, go!" he waved her on, and she clambered past him, Mithras reaching his empty hand as if to propel her even faster. She dropped to her knees in front of the open case. "It's not like a door lock," he told her, keeping his voice steady. "It doesn't have tumblers, just a catch, a way to turn the dial. We need to turn it off."

Her hands shook, the light trembling.

He slid down the rough mound, caught the god's shoulder to support himself. The hidden chain groaned, but the broken door didn't respond.

With another controlled fall, he let himself down next to her, taking the light from her hand. "You got this. You work with Caravaggios, Jacinta. You can do this."

"Can't you?" She darted him a glance.

He held the flashlight in his left hand, his right hand curled to the least painful shape.

Brows pinching together, she brought her attention back to the lock, to the string of three cases wired together. That much C4 would wreck the city for blocks around, but the control box was industrial, a demolition model rather than a terrorist's deadman trigger. If they pulled the wires, disconnecting the other two cases, the heart of the monster remained. How many people—

"Just focus on the lock," he told her, his voice carefully modulated. "You need it to turn, you need to apply pressure to the side, to trigger the catch."

"Ah!" She dug into her pocket, and came out with a monocle, tucking it into her eye as she leaned into the work.

He steadied the light, reached out with his right hand and tangled his fingers around the wires, willing his hand to close and yank them free. Knotting his jaw to hold back the pain.

She flinched. "Won't that—"

"No. It's meant for control. In his plan, there was nobody here, nobody would know where it was. Can you find the catch?"

She inserted one of the picks, tried a different one, then, "yes!"

"Keep that one, add the other."

Her careful hands maintained the pressure and she winced as she forced the ignition to turn.

It gave a sharp click, and Grant's body tensed, then, with a long beep, the clock blinked out and Grant praised the darkness.

Chapter One Hundred Two

Sweat slicked the tools in her hands, and Jacinta watched the clock suspiciously, in case it came back to life. The readout remained blank. She sank back on her heels.

Beside her, Casey shifted his position, placing his back to the bench, letting his head rest on the surface. He tucked his left hand under his right, lifting it to rest on his lap, the flashlight beam casting the shadow of Mithras against the lead Menorah.

"All of this, these lives lost, these injuries, and it's not even real," she murmured.

He didn't move. The first time she saw him, he wore another man's blood. Today, it was his own, and she didn't even know where to start with his injuries. No mere staunching of blood would do.

"Tell me about the fresco, Jacinta, his only one." His voice remained cool, and clear.

It was a strange time to be interested in Caravaggio. Most people, after all of this, might wish never to see another one, but if it distracted him from his pain..."On the ceiling at the Villa? What do you want to know?"

"Three gods, and an allegory. Del Monte said his interests would guide the path."

"Sì, the telescope, and the mirror you found."

"But his hobby wasn't that." He lifted his head, lifted the flashlight, and let it play over the Menorah, tracing the thick branches and blunt, awkward decoration.

"Alchemy," she murmured. "How to turn lead into gold."

"Lead's got a very low melting point. I saw Caravaggio's olive tree, not like any other. Just like you said, he painted from life. He painted the Menorah, then he concealed it, even here, where nobody should see. And even if they did, they wouldn't know what the saw."

"They chased him," she said. "The Spanish detained him, separating him from his final works, but the Zacariah wasn't among them. They hounded him for the secret, and when he wouldn't tell..."

"He died."

A Dio concede, nobody else would die for this.

Footsteps approached at a run, and Jacinta cast about for a weapon, but Casey shook his head, somehow grinning through the blood and the grime.

"Chief!" Nick bent his head, and managed the scramble between rock and ceiling. "Damn, Chief, but that's a lot of bodies." He carried a long, slender gun of a kind she'd never seen before, with a small light fixed to the barrel.

"Not our fault if it takes an army."

"I cannot tell you how I felt thinking one of them was yours." Nick stayed low, sinking to the ground in front of his friend. He slipped the flashlight away from Casey and held it out to Jacinta as he started a brusque examination, his large hands investigating the injured leg —"Maybe a greenstick, not a clear break"—eliciting a wince as he prodded Casey's ribcage—"these ribs now—ouch!"—finishing up gently clasping Casey's head, holding the damaged eye toward the light. "Probably won't lose the eye. Maybe have to wear a patch for a while."

"Thanks, doc," Casey murmured.

More footsteps, accompanied by shouting, orders to reveal themselves, to step out, to put their hands up.

"Carabinieri," Jacinta said. "I'll tell them." She started to rise.

Casey touched her hand, freezing her with a stare still sharp in spite of his injuries. "Good work," he told her. "All of it."

Even befriending a monster? And yet, it maybe saved his life. She would take a long time processing everything that had happened these last few days.

"What do you think, will I make a good pirate?" Somehow, Casey managed a smile. Jacinta wasn't sure she'd even manage to walk out to meet the police, much less to speak coherently when she got there.

"How come you get to play pirate when I'm the one with a peg leg?" Nick protested.

"I have believed you worse than that, Mr. Casey," Jacinta said. "I am sure you can do anything."

"Apparently, so can you."

She squared her shoulders, and strode out to meet whatever came.

Chapter One Hundred Three

Rome, Italy

"For cripes' sake, you go into that mess and you come out looking even more like a badass, Chief, and here I am, just a mess, like always." Gooney lay propped in his hospital bed as Grant limped in, supporting his splinted leg with a bone-handled cane Dom had selected from his uncle's shop.

"It's good to see you, too, man—and you, Jamie. I'm just glad any of us came out of this at all," Grant told him.

"You're telling me," Jamie Li Rizzo said as she vacated the chair by Gooney's side and perched on the edge of his bed, never letting go of his hand.

With a nod of gratitude, Grant accepted the offered chair and eased himself down. The hospital orderlies had taken one look at him and tried to get him a wheelchair, assuming he was there as a patient, but Grant refused. Three days in recovery at Naples had degraded his patience with being fussed over. The trip up to Rome by train almost made him reconsider that attitude. With his right hand broken, and the opposite leg in a splint there was no such thing as a comfortable position. Didn't matter: being here was worth it.

At least Gooney had Jamie to fuss over him. Gooney looked pale and bruised, but he'd mend. Eventually. As much as anybody ever did.

"At least I've got a view." Gooney gestured with his free hand toward the window overlooking one of the city's many churches. "I keep trying to convince J-Li to go get me some real manicotti, but she won't do it. Hospital regs, blah, blah, blah. Anyway, thanks for the upgrade though, Chief. Private room makes a big difference."

"If only so you're not cussing out your roommates for snoring," Jamie put in.

Grant rolled the cane in his left hand, his right in a cast to support the break. Be a few weeks until he was back. "You'll have to thank our client for most of this."

At that, Gooney frowned. "The Warden? Thought she'd gotten out one step ahead of the Mossad."

"She did," said a voice from the door. Dafne Chadad regarded the men with a little more humility than before, perhaps, as she said, "May we enter?"

"Depends. Who's we, and are you planning to fuck with us some more?" Gooney's free hand balled into a fist, and Jamie lost her smile, staring at the newcomer. Didn't even know the woman on sight, but took Gooney's cue that she wasn't a friend. Yeah, those two were perfect for each other.

"Come." Grant waved her in, and she walked quickly through, taking up a position at the foot of the bed as Nick and D.A. entered after her.

D.A.'s blue eyes sought Grant, then flickered away, her lips compressed as if she were still uncertain of her welcome. She, too, looked a bit pale. She'd lost some weight, and didn't have much to lose. Still here, just like he told her. Neither of them going anywhere.

Nick shut the door without a sound, then waved a greeting to Gooney and Jamie. "Great to get the band back together. Maybe we should've booked the conference room."

"Maybe, if they'd let me get up," Gooney replied, but he stuck out his hand, and Nick clasped it, grinning. "So. What's this about a client? And who invited her to the party?" He jabbed a finger toward Agent Chadad.

"She is the client," Grant said. "On behalf of the Israeli government."

Gooney did a slow blink, eyebrows arched about as far as they could go, then rubbed them with his thumb and forefinger.

"We have a civilian present, Mr. Casey." Agent Chadad aimed her finger at Jamie.

"She's with me," Gooney said. "I trust her more than I trust you, and I'm pretty sure the rest of the team agrees."

"Copy that," Nick said.

Chadad's expression turned stormy. "I'm uncomfortable with the discussion of classified information under these circumstances."

"Dafne," D.A. said, "Rizzo's law enforcement. She understands."

Grant cast a glance at Chadad, who, after a moment, nodded for him to continue. "The easiest way to tidy up a lot of this is for the Bone Guard to accept the commission of the Institute to recover a certain artifact—"

"Did you?"

Nick sighed loudly, and Jamie whispered, "Shut up, Tony. This is the part where you listen."

"Right. Sorry. Carry on."

"We'll come back to that," Grant said. "As contract agents to a foreign government, we're bound by some different rules, and the Italians are more disposed to look kindly on some of the things that've happened. Basically, the Institute covers us as part of covering their own ass. The contract is retroactive to the moment the Warden left a parcel in our car and Moishe got after it."

D.A. cocked her head, frowning slightly, but she didn't interrupt.

Grant stared at Agent Chadad, still mastering the gaze point of a single-eye. Couple of weeks on that, too, but Nick's assessment hadn't been wrong about his likely recovery. "Let's just say this client pays handsomely, has excellent health care benefits, and requests that we don't file with our own insurance for medical bills lest the Mossad be called on to explain or deny our story."

Gooney cleared his throat, and Grant said, "Go ahead."

"So we found your candlestick, and we can't tell anybody, did I get that right?"

Most of the others flinched at Gooney's blunt summary, and Chadad stiffened. "Moishe's group has primed a large number of people to believe that the revelation of the Menorah is the symbol of the coming Revelation, the spark to ignite the end of the world. Until we can deal with those implications, we can't reveal the truth of what your team has recovered."

She blew out a long breath, expelling some of her formality along with it. "What you've found, and the part that each of you played in it, it could mean the world to a lot of people, and no, we can't publicly acknowledge the debt that we owe you. I know that money can't really compensate for everything you've been through, but it's a start. The day might come when I welcome you to Israel as our guests and show you a little better treatment than you've come to expect..." She offered Grant a crooked smile, a sort of apology for the games she'd been playing ever since D.A. brought the Mossad in on the Bone Guard's mission.

Grant brought the tip of his cane to rest on the ground with a distinct tap. "There's a few things we need to hammer out about the contract before it goes through proper channels," Grant resumed, and Chadad's brow furrowed.

"I don't appreciate new conditions being imposed like this, Mr. Casey."

"Two things," he said. "I don't think you'll object."

"One?" she prompted.

"One. The painting. The last known owner was a mobster, now deceased. The painting stays in Italy, to undergo conservation and study. From here out, it's just a painting. We tell everybody that's what the fight was about, and restore part of Italy's lost heritage."

"Reasonable. Would I be wrong in thinking part of that condition is who gets to restore it?"

Grant smiled. "Nope. Given Jacinta's already got possession of the work, and has shown herself more than willing to fight for it, I think we've got the right woman on the job." She and Dom were holed up in an undisclosed location, probably sharing their own stories of everything they'd been through. "And she'll be discreet about the parts of the truth we're leaving out."

"I don't have any reason to object." Chadad folded her arms. "What's your second condition?"

"When you strip the lead from the Menorah, D.A. gets to see it."

D.A.'s eyes flared, and Grant kept his gaze on her. "She's one of the people it means the world to. And I don't think she's been back to Israel since the funeral," he added softly.

Her eyes turned glossy.

"Fine. I'll make those changes. Do I send it to you?" Chadad moved toward the door.

"D.A. handles the contracts. I'm sure she won't let you get away with anything." Grant rose, using his cane. Everything ached, in spite of the meds, but he needed a moment between position changes.

"Niiiiice," Nick said. He gave D.A. a sidelong hug, but her gaze remained with Grant.

"Come on, D.A., let's see your katsa out." He tipped his head toward the door, and all three passed through, walking a short way down the corridor to the elevators.

Grant couldn't really offer his hand, but he said, "Safe travels, Agent Chadad. Wish I could say it was a pleasure working with you... but I can see how it might be."

Her smile flashed and vanished. "Agreed, Mr. Casey. 'Til we meet again." She stepped into the elevator and it whisked her away to her next assignment, leaving Grant and D.A. alone.

D.A. cleared her throat. "Guess I've still got a job, then? For you?"

"With me," he told her. "Faith can make people do strange things. But they're not always the wrong thing."

"I want to say I'm sorry," she began, then held up her hands to forestall him and cracked a grin, "but Nick warned me not to. Maybe I can just say thanks? For keeping me." She blinked a few times. "For trusting me."

"They're not just your former employer now—they're a client. Hey--" He waited. Took longer than it should for her to look him in the eye, but she'd be back. "No more secrets."

"Do my best," she said. "Old habits..."

"I know."

She stared down the corridor toward Gooney's room where raucous laughter suddenly burst forth. "He was part of my first family, y'know. Moishe. I wish...there could've been some other way."

As if his own first family had been any less contentious. "We don't always get the closure we want."

"She asked me what to do with the body." D.A. took a deep breath. "Turns out, I'm listed as his beneficiary. His house in Sicily. His last requests."

Not surprising, at least, not to Grant. "Did he have any?"

She breathed a laugh. "Nothing."

That word again. Grant shook his head. "Should've known."

D.A.'s faint smile reset her posture, drawing her up, lifting her chin. "I think I'll bury him next to Avram. He was wrecked when he lost him. We both were."

He and Moishe'd always had more in common than Grant was comfortable with. Both knew how readily the shepherd became the wolf. "He lost the one thing he truly had faith in: his friend."

"More than that," she told him, and her eyes blazed as they met his, "his family."

They walked back down the hall together.

Thanks for reading! Please leave a review or rating on Bookbub, Goodreads, or wherever you buy books!

Want to know how Gooney got his name? Check out "The Chief's Boss"! The Secret Word and More Adventures collection is free for Tomb Reader subscribers! Get the first word on sales and freebies, research and new projects!

Plus, get a bonus story in your first issue!

author.boneguardbooks.com/SecretWord

More by this Author

Bone Guard Series

The Mongol's Coffin

The Nazi Skull

The Assassin's Throne

The Maya Bust

The Fascist Frame

The Roman Candle

Rogue Adventures (forthcoming)

The Blighted Mission

The Flaming Wreck

The Blasted Mine

Short Thrillers

"Windfall" in ThrillRide: Honor

"The Manky Head" in ThrillRide: Unlikely Partners

"Vanishing Act" in ThrillRide: NWWM

"Flight Risk" in ThrillRide: Betrayal

www.ThrillRideMag.com

"Sunny Day: A Bone Guard Adventure"

"The Sheriff's Man"

About the Author

Research junkie E. Chris Ambrose has travelled to India, Nepal, China, Mongolia, Germany, France and England in pursuit of great stuff for stories! In the process, E. C. learned how to hunt with a falcon, clear a building of possible assailants, and pull traction on a broken limb. A one time adventure guide, E. C. enjoys rock climbing, hiking, kayaking and coming up with new ways to push characters to their limits.

E. Chris Ambrose also writes dark historical fantasy novels as E. C. Ambrose: the Dark Apostle series about medieval surgery, from DAW Books. Developing that series made the author into a bona fide research junkie. Interests include the history of technology and medicine, Mongolian history and culture, Medieval history, and reproductive biology of lizards. Research has taken her to Germany, England, France, India, Nepal, China and Mongolia as well as many United States destinations. In the process, E. C. learned how to hunt with a falcon, clear a building of possible assailants, pull traction on a broken limb, and fire an AR-15.

Published works have appeared in *Warrior Women*, Fireside magazine, YARN online, Clarkesworld, several volumes of New Hampshire Pulp Fiction, and *Uncle John's Bathroom Reader*. The author is both a graduate of and an instructor for the Odyssey Writing workshop, and a participant in the Codex on-line writers' workshop.

In addition to writing, E. C. works as an adventure guide, teaching rock climbing and leading hiking, kayaking, climbing and mountain biking camps. Past occupations include founding a wholesale sculpture business, selecting stamps for a philatelic company, selling equestrian equipment, and portraying the Easter Bunny on weekends.

Visit the Rocinante Press Website Here: https://www.RocinanteBooks.com

9 781941 107416